Between the Raindrops

A Novel by Susan Schussler

Copyright © 2013 by Susan Schussler
All rights reserved.
ISBN: 0989033317
ISBN 13: 9780989033312
Library of Congress Control Number: 2013919093
Rocky Shore Media LLC
Saint Paul, Minnesota

Contents

I often look back on the past four years and wonder what I could have done differently. Could I have changed anything in any way to make a difference? Or is my life driven by fate, out of my control, and I'm just falling to the ground like the raindrops, only to be pushed and pooled into the eroded channels already carved before me? I'm not sure what I believe, but I remember the disastrous night four years ago that first made me question whether I was in control, and it changed my life forever.

At nineteen, my life was finally moving in the direction it was meant to go. I had endured my share of setbacks and failures for my age, but I'd had a decent run so far. Some might say I lived a privileged life, but it's all relative to where you start.

Growing up, my family life was stable. My parents had been married two and a half decades, which is unheard of where I come from. Where I come from, marriages are measured in months, or years, if they are successful enough. Los Angeles, Brentwood, Los Feliz, Hollywood—it's all the same. People always define themselves by where they live, but in reality, if you work in the business, it doesn't really matter where you call home. The only thing that matters is how successful your last movie was and if you have another one lined up.

My brother, Jack, and I practically grew up on my dad's movie sets, so it was natural for us to go into the business. I had my first acting job when I was six—a Play-Doh commercial. I don't really remember it much. I didn't have any lines. I just smiled a toothless grin and pushed down a handle, spewing fire-shaped Play-Doh out of a dragon's mouth. I get blindsided with clips of that commercial every once in a while. It's embarrassing to see myself in a TV commercial, but we all have to start somewhere, and besides, I was cute.

I was in my first movie at the age of twelve. I played the younger brother of a teenage psycho killer. I only had a few lines, but I had lines, and that was a big deal at the time.

By nineteen, I had acted in six movies. One of them was uncredited, as my scene never made it into the final cut of the film, but I had the experience of acting in it and got paid, so I still count it. I was the lead in two of the six movies, and my career was just taking off.

On that horrible night four years ago, my sixth movie hadn't been released yet. Its status on IMDb hadn't even been changed to postproduction. We wrapped the filming in Vancouver the day before, and I had just gotten back into Los Angeles that afternoon.

It was my biggest film yet. It had a huge budget—bigger than any movie I had ever worked on, bigger than any movie my dad had ever directed. Shooting proved grueling with fourteen- to eighteen-hour days. The days and nights blurred as filming consumed me. I did most of my own stunts. It was very physically demanding, but I was in the best shape I had ever been in, thanks to my personal trainer. The movie took almost six months to film, and postproduction was expected to take another year. I felt like my acting career was definitely heading in the direction of every actor's dream.

My brother Jack's career had taken off too. He'd stowed several financially successful films under his belt and had just been signed to play the lead in *The Houston Chronicles* with a $5 million contract. We went out to celebrate that night I got back into town. We were celebrating our successes of finally making a name for ourselves and were showing off a bit going to Club Priela. It was the place to be seen, where all of young Hollywood hung out. It was packed with celebrities and trust fund kids, and the sidewalk was packed with paparazzi. The paparazzi didn't care about me back then. My big movie hadn't been released, and no one really knew my name.

Jack, on the other hand, at twenty-one, screamed up-and-coming A-lister. He had worked all through high school and built a credible reputation. He'd successfully made the crossover from child actor into solid adult actor with his last film, and his fame was growing. His recent interview and cover shoot in *Men's Health* had fostered Jack Williams as a household name. Jack seemed to embrace the newly found attention, and that night didn't seem out of the ordinary to him. Maybe it was because I had been away filming and hadn't been exposed to my brother's growing notoriety that I was agitated by the photographers that night. But I could feel it in the air when we entered the club. The paparazzi were hungry, and something just didn't feel right.

Inside the club, the lights bounced off the walls in colorful, graphic patterns that gyrated to the beat of the music. The large booths with dim-colored lights emitting through the glass tabletops provided intimate seating for parties of six to eight. The club really was a good place to network with others in the business, and Jack introduced me to several people.

We met up with Jack's girlfriend, Camille Moss. They had costarred together in his last movie and been dating for seven months, but this was the first time I really had a chance to talk to her. A feisty redhead, she seemed to be a good fit for Jack. She stood thin, but not a waif. She possessed some semblance of a brain and big tits. She was exactly his type. Jack always fell in love with busty redheads. He knew what worked for him. I, on the other hand, had never found my type. I dated enough to know what was out there, but I had never been in love, never found that connection with anyone.

When we were ready to leave, the valet pulled Jack's silver Audi to the curb. I got into the driver's seat, and the smell of new leather filled my lungs as fifty or so paparazzi swarmed around us. Being under twenty-one, I was usually Jack's designated driver when we went out together. It's not like I couldn't drink at the club if I wanted to, but I had drank too much the night before at the wrap party and just wasn't in the mood to poison my body any further. As my father always said, when you live your life in the public eye, you need to be better than everyone else because the entire world will know about it when you screw up. It's good advice, and I was lucky I upheld it that night.

Jack and Camille posed on the sidewalk for a couple of minutes before sliding into the backseat. I was naive back then, not understanding the feeding frenzy stirred by an on-screen couple hooking up off-screen. The spray of flashes blinded us, and the intrusive questions the photographers hurled boggled my mind. I had seen this obnoxious behavior before, but not directed toward Jack or me. I inched the car forward cautiously as the camera lenses clacked against the darkly tinted windows. I didn't want to run over anyone's foot and be sued, so I took it slow. Once freed, we made our way down West Sunset Boulevard. Traffic was light, so we actually moved along, hitting green lights.

I didn't notice him right away, the paparazzo on the motorcycle. He pulled up alongside us when we stopped at a light. I remembered his long horse face and ponytail from the group on the sidewalk, and he hung way too close to the Audi for my comfort. When the light turned green, we picked up speed again, making our way through three more green lights.

The guy on the motorcycle hovered around my front-right bumper as if his hand rested on the car. I worried he would follow us back to the house, so I tapped the brake just a little to shake him off. The guy apparently decided that now was his chance. He pulled in front of us and whipped his camera out of his jacket. It all happened so fast that I didn't realize what he was doing at first. The idiot was attempting to take a picture through our windshield without crashing his motorcycle. He wasn't successful. He spilled his bike right in front of us, and his body skidded across the pavement. My first reaction was not to kill him, though now I wish I had. I instinctively slammed on the brakes and swerved to the left to avoid splattering the biker. But I forgot about the oncoming traffic, and when I saw the giant black Escalade barreling toward the Audi's passenger side, I panicked.

Even though time sped by so fast, I saw it in slow motion, just like the movies. Maybe the adrenaline in my body made everything around me seem to slow down, but I saw the mammoth SUV coming at us, and there was nothing I could do. At the same time, all I could think about was how Jack was going to kill me for destroying his new car. I didn't realize that things were much worse until I heard the screams from the backseat and the explosions of the side air bags. I heard a deafening crushing sound and a piercingly loud screeching of metal scraping against metal. The acrid smell of burning rubber grew in intensity as I sat unable to move, dazed in the moment.

I didn't feel any pain—not yet, anyway. I called out to Jack—no answer. I couldn't hear anything more, only the pounding of the blood in my head, and then I was on the ground, lying in the street. The heat of the pavement scorched my back. Someone had dragged me out of the car. A fireman, a paramedic, or just a guy on the street—I wasn't sure. I must have passed out then, because the next thing I knew, I lay in a fog in the emergency room, and I didn't even remember the ambulance ride.

Chapter One

The Internet, my fickle friend, my two-faced enemy, what would life be like without you? Where else can I be anonymously anyone and yet, have no anonymity at all?

J onathan pushed back from the oversized desk and glanced around his cluttered home office. Towers of half-opened cardboard cartons were stacked high against the wall behind his chair. The insides of the boxes intentionally strewed out over the rims to remind him of their contents. The disorganization of the room troubled him, but he couldn't fathom a practical way to fix it long term. As soon as he or his assistant cleared out a box, two more would arrive at the house, beckoning him to empty them. The packages of free merchandise were just one of the cursed perks that came with his celebrity status. He knew he was lucky to have any products sent to him at all, and he would never complain about the swag. Most actors only dreamed of such a privilege, but Jonathan felt overwhelmed by his fame and longed for a less complicated life.

He spun his chair around to face his open laptop and clicked on the icon that had become such a habit over the last few months. When the gossip website appeared on the screen, he uttered, "Wow, I really need a haircut."

He brushed the dark wavy hair off his face as he read the caption: "Jonathan Williams grabs a cup of joe after a late night of partying." The fan he had posed with this morning outside his favorite coffee shop must have tweeted the picture from her phone.

That was fast, he thought.

He sipped his coffee as he scanned the website for any surprises. Convinced he had a good handle on the day's gossip, he took out his phone to contact the website's manager. He had spoken to Paris Borel many times before. Every once in a while, he would feel so wronged by the gossip on her site that he would call her up just to set the record straight. Her site was one of the better ones—in his mind. Sure, it published gossip disguised as news, but it rarely put up paparazzi pictures and never leaked his whereabouts until after he had left. Paris didn't misquote him and usually gave Jonathan the benefit of the doubt when it came to the wild rumors that seemed to hound him lately. The latest one was about him getting engaged to Mia Thompson, his costar from the romantic comedy *Love Twice*.

He and Mia had gone out for a while, he couldn't deny that, but it wasn't anything serious. She was a riot to hang with and could handle herself in the press. Besides, his publicist, Remi Delano, didn't like it when he went to events alone. She said it was bad for his image. Mia didn't mind going out with Jonathan. She liked to be seen. She liked to be seen with Jonathan. He always brought a lot of attention, and that was what Mia liked most about Jonathan Williams.

At least the Mia story had some foundation. It wasn't relevant anymore, though. Jonathan and Mia both knew that the relationship had just been convenient. They were too different. Mia, a curvy, high-maintenance brunette, liked to live in the press, and Jonathan was too busy with his career to play press games. Mia was also known for hitting the LA nightclubs pretty hard, and Jonathan just wasn't into the club scene anymore. He would much rather hang out with friends at a house party or hit a concert than a club, and having his life unfold in the press did not excite him. So eight months ago, after the press tour for their movie had ended, they decided to remain just friends. They still went out for coffee once in a while, just to catch up, and used each other for dates to award ceremonies or charity events when they didn't have anyone else, but nothing more. They knew where they stood with each other, and that made it easier. Still, every time they were seen together, the rumors exploded. It kept his publicist happy, and Mia too, Jonathan thought.

Jonathan hadn't always drawn so much attention. But since his big break, his life had changed. It astonished him how one movie could transform everyone's opinion about him. His movie *The Demigod* became a blockbuster hit that made $687 million worldwide. Its release three years ago had skyrocketed Jonathan Williams to the actor's A-list.

His career sped from zero to sixty overnight, out of his control. The media took over, and the public wanted answers—answers about Jonathan's personal life. How many times could he endure the same questions over and over? "Do you have a girlfriend?" stood as the most common question asked, but "Boxers or briefs?" irritated Jonathan the most. He didn't see how his boxer briefs held any bearing on his acting ability. So one day, he decided to end the underwear debate. During a now notorious interview on national television, he showed just how frustrated he was with the senseless inquiry. Instead of his usual skirting around to something more relevant, Jonathan simply unbuttoned his trousers and let them drop, showing his choice to the world without a word. It became a joke, but at least no one asked him anymore.

His popularity cycled up and down slightly over the next three years according to the release of his films, but never wavered. With *The Demigod* sequel to start filming this fall, Jonathan's hype was climbing again. These days, he couldn't step outside without having his photo taken or someone tweeting his whereabouts. His fans stalked him, and some days, he was convinced that his hand was going to fall off from signing autographs. He rarely said no to fans and had signed some pretty crazy items and body parts.

Though the fans were exhausting, they didn't aggravate him like the paparazzi. The paparazzi hunted him. They dug through his garbage searching for anything they could use against him. They hid outside his condo or his parents' house in the heat and wind just waiting for him to leave. Then they followed him all day long with four-foot-long camera lenses, disappearing behind bushes and Dumpsters, all in the hopes of getting the perfect shot—a picture of Jonathan in a public display of affection with some random girl, or doing something illegal, or just compromised in some way. The worse Jonathan looked, the more money the picture brought. The paparazzi shouted in his face and blocked his way as he walked. They tried to provoke him into violence just so they could break the story about the hottie gone crazy. So far, he'd been good and managed to keep his cool, but it had been close a few times.

He realized that his love life was just as messed up when an aspiring actress recorded their date on her phone and posted it online. Though the picture was poor, every word was audible. The next day, it went viral on YouTube, tagged "A Date with a God." He had planned to ask the actress out again, until his publicist forwarded him the video link. At first, Jonathan laughed about it, because it wasn't too incriminating and it wasn't the worst date he had been on, but obviously, the girl didn't want to go out again. The incident convinced him that dating wasn't worth the headache. He shrunk deeper into his tight group of friends and rarely put himself out in the dating world. He always worried that his dates were just using him to promote themselves in the Hollywood press and wouldn't even go out with him if not for his celebrity status.

Jonathan found the website manager's number on his phone and pushed send. As he began chatting with Paris, he knew he would have to watch what he said to her. After all, it was her job to report breaking news about celebrities, but he felt comfortable because they had built some rapport. Jonathan also knew that he would have to give up a piece of himself to her. A small bit of his personal life would have to be sacrificed in order for him to get what he wanted. He knew which part it would be and thought it may help him in the long run.

"Jonathan, it's good to hear from you. Did you cheat on Mia last night and need some PR help? You looked a little tired this morning," chided Paris.

"Nooo," he said slowly, taken aback by her question. "I wasn't partying last night. I was home in my own bed. Besides, Mia and I are just friends. We're not back together, and we're not getting back together." That was the part he was giving up. He thought he might as well get it out in the open right away. He wanted her to take him seriously and recognize that there was nothing to gossip about when it came to Mia Thompson and him.

"I didn't say you were out," Paris snapped with a snicker. "I bet some of the best parties take place in your bedroom."

"You know I'm not the man-whore they make me out to be."

"Sure you are, Jon. I know you're not a saint. I've seen the pictures," she said shrewdly.

"You believe those rags? I thought you were better than them." He spun back around in his chair and glowered at the box towers. He bent down to pick up the green tennis ball off the floor in front of the stacks and ran his thumb over his portrait embossed in black ink on the ball's side.

"It's not just the rags. There are pictures of you all over the Internet. You're cozying up to a different beauty every night, by the looks of it."

"I just can't help it when they throw themselves at me." He laughed knowing this wouldn't help his cause, but he was having fun. "What's a guy to do? I'm only human."

"I thought you were a god."

"No, demigods are half-human." He knew it would be a while before he shed that label, and using his self-effacing charm to keep the conversation light, he said, "Honestly, they're just fans, and they only like my character, not me. They want my body so they can live out their character fantasies. The real me wouldn't interest them at all. Besides, I'd never hook up with a fan."

"Never say never, Jon," she lectured.

The corners of his lips turned up as he thought about why he had called. "Paris, I need a favor," he blurted out, knowing now was his chance.

"Anything you desire. You know that."

Her seductive tone made him chuckle. Though he would never act on it, they had always had a certain amount of chemistry as they spoke, and Jonathan enjoyed their banter.

"How is your husband?" Last he had heard, Paris's pro hockey player husband had been caught in the locker room with the coach's eighteen-year-old daughter. The incident had almost gotten him traded, but he got injured before the trade went through.

"His shoulder is healing, and we're still together, if that's what you're asking. I think revenge sex would help me get past my issues, though. You in?"

"I wish I could, but I'm saving myself for marriage." He chuckled again.

"Give me a week. I'm open to a second marriage."

"And mess up what we have? How would I survive?"

Over the years, Paris had manipulated stories on her website to portray Jonathan in a positive light, and he appreciated the unsolicited help with PR. In return, he provided her with tidbits of his personal life that he wouldn't share with any other journalist. Their relationship had helped Paris build a credible reputation, and she had once told him that his name alone was responsible for half her advertising dollars.

"What can I do for you, Jon?"

"I know you track your bloggers. You have to sign into the comment blogs with an e-mail and—"

"Are you sharing on my site?" she interrupted with a bit of sarcasm.

Her website allowed its readers to interact with one another on its blog threads to discuss the day's gossip, and over the years, Jonathan had come to the site many times—sometimes to read his fan's conversations and sometimes to participate in the blogging.

"You know I do. I just like to see what my fans are thinking—my real fans, not the ones on the other sites who are just waiting for me to screw up," he said. "Can I get an e-mail address of one of your bloggers?"

"That's against policy, Jon."

"You wrote the policy. Besides, you know I'm not a stalker."

"Never say never, right?"

"It's not like that." He realized he was going to have to lie just a little. He hated to lie, but Paris ran a gossip site, and he couldn't tell her the truth. "I think one of your bloggers may be Jack's ex," he stammered, "and I just want to reconnect. I haven't seen her since the accident." Jonathan knew that if he mentioned the accident, Paris wouldn't press him for more information.

"You know it wasn't your fault."

"Yeah, I know," he said, but in reality, he still blamed himself, and the guilt he felt plagued his every thought.

"OK, what's her username?"

He read off the username, and Paris keyed it in.

"You know most of these are fakes," she warned.

"I know," Jonathan admitted, "but it's worth a try." He smiled as he thought about what had driven him to contact the website manager in the first place. The girl from the blog threads that he couldn't get out of his mind, she was the reason for all this. He needed to know that she was real—flesh, bones, and a sweet voice to match her words. He needed to know that there was a woman in the world who really did understand him, and he wanted to meet her so badly that he was willing to talk to the enemy.

Jonathan wondered what the girl looked like. She said that she was two years younger than him, that she had dark hair and fair skin. She mentioned something about ex-boyfriends and had complained about the stupid pickup lines guys used on her, so she couldn't be too awful looking. In truth, her looks didn't really matter that much. Jonathan knew that, in Hollywood, anybody could be made to look good. It was inner beauty that was harder to fake.

The girl's inner beauty inspired him to find her. She was witty, yet sweet. She had a core confidence that emanated from everything she wrote in the blog, she wasn't shy about her opinion, and she seemed open-minded when she listened to others' ideas. He didn't know how to explain it, but Jonathan knew that this girl was special, not like anyone he had ever met before.

"I think you're in luck, Jon. This one looks legitimate, although I can't tell for sure." Paris interrupted his thoughts. "Do you have a pen?"

"Yeah, shoot."

She gave him the e-mail address and wished him good luck.

"Thanks, Paris. I owe you one."

"You do. Take care, Jonathan."

Jonathan didn't like owing Paris anything. He knew he would have to pay back the favor, but he had a feeling that it would be worth it in the end. He leaned back in his chair, putting his feet up on the desk, and sighed. He bounced the green tennis ball against the wall once and caught it, twice and caught it again. He kneaded the ball with his fingers as he contemplated. Months of anonymous chatting with Sarah had led to this. He was nervous about actually talking to her, and maybe a little intimidated by her, which was rare for Jonathan.

He remembered back to the first time he had run across her in the blogs. It was after a photo shoot he had done with four supermodels. During an interview following the shoot, reporters asked if he would be dating any of the models. He responded without thinking, saying, "They're beautiful, but not really my type." He had been through media training a couple of times, and at the time, he thought it was a decent answer. He preferred women who could think for themselves. Jonathan had never found much interest in models. He thought most of them were just a blank slate that could be molded into whatever someone wanted. "Where's the challenge there?" They were not his type at all.

Of course, the press twisted his answer, and the gay rumors flew. Every rag magazine had his picture with headlines like, "What IS Jon's Type?" or "Did Hanging with His Buds Make Jon Switch Teams?" or "The Hot, Steamy Truth About the Demigod's Secret Life." Then Remi, his publicist, called and insisted he get out and be seen with a woman. "Any woman, just make it public," she had said. Jonathan called Mia for some help. He went out with her a couple of times to very public clubs, hoping to make the rumors blow over fast.

Jonathan went on the gossip site's blog to see whether the sightings were actually working. The fans were usually very forthcoming with what they thought. That's when he first noticed Sarah. He had signed in with a username that he had used before, and he could still visualize the words from the blog threads on his laptop.

Cracked23: I thought this guy had a reputation for all the women he dated. Why would he all of a sudden switch teams?

Sarah A: You know those Hollywood types. He's probably just trying to set some new trend.

Cracked23: Yeah, because it couldn't be that he likes to go out to dinner with a girl who actually eats or that he's just not that into high-maintenance women?

Sarah A: Guys like you described don't exist. What guy would turn down a date with a supermodel?

Cracked23: I would.

Sarah A: Let me rephrase that. What straight guy would turn down a date with a supermodel?

Cracked23: Haha! I would.

Sarah A: No, you wouldn't. When was the last time that opportunity came up?

Cracked23: Last week.

Sarah A: So you're just as delusional as the rest of the people on this site. You were my only hope.

Cracked23: You should have known. My username IS Cracked23.

Sarah A: I'm usually more perceptive. Interesting username, I bet there's a great story behind it.

Cracked23: Nope, just my everyday supermodel-rejecting life.

Sarah A: It's too bad I'm a supermodel.

Cracked23: Oh? You don't sound like the usual high-maintenance model type. Maybe I'd make an exception.

Jonathan watched the blog site to see if he could catch her again. He didn't really know why, but she had captured his attention. The next time he found her, she admitted that she wasn't really a supermodel, and the two got so goofy on the blog that Jonathan felt like he was joking around with his high school buddies. His high school friends were the only people he considered his true friends. He trusted them. He had known most of them since middle school, and they never treated him differently when he became famous. When he interacted with Sarah, he felt like she didn't have preconceived ideas and expectations of him, like all the other people in the world. She treated him like any other person—like his high school friends treated him. Of course, she didn't know who he was, and knowing that might have changed her opinion, but somehow, Jonathan didn't think it would matter. She seemed different.

Over the next two months, he met up with her on the blogs almost every day. They would switch to chat rooms and privately message each other, but they always started on the gossip blogs. Their conversations progressed to anything and everything. They shared their most trivial thoughts on world economics, politics, education, dating, and music. They both liked some of the same bands. Jonathan told her that he used to play guitar and sometimes keyboard in a band in high school, but he didn't get to play much now that he had a real job. Sarah shared that she had spent years listening to her brother's band practice in her parents' basement and was overjoyed when they finally learned how to play.

Jonathan learned that Sarah was attending college and that she would graduate next spring with a double major in English and psychology. He told her that he worked on movie sets, but never revealed that he was an actor. Sarah didn't pressure him to give out information about himself. She seemed to know that it was something he didn't want to talk about. Jonathan felt a little guilty when Sarah asked him his name, and he answered, "My friends call me Will," which was true of his real friends, so he didn't feel that he was lying, just omitting information. The nickname came from his last name, and it was so obvious that he hoped she wouldn't figure it out, yet he didn't want to lie, either.

Though it was difficult to truly get to know someone on the Internet, Sarah seemed to understand Jonathan better than anyone he had ever met, and for some intangible reason, he trusted her. It was just a feeling he had. Yesterday, they talked about ex-boyfriends and ex-girlfriends, agreeing not to use real names. But when a guy chimed in on their private chat room suggesting that they take it to a hotel, they knew they really needed to find another way to communicate. So without sharing any personal information, Jonathan promised he would find a way to contact her.

Now here he sat, typing the e-mail that could change his life. Or not. It was no longer within his control. Once he sent the e-mail, it would be up to Sarah to call him. It had been a while since he worried about a girl returning his call, and it excited him, especially because she didn't know his true identity. He felt that she liked him for who he really was, not for who she thought he was, and that intrigued him. He kept the e-mail short. He said that he had been able to get her address through some connections his family had with the website and that he hoped she would call him so they could finally talk to one another. He gave her his cell phone number and chuckled out loud to himself.

He picked up the embossed tennis ball again and bounced it one more time, deliberately smacking his face hard against the wall before hitting send.

"The ball is in your court now."

Sarah didn't make him wait too long. She called the next night at eight, LA time, and said simply, "Hi. Will? It's Sarah." She sounded unsure and nervous, yet confident, and Will thought she sounded adorable. "I'm so glad you found me."

"I told you I would. I always keep my promises," he proclaimed.

"So what were you doing tonight? Anything exciting?"

"Oh yeah, I was thinking about you."

"No, you weren't."

"I was. I was starting to worry that maybe you were some middle-aged housewife just teasing me, and you weren't going to call because you didn't want your secret to be exposed."

"Sorry to disappoint, but I'm not a very good liar, and everything I told you is true. I am only twenty," she said with a chuckle.

"Good. At least no one will stare at us."

"Is that important to you—that no one stares?" she playfully antagonized.

"Not really, but I like to know what to expect—though the unexpected can be exciting." He stifled a laugh and hoped she would be open to surprises in the future.

"I didn't expect you to find me so quickly. You don't even know my last name."

All of a sudden, he felt like he might have been coming on too strong. "You wanted me to find you, right?"

"Very much, but I didn't realize you were so…resourceful."

"You'll have to get used to it. I have many talents, Sarah."

"So, Mr. Talented, you said that you like indie rock. Have you been to any concerts recently?" she asked.

"I haven't been to anything huge in a while, but I saw the Killers in Austin, in March. They were pretty chill. I've been to a couple of smaller concerts since then, but nothing that stands out. How 'bout you?" He consciously redirected the conversation back to her. Though comfortable talking to her, he was still leery of revealing himself.

"I've only been to three concerts in my entire life, and one of them was Ashley Tyler when I was fourteen—with my mom," she admitted.

"It was excruciating. My parents wouldn't let me go without an adult, and Jessica and I really wanted to go. My mom was dancing in the aisle and singing, as if she was onstage. I think she secretly wants to be a pop star. It scarred me for life."

Will laughed.

"I didn't go to another concert until I was in college."

"No doubt. Who would?" He chuckled, marveling at her openness. He liked that she could talk about humiliating moments and make fun of them.

"I know, right? Seriously, the whole pop-star-mom ordeal was very traumatic. I think it's the root of why I started taking psychology classes."

"So who would you go see now, now that you're starting to heal?"

"My housemates and I tried to get tickets to see EXpireD at the end of the month, but they sold out in ten minutes. Have you ever seen them?"

"Yeah, they're great. They're based in LA. They play here all the time. If you come out and visit me sometime when the band is in town, I promise I'll get us in." He suppressed another laugh. He couldn't believe that she'd mentioned the one band that he knew personally—better than personally. Two of his best friends were in it. He could arrange a private concert if she wanted.

"And you always keep your promises, huh?"

"Of course, like I said."

They chatted for three hours that first night. Neither one wanted to end the call. To them, it felt like they had known each other forever and were just catching up. Finally, they agreed to get off the phone, but only after Will had promised to call her the next night. And he did. Will and Sarah spoke to each other every night for three weeks. They gathered every insignificant little detail of each other's lives that they weren't allowed to talk about on the very public Internet—except Will's true identity.

By the end of three weeks, Will knew he had to meet her. He couldn't wait any longer. He was starting to feel like a liar, and that wasn't who he was at all. Will wanted to share everything with her. Sarah's birthday was next Friday—a week away. If he was able to organize it, he would be visiting her in Minneapolis the same day his buddies were doing the concert there. He might be able to arrange it so he could take her to the concert on her twenty-first birthday. He figured out the logistics of her birthday surprise and then called his buddy Nick to set up the concert details.

Chapter Two

Sarah sat at the reception desk in her dad's veterinary clinic. It was a slow day. Her dad scheduled most of the clients' wellness exams in the spring so they could start their pets on heartworm protection. By the time summer came around, the office visits were mostly emergencies or newly acquired pets.

There was nothing exciting happening at the clinic today. A nine-week-old German shepherd pup was scheduled for two o'clock, and a cat with possible ear mites was coming in at two thirty. Sarah had already pulled the file for the cat from the tall wall of shelves behind the desk that served as the clinic's filing cabinets and had gathered the paperwork that needed to be completed for the new puppy.

Sarah's dad was out in Hugo checking on a complication with a pregnant mare, so Dr. Anderson was covering the afternoon at the clinic. Sarah could hear her chatting in the back room with Cheryl, the vet tech, about the doctor's three-month-old daughter, and pictures were involved. As much as Sarah liked children, she just wasn't in the mood for another slide show. She had already cleaned the back kennels, hosing them out and disinfecting them first thing this morning. They were spotless. No animals were boarding for the weekend, and there was nothing else to do, so Sarah sat at the desk, behind the raised counter, thinking about her plans for the night.

It was her twenty-first birthday, and in truth, she was having a hard time concentrating on anything but tonight's plans. She had agreed to work on her birthday only so she could have off the following day. Today Sarah crossed the legal drinking age line—the last of her close friends to do so—and she wasn't sure how she would be feeling in the morning. The original plans for the evening had boasted club hopping in Minneapolis with her brother as the designated driver. Her friends had planned to initiate Sarah into her age by hitting four or five places for maximum exposure. She knew she would probably just end up getting drunk, throwing up on someone, and feeling awful the next day, which didn't really excite her. Sarah's friends had tried to convince her that this was what she was supposed to do on her twenty-first birthday, but she wasn't buying it. So she had been thrilled a week ago when the plans had changed.

Now, they were all going to the sold-out EXpireD concert at the Lindbergh Theatre. Tickets were impossible to get, but Will had assured her that he had it all arranged and they were going to celebrate her birthday at the show.

"Will," she whispered, thinking about their plans. She still couldn't believe she was going to meet him—the guy from the Internet. It just wasn't like her to be so reckless. She normally didn't talk to strangers on the phone for hours and hours, share her most personal secrets with them, and then agree to meet them in person.

Am I crazy? she pondered.

She knew this wasn't the type of thing smart girls did. She was usually so cautious. But in truth, she was tired of always doing the right thing. She wanted to listen to her heart, not her head, for once. There was something intriguing about relinquishing control and letting fate take over that just felt right this time.

"Will," she whispered again to herself, remembering back to how excited she'd been when she saw his username pop up on her screen after their first chat. She had just finished making a quick comment on someone's dissertation of the gossip site. A guy had written a three-hundred-word blog post about how celebrities deserved what they got from the press. The post was linked to an article about a well-known comedian who had gotten arrested after he smashed a guy's phone. Apparently the guy had taken a picture of the comedian using the urinal before the incident, but the comedian still got arrested.

The blogger's point was that celebrities got paid a ton of money; therefore, they should have to put up with people snapping pictures of them. It was part of the deal, in his opinion.

Sarah volleyed back. "Was the guy taking the picture paying the comedian?"

That's when Cracked23 joined in. "Good point, Supermodel."

His comment made her laugh. She couldn't believe he had remembered her. Quickly, it seemed as if they had slipped into their own chat room. She lost all track of time, spoke with him on the website for another hour, and ended up late for class, but she didn't care. She was thrilled just to have found him again.

She met up with Will several more times online over the days that followed. She logged on to the site a couple of times a day, searching for him, hoping to find him, and when she did, she relished in their conversations. She spent that whole first week walking around campus wondering whether each guy she passed on the sidewalk or in the hall was him. When Will admitted that he lived in Los Angeles, her heart sank. She knew she would never get to meet him. Though the distance disappointed her, it also freed her. She opened up to him in ways she had never done before with anyone, and it felt so right. She told him everything—how she didn't think she would ever trust a man enough to fall in love, how her biggest fear was never being taken seriously as a writer, and how she liked to sing pop songs in the shower—every single thought that burst into her head.

And now she *was* going to meet him. Without any walls to hide behind, she felt so exposed. He knew her better than most of her friends, maybe even better than her best friend, Jessica. It felt that way sometimes, the way he was able to almost read her mind. She felt a connection to him that she didn't know how to explain, and it scared her to death.

What did she really know about him?

He had worked for his dad, a director, when he was younger. But when she asked what he had done, he said it was nothing exciting, and seemed embarrassed to tell her. She knew that Will had not gone to college. He could have, his grades were good enough, but like most people, once he started working, he found it too hard to give up his paycheck to go back to school, and Sarah thought this might be why he was insecure about his job. She pictured him fetching coffee for Julia Roberts or holding up lighting shields to prevent shadows on Jake Gorboni's face. His dad had most likely gotten him the job, and that probably embarrassed him.

She knew that Will really didn't like to talk about his family very much, but she didn't know why. She figured he would tell her about them when he was ready. She didn't even know his last name. He said he didn't want to share that detail until he met her, since his dad was fairly well known and he didn't want her prejudging him because of some Internet story about his family. She'd tried Googling movie directors to figure out who he was, but nothing matched. Will didn't even have a social network account. He was kind of mysterious, and that was captivating to Sarah.

Sarah also knew that Will was super funny and always made her laugh. He was intelligent and enjoyed reading. He had read as many books as she had, which was rare for most of the guys she dated. He actually enjoyed talking about what was happening in other parts of the world and rarely bored her with sports talk.

She would be seeing him tonight, and there was one thing she was still uneasy about. Will had described himself to her as six foot one, "decent looking," but he didn't want to exchange pictures. He wanted it to be a surprise, and that was the part that made her the most nervous. She was worried that this guy she was so attracted to intellectually might not spark her attention physically—or worse, he might not find her attractive. She had been worrying about this for a week now, ever since she found out he was coming for a visit.

She contemplated this as she sat at the reception desk. She knew looks weren't everything. She had dated good-looking guys before, but never felt the attraction for them that she felt for Will. She had dated intellectual guys before, but never felt the connection she did with Will. So what if he wasn't a hottie? She knew she would give him a chance even if he had an evil twin growing out of his back, but she hoped he didn't.

Just then, her phone vibrated, and a huge smile spread across her face. She slid her index finger across the touch screen and raised the phone to her ear.

"Hey, Will."

"Hey, beautiful. Happy birthday."

"Shut up! You don't even know what I look like."

"I can tell you're beautiful inside and out. Besides, it doesn't matter. I think I may be in love with you."

"Quit saying stuff like that, or I'll think you're a stalker," she blurted out louder than she should have. This wasn't the first time he had said this. He had joked about being in love with her a few times over the last month. She fiddled with the papers in front of her. She was getting more and more nervous about their meeting, and his teasing wasn't making her feel any better.

"I'm just messing with you, Sarah. I know you're at work, so I'll keep to the reason I called. My flight is running late, and I'll have to meet you at the show. Just tell them your name at the door. The guys in the band are good friends of mine, so they'll take really good care of you. I promise! Only five of you, right?"

"Yep, six with you."

"Jeff's coming?"

"Are you kidding? My brother would disown me if I didn't bring him. EXpireD is his favorite band. He's been talking about it all week. Besides, he and Jessica are pretty inseparable lately. It's been a while since they've spent a Friday night apart."

"Sarah, I have a few surprises for you, so just take it as it comes, OK?"

"Not too many?"

"Only good ones. See you tonight, Birthday Girl."

"Can't wait."

As she set down her phone, Sarah melted back in her chair, anticipating what the night would bring, somehow knowing that her life would never be the same.

⁓

Meanwhile, Jonathan sat staring out the plane window, fidgeting with the phone in his hand. The plane was getting ready to take off, and he had just finished his call to Sarah when the announcement came prohibiting the use of electronic devices.

He wore his usual travel attire—a baseball cap, jeans, a vintage T-shirt, an edgy black jacket, and combat boots. He liked to be comfortable when he traveled, and he hoped no one would recognize him. He looked around the first-class cabin, keeping the bill of his hat down and making sure not to make eye contact with anyone.

Sam Kachinske sat next to him, and most of the other seats were filled with gray-haired couples or business travelers. Jonathan had traveled with Sam many times before, and he trusted him with his life. He was an ex–police officer who had quit the force after losing his partner to a gunshot wound. It was mostly his wife's persistence that had made him switch to a career in security, and now that they had children, he was glad he had made the change. Sam was a big man with broad shoulders and bulky muscles, the kind of guy whose sheer size intimidated practically everyone. He was thirty-one, had dark hair cut in a military flattop, olive skin, and a square jaw. He was pleasant, once you got to know him, and Jonathan chatted with him a little before opening his book.

"Big night ahead," Sam said in his husky voice. "You sure you want to go through with this, Jon?"

"I'm kind of committed now. We're pulling away from the gate."

"We've got the whole flight. There's still time to back out. I know security will be amped at the concert for you, but"—he looked at him inquisitively—"something tells me that nothing I say will change your mind."

"Nope," Jonathan said, reaching up to adjust the air valve that was blasting musty air in his face.

The FASTEN SEAT BELT sign flashed on, and the flight attendant came around to make sure everyone had what they needed before takeoff. Jonathan was too nervous to get anything out of the book, so he stowed it in the pocket of his chair. He couldn't concentrate on anything but tonight. He was excited to finally see Sarah, to connect a face with her personality. He wanted to study her face when she said something sarcastic like, "You think so?" or "Really?" He imagined she would speak with the slightest smirk.

As much as he anticipated the night ahead, he was also dreading it. He knew the horror he was about to release on Sarah's world. He lived with the destruction of the paparazzi every day and didn't want her to have to deal with it as well. He thought he was being selfish dragging her into his world. He wished he could protect her. He didn't want to share her with the photographers or the media. He didn't want them to stalk her or lie about her. He didn't want people to hate her just because she was out with him. Jonathan knew all this would happen if she was seen with him, and he loathed himself for involving her. But he yearned for her to be a part of his life, and he didn't know what else to do. Jonathan felt guilty about not really giving her a choice, yet he was sure she would say, "Bring it," and she would mean it—probably.

Jonathan and Sarah had spent hours talking about celebrities, their fans, and the press. She always said she didn't understand why people obsessed over celebrities. "They're just human and not any more special than you or me," she had told him. That's when Jonathan started to think he might be able to trust her with his secret. Now, he was certain he could trust her. She seemed to be such a part of him already. Jonathan knew tonight would be the litmus test, though, and there would be no going back.

Chapter Three

Sarah, Jessica, Jeff, Alli, and Megan inched their way closer to the front of the line. They had gotten there at six and followed the crowd all the way around the building in the scorching heat. It was ninety-four degrees, humid and sticky, with very little breeze breaking around the tall buildings that surrounded the Lindbergh Theatre. Heat emanated from the cement sidewalk, the street, and every rock set in the exterior of the old stone building—taunting them as they walked. Sarah was glad she had worn layers, but she was down to her last, a tank top with a flirty miniskirt, and as much as she yearned to be cooler, she couldn't remove any more clothing. She was carrying her blouse and her black fitted jacket over her arm, wishing she had worn lower heels. The rest of her friends were faring about the same in the heat, and everyone was complaining, especially Megan.

"I don't even know why I bothered putting makeup on before we left. It's dripping off my face. Seriously, can it get any hotter?" Megan grumbled. "You don't have an electric fan in that mammoth bag of yours, do you?" Her short blonde hair flipped back as she turned to her redheaded friend.

"No, but I have sunscreen and water if you want it," Alli answered, pulling a bottle of water out of her bag.

"Now you tell us." Megan grabbed the bottle. She gulped down about a third of the liquid before passing it to Sarah. As the bottle made its way around the group, Megan asked, "They have food in there, right? I missed lunch, and I'm starved."

"Yeah, I checked online," answered Jessica.

Ten minutes later, when the group approached the glass double doors leading into the theater, they could feel the cool air spilling out onto the sidewalk and were glad to be finally getting some relief after the last hour in the sun. The middle-aged woman at the ticket counter looked annoyed as Sarah and her group approached without tickets in hand.

"Tickets, please," the woman barked in a smoker's voice.

"We were told to give you my name and our tickets would be waiting for us at the front desk here?" Sarah questioned. She wasn't sure what the procedure was for getting will-call tickets.

The woman simply pointed to her left at a sign that read VIP ENTRANCE. There was no line there, so the group headed toward the other entrance, where a man in his early twenties sat wearing jeans and a band T-shirt. On the table in front of him was a pile of papers and a walkie-talkie.

Sarah spoke up. "I'm supposed to pick up tickets for Sarah Austin and friends."

The man looked on his list, and as he rummaged through the box at his feet, he said, "You should have come in through the VIP door. It's crazy hot out there." The group just looked back at him, dumbfounded. From the box, he pulled out five rectangular VIP backstage passes on black strings. The man smiled as he handed them out. "Let me get someone to bring you back," he said, then called back on the walkie-talkie.

Sarah and her friends slipped the passes over their heads and looked at each other, stunned that they were actually getting to go backstage.

A short guy with bleached-blond hair, wearing a black T-shirt that read *EXpireD Crew* in yellow letters, approached and proclaimed, "Hi, I'm Max. I'll take you back. Just follow me. There's only about an hour before EXpireD hits the stage, so there won't be much time to visit with the band. The opener is just about to start."

"I didn't know your friend Will was so well connected," Jeff said to his sister.

"He said he was friends with some of the guys in the band, but I didn't know we would get to go backstage," she admitted. "He did say he had some surprises for me, though."

Max turned around and smiled at her as if he knew some big secret that she wasn't in on. They followed him through an unmarked door and down a long cement hallway. The sound echoed as they clattered in their heels. Feeling a chill from the air-conditioning, Sarah paused to put her blouse and jacket back on. At the end of the hallway, Max led them through a second door that was guarded by a beefy woman in a black security T-shirt.

The smell of tacos and stale beer wafted through the air inside the large, open room. There were about fifteen people, some sitting in various chairs and some standing. On the couch in the center of the room sat a strikingly handsome man with long, dark cornrowed hair. He sat between two women—a tall, thin blonde and a shorter, obviously surgically enhanced, well-endowed brunette. Several people gathered around the couch and were talking animatedly to each other. Everyone was very casually dressed in jeans, and Sarah started to feel awkward in her mini and heels.

Sarah and her friends looked around the large room. They noted a long banquet-style table in the corner farthest from the door. A small steam table sat near a pile of plates on one end, and the rest of the table was cluttered with half-empty crystal platters. On the floor below the table sat a stainless steel cooler with a fluorescent-orange sticker that bellowed LOAD LAST. It was scratched and dented and obviously the band's own personal stash. The group couldn't see what kind of food was on the table from where they were standing, but by the way the room smelled, there had to be tacos somewhere. They were all hungry and dehydrated, so they felt relieved that getting some sustenance might still be possible.

As Sarah and her friends gawked at the food table, a tall, thin, pale man with perfectly messed black emo hair that hung in his eyes approached Sarah. Offering his hand, he asked with a very charming British accent, "Are you the Birthday Girl?"

Sarah nodded.

"I'm Nick Reyes." He cleared his throat and magically commanded the attention of everyone in the room. "This is Charlie"—Nick waved a hand around the room—"Marc, Amanda, Tiz, Hayden, Nacho, and everybody else. Hey, everyone, these are Will's friends."

The room echoed with a loud "Yo."

Sarah and her friends each held up a hand in a motionless wave, and the room returned to its previous chatter volume.

"Hi, I'm Sarah," she said to Nick, then introduced her friends.

Jeff whispered in Sarah's ear. "Unreal!"

"I know," she mouthed back.

"Hold on a sec. I need to grab something before I forget." Nick reached for a piece of folded fabric on the arm of the couch. "You're Jeff, right? Will says you are a fan of the band?"

"Yeah, huge," Jeff admitted.

"Here," Nick said as he handed Jeff a folded EXpireD T-shirt. "All the guys signed the back—thought you might fancy a souvenir."

"Thanks, man," boomed Jeff with a smile. He held up the shirt and gawked at the signatures in silver ink, pointing out Nick's to Jessica before refolding it in a quick roll.

Nick studied the group of friends. "Let me see if I can get this straight." He eyed the leggy girl with blonde hair and, winking his eye, said, "Megan?"

She smiled and nodded at him.

"And you're Alli?" he said, raising his eyebrows as he made eye contact with the bright blue eyes of the girl with wavy red hair pulled back in a loose ponytail.

"Yes," Alli admitted with a smile.

Nick turned to the last girl, with her pecan-colored hair to her shoulders and her deep-chocolate eyes. Staring at her ample chest, he said, "And lovely Jessica."

Jessica had been blessed with her double D eye magnets since the seventh grade and had dealt with many guys like Nick. "Up here." Jessica chuckled and pointed to her eyes. She turned with a look of *Can you believe this guy?*

"You're pretty good," said Megan.

"That's what they say," Nick confessed, unaffected by Jessica's correction.

"And not at all modest," added Megan, smiling and locking eyes with Nick. She loved bad boys, and he definitely qualified.

Alli spoke up. "I love your accent. Is it British?"

"It's hard to tell what it is these days. Originally, it was English—been here since I was thirteen. Our mate Will was one of the first blokes I met after I crossed the pond."

Just then, a guy with a two-day-old beard and spiked sandy-blond hair joined the chatting group. The tips of his hair were blonder than the dark roots. "Beer…soda…water," he offered, pointing to the food table. He twisted open a bottle of lemon mojito and handed it to Sarah. "It's your twenty-first birthday. You have to have something to drink." He smiled at her and continued. "I saw y'all eyin' the food table. Help yourselves—there's plenty."

"Thanks, we're starved. We were going to grab something once we got in the theater, but we ran out of time," admitted Megan as the group beelined for the food table.

Sarah stayed, talking with Nick and the guy Sarah thought had been introduced as Hayden. She was too nervous to eat.

"So, you and Will, huh?" Hayden asked, raising one eyebrow and looking down at Sarah's petite frame.

Sarah took a long draw on her mojito and smiled nervously.

"Did you really meet on the Internet?" questioned Nick.

She brought her free hand up to cover her eyes and peeked out between her fingers, embarrassed. She still couldn't believe it herself, and it sounded even worse coming from someone she didn't know.

"Yes." She grimaced.

Hayden chimed in. "And you've never met him in person, right?"

Sarah twisted the bottle in her hands and took a deep breath. Feeling a bit anxious about where the questions were leading, she gathered her courage and looked him in the eyes. "Your point?"

Nick cupped his hand on Hayden's shoulder. They looked at each other, and Nick confessed, "Oh, our little Will is in *so* much trouble."

Sarah lowered just a little as she considered their comment.

"So what do you really know about this bloke you met on the Net?" asked Nick. "You've never even seen a photo?"

"Isn't it too late to worry about th—why?" She stopped midsentence. She wondered why they kept asking whether she knew what he looked like. "Is he paper bag ugly or something?"

Nick smiled at Hayden with a knowing look, lifted an eyebrow, and then shouted across the room. "Hey, Amanda, is Will paper bag ugly?"

The blonde on the couch laughed and yelled back, "No, I'd do him—no bag!"

Seated next to her, Marc shouted, "Hell, I'd do him, and I'm straight!"

Laughter erupted throughout the room.

"I'll make sure to let him know you're pining for him!" declared Hayden.

"Oh, he knows," said Marc with a devious expression before slowly, purposefully wetting Amanda's entire left cheek with his tongue.

The room filled with hoots, shrieks, and moans. Sarah blushed. Her gaze caught Jessica's eyes, and they both chuckled.

"So, spill. What do you know about Will?" Hayden looked at Sarah with true curiosity on his face.

"Well," she began, taking another drink of her liquid courage, "I know Will is smart, hilariously funny, selfless—"

"I don't know about that," Hayden whispered to Nick.

"Honest—"

"She might change her mind on that one too," said Nick as he smacked Hayden in the gut.

Sarah studied them with surprise, hoping they would elaborate. They didn't. She was starting to feel that she was missing half the conversation. "I know his friends mean more to him than all else in the world. And I know I could tell him anything and he wouldn't condemn me." She could tell her face glowed with her feelings for Will. "He doesn't like gossip, and he doesn't blab secrets."

"Yeah, that's true," admitted Hayden.

"She might have him pegged, after all, Hayden," Nick said with a smirk. Seemingly satisfied with her answers, he moved on. "So, Birthday

Girl, which one of your friends is single?" They glanced over to her friends as the girls and Jeff approached with food plates in hand.

"Oh my gosh, you're Nick," she said with a sudden epiphany.

"That's me," he said, looking around the room as if she had a mental flaw.

Sarah took another drink. "Well, Will told me to keep them away from you. Apparently, you're a womanizer."

He brought his right hand to his heart like she had wounded him and, with a chuckle, said, "Me? I thought he didn't gossip?"

"He doesn't," stated Hayden. He looked over at Sarah's friends and back to Nick, shaking his head.

Nick faux glowered at Hayden. Then he turned to the group and, in his thickest, sexiest accent, asked, "Any of you ladies want to go out after the show?"

Hayden burst out laughing. Megan and Alli looked at each other and smiled. Jessica rolled her eyes. While Sarah's friends ate, they all discussed the must-see clubs in Minneapolis with Nick and Hayden.

"Prohibition is pretty hot right now. Parts of it are in the tunnels under the city," proclaimed Megan. "They say that one of the dance floors is in an area that used to be an old speakeasy and it's haunted. They have great live music—but not as good as EXpireD," she said, touching Nick's forearm, coaxing a bigger smile from him.

"Or Imposters is popular. I've never been there, but it got great reviews in *City Pages*," added Alli. "We were going to take Sarah there tonight, until this fell into our laps. We could all go out dancing to either club after the concert. They're both close. We could walk from here. They're closer than the car."

They all continued to discuss the evening's clubbing options until Sarah spoke up. "Will doesn't really like clubbing, and I'd rather go somewhere quiet where we can talk."

Her friends scowled at her, disappointed. But it was her birthday, and they would do whatever she wanted.

Hayden's eyes met Nick's, and he nodded. Then he announced that the band wouldn't be able to go with the group anyway, because they had to load onto a bus right after the concert and head to Chicago.

"You could come with us on the road. We can always find room on the buses," offered Nick. "I bet I could fit all of you in my sleeping quarters. We'd have to…stack up, you know, but I've done it before. It's quite cozy." He smiled a huge toothy smile, and everyone laughed. From what Will had told her about Nick, Sarah doubted that Nick was really joking. Will's friends had even admitted that Will didn't spread gossip.

Nick entertained them as he flirted with all the girls, making them laugh over and over. Even Jeff was charmed. As they interacted, Sarah noticed Hayden watching her. It wasn't in a creepy lurker sort of way, but more like he was subtly gathering information that he would be reporting back to Will. Sarah quickly became self-conscious.

"When is Will going to get here? Has anyone heard from him?" she finally asked.

"He'll be here soon. I'm sure he's just waiting to make a big entrance," Nick admitted, meeting Hayden's eyes again, and they both poorly concealed their smirks.

Just then, Nick's phone vibrated. He pulled it out to check it and quickly typed a response.

Then he leaned closer to Sarah, placing his arm around her shoulders and raising his eyebrows. "Hmm…You smell divine." He smiled as he checked his vibrating phone one more time, then let out a single devious laugh. Acting like he had coughed, he continued. "That was Will. He'll be here soon. You and your friends should probably take your seats, though. It's too bad, but it's time for us to get to work."

They said their good-byes to the band, and soon Jeff and the girls were led out into the dimmed theater. The opening act was just wrapping up as the group sat down. Their seats were in a roped-off section on the far right of the stage, in the front row, and the view was perfect.

Seated directly behind them was a local radio announcing team from KSWB. The two were easily recognizable from the billboards around town and were local celebrities of sorts. Megan pointed them out to the girls as the theater lights brightened and the opening band exited the stage.

"Your Will must have some pull if we're in front of them."

"I guess it pays to know the band. They were really interesting guys," stated Sarah.

"And hot," added Megan.

Sarah noticed there were two empty chairs next to them and wondered if Will was bringing a friend. He hadn't said he was bringing anyone. *But who wants to travel alone?* she thought. After about ten minutes, the lights over the stage brightened, and the theater lights dimmed again. The band entered the stage, picked up their instruments, and started to jam a song everyone knew from their first album. The theater went wild. Jeff knew all the words and was leaning across Jessica to sing them into Sarah's ear, just to annoy her.

Alli gazed at Sarah questioningly, giving her a look that asked, *Are you OK?*

Sarah glanced over at the empty chairs next to her and back to her friend.

Alli mouthed, "He'll be here. You look gorgeous."

Sarah smiled and ran her fingers through her hair nervously with a sigh.

The next song was from the band's new album, and it had a more hard-core sound to it. Sarah looked around the theater, scanning the dark spaces for anyone who could be Will. She was getting more anxious for him to arrive and was starting to worry that he wasn't going to show up at all. Maybe the band was checking her out for him and they warned him not to come.

When the song ended, Hayden continued a soft drum cadence in the background, and Nick began to speak.

"It's great to be here again, *Minneapolis!*" The crowd cheered, and Nick waited for the noise to die out. "Let me introduce the band." He introduced everyone else onstage and then continued. "And I'm Nick Reyes on bass. We have something very special for you tonight. Our next song is a ballad of sorts that my mate Will and I wrote, and he has graciously agreed to come out here and sing it with me. Let's all give it up for...*Jonathan Williams*, everyone!"

At first, there was silence as the audience tried to figure out what had just been announced. Then a tall man with a perfect angular, masculine silhouette and tousled brown hair joined the band on the stage. He scanned the crowd as he strapped on the bright blue Gibson guitar.

There was a shout from the back. "Holy shit! It's Jonathan Williams!" and the crowd went wild. The screaming grew and grew, until no one in the theater could hear anything, not even the band starting up.

The noise slowly began to level off, and Sarah just barely caught what the gorgeous man said into the microphone. "This one goes out to the Birthday Girl—you know who you are." And he smiled, showing his perfect white teeth.

Sarah looked at her brother and friends. They gawked at her. In unison, the girls mouthed, "Oh my god," with dropped jaws. Jeff just shook his head in disbelief.

Sarah couldn't make sense of it. Her head was spinning. She looked up at the stage, trying to concentrate on the song that was dedicated to her. The melody was gentle and sweet. The words flowed beautifully. Sarah was having a hard time catching all of them, but the lyrics were something about being lost and empty, searching the world and never finding what he was looking for, then stumbling upon her by accident and everything changing. Wow. Her head was really spinning now. She stared up at the stage, at the man she had never met, yet she knew so well. Then it all started to click—how he had been so vague when talking about his family and his job, why he hated the paparazzi so much. How could she have not seen all the signs? How could she have been so stupid? *It doesn't matter*, she told herself. After all, she had promised to be flexible and open to surprises, but she never expected this.

The song ended, and the crowd screamed wildly again as Will bowed, waved, and exited the stage. The band started up again, and Sarah noticed it was an upbeat song this time. That was about all she noticed until the song started to wind down and two people approached her group of friends.

Sarah watched as the gorgeous man from the stage scanned her friends. When his eyes met hers, she felt a zing of electricity buzz through her body. Their eyes remained locked in a silent conversation. When the men reached their seats, Will glanced down with a look of embarrassment, as if he just realized he had been staring.

He leaned over and spoke loud enough in her ear for her to hear. "Hi, Birthday Girl."

She looked up at him, shaking her head in disbelief. She was still in shock when Will leaned in again.

"We finally meet." He smiled. "See, I was right—you are beautiful."

Sarah felt a ting of relief from his words. He sounded the same as he did on the phone. *Could he really be the same person?*

"This is Sam. He's my personal security—our security." He paused. "Don't let him scare you, though. He's a decent guy."

Sarah waved at Sam, and he nodded back.

Will and Sarah's eyes locked again. They sat studying each other's faces. Sarah dissolved in Will's large ice-blue eyes. They were almost colorless in this light and were lined with thick lashes—the envy of every girl. She noted his dazzling crooked smile that gave way to a single dimple on his right cheek, and his hair, tousled chocolate brown, was just the right length to run her fingers through. She restrained herself, though. Time passed without them noticing anything but each other.

The band played on, and the crowd reacted to their favorite songs, but the two never noticed until Max, the short blond man who had led Sarah and her friends to the band's greenroom, came out and whispered in Sam's ear.

Will announced to Sarah and her friends, "We have to leave now, or we'll never get out of here."

The group promptly rose. The girls grabbed their purses, and they all followed Max back to the greenroom.

They stopped in the hallway outside the room, and Will declared, "Let me just grab my guitar and bag. I've got a car waiting out back for us."

"Uh, what about my car?" Jeff stammered.

"Sam, could you come back for Jeff's car after we get to the hotel?" Will asked as he reached for the handle on the greenroom door. He looked over his shoulder for Sam's reply.

"Yeah, no problem," answered Sam. Will came back out a minute later with his gear. "I'm all set." He smiled at Sarah. "We've got to go. We can talk in the car, OK?"

Sarah nodded, and they headed toward the back alley.

Chapter Four

They all swiftly exited the back of the theater and started loading into the black SUV. Just as Sarah was climbing into the car, two teenage girls ran around the corner of the building with cameras raised. They startled Sarah, and her heel slipped, causing her to fall backward slightly. Will caught her with his hand at the small of her back, and from where his fingers touched her, she felt warmth radiate through her. Her heartbeat quickened, and she closed her eyes, letting the heat linger. She scooted across the leather seat, still feeling the warmth fill her as Will squished in next to her. Sam closed the door behind Will and climbed into the front passenger seat next to the driver just as the fan-girls were approaching the SUV.

When they were close enough, the girls began pounding on the tinted windows, yelling, "Jonathan! Jonathan! Please!"

Will made eye contact with Sam in the mirror hanging on the car's visor above Sam's head, and Sam handed him a black Sharpie. Sarah realized that it must have been a security arrangement the two had worked out, because Will pushed the toggle button and the window slowly lowered, putting the girls within touching distance.

"I hate to neglect my fans." He smiled his perfect smile. "Hi, ladies. I'll sign an autograph for each of you, but no pictures, OK?"

Sarah noted how enticing his voice sounded—sweet, yet playful and confident. It drew her in. She had heard it on the phone too. She knew he couldn't help it. That was just how he sounded when he spoke. The fan-girls screamed with excitement and frantically agreed. Will hurriedly signed the autographs and wished the girls a good night as the driver pulled away.

"That's crazy. Does that always happen?" asked Jessica.

"Yeah, pretty much. It's usually worse. If you don't mind, could everybody buckle up? Things can get really cracked around me. After that, I thought we could all go back to my hotel and talk. Otherwise, we'll be mobbed anywhere we go." Will paused. "But it's up to the Birthday Girl." He handed the marker back to Sam.

They all looked at Sarah.

"That sounds great," she said, even though all she really wanted was to be alone with Will. She wondered if she was dreaming. She couldn't believe this man she knew so well was really a famous actor. She just never expected him to be the person they had been talking about when they first met. Celebrities didn't go on those sites. She fell silent for a second as she pondered the situation and then snapped back to reality. "Oh, where are my manners?" She introduced her friends and brother. When she was done, she turned to Will and whispered in his ear. "You lied to me."

"I'm sorry. I tried to be truthful." He continued to apologize with his eyes. "I just had to be sure I could trust you."

His expression changed to reverent, forcing her to ask, "What?"

"I knew you would call me on lying. It's who you are."

"Is that a good thing?"

He nodded and held his gaze.

Her resolve melted. She thought about all he had told her. She knew he really hadn't lied outright. She glared at him for just a second to make her point. "Never again." Then she smirked to tell him all was forgiven.

Sam spoke up. "Jon, when we arrive at the hotel, we'll be coming in through the garage entrance. I need you all to stay in the vehicle until I've checked everything out. I'll come back to get you when it's all clear."

The girls all looked at each other. "Wow, that sounds serious," said Alli.

Will sighed. "You don't know the half of it. There's a lot of crazies out there! I think we got away just in time tonight, but with such a public appearance, there will be hell to pay tomorrow. It's going to be a lot harder for us to get around the rest of the week."

Sarah bit her lip nervously and looked at him questioningly. "So I'll get to see you all week?" she asked with excitement. He had never really said how long he would be staying, so this was good news to her.

He tilted his head and stared at her, puzzled. "Well, I didn't come here to do the concert."

"So who did you come here to do, Will?" Megan asked, laughing.

Laughter broke out throughout the SUV. Sarah rolled her eyes.

"Not this again," complained Jeff.

"Again?" asked Will.

"Oh, it was nothing—just joking around with the band," Sarah answered quickly, not wanting to go into detail.

"Your friends are pretty witty," noted Will.

"Yeah, I know," Sarah said as she shot Megan the evil eye, saying wordlessly that she was going to pay for that comment.

They arrived at the hotel garage and made it up to the suite without any issues. The suite was large with beautifully polished granite floors and tall granite pillars that rose to the twelve-foot coffered ceiling. To the right of the door was a small kitchen area with a refrigerator, a microwave, and a fully stocked bar with a sink. A rectangular stone dining table, which could seat six in its black leather straight-backed chairs, divided the kitchen from the living area. The table was adorned with a huge bouquet of bright-pink peonies that rose three feet in height off the tabletop and was at least two feet in diameter. The flowers' sugary scent filled the air, and Sarah smiled, wondering if their presence was a coincidence. She had mentioned to Will that they were her favorite flower—but only once. In the living area, there was a long L-shaped beige couch and two oversized chairs arranged around a large black leather padded ottoman table. The girls all removed their heels, and everyone got comfortable on the furniture as they gawked at their surroundings.

"This is a really beautiful place," Sarah stated.

"Yeah," Will said, looking around. "My assistant always does a great job booking. She doesn't usually go to this extreme, but I think she was trying to impress you." He ordered some pizza and drinks from room service, and Sam left to get Jeff's car.

Will finally seemed to relax, and he started acting a bit silly, as he always had on the phone with Sarah. They chatted about the concert and the band for a while, and Megan admitted, again, that she thought Nick was hot. Will and Sarah shared the detailed story of how they had met online, and locked eyes, ice to emeralds, often as they spoke. Several times, they finished each other's sentences like an old married couple who had been together forever.

The girls shared with Will the story of how they had all met. Jessica and Sarah met the first day of seventh grade, in biology class. They sat at the same lunch table that day and had been friends ever since. In high school, Jessica got a job at the movie theater in Oakdale, and that was where she met Alli and Megan. Alli went to an expensive private school, but lived only a couple of blocks from Jessica. Megan, on the other hand, lived fifteen minutes east of the rest of the girls in a totally different school district.

Alli, Megan, and Jessica had worked behind the candy counter at the theater, filling buckets of popcorn doused with buttery topping and selling overpriced candy. Sarah spent most of her free time at the theater watching movies, waiting for her friends to get off work. All four of the girls ended up going to the University of Minnesota and were able to get into the same dorm freshman year. Last year, they all rented a house off campus, and their friendships had survived the trials of living together, so they figured they'd be friends forever.

The food came, and they ate as Sarah shared the story of how she had found out Jessica was dating her brother. Will sat down on the arm of the couch next to Sarah and watched her as she spoke. When their eyes met, they both broke into huge smiles.

Sarah explained how Jeff and Jessica had been trying to keep their relationship a secret, because Jessica didn't know how Sarah would react to the two dating. If it didn't work out, they didn't want her to know at all. Jessica had been attracted to Jeff since she was fifteen, but he was kind of aloof in his own world of friends. He had seen Jessica grow up in front of his eyes. She was always at the house, always at the lake cabin, and her mom had even become good friends with Sarah's parents.

Then Jeff went to the University of Wisconsin in Madison and was gone for most of four years, except one summer. Last year, when he graduated with his engineering degree, he got a job at Meditec in the Twin Cities. Jeff moved back home because he was debating going back for his master's degree and didn't want to commit to a house or a lease before he figured out his life. Sarah, not having seen her brother in a while, invited Jeff and a couple of his friends to a gathering at the rental house to celebrate the start of the school year. Two weeks later, Jessica started giving excuses why she couldn't go out with the girls.

"'I've got a paper due on Monday.' 'I don't feel good.' 'I'm not in the mood to go out tonight, and I'd just drag you guys down,'" Sarah mocked in her best Jessica voice. "We all knew she was dating someone. She did it all the time, didn't admit anything, and we would find out later that it was a guy. Well, several weeks later, Jessica was still putting on the charade, so we went out without her as usual. I ended up catching a ride home early from a friend, because I wasn't feeling well, and found my brother and best friend making out on the front steps. I threw up on the sidewalk when I saw them," Sarah admitted, "but it may have been because I was sick."

Everyone laughed.

"We saw the kind of skanks that Jeff used to date in high school, and Jessica is definitely an upgrade. We were stunned that she would go out with him," said Megan.

"Hey, that was a long time ago," boomed Jeff.

"Anyone up for some music? Jeff, I hear you play guitar. Does your band have a name?"

"No, it's not so much a band as a group of guys who like to hang out and jam," replied Jeff.

"That's what it's all about, right? Nick, Hayden, and Chris Hanson, from Invasion, and I used to play in Nick's pool house when we were fifteen. It was a blast, and now look at them," Will said as he squeezed in on the couch cushion next to Sarah. He held his hand out on his lap with his palm up and looked at Sarah as if asking permission to hold her hand. She smiled and pressed her hand into his.

Alli spoke up. "So why Will and not Jon?"

"My friends call me Will because my last name is Williams. When I met most of those guys, I was trying to distance myself from my acting career. I had just gotten the reviews back from *The Forgotten Year.*"

Sarah sighed, thinking about finally getting to hold hands with the man she'd been dreaming about for months.

He playfully bumped shoulders with her. "It was a movie I had done with my brother, Jack. Well, Jack got these great reviews on the movie, and mine…kind of sucked. I just wanted to forget that year, and I vowed not to act again. I didn't want to be known as Jack's talentless brother, as they printed in the press, so I got heavily involved in my music. My buddies and I started a band. We did some gigs, and my friends introduced me as Will so I wouldn't have to explain my acting career. It stuck—with my good friends, anyway."

"So what made you go back into acting?" questioned Jessica.

"Well, when I was eighteen, my dad said, 'You either get a job that actually pays money'"—Will raised both eyebrows, and everyone laughed—"'or you're going to college.' I didn't have a clue what I wanted to do with my life at that time, and he offered me the lead in an indie movie he had just signed on to called *Uproar*. It was a pretty good fit for me, and I liked the script, so I agreed. *Uproar* got great reviews. John Cranston saw it and asked me to read for *The Demigod*. That was my big break."

"So, Will," Megan said with a smile, "is your brother acting still?"

"Ah, no," Will stammered. "I killed him." His expression fell flat and distant. The group looked around at each other, unsure of what to say. After a very pregnant pause, Will continued. "You didn't know? I thought everybody in the world knew. It was all over the media. It happened four years ago." He looked into Sarah's face apprehensively. As he spoke, he slowly brushed his thumb nervously back and forth over the top of her joined hand.

"Jack and I were at a club with his girlfriend, Camille. We were arrogantly showing off going to that particular club. It was stupid, but it was the place to be seen, and at the time, that was important to us.

The paparazzi were all over Jack as we left. He had just signed a huge contract for the lead in *The Houston Chronicles*. When we left the club, one of the paparazzi from the sidewalk chased our car on his motorcycle. He just had to have one more picture. But instead of getting the shot, he spilled his bike right in front of us. I swerved so I wouldn't kill him, and crossed into oncoming traffic. An SUV T-boned us on the side Jack was sitting, so…He was in a coma for three days before he died." Will swallowed hard and whispered, "Three days." After another long pause, he looked into Sarah's eyes. "Camille broke some bones and had a bad concussion. I bruised my ribs and fractured my wrist, but survived."

Sarah squeezed his hand and leaned her head on his shoulder. "Wow, that must have been awful, but it wasn't your fault," she whispered, shaking her head against him.

Air escaped his throat, making a guttural balking noise, and he curtly said, "Yeah."

"I'm sorry, I didn't realize your brother was that Jack Williams," admitted Megan.

Tears pricked in Sarah's eyes as she tilted her head and spied Will's vacant gaze. She remembered hearing about Jack's death in the news. Girls had cried in the hallway of her high school after it happened, as if he was their boyfriend. At the time, she thought they were crazy. It was tragic, but they didn't even know him. Now, she wanted to cry—not for Jack, but for his brother's loss.

Just then, Sam returned with Jeff's keys. He came in using his own key, and Will looked up out of his daydream, nodding in acknowledgment. "Sorry, I'm not usually such a downer." He got up, got another beer, and opened it. "Sam, there's some pizza if you're hungry. Anyone want another drink?" He looked around for any takers. When no one showed interest, he said, "So how about we play some music? Jeff?"

The guys messed around on the guitar for a bit as the girls sat back and hashed the concert. After about forty minutes, Sam spoke up.

"I'm going to head off to bed if you don't need me. It's after three, and I can't pull all-nighters anymore. I value my sleep since I've had kids."

"Sure, we can reconnect about ten. No, make it noon—after we get some rest."

"Sounds good," Sam said, then explained to Jeff where to find his car and headed off to his hotel room next door.

Jeff looked around the room and announced, "We should probably get going too, or we're going to have to sleep here."

Jessica was sleeping, curled in the large chair, and Sarah could tell Jeff wanted to get her home.

"What are you, thirty?" Megan asked. "Do you see who is sitting in this hotel room with us? I'm not going anywhere."

"I have to work at the hospital in five hours. I would like *some* sleep— at your house, OK?" Alli added, ignoring Megan's comment. Sarah assumed Alli would be staying at her house. She always had, ever since high school, if they were out past midnight. Alli's parents didn't approve of her having a social life.

"You've got to be kidding! Can't you call in sick?" Megan glared at Alli.

"Some of us worked a full day before the concert. Do you even have a job, Megan?" Jeff asked in a condescending tone.

"I'll be here all week," Will added with a chuckle.

Megan met Sarah's eyes and settled. "Fine."

Sitting down on the arm of the chair next to Jessica, Jeff ran his fingers tenderly through her hair. "Come on, we're heading home."

Sarah watched her brother intently. Love had undeniably changed him. She remembered the girls he used to date before Jessica. She wouldn't call them girlfriends, because they were never around long. They were never his equal intellectually and rarely had any common interests with him. With Jessica, he was different—grown up, responsible, and half of an equal team. Sarah adored watching him take care of her best friend.

Jessica slowly opened her eyes and smiled up at him. "'K," she said, still half asleep.

Will spoke up, talking to the group. "Could you all do me a favor? Don't tweet about tonight or tell anyone what you did. Especially don't share where I'm staying. It's a safety thing, so *please?*"

Everyone agreed. The girls grabbed their purses and shoes, everyone except Sarah. Her eyes met Will's with a questioning look. He ghosted a smile and looked down.

"Aren't you coming, Sarah?" asked Jeff as he headed toward the door.

"No, I think," she said shyly, looking at her feet, "I'm going to stay." Then, barely moving her head, she glanced at Will out of the corner of her eye to make sure that she had read his body language right. She felt relieved when the dimple appeared on his right cheek.

Sarah's friends gasped in surprise. It was out of character for her to stay. She was always very cautious and conservative when it came to guys. She nodded to reassure them that she knew what she was doing.

"I'll be fine."

"If you need a ride, just let me know. I'll come back," Jeff assured her.

"Thanks." She smiled at her big brother. He was two years older than her and had always been a bit protective—in a good way, though, she thought.

Jeff and the girls said their good-byes and funneled out into the hallway. Will closed the door behind them and clicked the dead bolt as he turned to face Sarah.

Chapter Five

Alone together at last, Will slowly crossed the room, his eyes locked on Sarah. Seeing him advancing toward her, her heart began to jump out of her chest. It wasn't because he was even more gorgeous in person than in the movies. It wasn't because he smelled so good, fresh even without cologne, or that his ice-blue eyes were incredibly hypnotizing. It was because he was Will, the guy she connected with on so many levels intellectually, and she knew him so well.

As he reached her, he brought his hand to her face, and with the lightest touch, he tenderly brushed a strand of hair off her cheek, tucking it behind her ear. She involuntarily shuddered as his endless eyes poured into hers. He cupped her face in his hands, his grasp gentle. Bending to meet her, he brushed his lips against hers, barely touching, and again. A small moan escaped her throat. He wrapped his arms around her and pulled her flush against his chest to deepen the kiss. Their lips parted, and Sarah pushed up on her tiptoes, weaving her fingers through his silken hair. They stood kissing, forgetting that anything existed in the world but each other.

As their tongues slow danced, his hands leisurely skimmed down her sides, over her ribs, and stilled at her waist. Several minutes passed, or it might have been a week, before Will pulled back with a sigh, saying, "Hmm, I've wanted to do that all night." He combed his fingers through his hair as he caught his breath.

Sarah swallowed, feeling the butterflies in her stomach flutter back down out of her chest, and whispered, "Wow."

Then she smiled, and he leaned in again, meshing with her lips.

He led her to the couch, still kissing, and when he broke the kiss, he said, "You sit. I'll be right back."

"I'm not a dog," Sarah mumbled, pouting her lower lip.

Will smirked a barely there smile at her comment and disappeared into the bedroom. A minute later, he returned holding a rectangular package wrapped in silver paper with a shimmering blue satin bow.

"I have something for you—for your birthday."

"It's not my birthday anymore," she reminded him. Midnight was hours ago. "Besides, you've already given me everything I could have ever dreamed of." She smiled, looking up at him from under her eyelashes. She couldn't seem to get the smile off her face.

He handed her the gift. "Well, in reality, it's a present for me, even though it's yours."

"Selfish much?" she teased, pushing a loose tendril out of her eyes.

He laughed. "Just open it. You'll see."

As she mulled over in her mind what he'd said, Sarah started to get nervous. She couldn't think of anything a guy could give a girl that was really a present for the guy except lingerie. No. She shook that thought from her head. *Stop thinking about that*, she told herself. He wouldn't. Besides, the box was too heavy. She pulled off the wrapping.

"A laptop?"

"Yeah, I just thought we could Skype each other when we're not able to be together, so I can see those beautiful green eyes of yours."

"Oh," she stammered, feeling a bit overwhelmed.

"You said your old computer was really outdated and your webcam didn't work. This one has a large screen and a ton of memory. I even loaded it with mobile Internet service, so you can use it anywhere. I was going to get you an iPad, but I thought the computer would be more useful for school."

"You didn't have to get me anything," she said. "Thanks, though, it's really great. I did need a new computer. Mine is super slow, and my operating system is so outdated." Stopping herself, she repeated, "You didn't need to get me anything. This is too much, Will. I can't possibly accept it." Sarah had never gotten such an expensive gift from a guy before, and she wasn't quite sure how to react. She liked that he was practical and that the gift was well thought out, though.

"I wouldn't have gotten it if I thought it was too much. I want you to have it," he said in his mesmerizing no-one-can-argue voice.

"Thanks." She reached up and grabbed the bottom of his T-shirt, pulling him down on the couch next to her. She kissed him on the cheek and, fighting a yawn, asked, "Will you sing me the song from tonight? I couldn't catch all the words, and it was so beautiful."

Will looked at her questioningly, then rose without a word, went into the bedroom, and came back with a yellow vintage T-shirt. Tossing it to her, he said, "Put this on. You're not sleeping in that miniskirt. I'll grab my guitar and change myself." Then he vanished back into the bedroom.

Sarah slipped out of her shirt and tank top. She pulled the T-shirt over the top of her head. It smelled so good that she paused, taking in his clean, masculine scent before pulling her head completely through. She slipped off her bra, needled her arms into the T-shirt, and slid out of her mini. The bottom of the shirt fell to her midthigh. She neatly folded her clothes and placed them in a pile next to her purse. Sarah positioned herself on the couch, tucking her legs up next to her, just as Will reentered the room carrying his guitar.

"I wish I'd been quicker," he said with eyebrows raised.

Sarah blushed and looked up at him. Her jaw would have fallen to the floor if she hadn't caught herself. He was wearing a snug-fitting gray T-shirt and an exquisitely fitted pair of black cutoff cotton sweats that hung low on his hips. Through the clinging shirt, she could see the sinuous lines of his rock-hard abdomen and the lean, powerful muscles of his chest. But the picture-perfect curvature of his backside was what made her take a sharp breath.

And I was worried about not having chemistry—definitely not a problem and definitely no evil twin. She smiled.

Oblivious to her reaction, he waved the acoustic guitar back and forth, pretending not to know how to hold it. "Honestly, it's all smoke and mirrors on the stage. I'm not very good," he claimed in a sincerely humble manner. "If you knew how nervous I was getting up in front of the crowd tonight, you wouldn't make me do this."

He sat down next to her. His thigh pushed against hers and held as he positioned the guitar between his legs. The heat from Will's touching skin penetrated Sarah's entire body right down to the core, and she took a deep breath, savoring the rise in temperature, as he began to play.

His deep, sensual voice wrapped around her like a warm blanket, and the words were amazingly sweet. The song was more heartfelt than she could have believed, and when it ended, Sarah's eyes were moist with tears.

"It was so beautiful," she whispered. "Was that about me?"

"Every word." Will smiled and kissed the top of her head. He slid his guitar to the floor, wrapped his arm around her shoulder, and pulled her into an embrace. His sincere expression tugged on her heart. She fused into his strong but gentle grasp.

They sat in silence, each one relishing the comfort the other brought. No more words were needed.

She was almost asleep when he lifted her into his arms and whispered, "I'm not going to ruin this." She felt his warm lips press against her forehead. "Sweet dreams, beautiful."

When Sarah awoke at ten thirty, she was surprised to find herself in the large bed. She stretched and rose, looking around for any sign of Will. She quickly checked herself in the mirror and bent over, shaking out her hair to straighten it. When she was convinced there was not much more she could do to make herself look better with no makeup or a brush, she came out of the bedroom in search of him. He was sitting at the stone table eating scrambled eggs and mixed melons with strawberries. He had headphones down around his neck, and Sarah could hear a familiar piano composition flowing from the mini speakers.

"I tried to wait for you, but I was starving," he admitted with a big smile. He had obviously showered. His hair was damp and curled up on the ends. He had shaved and was sporting a long white hotel-supplied terry cloth robe.

Sarah swallowed hard when she saw him. She couldn't let him know how he affected her. "So what are we having?" she asked. Still wearing the large T-shirt, she approached the table, inspecting the food.

Will grabbed her waist and pulled her onto his lap. "Anything that's here," he answered, pointing to the eggs, fruit, whole wheat toast, and two large mugs of coffee on the tray. "Or if you don't see anything you want, we can order it."

"I want this," she declared, snagging a new toothbrush wrapped in plastic that was sitting on the table next to the food tray.

"You need that!" he proclaimed with a chuckle.

"Oh, shut up! Thanks, though, for getting it for me."

"Thought it would make your day," he said, taking another bite of egg.

"It did. What are you listening to? It sounds really familiar."

"It's just piano music. It keeps me grounded, relaxes me. My mom always played this album at Christmastime when I was growing up. It reminds me of Jack."

Sarah picked up his iPod off the table. Spying the artist, she proclaimed, "I listen to this same album when I study for finals. I have it on my iPod too."

Will set down his fork and brushed her hair off her shoulder. He began kissing her jawline, then whispered, "See, it's meant to be." When his kisses browsed the corner of her mouth, Sarah stood up quickly, waving the toothbrush in her hand. She wasn't going to kiss him with morning breath.

"I'll be right back," she declared as he chuckled.

Once she returned, she sat in the chair next to Will and helped herself to a plate of food.

"Where did you sleep last night?" Sarah asked trivially, pretending to be just making polite conversation.

He looked at her with a half smirk on his face. "In the bed. Don't you remember? It's a big bed," he revealed nonchalantly as he continued to eat.

Sarah smiled, embarrassed. She wished that she hadn't been so tired, but also was glad that Will was a gentleman. Not obsessively, though. He had slept in the bed, after all.

"So what's on the agenda today?" she asked.

"Anything you want, beautiful."

"I'd like a shower and a change of clothes for starters. Can we go back to my house?" She paused. "You'd have to meet my parents," she added hesitantly. She was embarrassed that she was living at home for the summer. He seemed so worldly, and she didn't want to come off as immature. "They'll be gracious. I promise." She wrinkled her face apologetically.

"Meet your parents?" He cringed, and then she cringed. He tenderly grasped her shoulder and admitted, "You know, I still kind of live with my parents too. I rent their guesthouse." He skimmed his fingers, featherlight, along her jawline and then kissed her cheek. "I used to have a condo, but I came home from the store one day and found some crazy fan lying on my bed, wearing nothing but her panties. It really freaked me out."

Sarah gasped. She couldn't believe that a woman would do that, though she knew he was telling the truth.

"I didn't know if she was a psycho killer, and I couldn't get her to leave, so I called the police. It became a media circus—a huge mess. I just didn't feel safe in the condo anymore, so I moved home."

"Wow. That's crazy," declared Sarah.

"Yeah, right? Welcome to my life." He downed the last of his coffee. "Let's check last night's damage before we go, OK? May I borrow your laptop?"

She continued eating while he checked the local news and then the gossip sites.

"Well, it doesn't look too bad yet. The rags know I'm in town, but it doesn't look like they know where I'm staying. There are some pictures of me onstage, but only a really grainy one when we were sitting. The pictures from the alley aren't out yet. No one will be able to tell who you are," he said, pleased.

"What, are you ashamed of me already?" she asked, jokingly on the surface, but still unsure of why he had picked her when he clearly could have anyone he wanted.

"No, silly. I'm protective of you. I don't want to share you with those vultures," Will admitted. "If the press finds out who you are, they'll hunt you down. They will lie about you—unbelievable stuff—and people will believe it."

"Not everyone believes them. None of my friends asked you about your pending wedding to Mia Thompson." Sarah laughed, but she was still nervous that the rumors might have had some relevance.

"Thank god! We're not getting married, by the way," he said matter-of-factly.

"Good. I'm not good at sharing—never have been," she muttered softly and took a bite of eggs. She saw a hint of his dimple appear on his gorgeous face before his brow wrinkled and a few choice cuss words escaped his lips.

"Damn it. I was hoping this wouldn't happen."

"What's wrong?"

"Oh, they're already putting on a full-court press to find out who you are."

"So?" Sarah said with a giggle.

"You don't get it, do you? I thought you got it, but how could you? They are ruthless, and they don't care who they hurt. I shouldn't have made this so public." He brushed his hand across the top of his head and exhaled loudly. "I can guarantee that if—no, when—they find out who you are, they will ruin your life. They'll call you awful names and say you're a home wrecker for breaking up a relationship that doesn't exist."

"Let them. I know that I'm not." She got up, kissed him assertively on the lips, and sat down on his lap, nuzzling against his chest.

"You better put some more clothes on if you know what is good for you." He wrapped his arms around her waist so she couldn't leave his lap. "You're just trying to distract me."

Pleased with his response, she gently ran her fingers through the hair on the back of his head. "Is it working?" she questioned. "You need to stop panicking. Just stop reading that garbage."

"You read it," snapped Will.

"I just go on those sites to antagonize people. It helps me understand people's psyches. It started as a psychology experiment for school. I told you that. I don't believe those lies. Most people don't have time to worry about the scandals in celebrities' lives." She gave Will a knowing eye. "Stop being so ridiculous! There are ways to get your voice out there—tons of different ways. I could name at least fifty. We could set up your own website. I had a couple of classes on Internet communication. I know a little, but I'm sure you have people who can do that for you. What about an interview or a press release?"

"The rags just twist what I say to fit their means."

"Then just forget about them and *live your life!*"

Will tightened his arms around her and started kissing the small of her neck. He pulled back for a second. "I like that you argue with me." His nose skimmed her soft flesh, and he inhaled deeply before kissing her again.

Sarah closed her eyes, enjoying the feel of his lips on her skin. She was so absorbed in his touch that she forgot the world again, until he whispered in her ear.

"You don't mind if we take this slow, do you? I really care about you, and I don't want to mess this up. Besides, you haven't even admitted that you love me." He glanced at her with a questioning look.

"Shut up."

"I'm serious," he said with just a hint of hurt in his voice.

"Does it matter?" she asked, taken aback.

"It does with you. You get me in ways no one ever has."

"You told me that you loved me before you even met me. How could you know that?" It sounded like a line to get her into bed, but that wasn't what he was trying to do, so she was confused by his words.

"I know it feels right—more right than ever before—and I can't stop thinking about you. I'm usually pretty levelheaded around women. I don't get infatuated."

"Do you always fall in love so easily?"

"Never before you. I've never even said it to another girl. And I know you're in love with me, but I'll let you figure it out," he whispered in her ear just before kissing it.

Sarah felt a shiver go through her body. She had never felt this way before, either. She had dated a guy for two years in high school, thinking it had been love at the time. Yet, she had never felt the connection that she felt with Will. She didn't know what to think. It was all happening so fast. She never thought love would be so complicated, yet so simple.

"Let's just take that slow, OK?" She kissed his lips and peeled herself off his lap. She smiled at him over her shoulder as she snatched up her clothes pile and headed out of the room to get dressed.

Chapter Six

At twelve thirty, they headed over to Sarah's parents' house so Sarah could change and Will could meet her family. A black SUV with a driver, the same driver as last night, picked them up in the hotel garage. Sam made sure they got off safely, but stayed behind at the hotel, per Will's request. Will wanted to meet Sarah's family on equal terms, and he thought it might be intimidating if he brought his bodyguard. Will carried a small bag of clothes to change into at the house. He planned to work out in Sarah's parents' weight room because, as he put it, "If I don't work out, they'll recast my role in *The Demigod* sequel."

The house, a two-story with a walk-out basement, was average sized for the older, established neighborhood. Situated on two acres of wooded land with a picturesque natural pond in the backyard. Sarah's mom often used the pond as a backdrop for photo shoots with customers from her photography studio, and Sarah hoped no clients were scheduled to be at the house today.

Sarah and Will walked around the house to the patio door that led into the basement. Sarah was putting off talking to her parents for as long as she could. The walk of shame was not something she ever wanted to do in front of her parents. And even though there was no guilt in what she had done, she wasn't quite sure what to say to them yet. She led Will through the large family room and down the hallway to the weight room. The weight room was small, with just the bare minimum of equipment—a treadmill and some free weights with a bench. It had a small television that hung on the wall in front of the treadmill and an iPod docking station with a radio that sat on the floor next to the door.

Sarah plugged in her iPod and turned on her favorite playlist. She set the volume low so she wouldn't attract her parents' attention and snuck upstairs to change into her workout clothes. By the time she returned, Will was hard at work on the free weights. Sarah smiled at him as she secured the door. Then she jumped onto the treadmill and pushed the buttons to set up her jogging program. She knew it wouldn't be appropriate to spend their entire workout gawking at him, so she shook her head and tried to look away.

After several minutes, however, he caught her staring at him, and said with amusement, "Stop ogling my biceps, Miss Austin."

"I'm not ogling your biceps."

"Oh, really?"

"I'm not. I'm ogling your pecs."

Will flexed his pectoral muscles, and they both chuckled.

Sarah left Will after about thirty minutes to take a shower, and Will moved to the treadmill. Sarah was just finishing up with her makeup, which she wore very little of, when Will wandered up to her room to use the shower. She had told him where to find it. He was glistening with sweat, and she thought that he looked like he had just walked off a movie screen. No, she thought he looked like a god. She showed him where the towels were, kissed him on the lips, and left him to his shower.

Sarah softly hummed an EXpireD song as she meandered down the stairs to fill in her parents on Will and the concert. Sarah's parents were used to having people make themselves at home in their house. They had a very relaxed attitude about houseguests. It probably came from owning a cabin on a lake up north. It was just part of the cabin mentality. There were always guests at the cabin—some were invited, and others would just show up. People the family barely knew would stay at the lake for days with Sarah's family.

Jeff and Sarah's friends were always at the house too. It was a welcoming place to hang out. They showered at the house, helped themselves to food from the refrigerator, and slept wherever they could find a space. That was just the atmosphere. So Sarah knew her parents wouldn't have a problem with Will working out and showering at the house, but she wanted to answer all her mom's questions before letting her have access to him.

She ran into her dad, David, as she entered the kitchen. He was helping himself to a slice of leftover birthday cake. Sarah had blown out the candles on the cake and eaten a couple of bites of it in her rush to get to the concert last night.

The few wrinkles surrounding his dark-brown eyes puckered deeper into his tanned skin as she entered the room. His short dark hair clung neatly around his ears, and his hip, rectangular-shaped glasses drooped low on his nose.

"Hi, Dad." Sarah tried to sound perky. She opened the fridge and looked inside quickly before closing it again. She was just surfing, not really looking for anything.

"We missed you at breakfast this morning. Your friends made it back safely," he commented in a judgmental tone. He leaned back against the counter, waiting for her comeback, with his cake plate and fork in his hands.

Sarah had hoped she would run into her mom first so her mom could explain the night to her dad. Her mom was easier to talk to about guys. But here she was, stuck—confronted by her father. Sarah knew she really hadn't been missed at breakfast. Even if she had been home, she wouldn't have been up to eat at seven o'clock—or even nine, for that matter.

Besides, her parents hadn't been home, anyway. They volunteered at the local animal shelter every Saturday morning when they weren't up at the cabin. Her mom took pictures to catalog on the Internet, and her dad checked on the animals. They had done it for as long as Sarah could remember. She knew that her dad's comment was just his way of asking why she had been out all night.

"We didn't have a chance to talk at the concert. You know, we've known each other for months, and this was the first time we had face time. Honestly, we just fell asleep talking." She looked up at him innocently.

David met her eyes and took a big bite of cake. He looked at her as if contemplating what to say next.

"Did you talk to Jeff this morning?" she asked, trying to sound as relaxed as possible. She needed to know where to start explaining that the guy in her shower was a movie star, and she was trying to change the direction of the discussion. She leaned back with her elbows on the counter and then twisted around when she smelled the chocolate behind her. She scooped a dollop of frosting off the cake and licked it off her finger, waiting for her dad's response.

"Uh-huh," he said with a mouthful of cake. When he had swallowed, he continued. "Jeff said you went backstage and met the band. He was really impressed with the concert. And then he said something about your Will turning out to be some famous actor? I didn't really understand what he was trying to say. He wasn't making sense. Maybe you could explain it better?" He raised his eyebrows questioningly and nudged his glasses up with his index finger as he took another bite of cake.

"Jonathan Williams. Your Will is actually Jonathan Williams, the actor. That's what Jeff said," added Sarah's mother, Kate, as she entered the room. The dark sunglasses perched on the top of her head held back her straight shoulder-length auburn hair. She was petite and slender like Sarah, though she was two inches shorter than Sarah's five-four frame. "So is it true? Or do we need to do a drug intervention on your brother?"

"No intervention needed," Sarah admitted guiltily.

"Oh, he's hot!"

"Mom!"

"I'm not dead, Sarah. He was in *The Demigod* and that movie with Mia Thompson. What was it? Um, we have it up at the lake." Kate paused, her brow furrowed, looking up as if she was concentrating.

"*Love Twice*," answered Sarah.

"That was a very sexy movie, and he was very convincing in it."

"Mom, you will not talk like that in front of him—ever!" Sarah said, mortified at her mother's reaction.

"I saw on the news that he sang at your concert last night, but I didn't realize you were the Birthday Girl he was singing to. He's up in your shower right now?" She eyed her daughter.

"Yes."

"So, how do you feel about him being a famous celebrity?" asked Kate.

"I really like him, and he's *so* handsome. He seems like the same person I met months ago. But I think it would be easier if he weren't a movie star. It's exciting, though."

"So, you really like him?" reiterated Kate.

"Why do you say it like that?"

"You never bring anyone to the house, Sarah."

Sarah rolled her eyes and shrugged her shoulders.

"Just be careful," advised David. "Those people in Hollywood don't have the same Midwestern values that we have. Honesty isn't a priority for them, and they move fast. Don't let yourself get swept up in all the excitement. Jeff says he has a reputation for dating a lot of women."

"Dad, he's really nice. He's not at all like they make him out to be in the press. If he were, you know I would be the first one to put him in his place. Just give him a chance."

"Let's hope he's here for just the weekend," stated David.

"All week, actually." Sarah beamed as she thought about the possibilities for the week ahead.

"Of course he is," David muttered, cutting himself another piece of cake.

"Don't worry, Sarah. We'll give him a chance," Kate said, making eye contact with her husband. "We know you have a good head on your shoulders, and we trust your ability to make good decisions." She wrapped her arm around Sarah's shoulder and squeezed. She looked back over at David, daring him to say any more.

He scowled at his wife. "I would feel better if we were able to get to know him just a little. Spend the afternoon at the house so we can see for ourselves what a nice guy he is, OK?"

"For a little bit, but if it starts getting weird, we're leaving. So behave— and no pictures, Mom," Sarah warned. She knew her mom always had her camera staged, waiting for just the right shot, and she didn't want Will to feel uncomfortable.

When Will was dressed, he joined them in the kitchen. Sarah introduced him, and Will's charm took over.

"So what brings you to the Twin Cities?" David asked.

"Your beautiful daughter invited me to celebrate her birthday with her."

"Really? I don't remember inviting you," Sarah said teasingly.

His jaw dropped with just a hint of a smile. "OK, so I invited myself, but you can't blame me for wanting to meet you."

His expression turned innocent and sincere.

The conversation flowed easily, and after the initial Hollywood discussion, it moved to deeper subjects, like the latest violence in the Middle East and corporate America's economic use of China. Sarah could tell David and Kate were impressed. Kate kept looking over to her with an awed expression, and David was actually agreeing with Will's assessment of the world's problems without his usual know-it-all superiority. No, Will wasn't just a pretty Hollywood face. He was well-mannered, grounded, and Sarah was definitely falling deeper and deeper under his spell.

Eventually, Kate took out the photo albums, and they all marveled at how Sarah could have blonde hair as a toddler and almost black hair now. It seemed that every important milestone of Sarah's life was recorded, and Will relished discovering every detail. He paid great attention to the albums and asked dozens of questions. He asked about relatives, family vacations, and the summers spent at the family's cabin. Will tried to pry out information about Sarah's past boyfriends without much success—just a few pictures.

Sarah could handle Will seeing the photo albums. Over the years, she had seen her face blown up half a dozen times to the size of a small billboard on the walls of her mom's photography studio. She was used to her picture being taken and exploited. She didn't like it, but she was used to it, and she had shared so much with Will on the phone that she didn't think there were any more stories to share. She was confident enough in Will's nonjudgment that she owned even the awful photos without apology.

For dinner, they ate grilled buffalo burgers with broccoli slaw and corn on the cob. Everyone teased Will when he ate three burger patties without a single bun. He defended himself by saying, "It's good protein. I don't need the fillers. I don't have anything against buns, but my trainer recommends just the patties, and I guess it's just become habit."

Jeff came home as they were finishing the dishes, and Sarah had a run-in with him in the back hall by the garage.

"Hey, slut, how was your night?"

Sarah's jaw dropped, and she glared at her brother with an audible gasp. "If, for some reason, it is any of your business, we just talked. We didn't do anything."

"Yeah right. I saw how you two were eye fucking all night."

"Eeerr!" she squealed in disbelief. She smacked his upper arm with the back of her fisted hand. "It's called self-control. You should try it sometime." She sneered at him as she threw her hands up in frustration.

"Just sayin'," he retorted, raising one eyebrow.

Sarah was fuming. She didn't know why. Maybe it was because part of her wished her brother was right. Not about being a slut, but about her being with Will. After all, she wasn't a virgin. She had been with her high school sweetheart, but he was the only one. At the time, she thought that she loved him, and that was what confused her. How could she trust what she was feeling now when her past had been a lie? She knew one thing for sure. Even though she hadn't known Will very long, what she had with him felt so right, and she wanted him.

Just then, Will came into the hall. Approaching them from behind and touching Sarah on the small of her back, he said, "I was hoping I'd catch you, Jeff."

Where his fingers touched her, a sense of relief radiated, releasing all of Sarah's tension, and she calmed down immediately.

"Your mom caught a clip of Sarah's song from last night's concert on the news this morning and is insisting that I play it for her," Will continued. "I don't think she's going to let it go, and since I'm not talented enough to sing it a cappella, I was hoping you had a guitar I could borrow?"

"Yeah, sure," Jeff agreed. "Come on downstairs with me, and I'll get it for you."

☙

As the evening wound down, Jessica showed up and snuggled herself next to Jeff on the couch. Will played Sarah's song for the family. Everyone was touched by its pure message and impressed by Will's talent. Will and Jeff took turns playing the guitar, and everyone joined in as if they were doing karaoke, using serving spoons from the kitchen for microphones.

At one point, Will stood up and started playing an Ashley Tyler song on the guitar. He glanced at Sarah with a not-so-innocent look and began singing in a high falsetto voice, swinging his hips back and forth. Sarah began laughing hysterically, and they both collapsed on the couch, unable to pull themselves back together.

"I need to go to therapy," sang Sarah.

As everyone else in the room speculated at their private joke, Will handed the guitar off to Jeff, powerless to stop laughing. Sarah loved to watch Will act goofy with her family, and she felt as if he really belonged there. He seemed so comfortable and uninhibited, as if he was already a part of her family. It felt so natural to be with him, and Sarah loved the feeling she got from his presence.

As Sarah's parents headed off to bed, Kate hugged Will, telling him he was welcome to sleep in the guest room overnight if it got too late, while David gave Sarah a look indicating she should be careful.

Having missed David's expression, Will asked Sarah, "Are your parents always so accepting of your boyfriends?"

"Are you my boyfriend?" Sarah asked with a smile. In her mind, a boyfriend implied some level of permanence, and for some reason, she was unsure of his intentions, but she liked that he considered himself her boyfriend.

"Aren't I?" he asked, sounding a little hurt by her reaction.

"Yes, they are pretty accepting of my boyfriends—usually," she said and kissed his cheek.

Jessica grinned at Sarah with a note of approval.

They all plopped down on the couch, and Sarah took out her birthday present to show it off to Jeff and Jessica. As Will protested, they Googled Jonathan Williams. They were amazed at how much had been written. There were sixty-three pages on Google of articles and websites associated with his name alone. They all laughed at the crazy stories they found. One article cataloged all his favorite places to shop, mentioning his favorite coffee shop, while another described Jonathan's dream date, including where he would take his date.

"Is that true?" asked Sarah. "Is that where you would take me?"

"I don't think so. I've never even been to Apollo's restaurant. Maybe it's a reference to Greek gods or demigods." He shrugged.

One article listed all the girls he had supposedly hooked up with in the last three years. There were twenty-seven people listed, most of them celebrities. Every single actress he had made a movie with was named, and the article had pictures of each of the women with Will.

"That's delusional. Those are just press pictures. I hardly ever date anymore. When would I have time to be with that many girls?" Will questioned.

As they continued their search, they found a site with an audiocast from the radio announcers who had been seated behind the group at the concert. The man-and-woman announcing team described Sarah and her friends in great detail. The announcers were frustrated because they wanted to talk to Jonathan, but they couldn't get his attention.

"He was completely focused on the girl with the dark hair. Though I didn't see any cuddling, they were definitely a couple. It was really cute," the woman declared.

"You mean nauseating, don't you? I expected them to rip each other's clothes off right there in the theater."

"It wasn't like that at all. It was really sweet. Why do you always have to turn everything into something dirty?"

"I call it like I see it," the male announcer said. "I was tempted to tap Jonathan on the shoulder and ask him to be on the show, but I was afraid his mammoth bodyguard would rip my arm off if I got anywhere close. He was pretty intimidating. But seriously, we have to get him on the show while he's in town. If anyone knows who this Birthday Girl is, call the station. We need to track them down," he added.

Jeff, Jessica, and Sarah all chuckled. They thought it was hilarious that the radio announcers were talking about them.

Will didn't laugh. Instead, he intensely studied Sarah's face and then asked, "Is that station popular?"

"Yeah. Everyone listens to it. It's the best local station," answered Jessica.

Will's demeanor changed. He was no longer relaxed and carefree. As they continued to look through the web for any more evidence of the concert, he kept silent. The next site they came upon had a close-up picture of Will leaning in to speak in Sarah's ear at the concert, and a second one of Sarah and her friends sitting with Will. There was even a picture of Sarah getting into the black SUV with Will's hand on her back. The pictures were tagged with the caption "Who is this Birthday Girl that stole Jonathan Williams's heart? If you know, tweet us," and it gave the Twitter address. The pictures were pretty clear, and they all froze staring at the screen.

Will cursed under his breath with a look of despair. Sarah saw something in his face that frightened her. The paparazzi seemed to possess power over Will. She didn't want him panicking again. Even though she hadn't known him long, she felt she could look into his ice-blue eyes and see his soul. There was definitely something more to his expression. He was in pain. She approached Will, her eyes still locked on his. She reached for his hand and wove her fingers between his, hoping to draw him out of his trance to find out what was causing him so much despair.

Will gently squeezed Sarah's hand. Then, raising their entwined fingers to Sarah's cheek, he achingly grazed her jawline, saying in a flat voice, "I need to make some calls." With a sigh, he released her hand and walked toward the back deck. Sarah watched him through the glass door as he made his calls.

His back was toward Sarah, and she couldn't see what he was saying. His body language was rigid, and he looked angry. She turned to her brother and her best friend.

"There's something he's not telling us. I know he doesn't want the paparazzi to find him, but seriously, what happened?" She paused and looked back at Will. "He started acting like this at the hotel too, after checking the Internet. I don't understand what's changed. I wonder who he's talking to—maybe his assistant or Sam."

When Will had finished his calls, he stood staring out over the backyard pond.

Sarah joined Will on the deck, and without a word, she rested her head against his shoulder. Will sighed and said nothing.

"What's going on, Will?" Sarah asked softly.

"I'm just trying to figure out my next move now that they're coming," he confessed warily.

"You sound so paranoid." She studied his face, wondering how his mood could change so quickly, and questioned him with wide eyes. "So what is our next move?"

Looking down, clenching his jaw tightly, he took a deep breath. "Sarah," he said, looking back up. Their eyes met briefly before Will closed his and continued. "I have to go back."

"That's OK. I could come with you to the hotel, or if you want, we could meet up in the morning." She paused. "Is everything all right?"

"No, not really," he answered softly.

She reached up and pulled his face down to meet hers. She looked desperately into his eyes, searching, and she felt a wave of pain. She wondered where it had come from. Sarah got the feeling from him that someone had died. Then she realized what he had, but had not, said.

"You're not just going to your hotel. You're going back to California, aren't you?" she asked with sadness, but still a little accusatory.

He took an audible breath and furrowed his brow. She saw in his face that she was right.

"Why? I thought that you had a week."

"I can't do this."

"What? What can't you do?"

"I can't be with you."

"You can't be with me? With the one person who actually cares about *you?*" she shrieked in frustration. "I was ready to give you a chance no matter what you looked like. You *get* me. I didn't know you were an actor. I didn't want you to be famous. It complicates everything."

"I'm sorry," he said softly.

"Sorry for what? Being a famous hot guy?" she said, still hoping to lighten his mood a bit.

Unchanging, he said with a scowl, "No, for bringing all this down on you. I know what's going to happen, and it's tragic. It's going to hurt you, and it's going to hurt me."

"I'm pretty tough, you know. The only thing that can hurt me right now is you leaving." Sarah was desperate, and she needed him to understand what his leaving would do to her.

"The only way I can keep you safe is to take those a-holes back to LA with me. I don't want you to end up like Jack."

"I won't," she pleaded. She knew what was coming next.

"Sarah, I have to go. I booked a flight back at nine fifteen tomorrow. The airport will be busy enough, and I'll find a way to get some press there. If they see me at the airport, if they see me leave for LA, they'll stop hunting you. It's the only way to keep you safe. I'm not going to risk your life. I never should have gotten involved with you. It was wrong."

"I don't understand. We're wr-wrong?" she asked, the words catching in her throat.

"I was wrong to think it could work. I know that now."

"Yeah, whatever," she said hopelessly. Sarah thought the last two days had been the best days of her life, and she didn't know how everything could have changed so quickly. It must have been a lie. Will must not have cared as much for her as he said, or he never would be able to leave.

Sarah began to shut down. She couldn't deal with this. It was too painful. Her heart screamed at her, but she pushed it deep down to follow her head. If he didn't care for her, she would have to let him go. There was nothing else she could do. It was better to end it now than prolong it. With an internal protection wall already building inside her, Sarah knew she needed to get away from this agony, to get away from here and distance herself. She calmly asked Jeff to drive Will back to his hotel. She knew she would never be able to drive with tears running down her cheeks, and she knew the tears would be coming soon. With a brave face, she hugged Will good-bye and headed upstairs.

♾

Will didn't want to bring this rabid animal into Sarah's life. He knew what would happen if he pursued her, and yet he had done it anyway.

He felt guilty and torn by his decision. This was not how he wanted things to end. He didn't want it to end at all, but he knew she would be better off without him—safer. He'd thought he could handle the paparazzi hunting her, but in reality, he wasn't ready to sacrifice Sarah. He thought she seemed to understand. She wasn't even crying.

Will and Jeff headed to the hotel in Jeff's Jeep.

"So what happened with you and Sarah? For someone who doesn't want to hurt her, you're doing a great job of hurting her," said Jeff.

Earlier in the evening, when Will and Jeff had gone downstairs to get the guitar, Jeff confronted him. He warned him not to hurt his sister. And Will assured Jeff that she meant the world to him, that he would never hurt her, and that he loved Sarah.

"What? What do you mean? She seemed to be handling it pretty well—better than I thought she would, anyway," said Will. He really thought Sarah understood why he was leaving. Maybe he was just too wrapped up in his own loss that he hadn't recognized her true reaction.

"You don't know Sarah, then. She doesn't get all quiet like that without something really bothering her. I don't think I've ever seen her that upset. So what's going on?" Jeff asked.

"Well, Jeff, I'm leaving for LA tomorrow."

"What? I thought you were going to be here all week. I thought she was the love of your life. I don't understand."

"She is the love of my life. That's why I'm going."

"I don't get it." Jeff shook his head.

"If I leave, the paparazzi will stop hunting her. It's the only way to keep her safe."

"So Jess and I are left to clean up after you leave? Thanks a lot! I told her not to trust anyone she met on the Internet, especially not a player like you," Jeff said sharply.

Will looked down, covering his face with his hands in helpless frustration. "Jeff, I don't want to leave her. I love her. I just don't know what else to do."

They sat in silence for the rest of the ride, until the Jeep pulled up in front of the hotel.

"Take care of her, Jeff," Will said as he grabbed his workout bag and stepped onto the sidewalk.

"Yeah," Jeff replied, shaking his head again.

Will headed to his suite, exhausted. He felt dead inside and didn't know if he was doing the right thing by leaving. He didn't want to hurt Sarah. He wanted to protect her. He was hurting her either way. In the long run, he knew she would be safe, and that was what mattered the most.

Chapter Seven

The next morning, Sarah was still in bed when she heard a tap on her bedroom door. She had been awake most the night thinking about Will. Her eyes were red and swollen from crying, and she didn't want to see anyone. She didn't know how she could trust her own feelings anymore. How could she have let this happen again?

She remembered back to the last time she had felt this awful. Vivid pictures still lingered in her head. It was a warm, sunny afternoon a couple of weeks after her high school graduation. She was supposed to spend the day with her boyfriend, but his dad was forcing him to clean out the garage, and he said it would most likely take all day. So Sarah met up with her girlfriends instead. It was rare for the four girls to have the same day off work, and Sarah was excited. They cruised to a pool party at a friend of Megan's just outside the city of Stillwater. The gathering was packed with graduates from Megan's high school, and Megan knew most of them.

After about thirty minutes of mingling in the house, the girls made their way to the backyard, where the music blared and the pool overflowed with barely clothed bodies refreshing themselves in the shimmering blue water. The weather was perfect for a pool party, and the atmosphere was energetic. Out on the wooden deck above the pool, the girls looked down at the chaos below. The slide at the deep end of the large pool was rigged with a garden hose duct-taped at the top, and a couple of guys at the bottom of the water slide were trying to convince a girl that it was safe to use.

Sarah and her friends helped themselves to some drinks from a huge white ice chest that creaked when they opened it. Then they descended down the deck stairs with drinks in hand, into the pandemonium of the poolside. That's when Megan started to act a bit out of character.

"We should probably get going," Megan said as she turned her back on the pool like she was hiding from someone.

The girls looked at her as if she were on crack. They were in their suits and eager to hit the water. Besides, Megan never wanted to leave a party, especially when she knew everyone there.

"Why? We just got here. Isn't Becca supposed to be coming? I haven't seen her in ages," questioned Sarah.

"Just trust me, we should go," Megan insisted as she tried to corral everyone back toward the house.

"What's up with you? Is Chase here or something?" asked Jessica, and Sarah and Alli chuckled. Chase was Megan's ex, who she fervently avoided.

As they scanned the pool for Chase, they all spotted what was making Megan act so strangely. Perched on the edge of the pool, near the shallow end, with his feet dangling in the water, sat Matt, Sarah's boyfriend, and in between his knees stood a cute little brunette with her tongue halfway down his throat. Jessica's eyes rose to Megan's, and they both sighed in despair. The girls looked toward Sarah. Sarah just spun around and stormed into the house. She was so shocked she couldn't say anything. She hadn't expected this. There were no signs that he was unhappy in their relationship. None. She gave him all of her. He was her future, and he'd just thrown her away without warning, as if she meant nothing, as if she was totally expendable.

It was Megan who confronted Matt, and of course, he ran after Sarah. He tried to come up with an explanation, but Sarah refused to listen to his lies. It wasn't the first time he'd lied to her, and she knew that, but it was the first time she'd caught him cheating. She knew she never would be able to trust him again. She'd thought they were in love, having been together for two years. She couldn't understand how Matt could do what he had—just disregard their relationship so easily. Or was he so stupid that he'd really thought she would never find out? *He can't really love me like he says and treat me like this*, she thought. She felt so betrayed, and she was convinced that she would never trust a guy ever again. Her heart sank deep into the pit of her stomach, weighing down her entire body. She was drained of all feeling, and all she wanted to do was run away from the hurt.

As Sarah lay in bed listening to the rapping on her bedroom door, she felt even worse somehow than she had that day at the pool, and she just wanted to hide. She began to wonder if men naturally possessed an innate ability to lie about their feelings. Will obviously had lied to her about his feelings. Sarah didn't want to think about either of them anymore—Will or Matt—so she covered her head with a pillow and ignored the knocking.

"I know you're in there. I can hear you moving around," the familiar voice called.

"What?" she shrieked, irritated.

"I need to talk to you," the man continued.

"Go away," she roared, but she got up anyway and unlocked the door. "What do you want, Jeff?" She pulled the door open and glared at her brother.

"Sarah, I'm pretty sure he's in love with you."

She scowled at him murderously, thinking he was being sarcastic. "Get out of here!"

"Just hear me out. I've been thinking about it all night. There are only two reasons a guy would fly across the country for a girl. The first one is that he wants sex"—he raised his eyebrow and looked at his sister—"but you said you didn't." Jeff apologetically stuck out his hands, palms up, and continued. "If he'd come for sex, he would never leave if he thought that he still had a chance to get some. Besides, I'm pretty sure he could have any supermodel he wanted, so that's not his motivation."

"Thanks. You're really making me feel better, Jeff," she snarled sarcastically.

"The other reason is love. Sarah, he loves you. He told me last night in the car."

"Well, he has a funny way of showing it, doesn't he?" she questioned bitterly, but as she thought about it, she realized that Will wasn't using her. He was the one who had wanted to take it slow. *What would he be using me for?* she thought.

"I think he's just scared—scared you're going to get killed like his brother. It sounds like Jack's death really messed him up."

"Jack. That would explain it. I can't imagine how messed up I'd be if I thought I'd killed my brother." She met Jeff's eyes. "It would end me." She paused as she considered his theory with all that had happened last night. "Did he really say he loves me?"

"Yeah. He had no reason to lie to me. He doesn't want to leave you, Sarah. He just thinks it's his only option to keep you safe."

"I know his brother's death must have screwed him up, but we always have options," she said with a renewed sense of hope. "I'll be downstairs in ten minutes. Would you drive me to the airport?" It would save time if she didn't have to park.

"Anything you need, sis," Jeff pledged.

Jeff drove Sarah to the airport, but he wasn't willing to leave her there, so he dropped her off at the terminal and promised to keep driving around the loop until she called. She was going to find Will before his plane boarded.

Right away, she checked the departure boards, and luckily, there was only one flight to Los Angeles around nine fifteen—Flight 2921 at Gate G22. Sarah knew she had only two options. Since she couldn't enter the concourse without a boarding pass, she could stand in line and buy a plane ticket. It would give her the most time to look for Will if she was able to get through the line quickly, but it would cost money, which she was short on. Besides, once he got to the concourse, he could easily disappear into the VIP waiting area. The other option would be to wait for him by the security checkpoint. He would have to go through it in order to get to his plane. This would be easier, but Sarah was afraid she might have already missed him. She didn't know what to do, so she said a quick prayer and looked for a good place to plant herself.

She picked a bench that had a clear view of the security area and sat down to wait. As she waited, she thought. She thought about the last three months. She thought about what Will had said last night. She thought about how she felt when she was with him. She thought about how electric his touch was and how being next to him made her feel fearless. Sarah wasn't sure what she was going to say to Will when she did find him, but she knew she couldn't just let him leave.

It wasn't long before she heard a loud commotion approaching the gate. The MSP airport was crowded for a Sunday morning, and at first, she couldn't see what was causing the ruckus. Then as it got closer, she could see three guys with cameras yelling at someone who was doing his best to ignore them. There was a constant stream of flashes coming from all directions. In the middle of the commotion was Will, and he had Sam. He was carrying his guitar case and a small carry-on bag. The group advanced fast. As they approached, she could make out what was being said.

"Jonathan, do you think Mia will take you back after your weekend lovefest?"

"Who is this new girl, Jon? Just another conquest?"

"One in every city, huh, Jon?"

Sarah tried to get Will's attention, but the paparazzi were too loud. Fans with cell phones raised huddled around the periphery, growing the mass, like a swarm of killer bees picking up energy as it moved down the corridor. Sarah couldn't get close. As Will loaded his belongings into the tub on the conveyer belt and removed his shoes, Sarah became desperate.

"Will, don't leave!" she shouted.

"Look! It's the Birthday Girl!" someone with a camera called.

"What's your name, sugar? How long have you known Jonathan?" asked the guy with a goatee wearing a Twins baseball cap.

"What's he like in bed?" asked another.

Sarah was doing her best to ignore the comments being shouted at her. All she cared about was stopping Will. She knew she could get through anything if he stayed, but she wasn't sure he would. She stretched up on tiptoe, hoping to see any sign of her prince, but he'd vanished. Her heart plummeted. He was gone.

❧

Will felt relieved when he made it past the scanner and had finally escaped the paparazzi, but then he heard Sarah's desperate cry. Will's head snapped toward her voice. He glimpsed her frightened eyes just as the photographers engulfed her. He couldn't see her anymore. Her small frame had been completely swallowed.

He swore under his breath as he turned to Sam.

"I have to go save her." He grabbed his shoes and sprinted for the exit door. "Can you get my stuff?" he yelled over his shoulder to Sam as he pulled on his shoes.

As he broke through the circle of press, he wrapped his protective arms around her, and she dissolved into his chest. He couldn't believe he had let this happen. Here she was, in the exact situation he had been trying to avoid.

Sarah looked up at him with innocence and urgency. "Please stay."

"You are so brave," he uttered in staccato, then kissed the top of her head. "But you don't know what you're getting yourself into being seen with me."

"I don't care. I couldn't let you leave."

He squeezed her in closer. "I guess it doesn't make sense to leave at this point. They're never going to leave you alone." He pulled the brim of his cap down over his eyes and stared off in the direction of the security checkpoint.

"Jeff is waiting outside," she whispered as she took out her phone.

"Great, let's go," Will said, spying Sam approaching.

When Sam joined them with the guitar case and the carry-on bags, Will filled him in on the change of plans. Sam held on to the bags and handed Will the pocket items he'd left in the bin. Will carefully fitted the dark sunglasses from Sam on Sarah's face. He knew her picture had already been captured, but he didn't want her any more exposed. They quietly discussed the logistics of the new plans as Sam maneuvered their way out to the curb. The paparazzi were still snapping pictures as they all climbed into Jeff's SUV.

They were almost at the point where the airport loop met the freeway when Will announced, "Can we go back to the airport? Sam, I think you can still make the flight. I would hate for you to be stranded here without luggage. Besides, we'll lay low, find somewhere to hide out that's not Sarah's house. It's idiotic to have you sitting around a hotel room when you could be home with your wife and boys. The photographers wouldn't have been at the airport if I hadn't tipped them off, and I really just needed you for the concert. I'll be careful."

"Hmm. If you're sure," Sam said with reluctance.

Jeff pulled the SUV into the left lane to follow the road back around to the passenger loading area again. They dropped off Sam to catch his flight and then headed toward Sarah's house in the suburbs.

"I made the loop six times before your call," Jeff confessed. "So what now?"

"I think Will and I are going to spend a few days up at the lake to get away from the cities," said Sarah.

"OK, but all I have in my carry-on is some T-shirts and a week's worth of underwear," Will said with a chuckle. "My underwear is always the first thing to disappear out of my checked bag, so I always carry it with me. Do you think I could borrow some things from you, Jeff?"

"Yeah, sure, anything you need. Sarah can show you my room. The dresser is stocked."

"Thanks."

Sarah snuggled into Will's chest. He nuzzled his nose into her neck and wrapped his arm around her shoulder, pulling her in closer. He squished his eyes together, shaking his head. *What am I doing?* He kissed her cheek before taking out his phone. Will made a call to his assistant to see what could be done about his luggage, while Sarah called to find someone to fill in for her shift at the clinic on Tuesday. She also called her mom to let her know the plans.

Both Sarah and Will knew that, whatever the future held for them, they needed to try to be together. It felt so right. They had less than a week to figure out how to make it work—and less than a week to be alone together.

Chapter Eight

Back at the house, Kate helped Sarah pack a cooler full of food and beverages to bring up to the lake.

"Sarah, I understand the whole getting away from the cities deal, but be careful and use your head, OK?" Kate said as she hugged her daughter.

"I will, Mom. Don't worry so much." Sarah smiled at her.

After reassuring her mother, Sarah headed upstairs to pack some clothes. When she was finished, she dragged her heavy pink duffel bag down the stairs, letting it thump on each step as she walked. Will immediately took it from her when it hit the floor, and effortlessly carried it out to Sarah's car. Together, they loaded the cooler and bag into the back of Sarah's red Honda CR-V. Like a gentleman, Will opened the driver's side door for Sarah to get in, and closed it with care behind her. He could tell she wasn't used to being pampered, and he wanted to show her how special she was. He jumped into the passenger seat, and soon they were headed toward Interstate 35. After a few minutes, the speed limit jumped to seventy miles per hour, and they were speeding out of the cities.

Sarah was driving, while Will relished watching her every expression. As an actor, he liked to examine people's faces, and he didn't think he would ever get tired of watching Sarah's. He thought she was perfect. She had a girl-next-door quality about her—beautiful, yet innocent, without expectations—and her emerald green eyes sparkled with a glow he had never seen before. Her alabaster skin was flawless and was such a contrast to her dark, cascading hair. Her lips formed the sweetest smile, and the way she looked out from under her long dark lashes made his heart skip a beat. He could probably lift her petite body with one arm. Yet, she wasn't meek. She was feisty. She was beautiful, that was for sure, and she didn't know it.

"So you get quiet when you're upset. That's good to know for the future," said Will. He had already committed this to memory and was just verifying his conclusion.

"Yeah, and you run when you get scared?"

"No, not usually. I guess I'm just a bit protective of those I care about," he answered with a sigh.

"I don't mind you being protective," she admitted. "Just don't make decisions that affect us both without talking to me. Please."

"I won't," he said, entertained by her directness. Just then, Will's phone vibrated. He checked to see who was calling. "I should probably take this." Answering the call, he said, "Hey, Remi, what's up?"

"I should ask you the same. You are all over the news, Jon. The office has been fielding hundreds of calls. It's great for business, but I just want to know what's going on. I feel out of the loop."

"I'm on vacation, just enjoying my private time."

"Private time? You made the network news. It doesn't seem too private to me. Who's the girl?" she demanded.

"Remi, I don't want her name all over the press. I really care about her, and I don't want to ruin her life, so just keep her out as much as possible, OK?"

"Her name is already out there. A local radio station made a contest out of identifying her, and some students at the university gave her up this morning. It's all over the Internet. There are interviews with students in her classes on YouTube. Someone even posted a video of her in an elementary school play. She sounds like a good girl—too good— nothing bad so far, anyway. So, Jon, what do you want me to tell them? The engagement is off?"

"Don't even joke about that. Tell them that she's the love of my life." He smiled at Sarah. "Or tell them nothing. I don't know. You're the publicist. That's what you get paid for. What should we do?"

"I wish you had told me about the concert. I would have had a lot more press coverage."

"That's why I didn't tell you," he confessed. "So, what do we do now?"

"Well, we could call that radio station. I could set up an interview. It wouldn't have to be long—fifteen, twenty minutes."

"I think our connection is breaking up. The cell service is terrible here. Remi?" He chuckled, knowing that the cell service was more than adequate.

"Fine, no interview. Regardless, we can't buy this kind of press. Serenading her at a rock concert? Writing a song for her? You never wrote a song for me."

"I never knew you wanted one," he said jokingly, as if it was no big deal to write a song.

"Running to protect her at the airport? It's great publicity. I always say keep them guessing—as long as it keeps your name out there. So I'll keep quiet for now, and I will do my best to shoot down any nuisances. You stay out of trouble, and don't punch any Midwestern paparazzi." She laughed. "I'll get back to you if anything changes."

"Thanks. Later, then," he said and hung up the call. Before Will could put his phone away, it vibrated again. He glanced at the screen— Isaac, his agent. He definitely didn't want to talk to him, so he turned off his phone without answering the call. Now he could concentrate on Sarah with no more interruptions. He turned to her and stated rather than asked, "So, beautiful, what a mess we're in now, huh."

"Together, anyway. That's supposed to make it easier," Sarah told him. "Your publicist?"

"Yeah. She's all right, but a bit annoying sometimes. Some of your classmates ratted you out to the radio station. So the vultures will probably be at your house soon. We should warn your mom."

"I already told her what to expect. I think she's ready. Hey, let's talk about something else," said Sarah.

"What do you want to talk about?"

"You," she said. "But first, tell me, when you wrote that song you sang at the concert, did you just recycle it from a past girlfriend? Be honest."

"No," he answered, unable to hide the hurt in his tone. "I started writing it the night we first talked on the phone."

Sarah glanced at him with a questioning look.

"I tinker around on the guitar. It helps me think. I had most the lyrics written before I showed it to Nick. He helped get the melody right, and he wrote all the accompaniments. He really is a music genius."

"It was...Wow," she stammered, shaking her head like she couldn't believe him.

"When I called him to get us into the concert, he insisted that we play it at the show. We didn't have time to run through it before the band went onstage. I was scared to death that it would sound like crap. I guess it was well received, because Nick sent me a text that night asking if I would record it with the band for their next album."

"So, what did he text you right before the concert? Was he checking me out for you?"

Will chuckled with a hint of embarrassment as he fished his phone out of his pocket and powered it up. He manipulated the phone and brought up the old text. He smiled as he reread it, unsure he should tell her what Nick had written. He bit his lip in hesitation.

"Just tell me."

He looked down at his phone. "He said, and I quote, 'She's a troll. Let me take her off your hands, mate. Save you the trouble of a brush-off.'" Will spoke in a British accent. "That's when I knew you were hot."

"I can't believe he said that."

"He wouldn't have said anything if you were actually a troll. My response was 'Piss off, she's mine!' It's usually best to be direct with Nick, in a language he can understand."

"Yours, huh?" she questioned with a giggle.

"Yep." His hand tenderly caressed her face, and she pressed her cheek into his palm. "What else do you want to know?" he asked softly.

"Tell me about your family."

"Where do I start?" Will questioned, perfectly willing to share anything with her.

"Tell me about your dad. What is he like?"

"Well, Zander is a pretty fun guy. He always has a funny story to share, though his sense of humor is Death Valley dry, and he's a bit too analytical. He works a lot. It wouldn't be unusual for him to be working heavily on a project for five months and only come home for twenty days total in that time. We used to spend a lot of time on the sets of his movies when we were kids, Jack and I, especially when he was filming in town.

"I have some really great memories of Jack from those days. I used to get him into so much trouble, and he would just take it without complaint. I'm pretty sure my parents knew that I had started most of it, but Jack would always get blamed because he was the older brother and he knew better. He was good that way." Will swallowed hard and paused to get back to talking about his dad. He knew he was going off on another Jack tangent, which seemed to happen more than he liked, and he needed to refocus.

"My dad always stands up for what he believes and doesn't take on movies just to make big box office dollars. He prefers smaller indie movies to the huge ones pushed by the big studios, because he has more control over the overall end product. He has done a couple of big ones, though, when he felt a great connection to the story. He tries to be a good person, honest, and gives pretty good advice."

Sarah smiled. "What's the best advice he ever gave you?"

Will squished his eyes shut. *Did I just admit that I listen to my dad's advice?* Furrowing his forehead like he was thinking hard, he said, "He told me to do what it takes to find you."

Sarah turned her head to meet his eyes just a second while she was driving.

"He could see that I was obsessed and wasn't able to stop thinking about you. So he told me to stop worrying about the consequences and just make it happen. That's when I sold my soul to the devil to get your e-mail address," he admitted.

"The devil?" she questioned with curiosity.

"Well, she's not really the devil, but they're related," he declared. "At some point, it will probably come back to bite me, though."

"What did you have to do?"

"I talked to the website manager where we usually blogged. I've known her for a while, and I know that she tracks her guests by e-mail. The site makes you sign in when you blog so only the real fans will use the site, or so they say. Well, Paris gave me your e-mail address—against policy—and now I owe her. Don't worry, it was worth it."

They sat in silence for a few seconds until Sarah asked, "So what is your mom like?"

"My mom...hmm. My mom...Well, I guess she's a little like you—beautiful inside and out, and a bit sarcastic." Will raised his eyebrows and watched her for a reaction.

Sarah scowled at him, and he continued.

"She's creative and a bit unorganized. She designs special effects. It's mostly on computer now, but some of it is still done on set. That's how my parents met. She worked on a movie with my dad, and they got married six months later. When I was young, she only worked part-time doing piecework. She always encouraged Jack and me to be ourselves and was never a momager." He paused with reverence on his face. "She worked really hard to keep our lives normal. We only had a part-time nanny, and I remember Mom always being around to do the day-to-day stuff, like Little League, soccer, and acting lessons."

Sarah looked at him questioningly.

"Don't look at me like that. I had acting lessons. It got me where I am today. It's really not that unusual in Hollywood. I had piano lessons too. The guitar is self-taught, which I'm sure you can tell."

Sarah chuckled and glanced at him with an admiring look.

"I think my mom is having an affair with her personal trainer," he blurted, wondering why he was telling her this. Something about her made him want to share his every thought. "I don't know for sure, but they seem really familiar with each other—more than they should be." Will took a deep breath.

"It's been really hard on her since Jack's death. My dad just threw himself into his work, like I did, but my mom doesn't function that way. She practically stopped working completely for close to a year when it happened. She just started working full-time again a year ago. My dad's gone all the time—*all* the time. I moved back home about eighteen months ago, but still, I'm never there. She was really close to Jack, and his death really destroyed her, destroyed all of us. I know she's lonely. It wouldn't surprise me if she was reaching out to someone else. I don't know, I'm probably imagining it."

"You must really love her to be so accepting of her stepping out on your dad," Sarah noted. "I don't know if I could be so mature about it."

"She's a great mom and a good person. People make mistakes. I don't think you can judge someone if you're not inside their head. How do you know what's really going on in anyone else's life? I'm not going to cast a stone," he said with a sense of righteousness. "Besides, I know my dad can be really self-focused sometimes. My mom's always been there when I needed her. She helped me get through everything when Jack was killed. She stayed at the hospital with me for those three days, even when we knew he was going to die. After he died, she forced me to keep going—to eat and sleep. She never blamed me for the accident, even when it seemed that everyone else did. She told me, every day, how much she loved me, and I knew I couldn't hurt myself without it killing her. She kept me alive. Jack was my dad's favorite, so it took him a while to stop blaming me for the crash. He finally realized that I had done the only thing I could, and he forgave me."

"How could he blame you? What kind of dad does that?"

"He was in the angry stage of grief. It was just how he coped. He got past it."

"I can't imagine what it was like. Tell me about Jack," she said softly and hesitantly.

"He outshined me, that's for sure." A slight smile broke across his face as he thought of his brother. "He was good at everything, and I wasn't. He had a tutor and didn't attend high school because he was working, but he still knew everyone in our school. He was really popular. He never struggled to get in shape, like I did, and he was a fantastic actor. It just came naturally to him. I was always in his shadow. I couldn't compete. He never rubbed it in my face, though—too much. OK, he rubbed it in my face all the time, but he was still a great brother, and I could talk to him about anything."

Sarah chuckled again.

"Growing up, we fought like all brothers do, but we were together all the time. He taught me how to surf, how to do a back dive, and how to talk to girls." A corner of his lips turned up, barely exposing his dimple. "He supported me when I gave up acting. He understood my thinking and explained it to my dad for me. He always looked out for me. He was a huge resource when I was having girl trouble. He would have loved you. I wish he could have met you." Will's voice softened. "He was pretty concrete when it came to girls and seemed to understand them better than I did."

"I wish I could have known him."

Sarah gently rubbed her hand on his knee, and he placed his hand on top of hers. They sat in silence for several minutes as they sped down the empty freeway.

"What kind of girl trouble could you have had?" she asked out of the blue, ending their long silence.

"Well, since all girls are crazy..." He paused, looking at her out of the corner of his eye and smirking. "Not you, definitely not you. You're not, are you?"

She glared at him, daring him to keep talking.

"Well, since all *other* girls are crazy, I had a lot of girl trouble. I wasn't born this charming. It's learned."

She made a balking noise like she didn't believe him, and then smiled, encouraging him to continue.

"I was just as awkward as everyone else in my teens, and I did stupid stuff. A few times, I got in…a little over my head. Jack used to say, if you're going to be with someone, you need to be with only that one person. Relationships are hard enough, and there is no way that they will work unless you give it all you have to give. I used to get in trouble with that when I was younger. Jack was pretty smart when it came to girls."

"So you don't believe in two-timing anymore?" Sarah asked with a grin.

"Not at all."

Her expression changing to confusion, Sarah asked, "What about your mom?"

"I didn't say I condone what she is doing, and I don't know what she is doing. Besides, I'm not her, and that's out of my control," he answered nonchalantly.

"So just me, then?" she asked.

"Yep." The word popped from his lips.

"That's good to know," she said as a big smile spread across her face.

"Is that OK—just the two of us?" he asked.

"Yes, I think I would like that."

Will studied her. He couldn't take his eyes off her.

"Are we there yet?" he asked as he continued to stare.

"Almost. We just have to go through this little town up ahead, and then we're practically there. Don't blink, though, or you'll miss it."

They had exited the freeway and were on a paved road headed west.

"My family always stops at that bait shop there." She pointed to a stark-white stucco building with gas pumps in front. "Jeff and I used to get a treat from there every time we came up to the cabin. It's like a general store inside. They have everything. I think my parents used it as a bribe so we didn't feel so bad about leaving our friends every weekend to come up to the lake."

"Didn't you get to bring your friends with you ever?"

"Oh, sure, as we got older. By the time I was ten, my friends were up here all the time. In middle school, Jessica was always at the lake with us, especially after her parents got divorced. It was really hard on her, being the youngest and all. Her sister and brother had already left for college when all the bickering started. She used my house as a refuge to get away from her parents' arguments. My parents practically adopted her."

"Yeah, divorce sucks. Nick's parents had a pretty nasty divorce. He moved here from London when he was thirteen, and his parents got divorced a year later. His mom moved back to England with his little sister. He spent most of his time here with his dad. Sometimes, I think that's why he's the way he is, or it may be genetic. He's just like his dad. The old nature-versus-nurture problem. No one knows where it crosses from one to the other."

❧

Sarah glanced at him with a smirk. She loved it when he philosophized.

They turned down a dirt road. On one side was a farm with spotted black-and-white dairy cows littering the hillside. Up on the hill sat a large white barn. On the other side of the road was a glimmering lake lined with cabins, a few of them spaced so closely together that you could barely see the lake between them.

"Wow, there are a lot of cabins on this lake," Will noted.

"Yeah, it's like its own little community," Sarah answered as she parked her car alongside the cabin. She pulled up on the grass, out of the view of the road, because she didn't want anyone to know she was there. Her cabin neighbors and relatives would drop by to visit if they saw her car.

The cabin was modern craftsman style, with a wood siding exterior, stone pillars, and a large stone chimney. Sarah's family had torn down the original 1950s-style cabin and rebuilt it six years ago. The new cabin had a screened-in porch on the lake side and a flagstone patio on the side opposite to where Sarah had parked. The property was splattered with hundred-year-old pine trees that towered high into the sky, making the new cabin feel like it had always been there.

Will and Sarah moved slowly as they unloaded the car. Neither had slept much last night, and they both really needed some sleep. The ninety-minute drive had made this fact more apparent, and they both yawned as they exited the vehicle.

Inside, the cabin was well lit. It had an open layout, with clean lines and simple styling. In the kitchen, the cabinets were made out of a light-colored hickory wood, and the floor was polished cement in a warm terra-cotta color. The natural colors blended into the cozy feel of an organized outdoors. Sarah kicked off her flip-flops, feeling the comfort of the cool cement floor on her bare feet. She made her way around the kitchen and family room opening windows, hoping to drain the cabin of the stifling heat.

Will set the cooler on the cement floor and started emptying the food onto the counter. Sarah joined him and began loading the food into the refrigerator. When he had finished pulling out everything, he leaned back against the counter with his arms crossed, watching her. She sweetly bumped her hip against his and grinned at him before returning to her task. She quickly tossed the rest of the items into the fridge, not caring where. She could fix it later.

Sarah turned around to face him and stated, "I'm so exhausted. I didn't get any sleep last night. Would you mind if I lie down and rest for a little bit?" She smiled at him, begging him with her eyes, hoping he would join her.

"No, I didn't get much sleep last night, either," he confessed.

Then Sarah grabbed his hand and led him up the stairs to her small bedroom. She was glad that her mom had insisted that everyone put clean sheets on their beds before leaving for home, because she was too tired to make up the bed now.

The room was warm and stuffy like the rest of the cabin, so Sarah crossed to the big dormer window, pulled up the blind, and slid the window up in its sash. She knew the breeze off the lake would make it bearable to sleep. The room was small, but efficient. It had a queen-sized bed with a pink comforter, a maple dresser with five drawers, and a closet. Covering the length of one wall was a built-in bench with a thick upholstered pad that could be used to sleep on if an extra bed was needed. Will sat down on the bench and looked at Sarah, as if he was waiting for her to take the lead.

Sarah looked him in the eye. "Would you like the bench or the bed? Slow, right?" she said, joking about his comment at the hotel.

"Well, since you're not sure of your feelings for me yet, maybe I should sleep on the bench. You got a pillow?" he replied with a smirk.

Sarah threw a pillow at him, hitting him in the head.

"Ouch!" He rubbed his head as she scowled at him.

Sarah surveyed the movie star in her bedroom. She had a hard time believing that she wasn't dreaming. She couldn't believe this was the same guy who knew her so well.

She took a breath. "Will you lie next to me? I want to make sure you don't leave."

He climbed onto the bed and patted the spot next to him. She settled in, and he wrapped his arm around her, spooning against her.

"Sweet dreams, beautiful," he said.

"Sweet dreams." She turned and kissed him on the cheek.

Chapter Nine

When Will awoke a couple of hours later, Sarah was no longer in his arms. He gazed around, admiring the quaintness of the room. On Sarah's dresser sat a well-played-with stuffed horse and an old spent firework robot with singe marks scarring the faded cardboard. They were obviously special to Sarah. Next to the horse sat a framed picture of Sarah holding a fluffy, round golden retriever puppy. Her toothless grin made him smile. Will wondered if it was the same dog she had mentioned died of old age a year ago. He noticed the four framed black-and-white photos above the bed. The little girl and the little boy in the pictures were playing on a distant beach. He knew right away that they were Sarah and Jeff. There was so much he knew about her, but still so much he didn't know.

He found her on the screened porch, curled up on the oversized wicker love seat, sipping lemonade and writing in a journal. The sun was high in the cloud-cluttered sky, and there was a slight breeze off the lake. He looked out over the water as he came onto the porch. The lake stretched as far as he could see from left to right, with cabins encroaching on the shore. Across the lake, structures dotted the hillside in an almost mirror image, but higher in the air.

"Hey, beautiful," he said and kissed her forehead. "I didn't know you kept a journal."

"Since I was twelve. I *am* majoring in English. It's sort of a prerequisite."

"Can I read it?" he asked, already knowing the answer.

"I'm sure you're capable," she said with a giggle as she finished up writing and closed the book.

"Excuse me, *may* I read it?" he said to appease her.

Sarah pretended to consider his request. "Mm…no." She smiled at him and took a sip from the tall glass dripping with condensation. "Lemonade?" she asked, holding up her glass.

Will took a mouthful from her glass and swallowed.

"Wow. It's really amazing here," he said as he looked out over the shimmering blue water.

The water moved constantly, with large waves that beat against the dock and shore when the boats passed. Massive speedboats rocketed one after another through the center of the lake, trailing thin ropes tied to brightly colored tubes that skipped across the water. Children flapped, prone on the tubes, attached only by their tightly gripped hands, while hip-hop music blared from the pontoon next to the neighbor's dock.

"But I didn't expect so many boats and people. I thought it would be more secluded," he admitted as he sat down next to her.

"It will be." She looked down at her watch. "It's two thirty now, and by four on Sundays, most of the boats are off the lake. By six, all the people will be loaded in their cars, heading back to the cities. You'll see. There are only three families that actually live on the lake, and they are all retired, so it will get pretty quiet."

"It sounds like you have it down to a science," he commented as he noted how the sunlight made her eyes look like jewels.

"I'm just observant. By tonight, we'll practically have the lake to ourselves. Most families only come up on the weekends," she said as she looked up at him through her lashes. Sarah ran her fingers across his stubbled jawline. "Sexy," she added, raising her eyebrows.

"Sexy?" he whispered. "I didn't shave this morning." He liked her choice of words and her playfulness. "Actually, I need to buy a razor or borrow a disposable one from Jeff. I checked mine, and some shorts would be helpful too."

"I'll show you where Jeff's room is, but you're keeping the scruff." She smiled back at him mischievously as she got up.

He grinned at her comment as he followed her. They went upstairs, and Sarah showed him Jeff's room. It was just down the hall from hers, about the same size, and decorated in a sailboarding theme, with a large sailboard balanced in the corner. Sarah sat on the bed while Will dug through the dresser and found some clothes he thought would fit. He was about the same height as Jeff, but thicker, more muscular. He changed into the shorts right in front of Sarah without any modesty. It didn't bother him at all.

Will and Sarah spent the afternoon lounging on the porch while they watched the activity on the lake. They talked and stole kisses from one another. It felt so good just to be together that neither one complained about being confined.

"So tell me what a typical day in the life of Jonathan Williams is like," requested Sarah.

"It's different every day. If I'm not working and I'm at home, it's pretty boring. I watch movies and read. I do my laundry and make meals like everyone else. I might have a business meeting over lunch, or dinner every once in a while, and I usually try to work out, just to maintain."

"How much?"

"Do I work out?" he asked, and she nodded. "An hour every day, if I can. I have to work out more before a shoot."

"Do you like working out?"

"Not always, but I have to, or I'll end up on one of those Beach Bodies Gone Bad shows on the Celebrity Network, and no one will hire me."

"Give yourself some credit. You're a great actor and super funny. You're so talented you could do anything you wanted, no matter what you looked like."

"So I should let myself go and become a comedian?" He looked at her skeptically as the corners of his lips turned up.

"If it makes you happy." She grinned back.

He playfully mussed her hair. "I actually enjoy acting, and working out isn't that bad."

"So what's a normal day when you're acting?"

"There's no such thing as a normal day on set. One day, I might be waiting around, sunning myself on a tropical island all day long just to shoot one line, and the next day, I could be standing up to my hips in mud and rain for fourteen hours with my toes so numb that I can't even walk. I guess that's what I like about it—no two days are the same. It can get monotonous sometimes if shooting isn't going well, but I think if I had to sit at a desk and do the same thing over and over every day, I'd go crazy."

"So do you get bored when you're not working?"

"I enjoy my time off," he said, beaming, while his fingers caressed her cheek. "What other job can you work a few months and take the rest of the year off?"

She looked at him skeptically.

"OK, I usually do a couple of movies a year, and then there's promoting, so I'm busy all the time lately. But I could take more time off if I wanted. I just want to make sure my career doesn't end."

"As long as you're happy." She chuckled and poked him in the side.

He jumped quickly into a standing position and turned to glare at her. "Don't do that. I'm really ticklish."

She chuckled again. "I barely touched you."

He bit his lip as he scrutinized her.

"Sorry, I didn't know. I won't poke you again. You can sit down."

"I just wasn't expecting that. It caught me off guard. Jack used to hold me down and tickle me until I peed my pants. I'm better at controlling it now, though."

"Peeing or being ticklish?"

"Both." He sat back down next to her.

As they sat talking, they watched the bigger boats disappear from the lake one by one. Sarah opened a magazine that was sitting on the floor and browsed through it while Will continued to survey the activity on the water.

Not long after the poking incident, Will stood up again, this time in utter amazement. "Holy crap! Did you see that?"

Sarah looked up to see what Will was so excited about. "What?"

"A bald eagle just picked up a fish this big"—he held his hand out in front of him about a foot and a half apart—"in the water, right off the end of the dock. It landed three docks down. See it? It's eating the fish. I want to get closer. Come on." He crept out the screen door. The door whined as he opened it and snapped back into place behind him with a clap. Crouching down, he snuck across the yard, hiding stealthily from the bird behind the large pine trunks as he crossed two more yards.

Sarah followed him outside, but hung back for a few minutes by the cabin. Then she slowly made her way across the grass to the side of the boathouse where he stalked the eagle. The wooden-slat boathouse pushed up against the water's edge provided the perfect cover to watch the fish's demise. They stood scrutinizing the predator's technique of ripping the flesh off the bones until their laughter frightened the bird and it spread its giant wings to fly. They could hear the pounding of its wings against the air as the bird took off, and they marveled that such a big bird could actually get up into the air.

"Have you ever seen that before?" Will looked wide-eyed at Sarah.

"No, never—just a couple of times a summer." Smirking at him, she picked up an old five-gallon bucket from the side of the boathouse and headed toward the end of the dock.

"What are you doing? Won't the eagle come back?" He followed her onto the dock.

"Probably not. I have to clean this off before it dries and stinks up the place," she said, bending down over the side of the dock and straining to fill the bucket with lake water. She pulled it up and poured the water all over the end of the dock. "This is my uncle Bob's cabin, and we look out for each other's property. If I don't rinse it, he'll have to scrape it off. Besides, the feeder fish will eat the debris."

"Here, let me help you," Will said, taking the bucket from her and bending down to dip it in the lake again. He could feel Sarah's eyes on his back as he hefted the water onto the dock, and he deliberately provided a show. He heard her mumble something under her breath, but he didn't hear what she'd said. When he turned around, she was shaking her head.

Mission accomplished, he thought.

"Once the lake is clear, do you want to go Jet Skiing or swimming?" she asked. "Hey, Will, come on," she added quickly as she spotted a bass boat trolling along the ends of the docks several cabins down. "We should probably wait it out on the porch until the lake clears. Sometimes the fishing boats come in pretty close to shore."

Will doused the end of the dock with the water and tossed the bucket to the side of the boathouse before they jogged back to the safety of the screened porch. They sat down on the love seat and watched the fishing boat glide by the end of Sarah's dock. The spindly bald man standing in the front of the boat cast his line nearly to shore as he silently floated to the next dock.

After he had passed, Will spoke up. "So I don't see any Jet Skis."

"Down there at my uncle's cabin," she said, pointing. "And my uncle Tom's cabin is the red one next to Bob's. He has a sailboat and a four-wheeler."

"Uncle Tom's cabin?" he questioned.

"Yeah, Uncle Tom and Aunt Sue. Both my dad's brothers have cabins on this lake. My cousin Ronnie and her husband, Nate, own the log cabin on the other side, that one with the rocky ledge there, straight across." She pointed. "They bought it two years ago. It doesn't have a beach, and the steps are pretty steep to get up to the cabin, but you can dive off the cliff ledge. The water is over twenty feet deep there. It's invigorating." Sarah paused and gazed at Will. "I know I'm rambling, but we have keys to everyone's cabins because we look out for each other's places. Uncle Tom has an old rowboat that we're always bailing out so it doesn't sink. It was my grandparents' boat, and when the water gets high on the lake like it did this spring, we have to put five-gallon buckets filled with water on Uncle Bob's dock to keep the decking from floating away."

"Buckets?" Will asked as he started kissing her neck just above her collarbone.

"Yeah..." She paused. "Um..." She took a breath.

Will stopped kissing her neck and looked at her, waiting for her to finish.

"Don't do that," she said. "I lost my thought."

"Something about buckets," he said, then started kissing her again.

"Stop," she said softly, without conviction.

He stopped, pulling back to see her eyes. "I just like to see that I can affect you the way that you affect me," he confessed, showing his perfect smile. "So you were saying?"

"Buckets," Sarah enunciated slowly as she ran her fingers through her hair and squished her eyes closed. "Uh, we all help each other, and we share toys like Jet Skis and our ski boat."

Will stared at her in amazement. "Have I told you that I love you?" he asked as his dimple pulled deeper into his right cheek.

"I believe you have," she whispered against his cheek before she got up, kissed his dimple, and strode inside the cabin.

Will paused for a minute, pondering Sarah's response. After all that had happened at the airport, she still was avoiding the subject. He knew he had only been with her a few days, but they had known each other for months, and he'd known pretty early on that he loved her. He followed her inside and found her in the kitchen taking food out of the refrigerator.

Without looking up, she asked, "Do you want to grill or chop?"

Will stood in the doorway, staring at her.

"Would you grill? I hate grilling," she said, turning toward him.

"Sure. Where's the grill?" he questioned, still staring at her.

Sarah pointed toward the kitchen patio door. Will walked out onto the patio, opened the gas valve on the tank, and pushed the igniter. The flame caught, and he adjusted the temperature dial. When he returned to the kitchen, Sarah was chopping peppers. Will walked up behind her and wrapped his arms around her waist, pulling her in toward him. He rested his chin on the top of her head, and his lips touched her hair in a kiss.

"So, what are we having?"

"Chicken fajitas. I hope that's OK."

"I love fajitas," he admitted as he took in the heavenly floral smell of her hair. "Can we go swimming after we eat? I'm not used to this humidity. And no air conditioner? Is it always like this?"

"No. Usually, it's only this bad before a big storm. And swimming sounds perfect," she answered. She turned around in his arms and kissed his cheek. Then she reached back, grabbed a ziplock bag of raw marinating chicken breasts, and handed it to Will. "I'll finish with the peppers, and I'll meet you outside."

He took a deep breath and sighed. Then, taking the bag, he headed for the grill.

Will browsed her silhouette with his eyes as she approached twenty minutes later. He was still trying to figure out why she couldn't admit that she was in love with him. He knew how he felt, and he thought she felt the same. He could tell by the way she looked at him. Nick had even mentioned that he thought she was in love with Will by the way she had spoken of him before the concert.

Women are so complicated, he thought. *I'll never figure them out. Maybe it was because I left. I'll have to gain her trust again somehow.*

"I think the chicken is ready."

"Good. I'm starving," Sarah admitted.

She handed Will a small cutting board and a knife for the chicken. When their fingers touched, Will felt electricity zing through his body. He envisioned pushing her up against the house and coaxing those three words from her with his body. He knew he would never gain her trust that way, though. Instead, he sliced the meat and resolved to give her some time.

"Let's eat," she commanded.

Sarah had found a third of a bottle of premixed margaritas in the refrigerator, and they finished it off, sipping from the same glass. They ate their meal outside, chatting about what it was like growing up in Hollywood. In the end, they decided that teenagers were teenagers, no matter where they grew up. When they were finished eating and had cleaned up the dishes, they changed into their swimsuits.

Will could see Sarah nervously hesitate near the top of the stairs. She shrank out of sight three times before finally slipping a T-shirt over her head and making her way down. It was too late. He had already glimpsed her tiny suit.

"What were you doing?" he asked.

"Just…I'm ready," she stammered. Looking up, her jaw dropped as her eyes slid over his body. "Hi," she said, as if she was meeting him for the first time.

"Hi. You don't need to cover up. It's just me, and my feelings aren't going to change," he said, gazing into her eyes.

"How do you know?" she whispered.

Will wrapped his arms around her. "I just know." He was feeling a little worried now about why she couldn't admit her love, and didn't want to pressure her about her feelings. "Let's go swimming," he suggested with a smile.

He grabbed her hand, and they walked down to the dock together. With the boats off the lake, the water seemed still, and the air was so quiet that they could hear a loon calling to its mate. When they reached the end of the dock, Sarah sat down, soaking her feet in the cool water. Will smirked devilishly at her and cannonballed into the water. Lake water saturated the entire end of the L-shaped dock, including Sarah. She looked at him in disbelief, with water streaming down her face.

"Thanks," she said sarcastically. "Now I don't even have to go in."

"I was just trying to get you to take off that shirt," Will confessed, now feeling guilty for what he had just done.

"I'm leaving it on," she declared and gave him a look as if to say, *So there.*

"Come on. You need the vitamin D. You're definitely deficient with your pale skin."

"I'll take a pill."

"Please?" He looked at her with puppy dog eyes and a pouty lip.

"All right, fine." She stood up, crossed her arms, grabbed the end of her shirt, and slipped it over her head.

Will stood in the water near the end of the dock, watching her.

Posing with one hand on her hip, she announced, "Last one to the raft sleeps on the bench." Without waiting for a response, she dove into the water and swam toward the yellow molded plastic raft anchored about thirty feet from the end of the dock.

Will stared after her for a couple of seconds, not realizing what she had said. Then as it sank in, he pushed off from the bottom of the lake and raced her to the raft. With her head start, Sarah was nearing the top of the ladder when Will reached up, grabbed her around the waist, and pulled her down on top of him. They both sank into the water, and when they came up, he glowered at her threateningly.

Hanging on to the edge of the raft with one hand, Will brushed the hair out of her face and said, "I didn't realize you were such a cheater."

"I'll give you a pillow. The bench won't be that bad." She grinned at him.

In truth, Will couldn't imagine sleeping on the bench, even if they weren't doing anything more than sleeping.

"That's not going to happen. I like the bed," he said, wrapping his hand around the nape of her neck and pulling her in for a slow, deep kiss.

They swam in the cool water, and Will taught Sarah how to do a back dive off the raft. The first time she tried, he stood crouched next to her with one hand supporting the middle of her back as she leaned out over the water and his other hand touching the back of her thigh, ready to flip her once she was airborne.

"Just trust me," he said.

She looked at him anxiously and took a deep breath.

He cocked his head, exuding sincerity. "On the count of three, OK? Just jump up and back. I won't let your head smash into the raft. I promise."

She nodded slowly, aligned the balls of her feet with the edge of the raft, and bent her knees.

"One, two, three," Will counted.

Sarah launched herself up and back, just like he had shown her. Will flipped her legs up into the air, and she flew backward. Then, just as she was supposed to do, she straightened out, landing in the water. When her head reappeared, bobbing above the surface, she brushed her hair out of her eyes and, with a smile, asked, "Should we try it again?"

"Sure, you're a natural," he replied, beaming at her.

Will helped her dive several more times, until she felt ready to try it on her own, and when she did, the dive was pretty close to perfect. They swam a bit longer, then lay on the hard plastic raft and watched the thick storm clouds grow more ominous as the sky appeared to sink down around them. A cool wind picked up, and the air seemed to take on a greenish hue.

"Look at those clouds. We don't get this shade of sky in LA. It's going to be a big storm."

"Yeah," Sarah admitted, "it will probably start pouring any minute. You can feel the cool air moving in."

Just as she was finishing her sentence, the sky opened up and pelted the two with large, heavy drops that stung their skin when they hit. Instinctively, they both jumped into the water to avoid the assaulting rain and swam for the dock. Sarah climbed the ladder, with Will right behind her. They could hardly see a foot in front of them with the wind blowing the rain so hard. Sarah reached for Will's hand and pulled him toward the boat lift.

"Let's wait it out under here," she yelled over the roar of the rain, and they climbed into the green-and-white ski boat under the canopy of the lift. Then they collapsed on the vinyl bench that spanned the back of the boat and laughed hysterically at their bad luck.

With their hearts pounding from the swim, they looked deeply into each other's eyes. Will cupped one hand behind Sarah's neck and pulled her closer to touch his open lips to hers. She leaned to meet him. In a smooth, deliberate movement, Sarah maneuvered onto Will's lap. Without breaking the kiss, she was now facing him, straddling his hips. Will wrapped his arms around her, and they kissed, feeling the vibrant energy of their wet, touching skin. Slowly, his hand found its way to one of her breasts. He tried to stop himself, but he couldn't. Sarah broke the kiss and reached up to untie the bikini string around her neck.

Startled, Will questioned, "What are you doing?"

She looked back at him, a bit surprised by his reaction, and conveyed, *Isn't it as plain as the nose on your face?* without a word.

"Don't...do that. I won't be able to control myself," he said, fighting himself internally.

"Why? Don't you want to?" she questioned.

"Of course I want to! Isn't it obvious?" He looked down at the front of his swim trunks.

She followed his eyes and smirked at him in disbelief. "Then why not?"

"OK, Miss Irresponsible," he said, shaking his head, "I don't have unprotected sex, because I'm not ready to have children yet, and even if we had something, I don't think you're ready."

Sarah looked into his eyes with a sense of acknowledged defeat. "You're right—about protection. I'll give you that. But what do you mean I'm not ready? Believe me, I'm ready!" she pleaded, wide-eyed.

"No, you're not. You can't even admit that you're in love with me. You're not ready!" he proclaimed, not believing that he was betraying his body's desires. "We are not doing that unless you are sure I am the one. I want everything to be right. Are you in love with me or not? Just tell me either way. Be honest. You know how I feel."

She paused, taking a deep breath. "I care about you more than I have ever cared about anyone before," she answered.

"But you don't know if it's love?" Will whispered.

She looked down with a worried expression, and her saturated hair fell forward, covering her face. The wet strands clung to her cheeks.

Will threaded his fingers through her hair and gathered it into a loose ponytail with his hands so he could see her eyes. "I just want to understand," he pleaded softly.

"I…" She struggled for words. "I don't know what to do. Are you Will or Jonathan? Who are you?"

Will looked at her, dumbfounded. He didn't understand where these questions were coming from.

"What's going to happen when you go back to LA? It is going to hurt so much when you leave. I can't. If I…" Tears built in her eyes until they leaked slowly down her cheek. "If I admit that I'm in love with you, it will only hurt more—more when you leave."

He pulled her into his bare chest, wrapping his muscular arms around her. "It's OK, Sarah," he whispered, scrunching his face in frustration. He didn't want to cause her so much pain. He grasped her shoulders gently and nudged her back so he could look into her eyes. "Sarah," he said as he wiped the tears from her cheeks with his thumb.

Looking into his eyes just made the tears flow faster, and she began to sob.

"Come on, you know it's not going to change what we feel in here." He pressed his palm over her heart. "I know it is going to be hard to be

apart, but I don't think I will be able to stay away from you for very long."
He flashed his perfect smile at her. "No matter what you call me—Will
or Jon—it doesn't matter to me. I'm the same person either way, and I
love you. I'm in love with you. You're right, we have a lot to figure out,
but my love is not going to change. You can take all the time you need to
figure out how you feel about me. I'm not going to pressure you again."

She rested her head on his chest, and Will wrapped his arms around
her again. He gently rubbed her back with his fingertips as they sat
listening to the roar of the pouring rain spattering on the lake around
them and pelting the green canvas above them.

When the rain started to let up just a little, Will asked, "Should we
make a break for it?"

Sarah looked at him, wrapped her arms around his neck, and sighed.
"If you…" she began, but just then, the sky lit up, immediately followed
by a loud crack of thunder that shook the boat. They both felt the hair
on their arms stand up when the lightning hit, and they could smell
the electricity in the air. Sarah looked at Will wide-eyed and nodded.
They climbed out from under the aluminum-framed lift, onto the dock,
and sprinted hand in hand to the cabin as the sky lit up again. They
burst through the cabin door, soaking wet, and Sarah headed right for
the stairs.

"Hey, where are you going?" Will asked, putting his palms up and
arms out as if to say, *What gives?*

"Towels!" she said, as if it should have been obvious.

"Wait! Come here." He flashed his big glacier-colored eyes at her.

"What?" She walked back to him. "I'm dripping all over the
floor here."

He bent down as if to kiss her and then shook his hair out like a dog,
splattering her with more rainwater. He couldn't help it.

"You're dead!" She sprung for his waist to tickle him.

He jumped out of her grasp. Backing up as she advanced on him, he declared, "I just didn't want you to dry off prematurely." He flashed his brilliant smile.

"You're going to wish for a premature death!" she threatened.

Trying to avoid Sarah's wrath, he placed his hands on her shoulders to keep her from reaching his ticklish waist and neck. Then Will quickly grabbed her around the waist and pulled her in, throwing her over his shoulder firefighter style. He carried her up stairs as she thrashed.

"Are you going to play nice?" He laid her on the bed and climbed on top of her. He straddled her waist so she couldn't escape, and smiled sheepishly at her as he gathered her hands in one of his.

With a forced scowl, she looked into his eyes and complained, "Now the bed is all wet."

"Just the comforter. If it bothers you, you can sleep on the bench." He smirked as he dramatically eyed the bench.

Still staring into his eyes, she blurted out, "God, I love you." A startled expression flitted across her face.

Will's eyes popped with surprise. He couldn't believe his ears. He had been waiting for her to admit this, but he never expected it so soon after their talk on the boat. He froze, staring at her face. He wanted to know whether she was aware of what she had just said.

Squishing her eyes closed, Sarah confessed, "It just slipped out."

He saw the vulnerability on her face and knew he would do everything within his power to never hurt this woman. He stared at her face a few seconds longer and then leaned over her. As his lips met hers, warmth filled his entire body. She'd finally acknowledged what he knew she was feeling. He kissed her slowly and fervently on the mouth for several minutes, forgetting the world around them.

When the kiss was broken, they were both out of breath.

With a huge smile on his face, he whispered into her ear. "There are some things in life that you just can't control." Then Will rolled off her and sat down on the bed next to her. He continued staring and continued smiling.

"What?" she asked with a chuckle in her voice. "OK, I admit it. I love you."

"Finally," he said, filled with relief.

"So what now?" whispered Sarah.

"Let's wait and see," he answered smugly. "Nothing has changed between us. I knew you loved me."

Even though he said nothing had changed, in Will's mind, everything had changed. He knew for sure that she loved him back, and he thought she had probably forgiven him for leaving this morning. Somehow, her admitting her love solidified their future together, and he knew that everything would work out. Her words had brought him contentment and hope.

Chapter Ten

The wind whistled through the tall pines outside the dormer window in Sarah's bedroom. The storm seemed to be getting worse as booms of thunder echoed back and forth across the lake. There would be no bonfire in this rain, and neither of them was in the mood to play cards. They agreed to watch a movie, but first Sarah wanted a shower "to wash the lake out of her hair."

Will offered to build a fire in the big stone fireplace to counteract the drop in temperature brought on by the storm, and headed downstairs. He was nervous about the evening ahead. The feelings he had for Sarah were so much more intense than anything he had ever felt before. He wanted to take it slow with her, to give her a chance to fully understand the baggage that came along with him. That was what his brain told him. He couldn't help it if his body didn't agree. He knew that if he'd had a condom stashed in his pocket this afternoon, he wouldn't have been able to stop himself. He wasn't that strong—not with Sarah. Now that Sarah had admitted her feelings, his control was completely gone.

He crumpled two sheets of old newspaper and stuffed them under the heavy oak log in the hearth, one on each end, trying to create a pocket where air could flow. Then he lit each wrinkled thread with the oversized lighter from the mantle and lightly blew on the flames until they trailed under the log. He waited for the bark to light and the flame to curl around the log before closing the metal chain doors.

As he watched the fire for a few minutes, he remembered sitting under the boat lift this afternoon, the feel of Sarah's fingers feathering across his abdomen, her touch so light yet so deep. He recalled the rain beating on the canopy above their heads, pounding like a drum calling him to act. And Sarah's face beaming with desire. Oh yeah, he was going to need a shower too—a cold shower.

He stood up with a sigh and wandered up the stairs. The bathroom door was open, so he knew Sarah was done. He knocked on her bedroom door and told her he was going to grab a shower as well, then stopped in Jeff's room, found what he needed from the dresser, and headed into the bathroom.

When he came downstairs again twenty minutes later, Sarah was sitting on a quilt that was spread across the floor. She was leaning on a pillow propped against the couch and writing in her journal. He wished he could read what she was writing. He knew by her blush that it was about him. He thought the quilt on the floor was a good sign. He couldn't help the smirk that came to his lips when he saw it or the way his eyes penetrated her as she innocently looked up at him. She closed her journal and popped up off the floor to greet him with a smile.

He wrapped his arms around her and pressed his lips against hers. Her stunning green eyes fluttered closed as he consumed her. He could feel tension building in her breath, and it matched his. His hands slid down the curve of her butt. What was she wearing? He pulled away from the kiss and stepped back to get a better look. The little black tank clung to her curves, leaving nothing to the imagination, and the tiny white shorts…

Oh god, they should be illegal, Will thought, taking a gulping breath. *She wore those on purpose.*

"You look..." He paused, trying to curb his words to girl-appropriate language. "Hot!" He peeled his hands off her hips and took another step back. He needed to slow himself down. He turned away from her so he could think. "So what do you want to watch?"

She chuckled like she could read his mind. "I don't want anything depressing. I've seen just about everything here, so you can pick, if you like. They're under the TV."

"Let's see what you have." He walked to the cabinet and opened it. There were four rows filled with movies. He opened a second cabinet and it was filled as well. "Watch movies much?"

"We don't have streaming—no Internet or cable—so we use DVDs. Every movie any of us buys ends up here because there's not much to do at night except watch movies, drink, or play cards."

He could think of some other activities. He ran his fingers through his hair, trying to refocus. "There's quite a library. Hmm. *The Summer Killing, Push, The Last Diamond...*How about *The Coven?*"

"No, not tonight. We used to watch that one every Friday in the dorms. I have it memorized. How about *The Demigod* or *Love Twice? Love Twice* is romantic."

He shook his head. "Not happening. That would be weird. I don't watch my own films. What about *Reckless?*"

"There's no romance in that one. I like romantic comedies. I'm sure you can find a good date-night movie, and I'll make some popcorn," she said, whimsically spinning and dancing her way to the kitchen.

"How about a horror movie?" he called across the room.

"No way, not at the cabin. Some young couple always ends up getting axed in their bed in a cabin."

While they're having sex, he added in his head.

"I wouldn't be able to sleep tonight," she yelled back.

"That works for me," he muttered, too quiet for her to hear. "That's a lot of noes. I'm just going to pick one." He chose one he knew well so he wouldn't have to pay attention to the film.

When Sarah returned with the popcorn in a big red bowl and two bottles of beer, the movie was just starting. The storm was picking up again outside, and the fire crackled in the hearth. The movie was fast-paced and scary in the beginning. Sarah adhered to his side like duct tape and clinched her nails into his arm as the first three victims met their deaths. The movie was a thriller with a romantic thread, but the first half hour was mostly a killing spree.

He leaned closer to her and whispered in her ear. "I thought you've seen all the movies here. Haven't you seen this before?" She smelled of cherry blossoms and vanilla—definitely dessert. He nipped her ear.

She turned her face toward him, but kept her eyes glued on the screen. "I have, just not for a while." She scrunched her eyes together and pulled his arm onto her lap as blood splattered on the wall of a dark alley on the TV.

This was definitely the right movie, he decided. He moved his arm behind her and drew her in protectively as he ticked off the on-screen killings in his head—five down, two to go. He didn't even have to look at the screen. He could tell by the sound effects and by the way Sarah tensed. He sipped his beer and popped a couple of pieces of popcorn into his mouth. It was much better watching Sarah than the film. More slashing noises, and she buried her face in his chest. He tucked two fingers into the waistband of her shorts as he waited for the killing to end and for her to relax. But when the hero's love interest crouched, hiding just a foot from the killer, there was a loud crack of thunder.

Kaboom!

The walls shook and the cabin went black—pitch-black, except for the hearth.

Sarah crashed her body into his, and he took full advantage. He drew her onto his lap, and as his hands lingered on her ass, his lips covered hers. Her lips were soft and inviting, and the kiss quickly turned hungry. Her hands ran into his hair, while his hands tugged at her thighs, pulling her closer. She was warm and mesmerizing, and he wanted her so badly it hurt. Right there, right now. There was no way he was going to rush this, though. He wanted it to last forever.

He broke off the kiss, pulling back to catch his breath, and she groaned in disappointment. He touched his forehead to hers and stared into her eyes. Her face pleaded with him not to stop, and her breathing was as shallow as his. He didn't want to stop.

He kissed her long and slow, taking his time to explore every aspect of her very sexy mouth. She tugged at his T-shirt, so with one hand, he reached back and dragged it over his head. Her hands fell to his newly exposed abdomen and smoothed over every inch of his tanned skin. When her fingers started to fumble with the button on his shorts, he knew he needed to take drastic measures to slow them down.

He covered her hand with his to stop her. "Sarah, do you have any candles?" He knew the question sounded obscure, but it was the only thing he could come up with.

She stiffened in his arms.

"I'm not going to drop hot wax on you or anything—unless you want that," he said with a slight laugh. That thought wasn't helping. "You're straddling my lap, and I'm sure you look incredible—you feel incredible—but I can't even see your face because it's so dark in here." It was true. There was some light from the fire, but it wasn't enough to catch all her expressions.

She nodded and climbed off his lap, muttering, "I'm not against hot wax. I'm really a pretty open-minded person."

Her comment made him chuckle, and getting her off his lap allowed him to think again. He didn't know what was wrong with him. He had been with more than his share of women and had never felt like this. All he wanted to do was please her. Love really did make a difference.

His eyes followed her as she reached up for the long lighter that he had used to start the hearth fire, and her top rose, exposing the small of her back. Straining on her tiptoes to spy the wicks, she began to light the candles that lined the length of the mantle. The glow from the fire and the candles hugged her perfect silhouette, and she was only able to light three of the candles before Will's arms wrapped around her from behind. He pulled at her tank until it was freed from the tangles of her body as his lips skimmed the back of her neck. His fingers glided under the strap of her pink lace bra, and he nudged it off her shoulder to give him better access to her soft, supple skin. He kissed with soft whisper kisses as his hands explored her bare flesh. When his hands covered her perfect lace-veiled breasts, she responded with quiet, throaty moans. Her soft noises drove him to unhook her bra with his teeth—his teeth, that was a first. His lips grazed her ear and hair, while his hands slid under her bra and the lace dropped to the floor. He cupped her full but very real breasts, earning him a full-body shudder from Sarah. She arched back against him as he tormented her, and he thought he was going to lose his mind. That's when he looked up and noticed her perfect form reflected in the window next to the fireplace. Lightening flashed every few seconds, but when the window was dark, he could see her beautiful figure entwined with his.

With one hand still on her breast, the other meandered down to the button on those flawless shorts. His fingers made quick work of the button and zipper before they slipped under the fabric. His hand splayed across her stomach, and he pulled her back against him. She needed to know what she was doing to him. Then his hand plunged lower and his finger sank into her. She ground her back against him as he teased her. Like a silent film, her image flickered on the window, tantalizing him with glimpses of her face. She looked so sweet, so innocent, as if she had never been touched before. He toyed with her until she could take no more. When her body quivered and slumped against him, he kissed the back of her neck thoroughly and whispered in her ear.

"You're so beautiful." And she was. He had never been with anyone who had exhibited the radiance that she possessed. Pure beauty poured out of her.

He lifted her into his arms and carried her to the quilt on the floor. As he laid her out below him, he stared into her emerald eyes, and she smiled up at him with a look of embarrassment.

"I love you, Sarah," he said, and her smile brightened, but she didn't say a word. "What? You're speechless? That good, huh?"

She nodded and wet her lips, and the look of embarrassment returned. He leaned down and kissed it away. After a long minute, he pushed back to look into her eyes again. She was so damn cute. He kissed the tip of her nose as her hands feathered lightly across his chest and then down to the button on his shorts again. When he felt his zipper give way, he quickly gathered her hands in one of his and pinned them above her head.

"Would you just let me enjoy you for a while?" His mouth found one of her breasts, and he took his time playing with it before moving to the next. When he finally released her hands, they tangled in his hair, and he leisurely kissed his way down her soft skin to those white shorts still hanging loosely on her hips. He pulled the shorts off in a single yank, then hooked his fingers into her tiny panties and slid them down her legs. He stared, taking in the splendor before him, knowing this was the visual that would stick in his brain—the one he would never forget. Oh hell! He wasn't going to be able to tease her the way he had wanted. He couldn't wait any longer. He grabbed what he needed from his pocket and shrugged off his shorts and boxer briefs. He planted one long, wet kiss below her navel before trailing kisses back up to her lips. His mouth devoured hers.

He broke the kiss and stared into her eyes one last time, and she whispered, "I love you, Will." Her words solidified his desire. And when he pushed into her, the look on Sarah's face and the noise that escaped her throat told him all he needed to know. This was exactly how it was meant to be. Perfect.

Her legs curled around him, and he moved slowly at first. He just wanted to get the feel of her. Oh god, she was tight. She arched up against him at just the right moment, as if they had spent hours working out their rhythm. He balanced himself on one arm and brushed the hair out of her eyes. He could stare at her forever and never tire. Her eyes were hooded, and the sweet little noises she was making told him he was hitting her in all the right spots.

He traced his finger over her collarbone and down her side, lingering on her breast. Her lips parted and the breathy sound that came out practically stopped his heart. When his mouth followed the same path as his hand, her fingers clawed at his back. He sucked and teased as she matched his now more fervent rhythm. She knew exactly how to push his buttons. She touched him in places he didn't even know were erogenous. He struggled to stay in control, but he knew she was close. He could feel the little tremors inside her. He shifted to get better leverage, switching arms. When he grasped her tiny ass in his hand and pulled it to meet him, he felt her surrender. Her body shuddered, and he thought he heard his name. He was too far gone to know for sure. He buried his face in her neck and followed her over the edge.

Hours later, the two lay listening to the rain sheet against the windowpanes. Will had gone back and taken his time to tease Sarah the way he had wanted. He was proud of the responses he had coaxed from her. He had more than enough experience to read a woman's body, and Sarah's was transparent to him. He didn't even have to think about what he was doing. It was all so natural, and his ego soared knowing he was able to push her over the edge three more times.

They had settled side by side, and Sarah lay nestled against him. They could hear the thunder moving farther away from the cabin, and lightning no longer lit up the room with flashes of light. The fire had died down, and the embers in the hearth glowed orange. The room was quiet except for their breathing and the occasional distant thunder.

Being with Sarah was more amazing than he ever could have imagined, and he had a good imagination. He closed his eyes, savoring the feeling of her fingers carelessly strumming back and forth across his chest. He was so relaxed it didn't even tickle. He relished the softness of her touching skin, knowing that this woman in his arms was the only one he would ever want.

"What are you thinking, beautiful?"

"I was just thinking how lucky I am," she answered. "How lucky it was that I was on that website three months ago at the same time as you. How lucky I am that I went to the airport this morning. I was thinking that God must have something pretty special in store for us, to overcome such odds."

"I think you're right," he said with a chuckle, "something pretty special." He drew her in closer and kissed her forehead. They lay listening to the rare crackling of the fire, enjoying the comfort of each other's arms while contemplating what the future held.

"Sarah, would you consider moving to LA when you're done with school?"

"I don't know. I've never really thought about moving away from here before." She paused. "I think I could do anything if I was with you. And I would have to find a job out there too."

"When does your internship start?" asked Will.

"Next Monday. Why?"

"I hoped you could come back to LA and spend some more time with me before you started it. I have to be back for costume fittings on Friday, but preproduction for the film doesn't start for two weeks. I have other commitments in LA and I won't be able to make it back here, but it would have been great if we could have had another week or two together."

"Damn, I would have liked that."

"Once preproduction starts, I'll be pretty busy with training for my stunts and going over my lines, but we'll find time. I'll fly you out, even if it is just for a weekend," Will said.

"I'll pay my own way, but a weekend? That just doesn't sound long enough."

He smirked at her "pay my own way" comment. She sure wasn't like most women. "You'll be working hard on your internship, and before you know it, school will be starting."

"Somehow, all that doesn't seem as important anymore," she confessed.

"I'm not going to get in the way of you finishing your degree. We'll make it work. Besides, I won't have a life anyway, once filming starts, for at least three months. By that time, it will be Christmas. What do you want for Christmas?"

"You," she answered as she ran her fingers along the stubble on his jawline and leaned up to kiss his lips.

"I think that can be arranged," he whispered against her lips before kissing them.

"Do you have any more, um…?" she stammered, pulling back.

"A couple." He pursed his lips, raising an eyebrow at her greediness. "I borrowed them from Jeff. They were in his dresser, and he said I could use anything I needed. I didn't bring any. I didn't want to assume that you would…want to, and I wanted to take it slow. I tried to force myself to take it slow, but they were right there, and I just can't control how I feel about you," he confessed without shame.

"Jeff is going to be mad, but holy wow, it was definitely worth it." She swallowed loudly and started to giggle.

Will laughed. "I'm glad to hear it was worth it. Do you want to go to bed?" Will stood up and offered his hand to help Sarah up.

She scrunched her eyes. "I don't think I can walk."

God, she's gorgeous, he thought.

"Come on." He bent down, grasped her hand, and lifted her to her feet. After she was standing, he picked up the quilt and wrapped it around her. He grabbed a candle off the mantel and extinguished the other two before they headed upstairs, laughing about Jeff and Jess's reaction when they couldn't find their box of condoms.

They made love again before falling asleep, and Will made sure Sarah thought it was worth it.

Chapter Eleven

Will and Sarah stayed in bed until early afternoon. Finally, the need to replenish supplies and growling stomachs forced them out of bed. Sarah teased him that he'd swallowed a bear, his stomach made such a loud noise.

"Hungry much? How did you work up such an appetite?"

He just smiled at her as he slipped on a pair of shorts and a T-shirt. The air in the cabin was much more bearable than the previous day. It definitely felt cooler. The humidity had blown out with the rain, and the sun shone brightly, high in the sky. Sarah and Will decided to go into town to get some supplies after they ate. Since the electricity was still out and could be out for days, according to Sarah, it was important to stock up before the stores ran out. The refrigerator would stay cold as long as they didn't open it too often, but it would be better if they bought ice. Since the cabin had a well with a pump that ran on electricity, they needed water, and they knew they should pick up some gas to fill the boat and the Jet Skis too. Will loaded the two big red plastic gas cans into the back, propping them up and securing them with a large black bungee cord before getting into the vehicle.

In town, they parked by the gas pumps and worked together to fill the five-gallon cans. Will wore his sunglasses and baseball cap to cover his face, hoping no one would recognize him. Sarah said she knew the family that owned the store. She had known them since she was a little girl, and they treated her like family. Besides, there were no other cars, so the store was probably empty.

Inside, the musty fish smell made it clear the store sold bait. Though the shelves were old and the floor warped in different directions, the store was clean. Will noted that Sarah was right about it having just about everything that was really needed. Besides the food, there was a Peg-Board wall covered with fishing lures. There were crossbows, arrows, and camouflage gear for hunting. Above the bubbling bait tanks swayed rows and rows of plastic yellow-and-white minnow buckets. There must have been about thirty of them.

Will even found an aisle with pharmaceuticals—cough drops, Tylenol, razors, and condoms. He picked up what he needed and then headed for the ice freezer. He grabbed two ten-pound ice bags. Balancing them on his shoulder, he carried them to the front with his other supplies and laid them all on the wood-and-glass countertop. He briskly rubbed his arms to rid them of the icy sting as he looked around to assess who was in the store. Intrigued by a big vat of live bait along the wall past the counter, he walked over and inspected the dark water. A large horde of fathead minnows huddled in one corner, wriggling on top of each other to hide from his cast shadow. He had been fly-fishing once and deep sea fishing a couple of times, but he'd never used live bait before. For a minute, he debated getting a fishing license, but decided it was best not to leave a paper trail for the media to track him.

Sarah was over by the cooler doors. She loved the fresh eggs from the farm just down the road, so she grabbed a dozen from inside the glass door and circled back around to find the water jugs. As she reached the front of the store, she loaded her groceries onto the counter next to Will's, then cautiously looked around for the clerk, and her eyes fell on the familiar face of a grossly muscular man in his twenties sporting a camouflage hat. His deep-brown eyes sparkled when they met Sarah's, and his always-smiling face animated.

"Sarah? Sarah Austin, how the hell are you?" the man's deep voice boomed from behind the magazine rack near the counter.

"Oh my gosh! Ryan!" She dropped her purse on the counter and walked to hug the marine. "You're home from the Middle East?"

"Yeah, I'm on leave, just filling in at the store today," he said, picking her up in a big bear hug. "I tried calling your house on your birthday, but your mom said you were out. I lost my phone and didn't have your cell. I've been thinking about you a lot lately. Do you ever think about us?"

"Sure, but you've been gone a long time," she admitted quietly, not really knowing what to say.

"That never stopped us before," he stated as he set her down. "Come out for a drink with me. You're legal now." A huge, infectious smile beamed on his face.

"Ryan, I..." She looked at him apprehensively.

"I know that you believe long-distance relationships don't have a snowball's chance in hell, but it's not like we really tried. What do ya say?"

"I can't. I..." She looked toward Will. She hoped Ryan wouldn't recognize him. With his cap obscuring his face, he could have been just some ordinary guy—a really off-the-wall gorgeous ordinary guy.

Ryan followed her gaze, and his eyes widened. Scowling, he gave Will a nod.

"Oh, I get it. So you're hiding out at the lake, huh?"

Sarah was stunned. "Um, just hanging out, enjoying the weather. There was quite a storm last night," she said in a jumpy voice, unsure if his comment was an innocent observation or all knowing.

"I saw you on *Celebrity News* last night."

"Really?"

"My mom had it on. I didn't think it was you. My mom was on the phone all night debating it. That's him?" he asked, tilting his head toward Will.

"Yeah. Why don't you come meet him?" She grabbed his arm and brought him over to introduce him to Will. "Ryan, this is Jon. Jon, Ryan." It felt weird for her to call him Jon, but calling him Will seemed too personal for this introduction.

The two guys shook hands as Ryan eyed Will skeptically.

"I wasn't sure if it was true, but I can see that it is."

"Don't tell anyone we're here." Will looked at Ryan with concern. "It really becomes dangerous when people know where we are."

"No problem. I know how that is. It's the same in the Middle East. Safety first, right?"

"I bet it's great to be home," Will said, making small talk.

"Yep. It's hell over there, either boring or deadly. Saw you in *The Demigod*. That was kick-ass," Ryan admitted.

They chatted for several minutes before Ryan started to ring up their groceries. He glowered at Will as he bagged the pharmaceuticals.

"Well, I'm just filling in for my mom while she runs to Sandstone for a prescription. She'll be back any minute, and if you don't want the world to know you're here, you should probably get going. Great to see you, Sarah."

"Thanks. It's great to see you too. Stay safe." Sarah smiled.

"Treat her right, Jon," he added.

"I will." Will wrapped his arm around Sarah possessively and kissed the top of her head, marking his territory, before picking up the bags of ice and the groceries.

Sarah grabbed the water jugs, and they headed toward the door.

"There are a lot of people who are protective of you," he said as they left the store.

Sarah just smiled innocently.

After loading their purchases, Sarah tossed Will her keys. "Will you drive, please? I'll tell you where to turn." She wanted to observe Will as he drove instead of him scrutinizing her. She knew he would ask her about Ryan. She hoped that Will hadn't heard her conversation with him, but judging by his possessive demeanor as they left, he probably had, and the expression on Ryan's face as he rang up the three packages of prophylactics had YouTube viral potential all over it. Sarah was embarrassed that Ryan knew, but was pleased that he didn't look at her until everything was bagged and his face had returned to normal.

Will closed the passenger door behind Sarah and climbed into the driver's seat. "So do you think he'll tell anyone we're here?" He started the engine and pulled out of the parking lot.

"No, I've known him for a long time. Ryan's grandparents are retired on Pine Lake, and his folks have owned the bait shop since I was a little kid. If his mom found out we were here, she might blab, but Ryan won't tell her. He's pretty loyal—like an old hound dog. He and I used to go out."

"I gathered that much," he said with a questioning look.

"It wasn't serious."

"Sounds like he thought it was serious."

"He joined the military, and I haven't seen him in over a year."

"Yeah. Long-distance relationships never work, right?" He shrugged.

"It's not the same for us."

"How so?"

"We love each other. We'll make it work. We don't have a choice," she declared.

He looked at her skeptically. "I didn't take you for the dumb jock kind of girl. I mean, I can see how some girls go for that bulky, giant muscle-bound kind of thing, but I pictured you with more intellectual types."

"We all have our vices, right?" She smiled at him jokingly, trying to erase the long-distance relationship comment from his mind. "Turn left at that public boat access sign ahead. Honestly, he's not that bad," she continued. "Besides, I'm with you, aren't I?"

"I'm not like *that*! He has fifty pounds on me. I'm more of a…sampler platter," he said, smiling.

"Yeah, nice to look at and a lot to offer," she added playfully. Her hand jetted out toward him and froze in midair as she realized it wasn't a good idea to poke him while he was driving.

Will laughed and then turned his head toward her defensively when he saw her hand. "I'm hungry. What do we have for lunch that's healthy? I start up with a trainer full-time next week, and he's going to kill me if I do too much damage."

"You're worse than a girl."

"I'd like to see how you would react if someone was taking close-up shots of you in your bikini, Miss I'm-Going-to-Leave-My-Shirt-On. Besides, I have some love scenes in this movie, and I'm going to be very exposed." He grimaced.

"How do you even do a love scene—I mean, with someone you don't really know or love?" she asked. "I know it's not the same, but I still think it would be weird."

"It is weird. You have to be that character in your head, and hopefully you have some chemistry with the other actor. You're on set wearing nothing but this privacy patch, which is basically a sock, and you're supposed to get cozy with this person in front of everybody. They wrap you in sheets, but they always fall off, so everyone sees what you have. You do get a chance to get to know your partner a bit during preproduction, though. Usually, you go out and do stuff together just to develop some understanding of each other, so that helps."

"You mean like a date?" Sarah questioned.

"Not really. Just hang out together, as friends. It makes it much easier when you're lying in bed with no clothes on kissing each other." His eyes met Sarah's. "It's just acting," he added quickly. "It's not me. It's the character."

Will parked the car next to the cabin and looked over at her as he got out. Sarah sat in silence. She was still contemplating what he had said. She had never really thought about it before, and it bothered her. She wasn't sure which part, though—the getting-to-know-each-other-in-preproduction part or the kissing-naked-in-bed part. She knew it was his job, but it still worried her. Will opened the back hatch to unload before Sarah joined him at the back of the vehicle.

"So how many of your costars have you ended up dating?" she asked in a worried voice.

He looked at her with concern. "Sarah, I love you. I'm not going to put what we have in jeopardy for anything, ever, but I have to do my job, so please trust me."

"I do. I think it will make me crazy, though," she admitted.

With a smile on his face, he said, "Don't let it. It's just a job."

"I know, but it's hard for us nonactors to wrap our minds around it," she confessed.

"You're cute when you're jealous."

She draped her arms around him, put her hands in his back pockets, and crushed her body against his. The closeness relaxed her. They held each other for several seconds before going inside to eat lunch. Will put away the groceries while Sarah assembled two salads tossed with leftover fajita chicken. They ate their greens out on the patio with two tall glasses of ice water and planned out the rest of the day.

Sarah's mom called to see how they were doing and to let them know what was going on at the house. There were photographers and possibly some fans staked out, but she assured Sarah that they weren't causing too much trouble as long as the drapes were kept shut.

"People have come to the door a few times and asked about you and Jonathan, but no one has told them anything. Someone even followed Jeff and Jessica thinking they were you," revealed Kate. "I got some great shots of them camped out on the lawn."

Will told Sarah that the press would eventually give up, but the fans were usually more resolute and harder to get rid of.

Over the next few days, Sarah and Will swam and boated. They went waterskiing, and Will was amazed at how good Sarah was on skis. They took turns tubing behind the boat, seeing who could hold on the longest. They went Jet Skiing and cliff jumping. Will played songs on his guitar for her. They talked for hours and held each other. Of course, they made love—in the tree house, on the boat, in Sarah's bed, and on the padded bench. If it weren't for the plumbing, or lack thereof, they wouldn't have cared that the power didn't come back on until Wednesday afternoon.

By Wednesday evening, when the sun descended low, trailing a colorful pink-and-orange banner across the surface of the lake, Will and Sarah sprawled on the ground in front of a bonfire. The fire wasn't needed. The air was warm, but the smoke kept the mosquitoes at bay.

Will leaned against a huge log bench, with Sarah nestled between his legs, and he adoringly ran his fingers through her hair as he spoke.

"I never thought I would meet someone like you—someone I wanted more with."

"What do you mean? Out of all those women you've dated, you've never been in love?"

"Not until now. I've told you, I've never said it to another woman."

"Really? You were with Mia Thompson for over a year, and you didn't love her? I don't believe you."

"Of course I love her, as a friend. We've been through a lot together."

"The media makes it sound like you can barely keep your hands off each other, and your chemistry with her is undeniable. I've seen it on-screen."

"Mia is just good at playing the press, and we do have a certain amount of chemistry. But I was never in love with her."

She leaned her head against his shoulder and looked into his eyes. "Then why stay with her so long?"

"It was easy. She was loyal, and I knew what to expect from her."

"I bet it was the sex." She straightened with a smirk and gazed out over the lake.

He laughed and kissed the top of her head. "She is nothing like you."

Sarah stiffened in his arms.

"I mean that in the best possible way. Trust me, I've never felt this way about anyone—nowhere close."

"What's going to happen after tomorrow? I don't want you to leave."

He pulled her flush against his body, wrapping his arms tightly around her. She leaned her head against his shoulder again.

"I don't want to leave, either. Maybe we should just turn off our phones and forget about everyone else."

"I'd smash my phone if it would keep you here."

"Promise me something, Sarah. Promise me that you won't believe the lies the media prints about me. I've seen the best Hollywood relationships shredded by gossip and innuendo. If you have a question, just ask me. I will always be honest with you."

"I promise," she whispered.

Before they wanted, it was Thursday morning. Will would be leaving for LA tonight at 9:35 p.m., and they both yearned to stop time. They planned to go straight to the airport because of the fans at the house, which gave them a little more time alone together. Sarah and Will spent the afternoon in each other's arms, talking and snuggling. It felt like they had known each other a lifetime, and they were already physically aching just thinking about being separated.

Will had to be back for the costume fitting, and Sarah needed the weekend to get ready for her internship at the web magazine, so they were going to have to be apart. As much as they wished, they couldn't stop time, and soon it was five thirty, time to load the car for the trip back to the cities. They locked up the cabin and settled into the car for the ride back to the airport.

The ride was sullen and intense. Once they were on the freeway, Will laced his fingers with her right hand. He stared at Sarah as she drove, as if memorizing her every expression. Whenever she glanced at him, she couldn't help the way the corner of her lips curled up just a little. He was sitting next to her, holding her hand, and she already missed him. They talked the entire drive, but it was subdued.

When they reached the airport, Sarah parked her Honda next to the curb. They looked deeply into each other's eyes. Sarah's were filling with tears, but not spilling yet.

She said simply, "I love you, Will"—she swallowed—"Jonathan." His given name making their week together more real somehow.

"I know, Sarah." He smiled. "I love you too."

He entangled his hands in her hair and gently touched his lips to hers. As Sarah's lips parted, the kiss grew urgent and consuming. They kissed without taking time to breathe for almost five minutes.

Finally breaking it off, Will said, "I've got to go." He kissed her again and whispered in her ear. "Stay safe, Sarah. I'll see you soon."

"Soon," she repeated softly.

He pulled his hat down over his eyes, put on his dark sunglasses, and stepped out onto the sidewalk. He grabbed his bag and guitar from the back. Sarah stared after him as he headed for the glass doors. Halfway to the door, he looked over his shoulder and smiled at her. She waved and smiled back as the tears in her eyes got too heavy and began to fall. Sarah watched Will walk into the big open tundra of the terminal. She knew it was going to hurt when he left, but never imagined that it would hurt this much. She waited a couple of minutes for the tears to slow and then pulled her Honda away from the curb.

Chapter Twelve

Sarah and her friends went out for dinner not far from Megan's house on Saturday night. The bar, known for its frozen drinks and giant sandwiches, showcased live music on the weekends in the summer. The girls planned to get immersed in the stories of Sarah's week with Will while they listened to the band. They were seated outside on the large wooden deck overlooking the St. Croix River. The sun burned warm, but a cool breeze blew lightly off the river, just enough to keep the mosquitoes away. The girls always tried to be seated outside whenever possible. They knew they needed to soak up the sun before winter hit.

After a few minutes, the waitress came over to take their orders. Sarah was the last to order. She asked for a turkey-cucumber sandwich with a frozen pomegranate lemonade. It was warm, and Sarah wanted to try one of the bar's specialty drinks. She had been twenty-one for just over a week now, and this was the first time she was legally able to order alcohol when she was out. It was a novelty, and it made her feel more grown-up somehow. After taking their orders, the waitress politely asked to see their IDs. The girls all reached for their purses and pulled out their driver's licenses. The short blonde waitress carefully examined each license, handing them back one at a time.

When she got to Sarah's, she took an extra-long time looking at it. "Your birthday was last Friday."

Sarah couldn't tell if it was a question or a statement, so she said, "Yes."

"Would you mind if I got a picture with you?" asked the waitress.

"What? Me?" Sarah asked, looking at her friends in astonishment.

"You're Sarah, the Birthday Girl—the one who's dating Jonathan Williams. I saw your ID. Can I get a picture with you?" The waitress took out her cell phone, fiddled with it, and handed it to Megan. "Please?"

Sarah looked at her friends questioningly.

Jessica said, "Why not?"

Sarah stood up and posed with the waitress as Megan snapped the picture. When the waitress left, Sarah sat back down and said, "Gosh, that was weird."

"You better get used to it. If you're going to date a hot famous guy, people are going to recognize you," said Alli.

"I don't even know what to say to people," admitted Sarah. "Will told me not to talk openly about our relationship, because what I say will probably get twisted into a lie. Pretty pessimistic, huh?"

"That kind of sucks. You're dating this super-hot guy that every girl wants, and you can't even rub it in the bitches' faces," Megan said dramatically, tossing her hair back, and everyone at the table laughed.

"How are you handling all this, Sarah? You seem pretty out of it tonight," said Jessica.

"I'm fine. I just…It's kind of overwhelming. I mean, it's all happened so fast. I'm pretty sure I'm in love with him, and he loves me back. That just makes it harder. Then there's this long-distance thing, and that never helps. We're living these totally different lives. I just don't see how this is going to work out. But I want it to because I love him and it feels so right with him. But what if he cheats on me like Matt did? I thought he loved me too. I don't think I could take it if he cheats on me," Sarah rambled on nervously until the waitress returned with their drinks.

After the waitress had left, Alli asked, "So, you two are exclusive?"

"That's what he said, and I agreed," Sarah shared with a smile.

"And you trust him?" questioned Jessica.

"Wait a minute. You agreed to that after a week? That doesn't sound like the Sarah I know. You usually just toy with guys," said Megan.

"No, that's you, Megan," Sarah replied with a mock glare. Ever since Megan ended her relationship with Chase years ago, she'd treated men like objects to be played with and put back on the shelf. She was always looking for new toys to add to her collection, not really caring whether she was done playing with the previous toy before adding a new one.

"No, I don't mean it like that." Megan smiled. "I mean you've never gotten serious, except with Matt."

"You shouldn't throw rocks from your glass house." Sarah scowled at Megan. "I never get serious *because of* Matt. Do you really think I can do better than Will? You met him. He's pretty…perfect," she said with a big smile on her face.

"No, I'm just saying that he lives in LA, and you're here. When school starts, I bet a hundred guys will be throwing themselves at you, after all your press exposure," said Megan.

"Shut up." Sarah rolled her eyes at Megan. "I'm still the same person, and I'm not interested in anyone else."

Megan persisted. "When Will's two thousand miles away and we're all out with our new boyfriends—"

Jessica shot Megan an evil glare.

"OK, when Alli and I are out with our new boyfriends, and Jess is out with your pain-in-the-ass brother, what are you going to be doing?" she continued.

"Hey, that's the man I'm going to marry someday. Be respectful," proclaimed Jessica.

"What?" Sarah said, turning to stare wide-eyed at her. "Have you guys talked about it?"

"Yeah," Jessica answered with a grin. She waved her left hand next to her face and added, "No ring yet."

"Wow. Welcome to the family," Sarah said with astonishment. She knew Jessica and Jeff were serious, but she didn't think they were ready to get married.

"I'm already part of your family." Jessica chuckled, and everyone laughed.

"So do you have a time frame?" asked Sarah.

"We just started talking about it. You'll be the first to know."

"Don't sound so surprised, Sarah. We all knew that was coming. We hardly ever get to go out without Jeff tagging along," asserted Megan.

"So, Sarah, you guys celebrated your love for each other, right?" asked Alli. "I mean, you were alone together the whole week."

Sarah tried to look innocent as she shrugged.

"You did, didn't you? You're a terrible liar," declared Jessica. "Did you see his glutes? I bet he's good."

Appalled that they would ask something so personal, Sarah motioned like she was zipping her lips. But as her friends all stared at her, she squished her eyes together with a smile breaking on her face and uttered, "Incredible!"

Laughter erupted around the table.

When the laughter died down, Megan declared, "You can't do that long distance, you know. Well, you can, but I know you wouldn't."

"Megan, you're not helping. I think Sarah's messed up enough. Do you really have to make it worse?" asked Jessica.

"I'm just being a realist. With all those girls throwing themselves at him all the time, is he really going to be faithful? There has to be some basis for his reputation. With him so far away, how will Sarah know? You know that long-distance relationships are really hard, and how well does she really know him?" Megan asked.

"I know him better than I know you guys, apparently." Sarah glanced at Jessica, thinking about her and Jeff getting engaged. "Besides, I don't really have a choice. It's like I'm not me anymore without him, and I trust him. I've got to try to make it work," she said, then took a long sip of her slushy drink. "Can we talk about something besides Will? Are you going to keep working once school starts, Alli?"

Sarah knew exactly why she was so detached from her friends tonight. It was her conversation with Will while Skyping yesterday. She couldn't get it out of her head, so as her friends continued to talk, she mulled it over in her mind.

"How's the love of my life today?" Will asked.

"You should probably ask her." The corners of her lips curled up as his gorgeous face moved closer into view on her computer.

"Funny. Really, how are you?"

"I didn't sleep last night. I missed having you next to me," she confessed. The comfort of his touch still lingered on her skin, and the smell of his skin still filled her lungs, but the vestiges of him weren't enough. In truth, she'd tossed and turned most of the night. She couldn't get comfortable without him. She even rearranged the pillows on her bed to trick herself into thinking he was next to her.

"I miss you too," he agreed. "Did you get the surprise I left in your bag?"

"Yes, but I didn't see it until this morning. It probably would have helped me sleep. Thanks. I'm going to wear it to bed tonight, or maybe I'll put it on my pillow," she said. He had snuck his favorite vintage T-shirt into her bag. It was from a 1980s band and said *Rebel* on the front in big faded letters, with the band's name on the back.

"It's just a loaner so you'll think of me. I want it back someday, OK? So, when do you think you can come out to see me?" he asked.

"I don't know. I'm probably going to have to work on the weekends, but I won't know for sure until they give me my schedule," she voiced softly, wishing it wasn't out of her control.

"Let me know when you get your schedule, or you may just find me on your doorstep one day."

"I'd like that." She smiled brightly into the webcam.

"Sarah, what do you see yourself doing in five years?" he asked with more than curiosity in his voice. There was definitely an agenda behind his question.

"What, am I applying for a job? Isn't that a question they always ask in interviews?" she asked, sitting back.

"I'm just curious."

"Well, I always thought I would be working for a reputable online magazine, writing my own column. I really like to write."

"Have you ever thought about having a family?" he questioned. His face grew again on the screen, and she knew he was trying to entice her out of the shadows so he could read her face, but she didn't want him to see her expression.

"Uh, yeah, I guess I want kids, but I always thought I'd have my career established first," she confessed, trying to figure out what he was thinking. "Why?"

"I don't know, just putting the puzzle pieces together," Will answered with a smile.

Guys never asked questions about having kids. She was sure of that. Will definitely thought differently than any guy she had ever met. Or maybe he wasn't really asking what she thought he was asking. She wanted to ask, "Are you feeling OK," but thought it sounded condescending.

Instead she asked, "What about you?"

"Well, I'm somewhat established in my career already, and I like acting. I don't think I'll be ready to direct in five years, maybe produce, but I'll be twenty-eight, and I'll definitely want kids by then," he said.

Sarah was quiet for a few seconds as she thought about how to respond. "Hmm, I guess that makes sense. You will be pretty old," she said, grinning sheepishly, closer to the camera.

After the conversation, Sarah realized that Will could be ready for the next step in life. Even though he lived with his parents now, he really had been supporting himself since he was eighteen. He lived in the guesthouse, which was like his own place. He had more money than he knew what to do with, and yet, he didn't spend his money on frivolous trinkets or toys. He always said if there was anything he actually needed, he would buy it, but he didn't need much, which was pretty mature for a twenty-three-year-old.

She wasn't in that place yet. Sarah had never lived on her own. She had lived in the dorms, which didn't really count, and her junior year, she shared a house with a bunch of girls off campus. She had never really had much money, and she still relied on her parents a great deal. Her parents helped her with her tuition, rent, and books, but she did have to work to cover her spending money and food. She had never had a real job. Working at the clinic didn't count as a real job in her mind. She always pictured herself having her own apartment and working for a while before she got married—and kids were way after that.

As she dwelled on the conversation, she thought about how her life didn't seem to be within her control anymore. She never expected to fall in love so quickly, or to fall in love with someone who lived two thousand miles away, or to fall in love with someone who already had his life figured out. She just couldn't get the conversation out of her head, and she definitely didn't want to share it with her friends. They would tell her to run. She knew they wouldn't understand.

"Hey, bring the shuttle in for a landing, Sarah. Are you?" asked Alli.

"What shuttle? Am I what?" Sarah looked up, making eye contact with Alli.

"Boy, you are spacey tonight. Are you coming to the state fair with us on the twenty-eighth?" asked Alli.

"Um, yeah, I think I can go," Sarah replied robotically.

"Sarah, are you OK?" Jessica asked, concerned, touching Sarah's arm.

"Yeah, give me a few days. I just need to clear my head."

Chapter Thirteen

On Monday, Sarah started her internship. She pulled into the parking ramp off Wabasha Street and checked the map again before getting out of her Honda. Since the weather was pleasant, she didn't bother with the skyway. Instead, she walked the four blocks on the sidewalk to the old sandstone building, and then she headed up to the fourth floor, to where the magazine office resided. TC LIFE AND ENTERTAINMENT MAGAZINE labeled the wall in bold silver letters behind the reception desk. The office was modern, with a large flat-screen television hanging to the right of the desk. The television was lit with the Internet cover pages of this week's main stories. On the other side of the desk, an L-shaped hallway led to brightly lit offices with tall ceilings only found in old renovated buildings.

Sarah checked in with the receptionist and soon was introduced to her mentor, Ellen Olsen. Ellen was about thirty, Sarah thought, with long blonde hair pulled back in a ponytail lying low on her neck. Ellen was personable enough, but spoke in an annoying nasal voice that was just a little too fast to allow people to understand her easily.

Ellen helped Sarah get her ID badge and showed her where to put her purse. She disclosed the ins and outs of the computer system and then assigned Sarah a username and password. Sarah was already familiar with the computer programs from school but was eager to learn how they integrated into the real world. She was given a tour of the magazine offices and, in the afternoon, was introduced to about twenty people at a staff meeting.

The first couple of days, Sarah mostly followed Ellen around and ran errands for the office. As the week progressed, the internship got a little more complicated. The rumors of Jonathan Williams and Sarah Austin filled the offices of the old building. They seemed to creep into every conversation Sarah had. She did her best to dispel the rumors and even went so far as to say, "It must be another Sarah Austin." But when someone printed a poster-sized picture from the Internet of her in Jonathan's arms at the airport and hung it on the break room door, she really couldn't deny that she knew him.

After it was out in the open, Sarah's supervisor insisted that she help work on several celebrity-related articles. She also mentioned that Sarah would be working on an article with her on the Teen FAV Awards next week and had told her to see if she could get some inside information about the awards since she had a source.

"It's not like I'm going to be there," she told Ellen.

"Well, you have a unique perspective into young Hollywood, and the magazine would be crazy to not utilize all our assets," Ellen spouted in her fast, nasal voice.

By the end of the week, Sarah was doing her best to complete her job without giving out any personal information. She just wanted to be treated like any other intern. She felt as though more was expected of her because of her and Will's relationship, and she was asked about him all the time. Even though she talked to Will every night and texted him during the day, she missed him terribly.

෬~୭

In LA, Jonathan was dealing with his own problems. Although his costume fitting had gone well on Friday and he didn't think that he would have to go back for more, he was expected to meet with his agent and publicist today. When he returned to town, he'd called to check in, and they'd insisted on the meeting. It usually wasn't good news when he was asked to meet with them together out of the blue, so he wasn't looking forward to seeing them. He knew his agent would have told him up front if there was a problem with the movie, so he had a feeling today's meeting had something to do with his trip and Sarah.

He took the elevator up to the twelfth floor of the posh building. As he listened to the drone of the mellow music coming from the speaker above his head, he thought about Sarah—her gorgeous smile, her soft skin, and her adorable laugh. He wanted to be near her, not here.

Jonathan was greeted by several individuals as he made his way through the agency to Isaac's office. Outside the office, he was welcomed by Isaac's assistant, Ann. Ann was a petite woman in her early twenties with pixie blonde hair.

"Good morning, Mr. Williams. Are you waiting on Leslie?" she asked in her perky voice.

"No, it's just me today," he answered. His assistant, Leslie, was working on some business details he needed taken care of, so she couldn't make the meeting.

"I'll let Isaac know you're here. Would you like something to drink?"

"You got a beer? I think I may need one for this meeting."

"Heineken or Blue Moon? I know it's one of the two, but I'm sorry, I forget which one," she said apologetically. "You don't usually want beer."

"You're slipping, Ann." He flashed his dimpled smile. "Nah, I was just joking about the beer. My trainer would kill me. Water would be great, though."

She disappeared for a minute and returned with an ice-cold glass bottle of springwater. She graciously handed it to him and said, "Isaac is ready for you if you want to go back."

Isaac's office was mostly glass with a wooden door. A couple of leather club chairs sat in front of the large mahogany desk, with their backs to a wall of windows overlooking the palm-lined boulevard and the hills. One wall of the office was lined with a dark wooden bookshelf from floor to ceiling, and framed pictures of Isaac with different celebrities cluttered the shelves. Jonathan had been here many times before, but today, he was not in the mood to deal with being tag-teamed, and it irritated him to have to come. Maybe it was because he missed Sarah so much, or maybe it was because his trainer had worked him into a puddle this morning. He wasn't sure.

Isaac, his agent, and Remi, his publicist, were both seated when Jonathan arrived. Isaac wore one of his Hugo Boss suits with a purple button-down shirt and no tie. His dark hair was cropped short, but long enough to curl in ringlets on the back of his head. Remi looked sharp in her tailor-fitted chartreuse skirt, crisp white blouse, and designer heels. She sported her signature short black razor-cut hair, spiked in all directions, which even made her shadow easily recognizable. They both stood up when Jon entered wearing his normal jeans, T-shirt, and edgy sports coat.

"Hey, Jon, how are you doing?" Isaac walked around the desk to shake his hand in a man-hug. "Did you have a good vacation?" he asked with a chuckle.

"Yep, best one ever." Jon leaned over and kissed Remi's cheek in greeting. "What's up?" he asked quickly, before taking a swig of his water.

"Well, I was talking to Remi about this past week and next week's Teen FAV Awards. We just want to make sure we were all on the same page about your public appearances," he declared.

"In what way, Isaac?" Jon asked, cocking his head questioningly as he unfastened the one button on his jacket, sat down, and stretched out his legs.

Remi spoke up. "Jon, we were just wondering about this girl you were with this past week—Sarah, is it? Were you serious when you said she was the love of your life, or were you just saying that because she was sitting next to you?"

"Well…" He paused, trying to figure out where this conversation was headed. "We're getting married next week in Vegas. You're both invited, of course." He was getting more irritated. "We're going to Beatrice Island for the honeymoon, but don't worry, I'll only be a week or two late for *The Demigod*'s production."

Isaac and Remi looked at each other. "Wow. Where is all this hate coming from? We're just wondering where you stand with her," confessed Remi.

"Sorry. I guess I'm a bit sensitive about her. Honestly, she means the world to me, and I can see myself marrying her, but I don't have any plans—yet," Jon admitted. "What does Sarah have to do with anything?"

"Really? Marriage? You?" Remi twisted her long neck questioningly.

"Why is that so hard to believe?" Jon asked, looking at them, and they both rolled their eyes at the same time.

"Well, you don't usually let anyone get close to you." Remi held up her hands apologetically and gave him the look.

"Don't give me that look. She's not after my money or fame. She didn't even know who I was when she met me."

"Does she live in a shack in the woods?" Isaac said, poorly hiding his amusement.

"No." Jonathan paused. "If either of you ever repeat what I'm going to tell you or make any rude comments, you're both fired." He glared at them and continued. "I met her on the Internet." He noted the change on their faces, then added, "Not on one of those sites. It was totally innocent. I've known her for months. She didn't know who I was until the concert."

They both looked at him skeptically, but didn't say anything at first.

Then Isaac couldn't help himself and, with a smile, said, "You know, if you wanted to meet a coed, even one from the Midwest, I could have hooked you up. You didn't have to actually go there."

"I was serious, Isaac," Jonathan stated, and Isaac stopped smiling.

Then Remi spoke up. "At the very least, you had her sign an NDA, right? I know Leslie sent some with you."

He collapsed onto the back of his chair, frustrated. "No, I didn't," he answered curtly. "That turns it into a business deal. This is not business." Jon knew the nondisclosure agreement would protect him from Sarah ever discussing their relationship with anyone, but the legal contract was far from romantic. He felt he was bringing enough baggage to the new relationship that he didn't need to make Sarah more uncomfortable by involving lawyers.

"It's your funeral," stated Isaac. "You're going to wish you had one, though, when filming starts and she finds out that you hooked up with Rachel Marrero. Rachel, she is one hot piece of..." He trailed off as he caught Remi's glare.

Jon closed his eyes and sank deeper into the chair with a groan. He wanted to get up and walk out, but he knew it wouldn't help. So, with his eyes still closed, he thought about Sarah's sweet smile, and it relaxed him. When he opened his eyes, Remi and Isaac were both staring at him wide-eyed.

"Regardless, this week was great publicity. Your name and face were all over. You looked like Prince Charming the way you were courting this girl. I didn't even know you could sing, Jon. I saw the footage. You were good." Her tone became slightly cross. "I'm still mad at you for not letting me know about your singing debut. We could have milked that concert."

"That wasn't my intent. The song was for Sarah, but if it makes you feel any better, I agreed to record it on EXpireD's next album. You can milk it then."

"Oh!" She perked up. "We could film the recording. It would be good for both you and the band." The smile grew on her face, and she nodded several times. "I think we could get you some gigs if you want. Isaac's been fielding some offers."

Jonathan shook his head no.

"How about Bono? I have a great screenplay here somewhere on the early days of U2," Isaac added as he dug through his desk drawer.

"Aren't I a little tall for that role?" inquired Jonathan.

Isaac stopped digging, and Remi asked, "Tell me, what was that all about at the airport? You abandoned your flight for her?"

"She was being swarmed by paparazzi. What's there to understand? I guess I wasn't ready to leave her with that," Jonathan said as he brushed the hair out of his eyes. "I could have told you this over the phone. Why am I here?"

"With you presenting at the Teen FAV Awards on Sunday, we were wondering if your plans had changed. Are you planning to bring Sarah? Because Isaac and I don't think that would be the best idea. It is a very public appearance, and your fans don't want to see you with some nobody, Jon. If she were a model or an actress and had media training, it wouldn't be an issue. Besides, you're going to get slammed with questions about her as it is, and if you were worried about her being overwhelmed by a few photographers at the airport, that was nothing compared to what she would face on the green carpet of the Teen FAV Awards."

"I know that, Remi, and she's not a nobody. Don't worry, I wasn't planning on bringing her. I'm not ready to put her through that. I'm still going by myself. I know just about everyone who's presenting, so I'm sure there will be someone there I can talk to. You can sit with me, if you like."

"I'll sit with you, Jon, and I'll meet you at the stylist's at one o'clock the day before, like we planned. You know, Mia will be at the awards too. Any chance I could get you two to walk the carpet together?"

Jon knew that anytime he and Mia were spotted together, it doubled his exposure. He laughed. "I can't believe you just asked that. No, *actually*, I can. But the answer is no. I'm done living lies."

"Just keep your contract in mind," said Isaac. "You can't do anything that could undermine the promotion of *The Demigod*'s sequel. You've got until next fall before that commitment is up, so keep your head in the game."

"What does that mean, Isaac? Are they dictating who I can and can't date now? Because I don't remember that line in the contract," Jon asserted accusingly.

"I'm not saying that." Isaac moved to the front of the desk and leaned against it, facing Jon, his hands stirring with exaggerated movements like a motivational speaker as he continued to speak. "I just want you to be careful. Remember, acting is just half the job. The other half is promoting. Your image is what sells and gets you work. You go tying yourself to some unknown girl, and your image will suffer. The fans want to see you with someone worthy of Jonathan Williams." He emphasized Jonathan's name in a commanding voice. "Just keep it on the down-low. That's all I'm saying." Isaac tucked his hands into his suit coat pockets and shrugged his shoulders. "Just being honest. The studio has expressed some concern. Nick Paulson called asking about your erratic behavior. They don't want some nutcase on the film. It's a twelve-million-dollar-plus contract. Are you ready to give that up?"

"How much of that is yours, Isaac?" Jon rolled his eyes, still irritated by their insinuations.

"You know I'm only looking out for you. You're my number one priority," Isaac backpedaled.

"Are we done here?" Jon stated with tight lips.

"Are we on the same page, then, Jon?" Isaac asked, tapping his fingers on the desk behind him.

Jonathan combed his fingers through his hair. "Yeah," he said, then left the office without another word. He knew that they were just managing his career, doing their jobs, but he wanted to live his own life, the way he wanted to live it—with Sarah. He didn't see how he could wait a year until his commitment to *Demigod Forbidden* was over to be with her. He got into his BMW, sank into the tan leather seat, started the engine, and turned up the music. He needed to clear his head. He knew Isaac was right. Being with Sarah could hurt his career, and he needed to ensure it didn't, but he wasn't going to give her up. She meant everything to him.

In reality, Jonathan knew that, once he started filming, the press would link him to his new costar, Rachel Marrero, and the hype about Sarah would blow over. He just hoped Sarah could get past the hype about Rachel. She knew about the pressures of acting—the gossip, the ridiculous hours—but Jonathan wasn't naive. He recognized that knowing about something and being able to deal with it were miles apart. It had taken him almost two years before he was comfortable on the red carpet or doing an interview, and he had grown up on movie sets. Maybe it was best if he and Sarah did take it slow. It would give her a chance to ease into the craziness. If he really was going to make this relationship work, he needed to do all he could to make it easier on Sarah.

At the Teen FAV Awards, Jonathan was questioned endlessly about "the Birthday Girl." He answered by saying that he didn't talk about his personal life. He made jokes and very diplomatically steered the questioning to his career or the awards show. He got away with it by using his charm and quick wit, but there was much speculation about Sarah in the press after the show.

❦

Will gave Sarah some information about the awards show for her article. It wasn't anything outrageously embarrassing for anyone, but it was something Sarah never could have found out on her own. The host, Alyssa Mason, accidently ripped a chunk out of her skirt during a dance sequence onstage. Her dance partner, rapper TZ, grabbed her skirt and purposefully ripped it into a miniskirt, all while they were still dancing. It was like a scene from an old movie. The audience thought it was part of the show, but when Alyssa got off the stage, her skirt practically disintegrated. She needed to make an unscheduled costume change, as the show was targeted toward teens. Will and two other male celebrities were backstage preparing to present when they were asked to be a human privacy shield for Alyssa's costume change. The story helped Sarah, but she felt bad that she was using Will. He assured her that the show's host had talked about the incident in an interview after the show and that he had just added more details. The article made Sarah a hero for the week, but it also escalated her problem of people asking about Will. She wanted to be with him, more than anything, and it hurt just to hear his name.

She ended up having to work the next two weekends, so by the time she was able to visit Will, he was in preproduction. He was busy training to do his stunts for the film and rehearsing lines with his costars. Sarah remembered what he had said about getting to know his costars. Even though they talked every day and had video chats whenever they were able, Sarah was nervous about Rachel. She tried not to make it obvious how much it bothered her, but he could tell. Will was honest with Sarah and told her everything. He and Rachel spent several days together going over lines and went out to dinner with other cast members. Will even introduced Rachel to Sarah on the phone one day, and Sarah talked to her for about fifteen minutes. That helped. Sarah trusted Will, but being away from him was making her crazy.

By the beginning of the third week of her internship, Sarah's supervisor was getting greedy and wanted her to dig up dirt on celebrities. She was supposed to scour the Internet to locate articles of interest, then try to confirm or refute information through the various networks she was provided. Sarah didn't want to do this kind of reporting—it wasn't writing. She wanted to be working on real stories, not following up on gossip. Sarah had thought the internship was going to be more writing than reporting garbage. She wasn't a journalist. She had expected to be an unpaid, abused gofer, not someone who actually contributed to the gossip problem.

That night, she spoke to Will and told him all about what was happening at the magazine. She complained just a little too much about her situation, and his curt response shocked her.

"If it's that bad, why don't we just break up?"

"What?" Sarah asked, confused.

"Why don't we break up? Then your boss won't bug you so much."

"Shut up!" she replied. "Why would you say that?"

"Not for real, Sarah, just a break. I'm not letting you get away that easily. We'll just take some time off. We won't be able to be together anyway. If people think we broke up, then they won't ask you about me. You can do what you want. Our relationship won't hinder you."

"Do you really want time off from each other?" She stared into an empty corner near the ceiling of her room, wishing they were Skyping and not talking on the phone.

"No. I'd rather be with you, but since we can't see each other anyway, what difference will it make?"

She was so confused. *A break? What does that mean?* she wondered. She wished she could see his face and read his beautiful pale eyes. She didn't know what to think, so she stayed silent, listening for any clues in the inflection of his voice.

"I'm going to be gone for more than two months filming halfway across the world in a few weeks. It would help me out too. My head is so messed up thinking about you all the time that I can barely concentrate. Maybe if we only talk once a week, I could get into my role better."

"We'll be together in the end, when you're done filming, right?" Her voice was almost inaudible.

"Yes. It's just a break, because we're on a forced break anyway. Just tell everyone that you couldn't handle the stress of the long-distance relationship and you broke it off. Then they'll leave you alone. Don't forget to tell them I was devastated, you heartless shrew," he said with a soft chuckle.

"Just until we can be together?"

"Not a second longer. It will go fast, you'll see."

"I love you, Will," Sarah said seriously.

"I know." Will sighed.

The next day, Sarah told everyone she knew that the distance was too much for her and that she had broken up with Will. She tried to sound like it was the toughest decision she'd ever made. In reality, this break wasn't what she wanted. She was genuinely sad about it. It was easy at the magazine office to convince everyone that they had broken up, and her supervisor even gave her the afternoon off. The magazine put a two-sentence blurb on their celebrity gossip page, and that helped to give Sarah's story credibility.

Back at her parents' house, Sarah contacted Jessica with the bad news and let her call the other girls. Of course, they all came over to console her and get the details. She thought about being honest with her friends, but they were half the problem, so she stretched the truth.

"No way did you break up with him. You were way too into him," said Alli.

"I thought you guys were in love. He must have cheated on you. Did he cheat on you? He cheated, didn't he?" Megan asked, smugly wrapping her arm around Sarah.

"No, he didn't cheat on me. You were right. The distance is just too much," Sarah told them. "It's too much stress being with him and not being able to see him. People are always bugging me about him, and they won't leave me alone. Long distance just doesn't work."

None of her friends believed her until she locked herself in her room and wouldn't come out. They knew she wouldn't talk to anyone when she was really upset. So, as they tried to coax her out of her room, she pondered what Will had said. Did he want a break for her, as he said, or was that just an excuse so he could have a break? What did a break mean? Not being with him was bad enough. Now she wasn't even going to talk to him? How was that going to make it better? At least her friends would stop asking her about him.

The day after the breakup announcement was easier. Only a few people asked her about Will, because no one wanted to upset her. It got easier and easier as the news perpetuated itself. She felt relieved not having to talk about Will all the time, though not talking about him didn't stop her from thinking about him.

Her internship ended two weeks later. Ellen gave her a glowing letter of recommendation. She completed all the paperwork for Sarah to get full credit at school for her month of work and offered her a job even before she finished her degree. Sarah had gained a ton of experience in the real world of web magazines and felt like she had a better understanding of what she wanted in a job, though she wasn't sure she wanted to work for a magazine at all anymore.

Chapter Fourteen

The evening that her internship ended, Sarah was feeling especially out of sorts. The magazine office had taken her out to happy hour for a going-away party, and she found herself in a posh downtown bar seated next to a bunch of people she didn't know. The ones she knew, including Ellen, were seated at the opposite end of the long table—the couples section. When the significant others joined the group, the single people, somehow, had been segregated to the other end. Sarah longed to be able to bring Will to this kind of gathering, but deep inside, she knew that it would never happen.

She sat next to Brandon from marketing, which was a big mistake. He kept touching her. It started off innocently enough. He grasped her arm to get her attention. But as she listened to him drone on about himself, she realized his touches were not so innocent. Each time his hand lingered just a little longer, and by the fifth skin-on-skin contact, Sarah was irritated. Feigning that she had forgotten to tell Ellen something important, she grabbed her drink, politely excused herself, and beelined down to the other end of the table.

After about thirty minutes, when Sarah was seated with the couples and immersed in conversation, she felt a large hand on her shoulder. She looked up, and there was Brandon, her phone clinched in his hand.

"I think you might want to hold on to this. It buzzed a couple of times, and then *he* called."

"Who?"

"The Demigod. His picture popped up on your phone. I had to wrestle it out of Keera's hand. She was going to answer it." He raised one eyebrow as he handed her the phone. "Funny, *my* exes never call me."

"Um, thanks." All the conversation at the table had stopped, and Sarah shrank under their stares. "We're still friends," she said, hoping no one would see through her ruse. How could she have forgotten her phone on the table? She needed to be more careful and needed to figure out how to set the password lock on it. She read the texts that Will had sent, aware that everyone was still watching her. Then shot him a reply, letting him know she still wanted to talk, but she wouldn't be home for another hour.

When she finally looked up from her phone, Brandon was back at the other end of the table, his expression sullen. Most of her coworkers were chatting again, but Keera was glaring at her with venomous hate in her eyes. She had probably read the tabloid story that came out on Monday—the one that claimed the Birthday Girl had shattered Jonathan's heart. Either people hated her for dating him or they hated her for not dating him. Sarah couldn't win.

She tried to get back into the conversation, but all she really wanted was to go home and talk to Will. She stayed another half hour before thanking everyone for the card and the party. After another ten minutes of hugs and good-byes, she was finally headed to her car.

She quietly snuck into the house, avoiding her mother. If Kate saw her talking to Will, she would ask a million questions. The entire time Sarah and Will were dating before the breakup, Kate cut out magazine articles, newspaper clippings, anything she could find about Jonathan Williams and glued them in a scrapbook for Sarah. Every time Sarah saw her mom, Kate pressed her on the validity of each story. Sarah lectured her mom a couple of times about how little of the information out there was real, but it didn't seem to slow down Kate. After the breakup, Kate stopped paying attention to the tabloids, and Sarah felt relieved. If she found out that Sarah was still talking to Will, it would all start back up again.

No, thank you, she thought.

When Will's face flashed to life on her computer screen, all of Sarah's worries seemed to disappear. Their conversation flowed smoothly, as always. And Sarah finally felt relaxed as she listened to his sexy voice and watched his vibrant eyes follow her—that was, until Sarah's bedroom door flew open and Jessica plopped down next to her on the bed.

"Hi, Will," Jessica said curtly as she leaned into view of the camera on Sarah's laptop. "So what the hell are you doing to Sarah? I mean, you guys broke up, and here you are telling her you love her? You need to stop messing with her. She doesn't need this."

"It's great to see you too, Jess." He chuckled, shaking his head. "Maybe you should talk to Sarah."

Jessica turned to Sarah and accusingly asked, "So are you back together, then?"

"We didn't really break up. We're just on a break," Sarah said in a rush, not wanting to waste any of her Will-time.

"But you still talk to each other? How does that work?"

"Well, we don't talk every day, just once in a while. It helps us get through until we can be together again," Sarah explained with a look that she hoped blared, *Not now.*

Jessica scowled. "I'll let you guys talk, but Sarah, we're having a conference when you're done. Sorry I jumped all over you, Will," Jessica stated and rolled off the bed into a standing position.

❧

When Sarah came downstairs an hour and a half later, she was a little surprised to see her friends lined up on the couch waiting for her.

"Is it a break, or did you break up?" questioned Alli. "Are you getting back together with Will?"

"It's just a break until we can physically be together. We never intended to break up. We love each other."

"How convenient. You two take a break so he can cheat on you while he's in Europe," added Megan. "I suppose he still needs it, even when he can't get any from you."

"God, you're jaded, Megan. Did Chase really hurt you that badly?" asked Jessica.

Megan squinted her eyes. "That was three years ago. I'm over it. I guess I just don't understand the concept of a break if the reason isn't to date other people."

"It's not that kind of break," stated Sarah.

"What other kind of break is there?" asked Alli. "Is he the one who called it a break? Because dating other people is kind of the definition of a break."

"It's just to keep the questions at bay so I can cope while we're apart, and to give him a chance to get into his role," explained Sarah.

"So he can get into his role with his costar, Rachel Marrero? He's probably practicing those sex scenes for the movie," added Megan.

"Shut up, Megan," whispered Sarah. "Nothing has changed. It's not like we would get to see each other anyway."

"I think you're deluding yourself," declared Alli. "A break is just a pass to cheat."

"Think whatever you want. I know what it is!" Sarah uttered in frustration.

Even though she defended their break as just a way to cope, she was starting to have doubts. *Is it really just a pass to cheat while we're apart?* She couldn't believe that was true, but maybe that was common practice in Hollywood. That was how the tabloids made it sound. She didn't know what to think anymore. She recycled the thoughts over and over in her head.

Sarah missed Will more than ever after that night. She was starting to have reservations about their relationship. Her past told her not to trust that he would be faithful, but her heart didn't want to believe he would cheat. She knew that loneliness and cheating were the reasons why long-distance relationships often failed. Will had once told her that he didn't believe in two-timing, but would it be two-timing if they were on a break?

Sarah really wished she could see Will, to touch his face and ask him what a break meant, but she wasn't sure she wanted to know the answer. She craved to see him before school started, though she knew he was working and wouldn't have any time for a visit.

☙

On August 28, Sarah and her friends went to the state fair as planned. The sun burned warm without a cloud in the sky. The fairgrounds were filling up. Fair attendance had reached 160,000 people yesterday, and by the looks of it, today would be just as crowded. The streets swelled with endless strollers and tattooed bodies as Sarah looked out over the vast spread of the land. She was wearing Will's T-shirt tied at her waist, exposing just a hint of skin. His shirt made her feel at ease, as if he was there with her, strolling around the grounds and people watching with her and her friends.

The girls made their way to the coliseum and watched the first fifteen minutes of an English riding competition. The horses were majestic and beautifully adorned as they sauntered around the dirt arena, kicking up dust, but the girls weren't really interested in the horse show, so they decided to move on. They strolled through the animal barns on their way out of the arena, feeling sympathy for the farm and ranch kids who had beds made up in the empty stalls next to their show animals. The girls couldn't imagine sleeping with the gamy smell that lingered inescapably in the air of the large building, and of course, Megan couldn't stop complaining about the stench.

They meandered to the animal birthing barn, where they watched some piglets emerge from a giant sow on a large-screen television above the birthing pen. The crowd around the pen was too dense to allow them to see the birth up close, but the screen provided a better view anyway. The piglets were pink and adorable after they had been cleaned off, and the girls joked about sneaking one into Alli's massive purse. They petted the baby chicks that bounced around the raised chicken pen, and marveled at how large an expectant cow could get.

Next, the girls headed to the butterfly house, where they watched as thousands of butterflies and moths of all different colors and sizes floated elegantly in the exhibit around them. Beautiful, fragrant plants filled the room, and the delicate insects fanned the air as they clung to the florae. The girls enjoyed the serene atmosphere, away from the crowds outside, for several minutes, until a shiny blue-winged butterfly attempted to make a nest in Megan's golden hair and the girls were asked to leave because Megan was caught swatting the bug.

At lunchtime, they shared all kinds of food—after all, that was why they had come to the fair. The smell of it had been taunting them all morning. It was food they could only find or eat once a year—minidonuts, deep-fried cheese curds, foot-long corndogs, pork chops on a stick, and corn on the cob roasted right in the husk. They drank enormous glasses of ice-cold lemonade that were squeezed fresh as they watched.

After lunch, they relished the air-conditioning as they browsed the vendor booths beneath the grandstand. The climate-controlled building displayed boats, jewelry, makeup, vacuum cleaners, and even cookware. When they reached the second floor, Alli found a booth with leather goods that were actually made in the USA, and she bought a large lemon-colored saddlebag purse made of glove leather. The girls seemed obsessed as they all ran their hands over it, admiring the soft, smooth feel of the leather, and they wouldn't stop touching it until Alli shoved it back into the shopping bag. Finally, they stopped by the midway and rode a couple of overpriced rides while they reminisced about their trips to the fair as teenagers. They remembered how they used to scope out guys at the midway, and they shuddered at the memory of some of the gross guys they had met.

By seven o'clock, hunger, thirst, and exhaustion convinced the girls to take refuge at a beer garden to replenish. They stood in line, got their food, and grabbed a table from a couple loading up their double stroller, getting ready to leave. The band was just starting up inside the tent as they sat down, but their table was far enough away from the speakers that they could still talk.

After about ten minutes, three good-looking guys came over and playfully begged to share the girls' table. They each carried a stray chair, but there were no tables open. The guys hoped Sarah and her friends would be accommodating. The girls reluctantly agreed—some less reluctant than others. It sounded like a pickup line to Sarah, but she gave them an A for effort. The guys were seniors from the University of St. Thomas and seemed balanced enough. They flirted for quite a while with the girls, and when the guys got up to get another round of beverages for everyone, Megan ambushed Sarah.

"What is your problem, girl? These guys are really nice."

"I'm just not interested in dating right now," admitted Sarah.

"You're on a break, Sarah," said Megan. "That Drew guy seems to really like you. He lives here, and he's hot. He hinted that he wants your number. Why don't you give it to him?"

Sarah looked at Jessica and rolled her eyes. She took a deep breath, looked Megan in the face, and smiled insincerely. "I'm not ready to date anyone else."

"Why not? You can't just sit around moping. He initiated the break. Going out with other people is what he wants you to do, or he wouldn't have called it a break. Don't be a doormat." Megan paused to suck in a breath and then continued, not giving her a chance to respond. "What's stopping you? I'm going to put your number in his phone if you don't."

"Just let it go—please," pleaded Sarah. She looked wide-eyed at Jessica as if to say, *A little help here.*

"Come on, Sarah, why not?" asked Alli. "A good Catholic boy from St. Thomas? He doesn't seem to have any critical flaws. We could double-date." One of the other guys had been flirting with her. "It's just a date. If you're on a break, it's not cheating. It's just filling time. That's what you used to do before Will, anyway."

"Sarah, it's OK to date other people when you're on a break. That's what a break is for," declared Megan. "Otherwise, you'd just say you're in a long-distance relationship, which I noticed you didn't mention. You know Will's utilizing this break. You've seen the pictures."

Sarah's head flopped back in exasperation. Megan had showed her some pictures on a gossip site of Will out with his costar. It looked like they were having an intimate dinner, but Will said the whole cast had been out together that night. She wished her friends hadn't seen the pictures. Believing him was easier without their input.

Jessica looked at Sarah and muttered under her breath, "A break's a break."

Sarah glared at Jessica with a look of betrayal. *Et tu, Brute?* She thought Jessica understood, but now she was siding with the other girls.

"All right, I'll give him my number," she whispered, not believing what she was saying. She hoped her friends were wrong. She didn't know what to believe. Was she being naive thinking Will was ever faithful? Why would he call it a break? She was shredded inside. She knew she couldn't resolve it herself. She had always listened to her friends until Will.

Jessica touched Sarah's arm to encourage her. "Just enjoy yourself. They're nice guys—and you're on a break. Just try." Her expression twisted sympathetically.

They *were* on a break. He had called it a break. So Sarah put on her best poker face and tried to push Will out of her head.

Chapter Fifteen

By the time Sarah's classes started and a few weeks had passed, Will was going crazy not seeing her. They hadn't spoken in over a week, and their last conversation was really short—less than fifteen minutes. Although he'd been busy working, he thought about Sarah all the time. The last two weeks had been grueling for him. There were five hand-to-hand combat scenes in the film, and the director wanted them all fought on location, not on green screen. So Will worked what seemed like nonstop to learn the choreography well enough to reproduce it on set. He had spent the last two days in a wire harness, with the circulation in his legs cut off for hours, practicing jumps and flips. The harness cut into his skin, and he had a big bruise on his right shoulder that he wasn't aware of until one of the crew pointed it out to him. Even with all the prep work and training he had done prior to preproduction, Will was still exhausted. Every muscle in his body ached, and the director had ordered him to rest on his day off. He wasn't going to rest, though. He knew what he needed to do—not just because he missed Sarah, but because he needed to know the truth too.

He unfolded the picture from his wallet that he had printed off the Internet. He didn't want to believe it was real, but it looked too good to be a fake. There she was, his girlfriend, in the arms of another man. The guy was so close to her ear that he could have been leaning in to kiss her. That's what it looked like, anyway. He read the tag again: *It looks like the Birthday Girl has moved on from Jonathan Williams.* The candid shot had been posted on a celebrity photo dumpsite, where he'd run across it by accident.

He knew how deceiving photos could be, but he didn't know what to make of it. So on his one day off before he left for filming in Greece, he jumped on a flight to see Sarah and gain back his sanity. He figured he would have eighteen hours of actual time with her, and he didn't really care what they did as long as they were together. He needed to see her eyes when he asked her. This wasn't something he could bring up on the phone or online. Sarah's face, her body, always revealed what she was feeling. He needed to know, and he longed to be with her.

He called Jessica to make sure Sarah would be home for his surprise visit, and arranged to have Jessica pick him up at the airport. He made it through the airport fairly easily. He was only recognized a couple of times. He graciously signed autographs and smiled for a couple of pictures. Jessica met him at the curb, and as soon as they pulled away from the sidewalk, he felt the relief he'd learned to appreciate that came with leaving a very public place.

⟋⟋⟍

When Sarah got home from class, Jessica revealed that there was a package waiting for her on her bed. Immediately, Sarah hustled up the narrow hundred-year-old stairs to see what it was. She knew it had to be from Will. Her mother hadn't mentioned mailing anything to her. She flung open the heavy white six-panel door and saw not a package, but Will lying on her bed with his arms folded behind his head. He wore jeans and a blue button-down oxford with the sleeves rolled up. His shirt color made his eyes pop with an irresistible luminosity, like the ocean on a sunny day. With a huge smile on his face, he held out his arms, and she jumped into them, dissolving into his torso. They held each other for several seconds without a word, just enjoying the comfort of the other's touch.

She couldn't believe he was actually there. She crushed her face into his chest. "Don't wake up. Don't wake up," she whispered softly. "I must have fallen asleep on the bus. It's OK. I can ride the bus all day. Just… Don't. Wake. Up."

"Sarah, I'm really here," he whispered, his lips softly caressing her hair.

"Hmm, that's exactly what he would say. This is such a good dream. I can even smell him, and he smells *so* good, just like I remember. Please don't wake up," she muttered softly.

"I'm really here, beautiful," he said with a chuckle. "I'm real," he whispered in her ear before nipping it.

Finally, Sarah slowly opened her lids and saw his magnificent blue eyes with the thick lashes staring back at her. "My dreams are never, ever this good," she uttered with a smirk. She shook her head. "How?"

"I'm just living my life, like you told me to do."

"But you leave for Greece tomorrow."

"Yeah?"

"You'll be on a plane for, like, ever."

"So? I get to see you. It's worth it," he said sweetly with his perfect one-dimple smile.

"Thanks." She sighed. She knew the sacrifice he was making to see her, and she was truly grateful.

"I love you, Sarah," Will declared intensely.

"I'm glad, because I missed you so much." She snuggled into the crook of his muscular arm and squeezed her arm across his chest.

"That's why I'm here." He turned to look at her and brushed her hair out of her face. He stared into her eyes like he was studying her—his eyes vibrant, but questioning.

With her middle finger, she reached up and touched the dimple, which still lingered on his cheek. Then, slowly, she moved her hand to the stubble on his jawline, pausing there a few seconds, drawing circles, before she progressed to his mouth. She traced the pad of her finger gently across his lips until he kissed it. Then she brought her hand to his head and ran her fingers through his darker-than-usual locks as she lost herself in his eyes.

"Do you like the color? It's Perseus's, for the film."

"I like yours better, but I can deal. It feels the same." She grinned devilishly, then rolled on top of him, straddling his hips. "So how long do we have?" As she spoke, she slowly ran her finger down his well-developed chest in a zigzag pattern.

Will shuddered under her touch. "My flight leaves at ten fifteen tomorrow morning. What do you want to do until then?" he asked, raising one eyebrow questioningly.

"I have some ideas," she admitted as she pinned his shoulders with her hands and started to kiss his neck. She continued to kiss him while her hands moved to unbutton his shirt.

He squished his eyes together and cringed, taking in a deep breath and holding it. She kept kissing him, pretending not to notice his reaction, until he forced his way out from under her and pinned her to the bed.

"You know how ticklish I am, and yet, you use it as a tool to take advantage of me."

She looked up at him with a Cheshire cat smile, and he leaned down to kiss her.

They spent the next two hours getting reacquainted in Sarah's bedroom. It was dinnertime before they came out for some air.

"Let's take a walk."

"You're breaking up with me for good, aren't you?" Sarah said jokingly.

"No. After what we just did? What kind of douche lord do you think I am?" He looked at her with mock contempt. "I just want to walk as much as I can before I'm stuck on a plane."

"I was just kidding, Will."

"I know. Actually, this break thing isn't working for me, and I was wondering if you would visit me on set in Greece. You could come with me tomorrow. We'd have the whole flight together. The Greek islands are gorgeous, and I know I could squeeze in some time for you if you come. I don't want you to miss class or anything, but I want to see you."

"I'd love to—I want to—but I don't even have a passport," she lamented.

"You don't have a passport? I thought everyone had a passport."

"Well, I don't. I never needed one before."

"So I'm really not going to see you until Christmas." Disappointment filled his voice.

"Don't you get any time off for Thanksgiving?"

"It's only a holiday here in the States. I'm going to be in New Zealand. We're filming there after Greece, and when we're on break, I'm booked for a photo shoot. I won't have time to come home before filming starts again."

"Are you kidding? You need a better agent, Will!"

"No, Isaac is the best. It wasn't a problem when he set it up six months ago."

"I'm going to miss you," she declared.

"Sarah, you'll wait for me, right?"

"I don't know. Do I have a choice?" She skimmed her fingers through the hair on the back of his neck and smiled brightly at him. She thought he was joking, but his expression remained serious.

"You won't get bored and find another guy?"

"Where is this coming from? Do you doubt my love?" She looked at him with a knot turning in her stomach.

"Well, it's stupid, I'm sure."

"Come on, just tell me what's on your mind," she said. She laid her head against his shoulder as they walked. It felt so good just to touch him, and she didn't want anything to come between them.

He sighed. "I saw a picture on the Net a couple of weeks ago—of you and a guy. He had his arm around you and was leaning in inches from your face. You were laughing, and you looked pretty comfortable together. I didn't recognize him. It looked like it was at a bar," he finally admitted.

Oh crap. "Me? Are you sure it wasn't old or Photoshopped?"

"You were wearing my shirt."

"Oh yeah, I'm going to wear your shirt on a date with another guy. Really?" She knew instantly what day she had worn his shirt, and she knew who the guy was.

He stopped walking and turned to her. "I didn't say you were on a date. I trust you." His eyes scoured hers as if searching for the truth.

"Trust? We're on a break." He was the one who'd initiated the break. He didn't have the right to be jealous. It was his idea. Unless…

She glanced at his expression, and what little resolve she had vanished.

He stared at her in disbelief. "I thought you understood that it wasn't that kind of break. Did you go out with other guys?"

She scrunched her face nervously. This was exactly the reaction she'd hoped he would have, but now she felt ashamed. She never should have listened to her friends.

"The girls told me that's what a break meant. You date other people while you're apart. They convinced me that was why you wanted a break—to alleviate your guilt."

His face wrinkled like he couldn't believe what she was saying. "You dated other guys?"

"No, not really. The picture must have been from the state fair. Remember, I told you about those guys and how flirty they were at the beer tent. This one guy kept asking me out, and Megan threatened to give him my number because of our *break*."

"You didn't mention that he asked you out."

"When was I supposed to mention that? We had so little time to talk. It wasn't a priority."

"So what the hell does 'not really' mean? You went out with him, didn't you?" he questioned, frustration and anguish building in his voice.

"He and his friends joined us at an outdoor concert at the U. Jeff and all the girls were there. It was just a group thing."

"Yeah, like our first date." His voice dripped with disappointment. "Did you kiss him?"

"No," she exhaled too quickly.

He looked at her skeptically. She wanted him to say something so she would know what he was thinking. But he held silent, as if waiting for her to continue. She knew she couldn't keep anything from him.

"He tried kissing me, but I started crying," she admitted, cringing at the truth. "I couldn't stop crying. He must have thought I was crazy. I just wanted you to be there with me, and it wasn't you. I wanted you to be kissing me. I love you, and I want to be with you, not anyone else."

In that moment with the other guy, Sarah realized that she would never again be able to kiss any man other than Will. She couldn't tell him that, though. She didn't know what Will was thinking. What if this was a deal breaker? What if he didn't want her anymore? She felt nauseated that she had let herself get into that situation, and she was afraid that Will would never forgive her. Tears filled her eyes. She looked down, unable to face him.

"No more break, Sarah," he proclaimed sternly, cupping his hands on her face and turning it to his. "It was just semantics. What more do I have to do to show you how much you mean to me?" He bent down to kiss her, wrapping his arms around her waist. They stood on the sidewalk kissing fervently for several minutes, until a passing car honked at them, pulling them back to the real world.

"So, which one of your friends posted the picture?" asked Will.

"No way. They'd never do that to me. It wasn't any of them," she said with conviction.

He smirked, cocking his head.

"No, it wasn't one of them!"

Giving up with a sigh, Will asked, "Is there anywhere around here to eat?"

"Out?" she asked with surprise, as they had never done anything out in public before—at least on purpose.

"Yeah. Can't we eat out?"

"Well, no one is going to recognize you here on the street unless they get close, but if we go to a restaurant, that'll be different. It won't help me convince people we broke up."

"Just tell them you had a relapse, like an addiction. Come on, I'm hungry," he pleaded as he looked at her with big blue puppy dog eyes.

She gave in to his begging charm. "You *are* an addiction." Shaking her head, she grinned and added, "There's a Chinese place not far from here. We can walk."

"Lead the way," he said. He turned his baseball cap around and pulled the bill down over his face. He reached for Sarah's hand and intertwined his fingers with hers. She smiled up at him, and they set out for the restaurant.

They walked on the old buckling cement sidewalk along the treelined streets. The weather was a perfect seventy-four degrees, and the trees were just starting to change colors. Small patches of vibrant orange, yellow, and red leaves danced among the green ones in the breeze above their heads. Will and Sarah enjoyed the ten-block walk to the small Chinese restaurant. Positioned in Dinkytown, a commercial area of Minneapolis, the restaurant mostly served the University of Minnesota students. It was off the main strip, and Sarah knew it would be less crowded than some of the bigger places to eat.

The food was served family style, so they shared an order of spicy General Tso's chicken with vegetable lo mein, and they drank hot green tea that came to the table in a small black ceramic teapot. Sarah giggled at Will's rendition of an old English lady drinking tea with her pinkie finger sticking out. Although the handleless cups clearly were not English, Sarah thought his accent was spot on.

They enjoyed most of their meal before anyone in the restaurant, other than the waitress, had the courage to approach their table. They noticed the gawks and pointing, but no one had the nerve to disturb their meal right away. Slowly, groups of two and three fans at a time approached the table. Sarah was infinitely patient as she watched Will sign autographs and pose for pictures with half of the patrons of the small restaurant. It was such a foreign experience for her that she marveled at how comfortable he looked conversing with these complete strangers.

When a young teen in that awkward stage dragged her twentysomething brother with her to the table, Will turned on the charm. He leaned in close to the girl. Taking her cell phone from her and handing it to Sarah, he said, "See my girlfriend over there?" He looked over at Sarah with a raised eyebrow and placed his arm around the girl's shoulder. "If she didn't get so jealous and I weren't so in love with her, I would definitely tell you how gorgeous I think you are."

The girl's smile brightened, showing a mouthful of braces, and Sarah snapped the picture.

Her brother spoke up. "We hate to bother you, but she's been driving my parents crazy since she spotted you."

He motioned toward a middle-aged couple sitting about four tables away, and the couple waved. As Sarah handed the phone back to the girl, she glanced up at the blond guy speaking. She recognized him. He was in her social psychology class. She had spoken to him just yesterday, but couldn't remember his name.

"Hi, Sarah," the blond guy greeted.

"Hi." Sarah smiled back, and Will reached across the table, covering Sarah's hand with his.

"I guess I'll see you in class on Tuesday," the blond added as he and his sister walked back to their table—the teen still smiling from ear to ear as she gaped at her phone.

"Who was that?" Will asked with a half joking, half serious expression as he picked up a piece of broccoli with his chopsticks and stuffed it into his mouth.

"You can't be jealous. I don't even know his name. He's in one of my classes. Besides, what kind of sick human being *are* you? What was she—twelve or thirteen? You'd go to jail."

"Now she'll have something to tell her friends. I was going for sweet and irresistible. Did it come off as perverted?"

"It was sweet," Sarah confessed. She especially liked the part where he admitted being in love with her.

Ghosting a smile and downing the last of the tea in his cup, he glanced over at the teen typing on her phone, probably tweeting the picture, and then scanned the restaurant. Seeing a large number of cell phones in use, they knew they would soon be swamped, so he and Sarah quickly finished up their meal and left before more fans could arrive. They walked back to the house without anyone following them that they could see.

While they walked, Sarah asked, "Aren't you worried what the executives at the studio will say about us being in the press again?"

He rolled his eyes. "Screw 'em. Filming starts in a couple of days, and I've been stunt training for weeks. I doubt that they'll replace me. It is a sequel, and I was the lead in the first film—the fans demand continuity. Besides, I'm not doing anything that any other twenty-three-year-old male isn't doing—or wanting to do." He raised his eyebrows and looked playfully at her.

They made it back to the house and spent some time talking to Sarah's housemates before disappearing into Sarah's room.

The next day, when Sarah dropped off Will at the airport, the emptiness left by his absence filled the car. It drained her of all feeling, leaving her raw and numb. She didn't know how she would make it until December not touching the stubble that lined his jaw by the end of the day, not feeling the warmth of his hand as it intertwined with hers, not staring into his big blue eyes. Sarah didn't know how she would make it so long, but it was out of her control, and there was nothing she could do to change it. If they were meant to be together, it would all turn out fine.

That afternoon, Sarah's roommates teased her that she'd had a booty call from Will before he left for filming overseas. Sarah knew it wasn't like that. It was more than a booty call. Somehow, Sarah and Will's relationship had progressed with this visit. They had gone out in public together, and he had held her hand walking down the street. He had told a total stranger that she was his girlfriend. It seemed more like they had a normal relationship, and Will wasn't as tense about people finding out that they were together. The break was over. It was definitely over.

He'd given her a different T-shirt from his vintage collection and taken his Rebel T-shirt to wear on the plane ride. Even though the shirt was clean, he said it still smelled like her, and he wanted to have her scent fill his head on the flight. It made her smile just thinking about it.

Over the next couple of weeks, the Internet was flooded with rumors about another sighting of Jonathan and the Birthday Girl. There were pictures of her and Will at the restaurant, including one of their backsides as they walked down the sidewalk. Fans had overwhelmed the Chinese restaurant shortly after they left, and there was a big write-up about it in the *University Press*. The gossip columns were full of speculation, and some of the pictures had even made the cover of the supermarket tabloid magazines.

It didn't take long for the rumors to blow over, though, with Will out of the country and sightings of him with his *Demigod* costar in Greece. Sarah still had people asking about her involvement with Will; even total strangers pestered her. She mostly reacted by joking about it. She rarely gave a real answer to the inquiries, except to her real friends.

A month passed and then another. Sarah and Will spoke as often as filming and school would allow, but it wasn't the same as being face-to-face. Christmas was approaching, and they were both looking forward to finally spending some time together. Sarah would have almost a month off for winter break, while Will had only a few weeks off before he was expected to resume filming again back in Los Angeles. They weren't going to waste a single minute of their time off.

Chapter Sixteen

"So what do you think?" Will asked his assistant.

"I've seen it before. It's perfect. She'll love anything you give her, Jon. Stop sweating the small stuff."

"Small stuff? Way to calm my nerves. Thanks." He set Sarah's gift on the bed next to the suitcase he was packing for his ski trip. "Everything is set for the trip, right?"

"The condo is just sitting there waiting for you." Leslie handed him the envelope with his boarding pass and itinerary. "I could come with you, if you want. There are four bedrooms, and with only Sarah's brother and his girlfriend joining you, I'm pretty sure only two of them will be used."

"That's all I need, your sarcastic butt following me around. The last three months of tripping over each other not enough for you?"

She laughed.

"You haven't seen your family since before filming started. Enjoy the holidays with them while you can. Sarah and I will be just fine without you." He cocked his head and asked her again. "Everything's set, right?"

She knew what he meant. Why was she avoiding his question?

"Yes. It's all on the itinerary. I talked to the guy yesterday. It will go perfectly, and you can thank me when you get back." She smiled and flipped her blonde hair back as she strode out of his bedroom.

Will grabbed a stack of vintage T-shirts from his closet and set them on the bed. He had just emptied his suitcase this morning, and now he was reloading it. Luckily, he had enough clothes that he didn't need to worry about doing laundry. He returned to his closet and found two thick sweaters and added them to his suitcase.

Leslie's head popped back through the doorway. "You're not bringing your snowboard?"

"No. Sarah only skis. I won't need it. I've got my skis."

"You're going to Vail, and you're not even going to board? Maybe you could teach her? You should bring it."

He looked at Leslie, shaking his head. "I haven't seen her since September. It will be a miracle if we hit the slopes more than a couple of times."

"I'm going to pack it, just in case." Leslie smiled annoyingly back at him as she plopped down on the bed and cracked open one of the two water bottles in her hands.

"I'm not bringing it." He scowled. He really needed to get away and spend some quiet time with Sarah—alone.

"You're cranky today. Too much to drink last night?" She handed him the bottle she had just opened.

He took the bottle and guzzled it until it was empty. The cold water soothed his dry throat. He was definitely off today. Last night's drinking *had* dehydrated him.

"Thanks. You should have come with us. It was guys' night, but you could have come."

"Why, so your buddies could hit on me all night? And you know Liam would just blab all the details to my ex. No, thank you."

"They're not that bad." He smiled, knowing they were that bad, and she rolled her eyes.

"Your mom wants you to have dinner with her tonight. I think she's upset that you're not going to be around for Christmas."

"I just have to finish packing. Dinner is doable. Can you tell her? I've got to check in with Sarah." He sat down on the bed next to Leslie and grabbed his phone. She bounced off immediately and headed out of the room, pulling out her phone as she exited. He lay back on the bed with his feet still touching the floor and started typing.

Can't wait to C U tomorrow. Call me. Luv U.

He hit send and waited. Her last final had ended a couple of hours ago, so she was probably getting ready for the trip too. His phone vibrated, and her face popped up on the screen. He loved the picture of her. Though she wasn't exactly smiling, her eyes were full of mischief, and he knew she was smiling inside. How many times had this picture gotten him through the day over the last three months? He couldn't wait to see her.

He tapped the screen and said in his sexiest voice, "Hey, beautiful, are you packed yet?"

There was a pause and a woman who wasn't Sarah began to speak.

"Will, it's Kate. Sarah's been in a car accident. I'm at the ER right now."

The air sucked from his lungs, as if the room had become a vacuum. "Is she...OK?" was all he managed to choke out.

"She's alive, but I don't know anything yet. She was having difficulty breathing, and they asked me to leave the room. That's all I know." Sarah's mother sounded panicked.

"Oh." He was silent for several more seconds. He couldn't catch his breath. With a shaky voice, he said, "I'll be in on the next flight. Keep me posted, would you?"

Something clicked in him. The next thing he knew, he was pulling out his duffle bag and transferring his clothes from the open suitcase.

"If I don't answer, it's because I'm on the plane, so leave a message or a text, please. I'll call you when I get in."

The call ended, and just like that, his life had spiraled into a tailspin again. Just when he thought he had pulled it together, it fell apart. He found his travel bag with his electric razor and pushed it into the duffle. He stumbled out of the bedroom as he flung the bag over his shoulder.

"Leslie, I need the next flight to Minneapolis, and if there isn't one, I need you to charter a jet."

"Oh god. Did she break up with you?"

He shook his head. He wasn't sure if the lump in his throat would allow any words to escape from his mouth. He swallowed hard and the lump lodged deeper in his chest.

"Sarah's been in a car accident. I spoke to her mom. She's having a hard time breathing. I need a flight. Can you help me?"

Leslie mumbled something into her phone and ended her call. He followed her into the office, where she opened her laptop and began typing.

Two hours later, Will sat in the VIP lounge at the airport, waiting for his flight to board. Freezing rain in Minneapolis had delayed the flight. The ice had probably caused Sarah's accident, he realized. If the flights in Minnesota got too backed up, his flight would get diverted to Atlanta. That was what the airline's agent had said, anyway.

He had just gotten off the phone with Kate. Sarah was in surgery. Her lung had collapsed because of internal bleeding. The doctor told Kate that a broken rib had most likely punctured a vessel, but since they couldn't get the bleeding to slow, she needed surgery.

Will fiddled with the phone in his hands. Kate had promise to call as soon as she heard anymore news. He typed *Hemothorax* into the search engine on his phone. That was what Kate had called Sarah's condition. As he read, he felt a little better. As long as they could stop the bleeding, she would be all right. He should have stopped reading after the first paragraph, though. The next several paragraphs described every complication associated with this form of collapsed lung. It was a long list—from shock to respiratory failure and death. He couldn't waste his mental energy on possibilities. He would go crazy. He stuffed the phone back into his jacket pocket and began to pace.

Forty minutes later, Will was on the plane as it taxied to the runway. He stretched out in his seat, his dark sunglasses covering his eyes. He knew the glasses only made people study his face more closely, but he didn't care. The woman next to him wrapped her hand around his. He tried to smile at her. He saw the familiar dimple that he had inherited appear on her cheek, but her smile looked forced.

He squeezed her hand. "Thanks, Mom."

She nodded, and they sat in silence. Will knew most people would try to reassure him that Sarah would be OK. His mother knew better. She knew as well as he did that life was fragile and promises couldn't always be kept.

The flight dragged on and on, in almost complete silence. When it finally ended, Will flipped his phone off airplane mode, and two texts appeared, both from Jessica.

Sarah's out of surgery and in the ICU.

The second text was the hospital's name and address. There was no more information. What did that mean? He showed it to his mother with a questioning look.

"She's alive," she whispered in his ear. "That's good news, Jon."

He pressed send to connect the call.

"Jess, my flight just landed. What's going on?"

"Sarah is breathing easier, and they stopped the bleeding. But she hasn't woken up since the surgery." Her voice caught and she paused. "She lost a lot of blood, and they gave her a couple of transfusions. The next few hours are critical."

"When is she going to wake up?"

"They don't know. But don't worry, I'm sure she'll be all right."

And there it was—a false promise that shouldn't have been made. He had heard it before, and it didn't bring him comfort.

By the time Will arrived at the hospital, Sarah had been in the ICU for a couple of hours. As the glass door pulled open in front of him, he felt a blanket of dread engulf him. He hadn't been in a hospital since Jack's death, and he wasn't feeling very optimistic. When he stepped off the elevator onto the third floor, the institutional smell filled his lungs, and the rhythmic beeping of the monitors took over his head. With his senses overwhelmed, he froze, paralyzed in the memory of his brother's death, paralyzed with fear of what he may have to face.

His mother reached out and wrapped her arm around his shoulder. Squeezing gently, she said, "You can do this, Jon."

He looked into her encouraging face and took a deep breath. Then, together, they walked toward Sarah's family.

"Kate. David," Will said as he hugged each of Sarah's parents. "How is she?"

"Well, not much has changed since your last update. She still hasn't woken up, and they don't know why. Her heartbeat is strong, though, and she isn't struggling to breathe," answered David.

"May I see her?" Will asked, looking at Kate. He noticed for the first time that her eyes were the same bright green as her daughter's, and his breath hitched in his throat.

"Follow me. We'll have to kick Jeff and Jessica out. They only allow a couple of people in the room at a time," said Kate. "Will you be coming too?" she asked the tall blonde woman.

"Oh, sorry, this is my mother, Lara. She wouldn't let me come by myself." Will glanced at his mom and forced a quick smile. He noticed Sarah's housemates lined the far wall, and he held up his hand in acknowledgment as they looked up at him.

"I would like to go, if you don't mind. Sarah is all Jon has talked about for months, and I don't want him to face this alone," Lara answered.

Kate nodded and led them to a small room with big glass windows facing a main nurse's station. The door was open. Jeff and Jessica came to greet Will outside the small room. Will hugged each as he spied Sarah's motionless body in the center of the raised hospital bed. She looked like she was almost sitting up, and had tubes and wires attached to her all over.

Will slipped into the room, leaving his mother outside the door with Jeff and Jessica. He stood just inside, taking it all in. The smell of adhesive tape, the blinking lights on the monitor, the white sheets on the metal bed—all flashed through his brain like an old black-and-white film, conjuring feelings he had buried deep inside.

This can't be happening, he thought.

He felt his mother's arm wrap around him, and he rested his head against hers.

That's when Will lost his composure and his eyes glossed over. It reminded him too much of the hospital four years ago. He could picture Jack lying in the hospital bed, and a feeling of helplessness about Sarah's condition choked him. He couldn't bear to lose her. She was the one who loved him for who he was, not his fame. She was the one who was meant for him, and he would not survive if she didn't. He knew this in his heart. He stepped forward, and leaning over Sarah, he gently kissed her forehead, being very careful to avoid the tubes coming from her body.

"Hi, beautiful. I missed you," he said softly.

Still leaning over her, he closed his eyes and touched his cheek to hers, letting her warmth penetrate his face. He held it there for a minute, enjoying the comfort being close to her brought him.

"I love you," he whispered, "but you know that." Will kissed her forehead again and stood up. "This is my mom. I know you've talked to her before on the phone, but she came all this way to see you. It would be great if you two could talk face-to-face." He unzipped his ski jacket and slid it off, not wanting to chill Sarah with his winter wear. He pulled the beanie from the top of his head and tossed it, with the jacket, onto his duffle bag, slumped on the floor behind him.

"It's nice to finally meet you, Sarah. Jon talks about you all the time. I think he was going a little crazy not seeing you, though," Lara admitted. Tears filled her eyes as she looked over at her son.

Lara and Will had experience with these one-sided conversations. Jack's nurse had encouraged them with Jack. "A person in a coma is aware of his surroundings and can hear everything. Hearing is the last sense to leave a person," the nurse had said.

"I'll let you have some time alone," Lara stated. She kissed her son's cheek and slipped out of the room.

Will pulled the square padded chair up to the bed and intertwined his hand with Sarah's. He sat for a while just holding her hand and staring at her bruised face. As the minutes ticked by, his hands began to quiver. He needed to distract himself from all the negative thoughts filling his brain. So he started talking, babbling about all the things they were going to do when she got out of the hospital, about filming, and about the endless waterfall he'd seen in New Zealand. He told her about a fantastic hole-in-the-wall restaurant he'd found in the Greek islands and how she was going to have to get her passport because he was going to bring her there. Talking to her was helping him cope. Will divulged all the details of last night's outing with Nick and his other buddies. They had gone to a sushi bar for dinner and drinks and been mobbed by fans. He told her how Nick had worked it to his advantage to pick up women, even though they had all agreed on a no-girls-allowed night.

"It was Nick, Hayden, Chris, and Liam. It was hilarious. Chris is married, so he and I were just sitting back, laughing, as these girls kept coming up and buying us drinks," he told her.

Will was feeling guilty about having taken time to spend with his friends while they were all in town for the holidays. If he had known his time with Sarah was limited, he would have been at her side last night, and this decision to spend time with his friends was weighing heavily on his mind. Will continued to ramble on until the ICU nurse entered the room, forcing him to pause his monologue.

Will sat quietly holding Sarah's hand while the nurse tried to make superficial conversation with him. As she spoke, she darted around the room, checking various monitors, recording fluid levels, and listening to Sarah breathe. She checked Sarah's pupils and her reflexes. The nurse pretended not to recognize him, and he appreciated her discretion, but he could see it in her eyes as she spoke.

"Are you holding up all right?" she asked as she rubbed the IV port with alcohol and slowly injected a clear liquid into the tubing. Monitoring her watch as she pushed the plunger, the nurse continued. "Are you her boyfriend?"

"Yep," he said with a nod, answering both questions and avoiding eye contact. He really wasn't in the mood for a conversation with a stranger.

"Let me know if there is anything I can do for you or the family," she added.

Will nodded again, and the nurse left the room. He sat quietly listening to the bubbling noise coming from the machine at his feet. The noise was loud and monotonous. The machine looked like a multichambered ant farm flooded with water, and from it ran a long clear tube that went directly into Sarah's side. Will lifted the blanket to check. All he could see was the tube leading to her side, and the place where it entered her skin was covered by a gauze pad and clear tape. He was going to ask the nurse about that machine the next time she made rounds. Still holding Sarah's hand, he leaned in and laid his head on the bed. He was beyond his coping limit and was trying to gather strength.

Sarah's mom came into the room, and gently squeezing his shoulder, she said, "You should get some sleep. Why don't you come back to the house and rest? The nurse will call us if anything changes. It's only a fifteen-minute drive."

"I can't, Kate. I can't leave her." He was adamant.

"I really hoped that...she would...wake up when she heard your voice...but I guess...she just needs more time to heal," Kate stammered.

Will placed his hand on top of Kate's hand. "I'm sorry."

"Don't be. It was just silly of me," she added. "I've convinced your mother to stay at the house with us. It will be easier in the long run. It would be idiotic for her to be stranded at a hotel. I'm heading back to the house too. I'll go nuts if I'm just sitting here idle. Are you sure you want to stay?"

Will looked up at her, unwavering. Kate kissed her daughter's cheek, said good night, and left. Will sat alone again with Sarah, listening to the bubbling ant farm that drowned out all other sounds in the room. He didn't know where the night would take him, but he knew that he would be with Sarah, whatever happened.

Chapter Seventeen

As the next three days passed, Will watched Sarah get poked and prodded. The hospital staff drew blood, took X-rays, connected her to electrodes, emptied bags of fluid into her, emptied bags of fluid from her, and ran test after test on her. There were very few changes in Sarah's condition. She was still unconscious, and she seemed oblivious to all the intrusions to her body. Will stayed at her bedside as much as he could over the three days. He never left the hospital floor despite the persistent berating from his mother to take a shower. His clothes were wrinkled, and his hair was curling up in odd directions. His unshaven face was taking on a new identity, but in Will's mind, nothing mattered except Sarah.

Although Will spent more time with Sarah than anyone else, he let others have a little alone time with her. He used this time to make phone calls, check his e-mail, and read. Kate and Lara made sure he ate some meals. They brought him food to eat in the family waiting area, but he always slept at Sarah's bedside. He slept leaning forward against Sarah's bed the first two nights, but last night, one of the nurses, feeling sorry for him, dragged a reclining chair into the room, so he slept there. In reality, he hadn't slept much the last three nights, and that fact was visible on his face. He had read up on Sarah's condition on the Internet most of last night, but couldn't get his mind to shut off when he did try to sleep.

This morning, Sarah's lung was deemed to have healed enough to have the tube leading to the bubbling ant farm removed from her chest. Will watched the procedure and was amazed at how much tubing was actually shoved inside Sarah. He watched most of the procedures that were performed on her. He found if he was quiet enough and pinned himself to the back wall, no one would ask him to leave. He had gotten to know most of the staff in the ICU and was fairly confident they weren't passing information to the press. No fans had shown up on the floor looking for him, at least.

By noon, Will and Kate were in Sarah's room talking about what Sarah had been like as a child. Kate told him how Sarah would write plays and have all her friends act them out while she directed. She had started doing it before she even knew how to write. She would tell them what to do and say, and where to stand.

"She is very creative, and the plays were elaborately detailed," Kate said. "I always knew Sarah would do something that involved writing. She got a short story published back in April in one of those literary magazines. It was really good. It helped her get the internship at TC last summer."

"She never mentioned getting anything published. I wonder why," Will commented, pondering what else he didn't know about her.

"Sarah isn't one to boast," Kate admitted with pride. "Unless she's specifically asked, she doesn't mention it to anyone."

The room was eerily quiet with the bubbling ant farm removed, so they heard every drip and beep as if for the first time. While they continued to chat, Sarah's heart rate monitor began to alarm, startling them both. The nurse came into the room to assess Sarah. She listened to Sarah's heart with her stethoscope, repositioned her on the bed, and checked the monitor leads. Sarah's heart rate quickly returned to normal when she was repositioned.

"Darlene, is it normal for someone's heart to do that all of a sudden?" Will asked the scrappy older nurse.

"Well, it isn't unusual, Jon. But, honestly, it may not be the best sign. We will keep monitoring it, and her previous tests haven't indicated any reasons for concern," the nurse offered. "We'll do more tests if it continues."

"What do you mean it may not be the best sign?" questioned Kate.

"Well, if it continues, it may indicate a new problem has arisen. It could be the first sign that her body may be shutting down, or it may mean nothing at all. We will just have to take it as it comes," Darlene answered candidly.

By two thirty in the afternoon, Sarah's heart monitor had alarmed two more times, and Will hovered in her room, ignoring his growling stomach, refusing to leave her side to eat lunch. He sat in the vinyl recliner reading a movie script that he had been given to consider. He was reading it out loud to Sarah, and he made funny voices for the characters as each spoke. It was a romantic comedy, her perfect date-night movie, and it reminded him of the night of the summer rain when she first admitted she loved him. He was at a point in the plot where the characters were pulled apart with no hope of getting back together when he looked up at Sarah's face and noticed a tear rolling down her cheek.

He got up and moved to the chair next to the bed. Will reached up and wiped the tear away with his thumb, not sure at first whether it was real. Then he gently brushed a loose strand of hair off her face and whispered, "Sarah?" He wasn't sure if it was normal for a comatose person to have tears, but he was a little apprehensive to ask about it, dreading more bad news.

Will sat holding her hand and watching her face in silence, hoping for a miracle. He had silently prayed off and on during the day, but his prayers had never saved Jack, so he didn't put much stock in them. He watched and waited. He stared at her face, searching for a sign—a sign that she would come out of this.

After ten long minutes and no miracle, he said, "Sarah, I'm scared." He took a deep breath, fighting the moisture in his eyes. He chuckled, adding, "And look, I'm not running." He took another deep breath. "I'm scared, Sarah, that I'll never hear your laugh again, that I'll never see those beautiful green eyes of yours. I'm scared that we'll never see our children jumping off the dock at your parents' cabin, that we won't get to grow old together. I can't live my life without you. Please wake up, beautiful. I need you." His breath caught in his throat. "I need you," he whispered a second time.

Emotionally and physically exhausted, he laid down his head on the bed next to their intertwined hands. He closed his eyes. His head felt like lead as he envisioned the third day after Jack's accident—the day that he died. Will remembered watching the heart monitor as Jack's heart started to fail, how the beats slowed and spaced apart and eventually stopped altogether. In his mind, he could still hear his brother's last gasping breath and could still picture his mouth opening, struggling to suck in air for the last time. He couldn't get that memory out of his mind. He didn't want to see Sarah die that way. He didn't want her to die. The tears started to leak out of his eyes, and he could feel the moisture drip down the side of his hand. He crushed his eyes together, willing the tears to stop, and then he felt something brush his cheek. Will lifted his head to make sure he wasn't imagining it. He looked at her hand, and there was no movement.

He glanced up at her face. She still looked like she was sleeping. Her breathing was steady. Her eyes were closed.

"Sarah?" He paused. "Did you just touch my face?"

He watched her intently for any kind of reaction. After several seconds, the corners of her lips turned up just a little, and his heart leapt. Ecstatic now, he chuckled.

"Sarah, you smiled at me. Beautiful, open your eyes. I want to see those gorgeous green eyes." Feeling a glimmer of hope, he brushed his fingertips from her chin to her temple and cupped her cheek in his hand. "Please?"

Sarah slowly opened her eyes and looked at the hand that was still touching her face.

"Sarah," he bayed in a huskier-than-usual voice.

She moved her eyes to his, and his heart jumped in his chest. Will stood to lean over her, and he gently touched his lips to hers. With Sarah still staring wide-eyed at him after a couple of seconds, he pulled back.

"Please tell me you know who I am."

Sarah nodded and said in a raspy voice, "Um…"

He looked at her in panic. "You know who I am, right?" he asked again, louder.

"Yeah," she said with a hoarse laugh. "Ouch." She instinctively moved her hand to her right side. "Don't make me laugh anymore. You should have seen your face."

He just smiled at her, happy to have her back.

The nurse interrupted Will's bliss by entering and announcing, "It's so good to have you awake, Sarah. My name is Darlene, and I'm a nurse at St. Mary's Hospital. You were in a car accident. How are you feeling?" She flitted around the room, asking Sarah questions and recording information from various instruments. The nurse checked Sarah's eyes with a small flashlight. She listened to her heart and began to check her over from head to toe.

Will slipped out the door, saying, "I'm going to get your mom. I'll be right back."

He sprinted down the hall to the family area. Kate and Lara looked up with a start as he paused a moment, taking a breath. He could feel the positive energy radiating from him.

"She's awake," he announced.

Kate squeezed past him in the doorway and raced toward Sarah's room.

Lara stopped to hug her son, and Will said, "Thanks, Mom, for being here. It means the world to me." Then he smiled his brilliant one-dimple smile. He was genuinely happy for the first time in days.

When he returned, Sarah was sitting forward in bed, splinting her side with a pillow, and the nurse was listening to Sarah's back with her stethoscope. Sarah's eyes met Will's, and she silently mouthed, "Love you."

Will's face lit up.

Kate asked the nurse how Sarah was doing, and the nurse responded, "She's doing great considering all she's been through. I figured she was awake—at least I hoped—when I looked up and saw Romeo over there making out with her."

Kate and Lara turned and looked accusingly at Will.

"What? It was just one kiss—a peck, really," he explained.

They all laughed.

"I'll talk to the doctor as soon as possible, and we'll run some more tests. Sarah will probably get moved out of the ICU today. I don't think she'll get to go home for Christmas, but we'll see what the doctor says." The nurse finished examining Sarah and left the room for the computer poised right outside at the nurses' station.

Over the next couple of hours, Sarah continued to get assessed by every discipline at the hospital. She saw respiratory therapy, neurology, cardiac, and dietary. Every field squeezed in her assessment because they knew tomorrow was Christmas Eve and staff would be low. The nurse explained that no one wanted to be called in for an assessment that could be completed today. At one point in between evaluations, Darlene asked everyone to leave the room so she could remove Sarah's urinary catheter.

Sarah reacted by saying, "My what? Are you serious?" She leaned over the side of the bed, which was quite a feat for her, to spy the bag of yellow liquid dangling on the bed frame. "That's so gross," she declared with a look of utter horror on her face.

"That's nothing, Sarah. You should have seen what was collected in the bubbling ant farm. That was gross." She seemed mortified at the thought of all that Will had seen while she was unconscious. Will chuckled as he mussed her hair gently. Then he left the room with a huge grin.

While Sarah was being assessed, all the important people were notified of her recovery. Will's dad, Zander, was boarding a plane from Toronto and would be meeting everyone in Minnesota for Christmas. Lara and Kate had decided that the two families would spend Christmas together, since Will would not leave Sarah's side and Lara wouldn't leave Will. They would all have Christmas dinner at the Austins' house or the hospital, depending on Sarah's condition. Now that Sarah was awake, they hoped that it could be at the house.

After all the assessments had been completed, Sarah was moved out of the intensive care unit to the medical/surgical floor, one story up, and was placed in a room at the far end of the hallway. Will had used his charm with the charge nurse to get a private room away from the commotion of the floor. The room was as close to a presidential suite as the hospital possessed. The charge nurse agreed that if Jonathan Williams was going to be in Sarah's room, she needed to be away from the rest of the floor, or more security would be needed. The nurse knew that if word got out that he was at her hospital, it would be utter chaos on the surgical floor, so she assured Will that his presence would be kept confidential and that Sarah would be assigned the most trustworthy staff.

Chapter Eighteen

Once Sarah was settled in her new room, she was really too tired to converse very long with her visitors, so everyone headed back to Kate and David's house to celebrate her awakening, except Will. He still wasn't willing to leave Sarah's side. He would let her sleep, but would not leave her. She smiled at him as he kissed her forehead. She couldn't keep her heavy eyelids open any longer.

"Thanks for staying with me, Will," she said as her eyes closed.

"Anytime, beautiful," he told her, just happy to have her back.

Will settled into the plum-colored recliner and relaxed for the first time in days. He fell asleep quickly and slept for several hours before opening his eyes again. Slightly disoriented, he looked up at Sarah, and she was staring back at him, smiling.

"Hi." He stretched his arms straight out and then as far back as he could manage. "You awake long?" Will asked with a yawn. He checked his watch. It was eleven fifteen.

"No, not really. You looked so peaceful that I didn't want to wake you," Sarah admitted.

He smiled back at her, rubbing his face. "I guess I needed some sleep. Do you want to talk?"

"Yeah, I'd like that," she said.

"Do you remember the accident much?" he asked as he moved to the smaller chair next to her bed.

"Most of it. My car was totaled, right?" she said.

He nodded his head in affirmation. "The cars just kept piling into you."

"I don't remember being pulled out of my car or the ambulance ride," Sarah confessed.

"Your mom has all the newspaper clippings and some pictures of your car too. I'm sure she'll show them to you. You'll be amazed that you survived."

"She is really good about documenting everything in scrapbooks."

"Sarah, I thought you were never going to come back to me," Will blurted out, searching her eyes for some kind of explanation as to why this kept happening to the people he cared about the most.

"Well, I didn't come back on my own," she replied, sounding nervous.

"What do you mean, not on your own?"

She hesitated and whispered softly, "Jack told me I had to come back."

He gaped at her in disbelief, not knowing whether she was trying to make a joke. "What?" he asked, shaking his head, unable to process what she had said.

She looked at him with a very serious expression. "Jack told me that you needed me and that I had to go to you. He said you wouldn't survive if I didn't wake up." Tears were building in her eyes. "He said you and I were meant to be together and I wasn't meant to leave you. That—" She stopped and studied Will's face. "Are you all right, Will?"

He stared at her face in disbelief, wanting to believe her, but not knowing if he could. His heart was beating faster, and he sat as rigid as stone.

"It may have been a dream," she said, studying him again. "It was probably a dream." Her eyes met his, and she revealed all the sincerity she was feeling.

"How was he?" Will whispered as he regarded her.

"He was happy. He loves you and has never blamed you for the accident. He wants you to be happy too."

"I miss him, Sarah."

"I know." She intertwined her hand with his, and the corners of her lips turned up slightly. "He's always watching out for you, though. He called you Jon-a-thon."

A smile broke across Will's face. He had forgotten that Jack called him that. He cocked his head, staring at Sarah in amazement. "I never told you that." He was sure he had never shared that information with her.

She shrugged her right shoulder slightly and smiled lovingly back at him.

"You know, I used to dream about him all the time, especially the first year after he died. They were always good dreams, not nightmares. I hated waking up from them. I haven't had a dream about Jack in a long time. Every time my phone would ring that first year, I thought it was him. I knew he was dead, but just for a split second, I'd think, 'Oh, that must be Jack.' Weird, huh?" he admitted.

She smiled and squeezed his hand.

"It doesn't happen anymore," he assured her. He didn't know what to believe, but he wanted to believe that Jack was looking out for him and Sarah. It comforted him. "I'm glad you came back to me."

Just then, a perky little blonde nurse peeked into Sarah's room. "I didn't think you would be awake. I'm Paige. I'll be your nurse until eleven tomorrow morning. How are you feeling?"

"I'm OK," Sarah answered.

As she assessed Sarah with her stethoscope and evaluated her bandages, she asked, "You look like you're guarding yourself a bit when you move. Are you in pain?"

Sarah nodded.

"You're due for some pain medicine. On a scale from one to ten, with ten being the worst pain you've ever felt, where would you rank your pain right now?"

"I don't know. Eight?" she confessed.

Will looked at Sarah in disbelief. "Why didn't you say something?"

The nurse looked at him and smiled.

Will offered his hand to the nurse to shake. "Hi, I'm Jon."

"Nice to meet you, Jon. *The Demigod*, right?" Paige said, still smiling.

"Yep," he admitted as he turned to Sarah. "Why didn't you tell me you were in pain?"

"It only hurts when I move—or breathe."

"I'll go get some medicine. Then, after it starts working and you feel some relief, I'd like to get you up and walking, if you're up for it," stated the nurse.

Paige left and returned a couple of minutes later.

"This should work for now to get you back on track, but if you want to go home by Christmas, you're going to have to get your pain managed with oral medicine," she said as she injected the medicine into Sarah's IV tubing.

"There is still a chance she can make it home for Christmas?"

"It's possible, but she has to be up and moving around." She turned to Sarah. "You can't allow your pain to get past a three or four anymore. It's important that you stay on top of it. If you don't, you end up having to take more medicine than you would if you just took it on a regular basis. OK?" She smiled. "No more lecturing, because you're newly awake, but you're due for more medicine at four a.m., and you will be taking it orally—pill form. If your pain gets worse than a four before then, tell me. Are you feeling some relief yet?"

"Yes, I feel better," Sarah admitted. "I could feel it spread through my blood the second you injected it."

"Do you want to try getting up?" asked Paige.

"Sure, if it will help me get home by Christmas."

"You were up walking earlier today, right?" the nurse questioned.

"Just once in the hall. It hurt," Sarah confessed.

Paige smiled at her and helped her slowly get out of bed, into a standing position. "Are you dizzy at all?" she asked. Sarah shook her head, and Paige added, "Jon, I'm going to have you walk with her. The halls are dead, so no one will see you. It will be good for you to get out of this room too."

She showed Jon how to support Sarah as she walked, and the two headed into the hallway, dragging Sarah's IV pole with them. They walked the length of the hall two times before Sarah admitted she was tired. They returned to the room, and he helped her back into bed.

Will slept in the recliner chair next to Sarah's bed, and Sarah took her pain medicine orally at four without waking Will. In the morning, they were both surprised when Nurse Paige came in, closing the door quickly behind her.

"We have to get you out of here this morning. I have orders."

Sarah and Will looked at each other excitedly.

"That's great!" Will said.

"There's a group of about eight girls roaming the halls of the hospital looking for you," Paige added.

"I take it they're not my friends. They're looking for Jon, right?" Sarah asked, rolling her eyes.

"Both of you, actually—at least that's what they said. They are asking everyone in the hospital if they know where to find you. I'm sure it's only going to get worse, so as soon as the doctor comes in and gives her OK, we will send you on your way," Paige said.

"Only if she's really ready, right?" asked Will.

Sarah shot him the evil eye.

"Jon, we would never send her home if she wasn't ready." Paige smiled at Sarah.

Twenty minutes later, the doctor came in to assess Sarah's condition. She told Sarah she was ready to go home, but would have to see her regular doctor on Monday for a follow-up visit. The doctor wrote her several prescriptions and instructed her on how to take them properly. After the doctor had left, Nurse Paige gave Sarah more instructions and reminded her to stay ahead of her pain when taking her medicine. Almost immediately after hearing she was being discharged, Will called Sarah's house to notify her family.

Soon David arrived with some clothes for Sarah to wear home. The clothes she came into the hospital wearing had been cut off her in the emergency room, and it was too cold to walk outside in a hospital gown. Sarah changed in the bathroom with Paige's help and bundled up in a coat, hat, scarf, and mittens before climbing into a wheelchair for the ride down to the car. David left to pull the car up while Sarah got ready.

"Wow, you need a new coat, Sarah," Will said jokingly.

"Yeah, I think this one is from junior high. I thought Mom donated it years ago. This is probably the best he could come up with. All my clothes are at the rental." The sleeves hung an inch too short, and she couldn't get it zipped over her now developed chest. "It must have taken my dad a while to find. It was probably on the bottom of the coat closet. I wonder where my coat ended up," she said.

"When you feel better, we can go shopping and replace all the items you lost in the accident. You're going to need a new car too." Will smiled deviously at her.

"Don't get any grand ideas. My insurance will replace everything," she stated, looking up at him. Will just kept smiling as he contemplated what kind of car he was going to buy her. "You're not buying me an expensive car! I liked my Honda," she added.

"We'll just look," he said, chuckling. "Besides, you probably won't need one until we get to LA." He stepped into the hallway in front of the wheelchair. He wanted Sarah to contemplate that on the ride home.

"How can...? I..."

He could feel her eyes burrowing into the back of his head, willing him to turn around. A smile flickered on his lips. They obviously had a lot to discuss.

Paige pushed Sarah to the elevator as Will fiddled with his hat and jacket collar, trying to disguise himself and trying to avoid Sarah's questioning expression. The elevator was empty, and they descended two floors before the door opened. On the platform stood two teenage girls looking just as Paige had described earlier.

Before the door was completely open, Paige announced, "You're going to have to take the next one. She's very contagious," and she pushed the close-door button before the girls had time to react.

"You're good!" Will commented after the elevator door had closed. He stepped out from the corner by the control panel.

"Thanks," Paige said with an energetic smile.

They made it out to the curb and loaded the car without any more fan encounters. They thanked Paige for her help and headed back to the house. Sarah was finally out of the hospital and ready to go home. She and Will sat in the backseat of the car holding hands, as if they were fourteen again, being chauffeured around by her father. Will breathed a sigh of relief and nodded at David's reflection in the rearview mirror.

Chapter Nineteen

When they arrived at the house, it was quiet. Zander sat at the dining room table typing on his laptop—an iPad and a few piles of papers spread out around him. He looked up from his work to see his son's scowling face.

"Dad, give it a break. It's Christmas Eve," proclaimed Will.

"There was no one here, Jon. I was just taking advantage of the quiet."

"Honestly," David interjected, "he's been the life of the party since he got here. You should have seen him last night. He shared some really great stories about you and your dealings with the press. Like when you dropped your pants on national television and ended up getting twelve different underwear modeling offers."

"Great," Will said, rolling his eyes.

Will introduced his dad to Sarah. He knew Sarah would see the resemblance right away—the strong jawline, the height, even his eyes. Though Zander's were light brown, almost amber, not ice blue, they were lined with the same thick lashes. Zander's hair was lighter than his, and cut short, with a peppering of gray throughout.

David, Zander, Will, and Sarah all chatted about spending Christmas together and how well Lara and Kate were getting along. The moms and

Jessica were out doing some last-minute shopping before all the stores closed. Lara hadn't brought any gifts with her on the plane, and she wanted to pick up a few items.

After visiting for an hour, Sarah was exhausted again and needed a nap. She still had a long recovery ahead of her and needed to take it slow. Will reminded her to take her pain medicine first. Then he helped her upstairs to her room and got her settled into bed.

He kissed her forehead and was getting ready to leave when Sarah asked, "Will you stay with me, Will?"

"Sarah, I don't think your dad would allow that. Didn't you see the look on his face as we were going up the stairs?" He raised his eyebrows and smiled at her.

"Just for a little bit, please?" she pleaded.

He climbed up on the bed next to her and wrapped his arm gently across her hip.

After about ten minutes, David knocked softly on Sarah's door. Will jumped off the bed and met him.

"She just fell asleep," Will whispered as he slipped out of the room.

David put his arm around Will's shoulders. "You look tired. Your parents have the guest room, but you can lie down on the couch in the basement. It's quiet there. I can get you some blankets and a pillow, if you like."

"No, I'll be fine. Thanks, though," Will said as they headed downstairs.

Will spent the next hour catching up with his dad. David had to run to a local animal shelter for an emergency, so Will and Zander were left alone to talk.

"You're serious about this, Jon?" asked Zander.

"Yeah, Dad, I love her."

"I can see that. Do you think she is ready to take on your life, though? It can be much crazier than the life she is used to here," Zander said, looking around the living room. "It's pretty quiet here—not like your life at all. Her family seems grounded, but will she be able to handle Hollywood?"

"She thinks she's prepared, but I don't think she has a clue what it's going to be like."

"Well, you better find a way to prepare her, or you're going to lose her, Jon." He probed his son's eyes with a very serious look.

"I know, Dad," Will said with a worried expression. "But how?"

"Talk to her. Tell her everything you know. Then ease her into it slowly. You do not want to spook her," he said as he closed his laptop and gathered the papers spread across the table.

"She's seen some of the craziness, but nothing like Hollywood, or worse, a red carpet. I think you have to experience that—the screaming and crying fans, the blinding flashes, the paparazzi—to understand what a cracked life I have."

"Not every actor has to deal with your wild circus. It will slow down someday."

"I'm actually looking forward to that day—I think."

"Save your money, because when your life slows down, so do your paychecks," his dad reminded him.

"I'm not a spender, Dad."

"Yes, you *are* pretty responsible." He stood up and walked over to the couch. "Come sit down." He patted the cushion next to him.

Will sat down and turned toward his dad, placing his arm across the back of the couch. "Even if I can prepare her, how do I keep her safe? I almost lost her this week. What if my crazy life kills her?" He pleaded for some help.

"Well, there are two philosophies right now. I have seen them both fail, though. In the first one, you do not tell the press anything. You live your life avoiding direct questions, and the paparazzi are so focused on whether you are together they can't move on to harder questions. Still, it can backfire and make the paparazzi more relentless in trying to prove what you won't admit." He met his son's eyes and continued. "In the other, you give press releases, and you deal with issues as they come up. You admit what you want in interviews, but the paparazzi still stalk you with even more intrusive questions. I don't think you can win either way, and I do not know if you can completely protect anyone— ever. Sometimes things are just out of your control. You do what you can to avoid problems, but you can't orchestrate everything, Jon."

Will looked at his dad, wishing he would have given him a better answer, something more tangible, something that would solve all his problems. He already knew these philosophies, probably better than his dad. He had been dealing ceaselessly with the press for four years now. Realizing that this was the only answer he was going to get, he pressed on.

"Dad, you know, Mom really misses you. You leave her alone too much."

"Yes, I know. It's not entirely my fault. She is always welcome to join me on location."

"She'd still be alone if you're working, whether she's physically with you or not."

He scrunched his thick eyebrows. "I'm going to take some time off here in January. Maybe we will take a trip. What do you think—Paris or Milan?"

"Better make it a secluded island resort—Caicos, maybe. She'd like that better."

"We're not you. We do not need to rent an entire island, but you're probably right about her liking it better," he admitted, patting his son on the shoulder. "So, tonight or tomorrow?"

"I don't know—sometime when I can get her alone and awake." Will chuckled nervously.

"Well, good luck, son."

"Thanks. I think I'm going to go lift some weights and grab a shower before everyone gets back. I must have lost ten pounds. My director is going to kill me, if my trainer doesn't beat him to it." Will smiled at his dad, grabbed his bag he had been dragging around the hospital, and then headed downstairs.

He had a lot of worries on his mind. He didn't know if he would ever be able to prepare Sarah without scaring her off and was more worried than ever before about keeping her safe. Having almost lost her once, he didn't see how he could ever let her out of his sight again. He really wasn't looking forward to being tortured by his trainer to gain back the weight, and he was a little nervous that Sarah wouldn't like her Christmas present.

Chapter Twenty

When Will entered the family room, the smell of cut pine assaulted his nostrils, and he took a deep breath, enjoying the pleasant burn. The large front window, blocked by the tall lit fir, bounced back bright, blinking colors, filling the room with shifting ambient light. Will had never had a real Christmas tree, and the shadows produced by the large flashing bulbs fascinated him.

David's collection of colorful German nutcrackers animated the walls of the room as the lights' strobe hit them. The wooden faces peered out from the built-in shelves with bright jewel-toned eyes like a wooden toy army. Will picked up one of the crackers, examining it more closely. It was old. It felt solid and well-constructed—not like one of those cheap ones assembled in China. Will ran his finger over the brass plate that read THE MOUSE KING and playfully opened the crowned mouse's mouth with the handle, pretending it could talk. He caught himself, looked around the room to make sure no one had spotted him talking, and set it back on the shelf.

He wandered around the room, examining the decor, wishing Sarah was awake. She had been sleeping all afternoon, and he was starting to worry that she would sleep right through dinner. Will was hoping that he could talk to Sarah tonight, since there would be fewer people in the house. Jeff and Jessica were at her grandma's house in Rochester and wouldn't be back until tomorrow morning. Will had planned out what he would say to Sarah. He had even practiced it in his head. He just needed to get her alone, and with Sarah's relatives coming to the house tomorrow for Christmas dinner, tonight would be his only opportunity.

Kate found Will in the family room as he was studying a handmade ornament from the tree. It was a two-inch-tall book bound in homemade paper. The cover of the book was titled *Santa's List* in minute gold letters. Inside, ten or so names were printed in a child's writing under the headings "Naughty" and "Nice." Will chuckled when he saw that Jeff's name was the only name listed on the "Naughty" page.

"Sarah made that when she was seven. It's one of my favorites," Kate stated as she approached. Her voice startled Will, and he froze with the decoration in his hand before turning to her.

"I can see why," Will said, hanging the ornament back on the tree. He wondered what Jeff had done to tick off a seven-year-old Sarah.

"Did you find everything you wanted this afternoon?"

"Yes. Thanks for letting me use your car. I really appreciate it." He smiled at Kate and then asked, "Do you need any help with dinner?"

"Everything is ready. I was just waiting on Sarah. Would you mind running upstairs and waking her?"

"Not at all," he answered and eagerly took off up the stairs.

He knocked softly on the door and opened it slowly. He was surprised to see her out of bed.

"I thought you were still sleeping," Will said apologetically. "Your mom asked me to fetch you for dinner."

She stood wrapped only in a towel with her back facing him, her hair damp. As she turned around, the grimace on her face told Will something was wrong.

"Are you all right? I can leave."

"No. Please stay. I need your help."

"You're in pain," Will stated, knitting his eyebrows in concern.

She nodded.

"I'll be right back."

He sprinted down the stairs and found her purse on the counter in the kitchen. Next to it sat her pain pills. He retrieved the tan prescription bottle, filled a glass with water, and headed back to Sarah's room, ignoring Kate and Lara's gaping.

When he reached the bedroom, he said, "Here," handing Sarah the bottle and then the glass.

She thanked him with her eyes as she took the medicine and, still grimacing, asked, "Will you help me get dressed? I've been trying, but I just can't do it by myself."

Will leaned back and clicked the door shut. "What do you need me to do?"

"Help me with my bra and underwear?" She looked at him anxiously. "I can't bend down. It hurts too much."

"I'm not used to putting them on you. My mind is set to work in the other direction," he admitted with a grin as he took the pair of pink lace panties from her.

She attempted a smile, but he could tell it was pained. Sarah sat on the edge of the bed as Will slipped the leg holes around her feet. He extended his hand to her and slowly, gradually, helped her back into a standing position. Then, bending down, keeping his eyes glued on her eyes, he gently pulled up her panties the rest of the way.

With sorrow dripping in his voice, he stated, "I wish I could take all your pain away."

"It helps just having you here," she whispered as she gingerly turned back toward the wall. She let go of the towel, and it dropped to the floor with a dull thud.

The sight of her practically naked backside made Will wish even more that he could take all her pain away.

"Argh," Sarah groaned, her arm trembling uncontrollably as she threaded it through the strap of the pink lace bra.

Will cringed. "Here, let me do that." Walking around her, he took the other end of the bra and tenderly eased her arm through the strap. Then he gently fitted the garment onto Sarah's breasts, being careful not to touch anywhere near her bandages, and fastened the two hooks in the back. "I think pink is my new favorite color. What's next?" he lovingly asked.

"My blouse and skirt." Her eyes flitted to the bright-red blouse and black skirt on the end of the bed.

"You're not wearing that. You'll be too uncomfortable. It's just our parents. You don't have to impress anyone." He dug through her dresser and pulled out a pair of black yoga pants and a pink T-shirt. "You'll be happier in this. No one is expecting your A-game, Sarah."

Her mouth dropped open, as if she was ready to argue, and then closed again. Will carefully helped her with the clothes, and when she was dressed, he smiled at her. "Are we ready?"

"Almost." She dragged him to the closet and pointed the best she could to a charcoal-colored sweater high on a shelf. "I'm cold. Most of my clothes are at the rental house. All that's here is stuff I don't like, but that one isn't totally awful."

"My parents aren't the fashion police. You look beautiful. It doesn't matter what you wear."

He helped her with the sweater and gently wrapped his arms around her. He kissed her cheek softly, still holding her in his arms, and she whispered, "Thanks."

He leaned down and pressed his forehead against hers. Pinning her with his glacial blue eyes, he declared in his most tender voice, "I love you, Sarah. I'll do anything for you."

Her face lit with a genuine smile. "I know."

She grabbed Will's hand, and together, they slowly negotiated each step of the staircase until they reached the main floor.

∾

Kate had made her traditional Christmas Eve dinner—Italian lasagna with garlic bread, asparagus sprigs, and a large green salad with pears and walnuts. Will declared it the best meal he had ever had and ate three helpings. Everyone was stuffed by the time the dishes were cleared, and they all sat around chatting in front of the tree, digesting their meals.

As the evening progressed, David, Kate, Zander, and Lara left for the candlelight service at Sarah's church. Sarah didn't feel up to going, and Will didn't want to leave her alone at the house.

As soon as everyone had left for church, Will gently scooped her up into his arms, saying, "Come on, we don't have much time," and he started carrying her down the stairs.

"I can walk," she proclaimed.

"Not fast enough."

They rounded the corner to the family room, and Sarah couldn't believe her eyes. The room was illuminated by at least fifty crystal candles that cluttered every flat surface. The dancing flames threw off intertwining refractions of light that shimmered on the ceiling and walls.

Sarah, overwhelmed by the beauty of the lit room, said, "Wow, I can't believe you did this. How did you pull this off?"

Will set her down on the couch and, looking at her, inches from her face, he said, "Sarah, I have many talents." He smirked playfully at her, then added in a serious tone, "I want to give you your Christmas present."

"But I don't have your present. It's back at the rental," she admitted.

"You are my present. I don't need anything else," he whispered and kissed the top of her head.

"I do have something I can give you tonight, though. Would you get my purse?"

Will rolled his eyes. "Really?" He shifted back and forth on his feet for several seconds before sprinting up the stairs. When he returned, he handed the purse to her, panting to catch his breath.

"Close your eyes," she said. "I haven't wrapped it."

His lashes fanned across his cheeks as he held out his hands in front of him.

She placed the gift in the palm of his hands. "You can open them now."

He looked down at the small booklet in his hands and, with a smile, said, "You got your passport—that's perfect."

"It's not your real present, but I thought you'd like it," she admitted.

"No, it's perfect," he said. "Thanks." He kissed her cheek and continued. "Now, for your present...You know, I was planning on giving you this on the slopes of Vail, but since we're not going to make it there, I had to improvise. I can't wait any longer to give it to you. I did what I could, but..." He reached into his back pocket for the present.

"What is this all about, Will?" she asked, looking out from under her long dark lashes. She was getting anxious with anticipation.

"Close your eyes. It's not wrapped."

She squished her eyes together and declared, "We should make this our tradition. Think about how many trees we could save."

"OK, it's our new tradition. You can open them now."

Sarah opened her eyes to see Will before her. He was on one knee with his hands extended in front of him. Cupped in his palms was a lacquered wooden box, and perched delicately in the black velvet lining was the most beautiful ring Sarah had ever seen.

"Ahh," she gasped as all the air rushed out of her lungs. She sat looking at it for several seconds in silence. Tears welled in her eyes. "It's so beautiful."

The ring had a huge square-cut diamond. *It must be four carats*, she thought. It was set distinctly in swirling white gold with two emeralds, in descending size, set asymmetrically in one side of the band.

Will pulled the ring from its protective case and caressed her left hand. Then he looked deep into her eyes and declared, "You know that I love you, Sarah. I knew you were the one meant for me before I even laid eyes on you, and I can't imagine living my life without you. Will you marry me?"

She stared at him in disbelief. "Yes, of course."

She was still stunned in the moment as Will gently slipped the ring onto the correct finger, kissed her hand, and then kissed her passionately on the lips, as if he had never kissed her before. His kiss was gentle, but oozed with more than desire, more than love. The electricity filled the room. When Will pulled back from the kiss, Sarah opened her eyes, and she swore that the candles were glowing even brighter. Maybe it wasn't the candles. Maybe it was Will.

He stared into her green eyes with a huge smile on his face. "I thought the emeralds matched your eyes. I had it designed especially for you."

"I love it. It fits perfectly. How did you get the right size?" she questioned, thinking that Jessica or her mother had to be in on it for him to get the right size and must already know that he was going to ask her.

"I measured your finger while you were sleeping," he admitted casually as he rose from his proposal stance and sat down next to her, still holding her hand.

"When I was in the hospital?" she asked, confused, knowing he had never left the hospital.

"No," he said with a slight smirk.

"When?"

"The night before I left for filming in Greece."

"Oh." She swallowed as she organized his confession in her head. "So, you've been planning this for a while, then?" she asked. "And it's not just because I almost died?"

"No, I've known you were the one since the first time we talked on the phone," Will declared.

"Wow." She paused, processing again. "That's a long time."

"Yeah," he said, penetrating her daze.

She bent in to press her lips to his, and they kissed, forgetting about the world outside as they always seemed to do when they were with each other. Will moved gingerly around her. He was keeping his hands to himself, and it was starting to annoy Sarah.

She broke off the kiss, saying, "You know you *can* touch me. I won't break."

"I don't want to hurt you," he admitted.

"Touch me!" she growled jokingly.

With his eyes locked on hers, he lifted his hand and slowly touched his finger to the tip of her nose. They both broke out laughing.

"Ow! You're not supposed to make me laugh, Will!" Sarah shrieked.

"Sorry," he said, leaning down to kiss her side sweetly. His eyes sparkling with adoration, he sat up. "This isn't exactly how I pictured proposing to you. I was going to ask you to marry me using flares on a private ski run. We were supposed to ride to the top on the lift, and all the lights would suddenly shut off. Then, when you felt all vulnerable swinging forty feet off the ground in the pitch-black, you'd look down to see 'Marry me?' lit up in the snow. I had it all arranged. This doesn't even compare to what I had in my mind. I thought about waiting, but I just couldn't."

"This was perfect, more intimate. No one knows but us. It feels right, and I'm glad you didn't wait," Sarah admitted, nuzzling next to him.

"Almost no one," he said under his breath, then kissed her left hand again. "Does your dad hate me or something?" he asked. "It's been bothering me all day. I mean, he has no problem with Jessica sleeping over every other night in Jeff's room, but I go upstairs with you, and he's knocking on the door after ten minutes. Like I would try something right after you get home from the hospital. He must not have a very high opinion of me."

"I *am* his daughter."

"I thought Jessica was like a daughter to him."

"She was until she started dating Jeff. Now she's an in-law," Sarah admitted.

"Double standard?"

"It's not a perfect world."

"I would have asked him for your hand, but I was afraid he would say no, and if he had, it wouldn't have stopped me from asking you, so what's the point?" He chuckled. "How do you think your parents will react?" he said, pointing to her ring.

"I don't know. I'm only twenty-one, and before the accident, they thought we had broken up. I haven't had a chance to talk to them about us yet, but they usually support my decisions—at least to my face. We can find out what they really think in a week from Jess and Jeff. What about your parents?"

"My parents will be happy to hear that you said yes. They already know about the ring. My mom told me where I could buy the candles this afternoon. I had to go to three different stores to find enough," he admitted. "I explained our relationship to your parents while you were in the hospital. I think they can see how much we care about each other, but they might have a problem with you moving to LA."

"Wow, I can't believe I'm moving to LA. That just sounds so wild. I know we've talked about it, but to actually move will be surreal."

"I can't wait," he whispered as he began kissing her right below her earlobe.

"Keep doing that. All my pain is gone when you do that," she uttered, enjoying the feel of his lips on her skin. "I love you, Jonathan Williams," she softly added.

Will kept Sarah's pain away for several minutes before pulling back and saying, "I love you too, future Mrs. Williams."

"That sounds so weird. But I like it."

"So you'll change your name?" he asked, wide-eyed. "I know it sounds old-fashioned, but I want you to take my name with no hyphen. To me, it means that you're committed to being together forever. Will you take my name, Sarah?"

"If it means that much to you, I will," she vowed. "That's what everyone will call me anyway." She didn't have any strong attachments to the name Austin, and she never really wanted to hyphenate it with anything. Sarah Isabel Austin-Williams didn't sound right, anyway. "How many first names can one person have?" she thought out loud.

"Thanks," he whispered with a chuckle before he began kissing her ear. He worked his way around to her lips, and they kissed for several minutes, until they heard the garage door opening. Will anxiously looked around the room at all the glowing candles. "Should I blow them out?"

"No, leave them. They can deal. I like the candles."

Zander was talking loud and animatedly as the parents entered the house.

"Sarah? Will?" Kate called.

"Down here," Sarah yelled back.

They all slowly made their way down the stairs into the candlelit room. Sarah and Will looked over their shoulders as everyone approached from behind the couch.

"Look, Mom!" Sarah squealed excitedly, holding her left hand above her head, though not as high as she would if she weren't so sore.

"What is it, Sarah?" Kate asked, looking around the room at all the candles.

"Look!" she squealed again, waving her hand in the air. "We're engaged!"

"Oh my, it's gorgeous!" Kate took her daughter's outstretched hand and examined the ring. Tears filled her eyes. "Oh, baby, I'm so happy for you." She kissed Sarah's forehead and lovingly caressed the top of Will's head with her hand. "I've got to get my camera," she added as she scurried upstairs.

"So she said yes, huh? I tried to stall them for you," Zander admitted.

"Is that what you were doing? I couldn't understand why you felt the need to talk to every parishioner in the church. I thought maybe it was just a character flaw," David stated.

"Character flaw? I don't have any flaws." Zander chuckled, and the room filled with laughter. Zander kissed Sarah on the cheek and added in a very sincere voice, "Jon's a lucky man."

"I'm so happy for you two. I've always wanted a daughter." Lara beamed her dimpled smile at Sarah and then kissed her cheek. She turned to her son and lovingly touched his shoulder. Jon placed his hand on top of hers and grinned up at her.

"Let me see that ring, Sarah," commanded David. He scrutinized the ring on Sarah's left hand. "How did my little girl get so old?" He studied his daughter's face, then turned to Will and offered his hand. "Welcome to the family, Will, or do you prefer Jon? I don't think I've ever asked."

"Jon is probably easier, especially in public," he admitted.

When Kate returned with her arms full of cameras. She insisted that such an important event had to be documented.

"I'm wearing yoga pants, Mom. Can't we do this later?" Sarah questioned.

"It has to be as it happened. You'll appreciate it more," Kate declared as she layered Sarah's hair to cover up the stitches on her scalp and tried arranging the two into the classic poses. She snapped some pictures of Will and Sarah showing off the ring and, without prompting, assured everyone she wouldn't sell them.

They all chatted for a little while, but as the time was approaching midnight, everyone headed off to bed—everyone except Will and Sarah. They were sitting on Will's bed—the couch—and stayed awake for a couple of more hours, talking about what to do next and discussing how they would make their very different lives mesh.

Chapter Twenty-One

On Christmas Day, the house was filled with guests. Jeff and Jessica had returned from Rochester. Plus, joining Sarah's and Jon's families for a traditional Christmas dinner were David's brother, Bob; his daughter, Ronnie; her husband, Nate; and their eighteen-month-old daughter, Lilly. The dinner plans with David's relatives had been cemented long before the accident, so it wasn't too much trouble to add six extra people.

The long oak table had been elaborately set with Kate's best china and linens. The royal-blue-and-white plates rimmed with silver were perfectly placed and beautifully layered on the white damask tablecloth. The long-stemmed crystal water and wine goblets sat, filled in anticipation. Great-Grandma Hanson's silver was properly positioned, and the candles were lit. The smell of roasted ham and fresh-baked rolls filled the air as they all squished in around the adorned table.

The conversation was abuzz about the engagement. It seemed to be the only topic anyone wanted to talk about, especially Jessica.

"You've hardly spent any time together. How could you be ready to make that kind of commitment?" Jessica asked bluntly as she cut up her meat.

Sarah glanced to Will and took a small sip of her wine to gather courage. Then she dropped the bomb. "That's why we're moving in together."

Jeff looked over at his dad and, with a chuckle, said, "Whoa." That was all he said. He sat back in his chair as if waiting for the backlash to start. He didn't have to wait long. The silence lasted only several seconds before Kate started the questioning.

"You're finishing school first, right?" asked Kate. "Or is Will moving here?" She stood up and repositioned a couple of dishes around on the table. She looked like she was struggling to stay in control as she sat down and readjusted her napkin. "Because I can't believe you would quit school and not finish your degree. You only have a semester left, Sarah." She glared at her daughter.

"I'm moving to LA with Will," Sarah confessed unapologetically. "We don't have everything figured out yet, but I will finish my degree at some point."

Most of the dinner guests were eating quietly, trying to look like they weren't listening to the conversation that had taken over the space of the room. Sarah knew this would be a sticky point with her parents. Both Kate and David always stressed the importance of an education, but right now, she didn't care. Nothing was more important than being with Will.

"What does that mean, Sarah, 'at some point'? Because your mother and I didn't pay for you to go to school for three and a half years just so you could drop out right before you graduate. You're so close to finishing that it doesn't make sense to quit now. And what about graduate school?" David paused to take a breath and then rattled into his education lecture. "A person without a degree makes half as much as someone who has one. You're going to regret not finishing for the rest of your life. I'm sure Will—er, Jon—doesn't want you to quit school." He looked over at Will accusingly.

Sarah cringed at the surprised expression on Will's face. "I'll make sure she finishes her degree, David. I promise," Will stated, hardening his face.

Sarah slipped her hand into Will's hand under the table, knowing nothing he said would make a difference. It was best to let them calm down and then address the issue again, later.

"Well, good luck with that," David said caustically. "She doesn't seem to listen to reason or tell the truth since she met you."

That comment was too much for Sarah. "Dad, we can't fight it anymore. It doesn't work for us to be apart, and Will has to go back to work in a week and a half in Los Angeles. I will finish my degree. I only have six credits left, and I'll find a way to get it done. I have to talk to my faculty adviser and see what I can work out. Maybe I can write a thesis paper to get the credit or do it online and just come back to take the final. I'll have to see what my options are."

"We'll talk about this later, Sarah. Let's just enjoy dinner right now," David said, looking around the room at all the dinner guests silently staring at their plates.

The conversation started back up after a few minutes of quiet, and everyone joined in, speculating about wedding plans.

After hearing all the details of the engagement, Sarah's cousin, Ronnie, wanted to know more details about the accident. So after dinner, while the men cleaned up the meal, another Austin family tradition, Kate took out the scrapbook she and Lara had put together at the hospital. It was full of newspaper clippings, pictures of Sarah's vehicle from the police, and everything Kate had found on the Internet. The *Pioneer Press* had a full-page spread of the accident, and Sarah was visibly shaken when she read the article. She hadn't realized that someone died in the pileup.

"It wasn't your fault, Sarah," assured Lara. "Witnesses said the driver that died was the one that caused the accident. He crashed into you."

"Yeah, I remember. He slammed me into the cement barricade," she said, distracted. Sarah disappeared behind a blank expression, remembering the accident. After several seconds, she added, "Was anyone else hurt?"

"Not as seriously as you. The woman in the Suburban and the nineteen-year-old in the pickup both walked away. The family in the car that hit the pile last all went to the hospital, but only the ten-year-old had to stay overnight. The boy was fine, though—only a couple of broken bones—and he went home the next day," answered Kate.

Sarah felt some relief by this answer and returned her attention to the book. She skimmed the next couple of pages until she saw the pictures of her vehicle. "Is that my car?" she asked with alarm, staring at a photo of a red vehicle squashed beyond recognition, its roof removed.

"They used the Jaws of Life to get you out," explained Jessica. "I saw a clip of it on YouTube. Someone recorded it on their cell phone. It was surreal—kind of like your life is all the time now." She grinned at Sarah.

"You're right about that. You'll have to show me that clip," said Sarah.

As they finished looking through the scrapbook, Ronnie begged to know the details of Sarah and Will's beginnings. Sarah had told her about Will, but had never really explained how they had met. So Sarah explained an abbreviated version.

"Do you think Will would sing your birthday song for us?" Ronnie asked.

"I think he would do anything I asked right now," she admitted as she held up her pinkie finger and drew a circle around it with the index finger of her other hand. "They look like they're almost done, right?

Watch this," she whispered. "Will, would you sing my birthday song for everyone? I haven't heard you sing anything since that call from Greece, and Ronnie wants to hear the lyrics," she called over to him from the living room with a big smile.

He came out of the kitchen with a white dish towel in his hand and looked over at Sarah to assess whether she was serious. His eyes met hers, and a scowl ridge grew between his eyebrows. She looked up at him from under her lashes, and he exhaled, deflated.

With a nod of defeat, he said, "If I can borrow Jeff's guitar."

"See?" She giggled, and all the women started laughing, even Lara.

In the end, Will sang the song without complaining, and when his eyes met Sarah's during the second verse, she could feel his love for her pouring out of him. He tossed the hair out of his eyes as he strummed, and his dimple appeared on his cheek. He kept his eyes locked on her, and all she wanted was for her family to leave so she could have him all to herself. When he had finished the song, he leaned over and kissed her cheek.

"I do know other songs, but unfortunately, my contract forbids me from singing in public more than once every six months," he said with a chuckle, and everyone laughed.

Just then, Ronnie and Nate's eighteen-month-old daughter climbed onto his lap. She seemed fascinated by Will. She had been watching him intently while he sang and made her move on him as soon as he finished. He showed her how to strum the guitar while he fingered the guitar's neck. Sarah's heart melted to see how sweet he was with her, so patient and gentle. Everyone commented on it.

Lara observed her son with a smile. "He's always been irresistible to kids and dogs—oh, and women. It's like he has this inert magnetism that draws them in. But he doesn't see it."

"Wow, he's a keeper," remarked Ronnie.

"Yeah, I know," Sarah confessed with a smile.

Chapter Twenty-Two

O n Monday morning, Sarah argued with her parents—again. It was more of the same discussion from Christmas dinner, and Will tried to stay out of the conversation as much as he could. Sarah's parents made that virtually impossible, though. He ended up telling them he would reimburse them for all of Sarah's education costs when it was brought up again, but it just escalated the argument. After that, Will said very little, because he did not want to say anything he would regret. He knew from his parents' experiences that, in the world of in-laws, anything he said would be held against him, and anything Sarah said would be forgiven, so he did his best to stay quiet.

He listened while her parents reminded her that half of all marriages end in divorce and that she needed to take care of herself first. They rattled off statistics, which they had found on the Internet, about the divorce rate in Hollywood. They told her that she needed to find her own way before she could commit to someone else, because the real world did not have fairy-tale endings.

In the end, Sarah said, "This is me finding my own way. I'm an adult, and it's my decision," and it was left at that.

Later that morning, Sarah and her mother went for a follow-up visit to see Sarah's doctor. They planned to go out to lunch after the appointment and then shopping, if Sarah was feeling up to it. Will wanted Sarah to have a chance to act like a normal person before his crazy world overtook her life, so he stayed back at the house to work out. He hoped to get back on track with his training before he returned to filming.

When Sarah got back to the house after lunch and a couple of other stops, she filled in Will on what the doctor had said. Will was surprised to hear that she shouldn't do any lifting or have any physical activity for at least another three weeks, but being the talented actor that he was, he didn't let his disappointment invade his face.

She showed him her incisions, lifting her sweater and tank top as she spoke. "I'll never be able to wear a bikini again, but at least those ugly blue stitches are gone, even the ones on my scalp. The nurse took them out."

"I don't think your scars are going to be that bad. No one will know they're there but you, so don't give up your bikini," he said obstinately. He had fond memories of her in her bikini and couldn't imagine never seeing her wear one ever again. Besides, he knew that if the scars really bothered her, a plastic surgeon could probably get rid of them completely.

"Thanks, Will," she said and kissed him on the cheek. "You always know what to say."

❧

Later that afternoon, Will got a call from his publicist. He had been keeping in close touch with her during the hospital stay. He wanted her to know what was going on so she could keep the rumors to a minimum.

"Hey, Jon, how's Sarah?" Remi greeted.

"Better, thanks. So what's up?"

"I have a couple of things I wanted to talk to you about."

"Like what?"

"There are some crazy rumors out there right now. I was just wondering if there is anything you need to tell me?" she inquired.

"Crazier than usual? I can't imagine that."

"Not crazier—more believable, actually. Stop messing with me, Jon. You were spotted buying a hundred crystal candles on the twenty-fourth. What was that about?"

"Yeah, about that, I was just going to call you." He looked over at Sarah and smiled when they locked eyes. "You must have supersonic radar, Remi."

"I've been expecting your call ever since our last conversation," she admitted.

"You know, I just got the ring on her finger. We've barely told our parents. You're the first to know. I wouldn't leave you out of the loop. I haven't even told Isaac. We're still figuring everything out, so I'm not ready to go public with it yet. Besides, I'm still under contract with *The Demigod* promotion."

"I wouldn't worry about the studio so much. You know how dramatic Isaac can be. I had lunch with Darin Schwartz last week, and he didn't seem to have any concerns about your personal life as long as you're not doing something scandalous. They're not going to create problems with their biggest star over something that's just going to bring positive attention to the film."

"Well, that's good news," Will noted. "You know, I think Isaac wants me to stay single so he can keep finding me man-whore and superhero parts. I want to try a more serious role next."

"Can I be there when you tell him? I like to see him squirm," Remi confessed in a conniving voice.

"Sure. We can do a conference call. I don't want to tell him in person," he said with a chuckle. "I tried to talk to him about it last week and he acted like he would have me committed to a rehab center if it ever actually happened."

"Getting married will definitely change your image, and that may affect the movies you're offered. I've seen careers come to a halt when the actor gets hitched. Are you sure you want to do this?"

"Yes!" he exclaimed. "We'll just take it as it comes, I guess."

"It should slow your fanatical fans down a bit—at least after the news blows over—but it might be a little hateful for a while. You may need extra security until the fans accept the idea of you having a personal life that doesn't involve them. I still don't think the public wants to see you with someone not in the business."

"I'll talk to Sam and beef up security."

"I guess I need to congratulate you, you super-sexy, off-the-market man. When do I get to meet her?"

He chuckled. "I'll let you know when we get back into town—a couple of days?"

"Set a date yet?"

"No, I want to ease her into the lion's den slowly to give her a chance to back out." He looked lovingly at Sarah.

Sarah squinted her eyes and yelled across the room. "I'm not backing out!"

"So you think she'll back out?" Remi asked.

"Nah, she's tough. She better not," he admitted as he raised his eyebrows and looked over at Sarah again questioningly.

"Well, I can't wait to meet the girl who can keep you in line. Oh, one more thing, Paris Borel from Celeblife has been trying to get ahold of you. Normally, I wouldn't bug you with it, but I know you connect with her once in a while, and she was pretty persistent. She said you'd know what it was about," Remi added.

"I've got her number. I'll give her a call," Will said. "So no press releases for now, right?"

"Your call, but award season starts in January. It's going to come up on the red carpet."

"Wait, I know I haven't been nominated. I'm not scheduled to present, am I?" he questioned. "We're still filming."

"We can talk about it in a couple of days. Enjoy your time off, Jon, and keep that ring hidden. It will need its own coming-out party," she said.

"We'll keep the ring under wraps, but seriously, what have you got?"

"The big one—with the golden man."

"I'm surprised they're inviting me back, after what happened last year. Remember the prompter went out and I had to ad-lib?"

"What are you talking about? You were adorable. That's why they want you back," she countered. "You perform well under pressure."

He feigned a cough, scoffing at her words. "So what am I promoting, anyway?"

"Besides yourself? *Demigod Forbidden*, of course. But I heard that *Third Rung* might get picked up at Cannes. You knew that, right?"

"Yeah," he admitted. "I was actually hoping that one would never make it to the theaters. I filmed it four years ago. That whole year after Jack's death was pretty dark. It seems like a lifetime ago."

"I heard the film was good. Have you seen the final cut?" she asked.

"No."

"Well, it has to be good to be considered at Cannes, and it's never too late to sell a movie, especially with a big star like you attached," boasted Remi.

"If it does get picked up, Sarah is definitely coming with me to the South of France."

"So, do you think Sarah will be ready for the red carpet by the end of February?"

"Hell, I don't know if *I'll* be ready, but we'll figure it out."

He looked at Sarah, wondering how he was going to prepare her for the red carpet by February, and unsure whether he should put her through that torture at all. Most of all, he didn't know how he was going to keep her safe. Once they announced their engagement, it would be utter chaos. He also didn't know what Paris wanted, but whatever it was, he was sure it was not good and would complicate his life even more.

Chapter Twenty-Three

Later that same evening, Will made the dreaded call to Paris. He knew that this day would come. He had just been hoping that it wouldn't be so soon.

"Paris, it's Jonathan Williams. Remi said you've been trying to get ahold of me?" He held the phone away from his ear so he wouldn't accidentally end the call.

"Good to hear from you, Jon. How was your Christmas?" Paris asked.

"Great. And yours?" he responded automatically.

"Fine—busy, though. So I've been hearing some engagement rumors, Jon. Any truth to them?"

"I'm not surprised. I'm always engaged to someone in the rags. Where did you hear about it this time?" he asked, not wanting to answer the question.

"Blogging fans, mostly. A couple of different fans spotted you at a posh jewelry store just before Christmas, and there have been all kinds of sightings of you in the Midwest with some girl named Sarah."

"And you believe the bloggers? Wow, I didn't realize you were so gullible," he said, doing his best not to lie.

"You would be amazed at what you can find out from the bloggers. I went through some old blogs over the holidays and was flabbergasted at what they revealed."

"Really? Like what?" he asked smoothly, without emotion.

"You met her on my website, Jon. I went through the old blog threads. Her name is Sarah—the same as the girl in the blog. I gave you her e-mail address, for God's sakes."

"What do you want from me, Paris?" Will said, clearly irritated.

"I want an interview."

"You're talking to me now. Why do you need an interview?" he asked.

"Well, I like to post the truth, and I want it from the source. I've got all those blog threads, but they're dated, and my followers prefer current news. Although, I think they would be interested in your relationship's beginnings," Paris stated.

"You want our firstborn child too?" Will mumbled under his breath.

"You dirty dog, is she pregnant?"

"No, she is not pregnant!"

"Come on. I introduced you. You owe me, remember?"

"I'll have to talk to Remi. She'll have to put her seal of approval on it, and I have some conditions." He had been contemplating this situation for a while now and knew what he needed to do.

"I'm intrigued. What conditions?"

"I need you to delete the old blog threads with Sarah's name that you're referring to."

"So you admit it's her?"

"No, but if you delete the threads, you can have an interview."

"With both of you? I just want to see what kind of woman actually interests you, Jon."

His heart sank, knowing he had to make this work with Paris and knowing, if he involved Sarah, there would be no going back. He paused for a few seconds, then said, "Hold on."

He held his hand over the phone's mouthpiece.

"Sarah, do you want to do an interview with me?" he asked as he flashed his big pale-blue eyes up at her from across the room.

Sarah was sitting on the couch writing in her journal. She shrugged her shoulders gently.

He took his hand off the mouthpiece. "All right. Only because we're friends, Paris. But delete the threads first."

"They're so old no one even knows they're there."

"Someone might slip up someday and publish them, just by accident. I want them wiped. You completely get rid of them, and I will give you the best interview ever. And you can be our first interview. You can't beat that."

"OK, Jon. You know I'd do anything for you," she declared.

"I'll have Remi call you to set it up, and I'm sure she'll have some paperwork for you too." He knew Remi would make sure all the legal contracts needed to ensure the blog threads were erased were signed before allowing an interview.

"Talk to you again soon," she said.

Will hung up the phone and glanced across the room at his fiancée. He twisted his face with concern. Did she really understand what she would be facing marrying him?

"It's starting. So are you ready for this, beautiful?" he asked as he planted himself next to her on the couch.

She closed her journal, locked eyes with him, and said, "Bring it."

"No, I mean, are you *really* ready for this?"

"I think so." She looked at him skeptically.

"There is a ton of crap that we need to do before we announce the engagement."

"Like what?" Sarah asked, wide-eyed.

"To begin, you need to make a list of the people in your life that you can trust—I mean, really trust—not to go to the press with tidbits of our personal life. I can guarantee that one of your friends or a relative will contact the tabloids to sell them personal information about you. They'll make up stories about you and pass it off as inside information. You need to cut ties with anyone not on your most trusted list. Are you willing to do that?"

"You make it sound like I'm joining the Witness Protection Program," she said, cocking her head.

"It seems like that sometimes. You won't know who to trust. People will crawl out of the sewer and claim to be your best friend. Every unflattering picture of you growing up will resurface. The tabloids will contact your third grade teacher, your cousin Ronnie, your ex-boyfriends..." He trailed off, raising his eyebrows.

"Ronnie is on my list, but the rest sound awful."

"The next thing you know, your aunt Zelda is selling our Christmas picture to the tabloids and she swears someone stole it from her."

"I don't have an aunt Zelda."

"It's just an example. The point is that you have to eliminate people you can't trust from your life."

"So what does it matter if Aunt Zelda sells our Christmas picture to the tabloids? How is that really going to hurt us?"

"What if it's a picture of our newborn daughter that Zelda is selling?" He looked at her questioningly. "She gets ten thousand dollars, and our daughter's picture is plastered all over the supermarket shelves."

"So you want babies, huh?" she asked with a smirk.

"Yeah, I want babies." Will beamed back at her. "But do you understand what I'm saying?"

"I get it, but it's not like we have to cut everyone out completely. We just have to be really careful when we're around people not in our inner circle, right?"

"Sarah, you can't trust anyone. Do you remember that little blonde nurse that helped us escape from the hospital?"

She nodded. "Yeah, she was great."

"Yesterday, she tweeted that I was complaining about how you were dressed and that I planned to take you shopping to buy you better clothes. She said I couldn't keep my hands off you. I don't remember even holding your hand in front of her. It had to be her. No one else was near us when I was teasing you about that jacket."

"Seriously? She seemed so nice. What a liar!" Sarah fumed. "That's not what happened at all, and you've barely touched me since the accident."

He wrinkled his nose at her last comment, but he continued. "You're always on show. It's really tedious and can get a bit lonely. Someone always wants something from you, and no matter what you give, it's never enough. I could give them every stitch of clothing off my back, and they would still ask me to shave my head so they could have my hair."

She reached up and ran her fingers through his hair with a pouty lip.

"You have to get off all those social network sites too. They're not safe. They get hacked all the time." He looked apologetically at her. He knew this would be hard for her. "It's not going to be pleasant, Sarah. The tabloids will lie about you. As soon as we announce our engagement, they'll say you're pregnant. They'll manipulate pictures to make it look like you have a baby bump, and strangers will come up to you, touching your belly, congratulating you on your pregnancy." He playfully touched her stomach. "They'll say you're too skinny and too fat, all in the same week. I just want you to be prepared. They would be even more critical if you were in the business, but it will still be pretty bad. Are you ready to live in a fishbowl with the world watching everything you do?"

"You're worth it, Will."

He flinched at her words, not believing he was worth it. It was a lot for her to give up, and he knew that. He hoped that she was being honest with herself, that she could deal with his crazy life.

Then he smiled at her and added, "I'd like you to take a media training class. I know it sounds lame, but it does help—and defensive driving."

"Whatever you need me to do."

"Sarah, you don't have any sex tapes or nude pictures I should know about, do you?"

"Hmm, let me think." She scrunched her face as if concentrating hard. "*No!*" she said as she hit his shoulder with a pillow off the couch, using as much force as she could muster without hurting herself.

"That didn't even hurt. You're going to have to start lifting weights with me," he said mockingly. "So, no skeletons in your closet? Be honest. It's better to know what to expect up front. I won't judge."

"I told you about Matt."

"No pictures?"

"No!"

"That's not scandalous. He's an idiot for not realizing what he was giving up by cheating on you." He wrapped his arm around her, and she leaned her head against his shoulder.

She turned to look at Will as if contemplating for a minute whether she should tell him something. Her emerald eyes couldn't hide her secret.

"What is it, Sarah? What aren't you telling me?"

"It's nothing. I just don't want to deal with Matt's lies again," she said, looking down at her journal, away from his gaze.

He knew she was lying. There was something that she had left out. He grasped her face in his hands and lifted her chin until her eyes fluttered open to meet his. "You know I love you, and you can tell me anything, right?"

She blinked her eyes slowly and nodded. He wondered what kind of skeletons she could have hidden. It didn't matter, though. They could never be as bad as his. He kissed her softly on the lips and decided she would tell him when she was ready. He could wait.

Chapter Twenty-Four

The chaos started as they landed in Los Angeles. The paparazzi were waiting when they got off the plane. Sarah had taken off her ring before they left Minneapolis to avoid the obvious questions. Will knew that photographers always roamed the LAX airport seeking celebrities, so he wasn't surprised at first when he and Sarah were found.

"Just keep your head down and follow me," Will instructed. He didn't want to give the paparazzi any good pictures to sell. "Stick close, or they'll separate us."

At first, it was just a lone photographer who didn't even ask questions as he snapped pictures, and then it quickly grew into a mob as Will navigated their way through the airport. Soon Sarah started to lag behind him. She wasn't used to walking so fast and still wasn't up to her normal speed after the accident. Will had been checking over his shoulder frequently as they walked and reacted quickly when he noticed her falling behind. He knew what he was about to do would just add fuel to the fire, but he had to do it. He stopped, reaching back for her hand, and as their eyes met, he smiled encouragingly. The camera flashes exploded like popcorn in a fire.

Will looked back. Sarah was ashen, not her normal pale, and he worried she wouldn't make it to the car. He gripped her hand tighter and smiled again, trying to reassure her. They were almost to the curb, and he could see their liberator, his assistant, outside her forest green sedan with the trunk open. Leslie saw them, opened the backseat door, and jumped into the driver's seat. Will moved quickly. He helped Sarah into the car and closed the door behind her. He dumped the bags into the trunk and then joined her in the backseat on the other side. Within seconds, the car sped away from the curb, leaving the photographers behind in a mass on the sidewalk.

"Thanks, Leslie. Perfect timing as usual," Will said as he wrapped his arm around Sarah and settled back in the seat. He introduced her to his assistant and then asked, "Are you all right, Sarah? You don't usually look quite so gray."

"Yeah, I'm fine. I think I should have taken some pain medicine before I left, though. Is it always like that?" She rubbed her cheek. "Someone hit me in the face with a camera lens."

"Oh, I didn't even see that. I would have taken him out," Will declared.

"No. It was an accident. I'm fine."

"It's not usually that bad. There must be something going on in town tonight," he said. Realizing that he should have had Sam or another bodyguard traveling with them, he whispered to himself, "What was I thinking?"

Sarah looked at him questioningly. He shook his head as if it was nothing. He didn't want her to know he was freaking out inside. He had wanted to ease her in slowly, not like this.

"They're at the airport for all the holiday travelers, and there's also a huge charity event at the Nokia tonight that a lot of people are coming in for," Leslie stated. "We're going back to the house—no stops, right?"

"Yeah, I think we've had enough excitement," he admitted. "I just want Sarah to get settled today." He had no desire to go anywhere but to the safety of home.

Forty minutes later, Leslie pulled the car up to the gate and punched the code into the pad. As the black metal gate slid open, Sarah looked at Will.

"This is where you grew up? It's huge." She scanned her surroundings, gaping at the colossal Tuscan-style estate. The grounds were meticulously maintained, with giant palm trees, and there was obviously a staff just to take care of the outside of the house.

"Actually, the main house isn't that big by West Coast standards, but this is our place here. It's tiny." He pointed to a smaller house as they drove down a narrow drive behind the main house's garage. The main house was U-shaped, around a center courtyard. The guesthouse was at the back end of the courtyard and connected to the main house with a veranda-style walkway. "And, yes, I do pay rent," he added.

"I know. You told me that already." She looked at him questioningly. "Why does that bother you so much?"

"Liam and Chris are always giving me crap that I still live at home and I make more money than my parents. I haven't needed much in the past, but maybe you and I can find our own place."

"Don't rush into anything for me, OK? I think we have enough to do without looking for a new place to live."

"All right—for now."

The wooden garage door lifted, and Leslie parked her sedan in the empty space next to Will's dark metallic-colored BMW. When they reached the entrance to the house, Will pulled down the handle and propped himself against the door so Sarah could squeeze past him. She set her computer bag on the stone floor and looked around the dark kitchen, not really knowing what to expect.

Will flipped on the lights and stood behind her, placing his hands on her shoulders. "So this is our place, for now. I'm glad you're finally here." Then he walked over to the cupboard, reached up, and opened it to take out a glass. "Glasses are in here. You'll have to explore the kitchen if you're going to share in the cooking. There are only so many meals I know how to make. I'm sure you'll get bored fast."

He pushed the tall green glass against the dispenser on the fridge door until water brimmed at the top, and then he handed it to Sarah. Smiling at him, she set the glass on the counter and took out her prescription bottle. Once she had taken her pills, she glanced around the kitchen again.

It was a decent-sized room—not as big as her parents' kitchen, but plenty big for two. It had a dark wooden table that could seat four, and french doors that opened out into the courtyard. The cabinets were glossy white, with light-colored granite countertops, and there was a center island with a sink for washing vegetables. The walls above the counters were tiled with light-colored stone rectangles, and in muted tones, there was a mosaic picture of a sunset above the stove.

Will showed Sarah around the rest of the house, which wasn't nearly as small as he'd described. Besides the kitchen, the house had two bedrooms, two bathrooms, and an office. The master bedroom had a large four-poster king-sized bed and a small sitting area with a love seat. Above the bed hung a large brightly colored abstract oil painting with a white frame that coordinated with the fluffy white comforter. The master bath boasted a large soaking tub, a separate shower, and a large walk-in closet with shelves along one side. Sarah was amazed at how many vintage T-shirts Will actually owned. They were all neatly folded in color-coordinated stacks that took up most of the shelves in the closet. The bedroom was just as Will had described, and Sarah felt at home already as she searched for more insight into Will's world.

The second bedroom was more of a music room than a place to sleep. Its C-shaped, mustard-colored leather sofa filled the length of the wall farthest from the door as it hugged the coordinating upholstered ottoman. There was no bed. The long wall opposite the windows was arranged with seven hanging guitars of various shapes and colors— three electric and four acoustic. There were several black metal music stands and two large amplifiers pushed up against the wall by the door. The center of the room was void of any gear or furniture, and it looked like it was a place to stage more equipment. Sarah was excited when she saw the room. She couldn't wait to hear Will play again.

He showed her the office, and she was surprised at how disorganized the room looked compared to the rest of the house. Brown corrugated boxes were stacked three high and ten across. They were all different sizes, and they covered the wall behind the desk. Some of the boxes were open, with various items spewing out of the tops, and some were still sealed with tape.

"What is all that?" Sarah asked, pointing to the half-open boxes.

"Swag. You know, the junk that people send me hoping that I'll wear it out in public or use it and mention it in the press. There is all kinds of crap here—sunglasses, running shoes, clothes, body wash. They're just hoping I'll give them free advertising.

"I heard that the jacket I wore to the Teen FAV Awards sold out of stores the day after I wore it. I don't know. I can't imagine that I really influence anyone, but it's not like I ask them to send me the stuff. It just keeps coming, and I try to give it away when I can't use it, but it piles up. I rarely have to buy clothes anymore. All I have to do is mention I like a designer, and the next thing I know, it's in my closet. That's one of the benefits, I guess.

"After we announce our engagement, they'll start sending you stuff too. You'll see." He pointed to a large overflowing basket on the floor next to the desk. "That pile is junk my fans have handed me. It's crazy all the different stuff people give me." He bent down and picked up a heart-shaped pillow with his face hand-embroidered on it. He showed it to Sarah and rolled his eyes. "I have a hard time throwing it away. A lot of it is homemade. It's not all swag and gifts, though. A couple of the boxes are promotional items from *The Demigod.*"

"Really? Promotional merchandise? Do you have any action figures?" she asked with excitement.

"There are a few. Why?"

"I had one. Jessica got it for me so I wouldn't miss you so much, but I couldn't find it when I was packing up my stuff. I didn't mention it before because I didn't want to sound pathetic." She smiled at him apologetically. "My roommates used to hide him around the rental house. They made a game out of it. I was always looking for him. I found him in all kinds of places—the refrigerator eating leftovers, on the windowsill watching the raindrops, and in the shower just keeping an eye on everyone. He was quite active."

"How did you know what he was doing? He didn't talk to you, did he?"

"No, he had his own Connect.Me account like the gnome in that commercial. I had to log on just to find out where he was sometimes, and there was always an elaborate story about what he had been doing. I have a feeling the girls kept him so they could keep his adventures going."

Will reached into a box, pulled out a nine-inch action figure, and handed it to her. "I think I'm jealous," he admitted, running his hand through his hair.

"Don't be. Now that I have the real thing, he just reminds me of my roommates."

Will studied her face, and she smiled widely to reassure him. She knew he felt guilty for taking her away from her friends. She wanted this. She had no regrets. There was no reason for guilt.

They made their way back to the living room, with Sarah carrying her doll, and she asked, "Your mom helped decorate in here, right?"

"She pretty much decorated most of the house. How could you tell?"

"The monster head." On the wall above the fireplace hung a four-foot-wide green animatronic monster head with big round, bulbous eyes and stubby arms with three long clawed fingers on each hand. It looked like it was coming out of the wall.

"He's mine. I told you about Pedro."

"This is Pedro? I guess I didn't realize he was so...big."

"Wait. You have to see this." He reached for the light switch. "His eyes move. They follow you around with motion sensors. It's great for parties. He's from an old movie set. He doesn't freak you out, does he?"

"No, I think we're going to be good friends." She touched Pedro's rubbery skin and his eyes creepily moved to her. "Do you have any more special effects?"

"I have a few things on the bookshelves in the office, but the main house is full of them. We can watch a movie in my dad's viewing room later, and I'll show you around."

"Can you show me now?" she asked, excited to finally piece together all the stories Will had told her.

"Let's just stay inside and wait for the rest of your luggage. The paparazzi will be waiting outside the gate to snap pictures for a while, anyway. They're probably climbing the wall as I speak."

"You're not that special, Will. Why would they—"

He interrupted her words by leaning down and pressing his lips to hers. When he broke off the kiss, he said, "You're right. I'm not that special. It's your picture they want." His eyes sparkled with adoration as he leaned in to kiss her again.

"And as much as I love to hear you call me Will, now that you're here, you may need to start calling me Jon." He ran his fingers through her hair indulgently and whispered in her ear. "Except in bed."

A shiver ran down her spine.

"It will make life easier." He pulled back and smiled brightly. "Very few know me by that name."

"I'll try, but no promises, Will—er, Jon." She said "Jon" dramatically slow, as if she was trying out his name for the first time. She suppressed a smile and kissed his ear.

It wasn't long before Sarah's luggage arrived—three big suitcases. She had packed what she could. She knew she would have to take a road trip at some point to get the rest moved, and her parents promised to store what she wasn't able to take. Sarah, Will, and Leslie spent what was left of the day emptying Sarah's bags. Leslie helped her find a place for most of the clothes and promised to pick up some more hangers the next time she was out. While they all worked together to get her treasures put away in the house, Sarah questioned Jon about Leslie.

"Why haven't you ever gone out with Leslie? I mean, she's amazing," Sarah asked, then smiled hugely at Leslie. She had wondered about her many times before, but Will never showed the slightest interest in her—that Sarah could see, anyway.

"She is amazing, isn't she? Wow, I can't believe I never told you about Leslie and me." He smirked with a playful expression.

Sarah looked at him questioningly, a little worried that she might not want to know what he was going to say.

"There was a time in my life when I was convinced I was going to marry her." Will smiled at Sarah as he wrapped his arm around Leslie and mussed her hair. "I was devastated when my dreams were shattered."

"You touch my hair again, and you're dead, Mr. Williams," Leslie warned, twisting his name as she extricated herself from his grasp.

"I was." He looked back at her with a hurt expression. "I cried for days."

Leslie rolled her eyes.

"I know we were only five, but it still hurt. I couldn't believe it when my mom told me cousins weren't allowed to marry. She and Aunt Catherine were pretty adamant about it. I don't know what it's like in Minnesota, but apparently, there are laws in California that forbid that." He chuckled.

"Why didn't you tell me she was your cousin?" asked Sarah.

"Leslie doesn't like to talk about it. I think she's embarrassed by me. I always laugh when the paparazzi catch us out together and write a big article about me being spotted with a gorgeous blonde. They're so clueless."

After Sarah had gotten settled, they visited with Zander and Lara for a while before watching a movie that Zander suggested. Sarah was relaxed and just happy to be with Will. She didn't have any grand expectations about what was going to happen now that she was in Los Angeles. She knew she had a little money saved from working at the clinic, and she had the insurance money from the accident if she really needed anything. It would last her a little while. But she still needed to buy a car, and she wasn't going to let Jon pay for it, so she would have to be frugal.

⟨∽◯

On New Year's Eve, Will and Sarah went to a party at Will's friend Chris's house. There were quite a few people at the small house in the Valley, and Will enjoyed introducing Sarah to all his friends. The party was a tradition with his buddies, and they all worked hard to make it there every year. Nick and Hayden were both present, and Sarah enjoyed reminiscing with them about their part in getting her and Will together. Nick asked when her girlfriends would be visiting and joked about rearranging his schedule so he could get to know them better.

Sarah teased Nick for calling her a troll in his text to Will the night of the concert.

"Oh, I can't believe he shared that." He glared at Will across the room. "I just wanted you for myself." He feigned stretching and slowly draped his arm around her waist, drawing her in as he continued to stare, challenging Will.

Sarah glanced up and met Will's eyes. Her wary expression motivated him to cross the room quickly.

"I believe this one is mine, Nick." Will wore a ghost of a smile as he wrapped his arm around Sarah's waist and lovingly pried her away from him.

"I don't see your name on her."

Will smirked, cocked his head, and pointed to her left hand.

"Oh, I didn't notice that."

"You didn't see that?" Hayden questioned, snatching Sarah's hand and holding it in front of Nick's face. He let go and shook his head in disbelief. "It's not that you didn't see it. It's that you just don't care."

Nick shrugged his shoulders. "You used to be better at sharing, mate."

Will turned, crouched to her level, and looked directly into Sarah's eyes. "I have never shared a girl." Then, glaring at Nick, he chuckled. "Don't start rumors!"

"There was that one girl from the party Liam had when his parents went to Milan sophomore year," Hayden divulged, seemingly eager to share information.

"What girl? I never dated her!" Will pointed a finger at Hayden and gave him a death glare.

"Yeah, but you got to second base—or was it third?—at the party." He met Will's eyes with a sarcastic *Oh, I'm scared* look, disregarding his warning. "And Nick ended up dating her—for a couple of months, anyway."

"I remember her. You can't blame us. She was quite fit, and her tits were fantastic," Nick added, cupping his hands in front of his chest. "Breast man, I am," He reached out and squeezed Will's chest with one of his cupped hands. "You been working out, mate?" he asked with a chuckle.

Will scowled at Nick and lifted his arm, breaking Nick's grasp.

"She doesn't count. We were sixteen. I'm not the same person I was then." He continued to glare at Hayden. "Come on, guys, Sarah doesn't want to hear about ancient history."

"Yes, I do—as long as it's ancient," she professed with a grin.

"Don't worry, Sarah. Will flirts, but he's all talk. He really is a one-woman kind of guy, and he's yakked of no one but you since he met you. I have a hundred stories I could tell you, though, if you're interested," confessed Hayden.

Sarah enjoyed hearing stories about Jon growing up, and she reveled in the fact that most of the people at the party called him Will. It tickled her for some reason. Sarah really liked getting to know his friends. They were all so different, yet all seemed very genuine. That was the part she liked the most. She felt as if they were people she could trust in a place where she wasn't supposed to trust anyone.

Chapter Twenty-Five

Three days later, Will and Sarah were scheduled to meet with Paris for the dreaded interview. Even though Will didn't like the means that had led to it, the blog threads had been deleted, and he felt it was going to be a good day. The paparazzi were nowhere to be seen when they left the house, and that added to his breezy mood. Sarah was wearing her engagement ring, and she looked so beautiful in the snugly fitted minidress that Leslie had picked up. He was having a hard time keeping his hands to himself as they made their way to the hotel to meet Paris.

"We could just get a room and skip the interview," he said with a huge smile as they got out of his car in the hotel garage. He was excited to come out about the engagement, almost giddy. There had been so much misinformation in the press that he felt a sense of relief to finally share the truth.

Sarah was quieter than usual. Will thought she was probably just nervous about her first interview. She hadn't had her media training class yet, but he would be with her, so he was confident that it would go well.

Paris's room was a standard suite, the kind that Will had been to dozens of times for previous interviews. He leaned in, giving Paris a peck on the cheek, as he often did when he greeted women he knew. Then he introduced Sarah to the tall blonde. Paris welcomed them inside and froze for a second, shaking her head in disbelief as she spotted Sarah's ring.

"That's quite a ring there." Paris gawked, reaching for Sarah's hand and examining the ring.

Sarah just smiled and said, "Thank you."

Knowing that Paris would dive right into the heart of the interview if she could, Will reminded her, "We're going to have to wait until Remi gets here to start the interview. She's running a few minutes late but should be here shortly."

"That's OK. We can get comfortable while we're waiting. Would you like a mixed drink or a beer?" Paris offered. She directed them to a love seat where the video camera poised on a tripod could capture the interview.

"Sarah?" Will asked, admiring how beautiful she looked as they sat down.

"No, I better not. A pop, I mean, a Coke—would be great," Sarah answered.

Will chuckled softly. He adored her Minnesotan accent. It wasn't always there, but every once in a while, he would catch a glimpse of it. And if he asked her about it, she would deny she had an accent at all. "A Coke sounds good to me too."

"You better not? Are you sure that there isn't something to the pregnancy rumors?" asked Paris.

"No, Paris. Look at her. There are no pregnancy rumors. She was in a car accident and is still on medication. That's why she shouldn't drink."

Will knew he would probably mention the car accident at some point during the interview, so he didn't feel like he was giving anything away.

While Paris got their drinks, Sarah stared wide-eyed at the camera.

"That won't be turned on until the interview," Will said. He wanted to help Sarah relax, so he grabbed her hand and squeezed it gently as he looked tenderly into her eyes, trying to calm her. He could tell she was nervous. He wanted her to unwind and enjoy herself. After all, Paris wasn't really that bad. She had always stuck up for him in the past. This interview would be easy.

Just then, his phone vibrated. He checked it, thinking that it was probably Remi letting them know she had arrived.

"Oh, I've got to take this. It's my production manager for *The Demigod*. We've been playing phone tag for a week." He rose from the sofa and stepped out onto the balcony to get some privacy. Thirty seconds later, he returned.

"I've got to run to the car really quick. It might be ten minutes or so. Is that OK?" He looked at Sarah apologetically, and she nodded, but her eyes were wide with apprehension.

"No questions. The interview doesn't start until Remi gets here," he added just before the door clicked behind him.

◦◦◦

Sarah sat quietly for a few minutes until Paris brought her a tall glass of Coke with ice. Sitting down on the chair next to the couch, Paris immediately pounced on her with questions.

"So, Sarah, are you even old enough to drink alcohol?"

"Yes." She chuckled nervously. "I'm twenty-one," she answered, wishing Will hadn't abandoned her with this woman.

"You're pretty young to move so far away from home—to such a harsh environment as Hollywood. It's not really fair for Jonathan to ask so much of you. You've got to miss your family, your friends." Paris paused with a scripted look of concern. "You'll never find people who really care about you in Tinseltown. The best you'll ever be is arm candy."

Sarah didn't hear a question in Paris's statement, so she smiled, sipped her Coke, and shrugged. Paris fidgeted uncomfortably, and Sarah could tell she wasn't satisfied with the reaction she was getting.

"Do you really think you're good enough for him? I mean, he's a megastar, and what are you, some little college student from nowhere?" she asked nonchalantly.

Sarah stared at her in disbelief for several seconds. She was so shocked that she wasn't sure if she had heard her correctly, and she definitely didn't know how to respond. She wanted to say something sarcastic, but didn't want to come off as a bitch in her first interview. She didn't know if Paris was just trying to get a reaction from her, like the paparazzi, or if she was serious, so she sipped her Coke until the ice clattered to the bottom of the glass, hoping Jon would be back soon.

"You're never going to be enough for him. He doesn't stay with anyone very long. You have to see that you'll never be able to hold his attention. He's going to get bored and move on. I've seen it a hundred times. You seem like a nice girl, Sarah. I just want to warn you so you can go back home before you're all used up and tossed aside. Hollywood is brutal."

Sarah, stunned by Paris's words, rose from the couch. "I'm going to go find Jon."

Twenty minutes later, Will tapped on the suite door. "Sorry it took so long. It was only supposed to take a minute. Remi will be here any second now. She just sent me a text." He looked around the suite, confused. "Where's Sarah?"

"Didn't she catch up to you? She left shortly after you. She seemed upset about something," Paris admitted with a glossy smile. "You know how young girls are. They don't possess the prudence to cope with problems as they arise like mature women do. Why don't you sit down and have a drink with me? I'm sure she'll be back."

"What did you say to her, Paris?" Will questioned.

"Nothing, just small talk."

"I'm going to find her," he said as he opened the door and jogged toward the elevator. He thought maybe she had gotten upset about him taking so long. It wasn't like her, but it could happen.

Once in the elevator, Will took out his phone and sent Sarah a text: *Sorry I took so long. Where r u?*

She usually responded quickly, but he still hadn't gotten a response by the time he made it to the lobby, so he waited a few more seconds outside the elevator, thinking maybe there was bad reception. He looked around in the lobby and didn't see any sign of her. He asked the woman at the front desk, the concierge, and several random people he ran across in the lobby if they had seen her. He even showed them a picture of her on his phone, hoping to jog their memories, but no one remembered seeing her. He didn't want to make a spectacle of himself, but he needed to find her.

Will was starting to panic, anticipating the worst. He sprinted down the stairs three at a time to the car in the parking garage. He scanned the garage, and there was still no sign of her. He knew he wouldn't have missed her if she had made it to the garage, so he raced back up to the lobby.

With trembling hands, he sent another text: *Sarah, where r u? I need to know u r safe.*

This time, he got a response: *I can't do this, Jon. I'm going back to Minnesota. Please don't come after me. I will call you when I'm ready to talk.*

Will flipped his phone over, checking to see if it was really his. *This is ridiculous,* he thought. What could have happened to spook her so badly? He racked his brain trying to make sense of her actions and decided that the accumulation of all that had transpired since they met was definitely enough to make any normal person run in terror. But he still couldn't believe that she would leave without talking about it—unless she was so upset that she wouldn't talk to anyone. He had seen that before. His mind kept racing in circles. Will just couldn't make sense of anything.

"Screw that." He made his way to the hotel bar. She couldn't have gotten far. He scanned the mostly empty bar for Sarah, hoping she hadn't left the building yet, but she wasn't there, either. He tried calling her, but she didn't answer. Will made it back to the lobby. Breathing shallow, erratic breaths, he tried to think about what he should do next. He brought his hand to his forehead and squished his eyes together, demanding his mind to figure a way out of this. He knew that Sarah would most likely head back to the house before leaving for Minnesota, so he needed to head there first. Once they talked, they'd work it out. He just needed to catch her before she got on a plane.

As he was getting ready to leave, Will looked up and saw a familiar figure standing by the elevator. Hoping to snag her before she got on the lift, he called her name across the lobby.

"Remi!"

The woman looked up in surprise. He walked over to meet her and spilled.

"I've got to go. Can you tell Paris that we'll have to reschedule? I'll explain later."

Once in his car, he felt a little more relaxed. He knew it would all work out. Sarah wasn't unreasonable. She was probably just scared. After all, he had taken her away from her friends, her family, everyone she knew. He had dragged her across the country into his crazy world, where strangers stared at her and chased her with cameras. Will knew it had to be hard for Sarah to be in such unfamiliar surroundings. She had never even been out of the States. He thought about how he could make the transition easier for her. He could fly her friends out next weekend, or her parents, though he didn't really want to see her parents quite yet. Her friends, he thought, they would make it easier.

When he pulled up to the guesthouse, he had thought it out. He knew what he would say to her. If she needed more time, he could give her more time, but he wasn't going to let her leave without talking and making a plan. Leslie's car was out front, and he wondered if she had picked up Sarah from the hotel.

"Sarah?" he called as he opened the door into the house.

"No, it's just me. I thought Sarah was with you at that interview. Did she escape?" Leslie stopped her teasing when she saw his shattered face. "Jon, what happened?"

"Sarah left the interview. She's going back home to Minnesota."

"Why?"

"I don't know. She won't answer my calls. She probably just got scared. I don't blame her. My life is so crazy." He sat down on the couch and buried his head in his hands.

"What scared her?" Leslie asked, sitting down next to him and wrapping her arm around his shoulders.

"I left her with Paris while I took a call. Maybe Paris said something. I don't know. She was pretty quiet this morning. Maybe it was something else. She talked to her parents for at least an hour last night." He paused, worrying what her parents could have said, and then he stood up. "I have to catch up to her before she leaves town," he said in a rush. He knew Sarah couldn't have beaten him back to the house. Leslie would have seen her. She had been at the house for a couple of hours. Sarah must have gone directly to the airport.

"Go find her," Leslie said. "I'll stay here and check the departure times for the outgoing flights to Minneapolis. I'll call you."

As Will got back into his car and set his navigation system for the fastest route, avoiding traffic on the 405, he called Sam.

"Sam, would it be possible for you to come with me to the airport? I'm about twenty minutes from your house. I could pick you up?"

"Sure. Are we flying out?" Sam asked.

"No, there's no need to pack. Something is going on with Sarah, and I just need some help to get through the airport. It won't be an overnighter. I'll explain when I get there."

Leslie called as Will stopped to pick up Sam. She informed him that the next flight out wasn't for two more hours and confirmed that Sarah had not been at the house yet. With Sam in his BMW, they sped toward LAX. Will explained what had occurred at the hotel the best he could. As they continued on their way, Sam began to ask questions.

"Is it normal for Sarah to run off like that? Has she ever done it before?"

"No, but I've seen her clam up and not talk to me when she was really upset."

"Can you think of any reason why she would want to go back to Minnesota?"

"I know she wanted to finish her degree, but I thought we had worked through that."

He wondered if her parents had pressured her last night on the phone to come home and go back to school. She hadn't said anything.

"Actually, there are a million reasons. Would you want my cracked life?" Will added. If he didn't catch her at the airport, he knew he would have to call Sarah's parents or Jeff to make sure she was all right.

"Yeah, I see your point." Sam nodded in acknowledgment. "Does she know anyone in LA that she would trust enough to call for a ride?"

"No, she doesn't know anyone."

"What about your parents? Would she call them?"

"They left for Belize this morning. They're not even in the country." As Will thought harder about who Sarah knew in LA, he came up with a name. "Sarah could have called my buddy Chris's wife, Toni. I think she gave Sarah her number on New Year's. I'll call her and check."

Will called Chris's wife using the hands-free connection on his steering wheel. She said she hadn't heard from Sarah. Even though the conversation was on speakerphone, Will shook his head, emphasizing her answer to Sam as he wrapped up their conversation. When Will was off the phone, Sam started his questioning again.

"So, Jon, let me get this straight. Sarah, not knowing anyone in LA to call and pick her up, caught a cab from the hotel without any help from the front desk or the concierge and without anyone seeing her, and she did this all in about thirty minutes? Does that make sense to you? Let me see that text she sent you."

Jon handed him the phone.

"Does this sound like her? Is it her voice, something she would say?"

"I don't know. I can't remember it exactly."

"Let me read it to you. 'I can't do this, Jon. I'm going back to Minnesota. Please don't come after me. I will call you when I'm ready to talk.'" Sam looked at the texting thread above the one he had just read and continued. "Would she normally abbreviate words like you did in the text you sent? Because she didn't abbreviate at all on this text."

"Shit! *Shit*! How could I be so stupid?" Will berated himself as a horn blared loudly.

"Jon, pull over." The BMW was swerving between lanes and barely missed the sports car next to them. "I'm driving. Just pull over!" Sam boomed in his commanding voice.

Will pulled the car to the shoulder, and as he got into the passenger seat, he confessed, "She almost never calls me Jon except when we're in public—never in a text. She always calls me Will, and she abbreviates more than I do. Sometimes I have to ask her to speak English because I have no clue what her texts mean." His whole body shook as his head fell into his hands. "Someone's got her, don't they?"

"We don't know for sure what has happened, but it's starting to look suspicious, Jon. We're heading back to the hotel. I think we need to start there, and we need to contact the police."

"No police! It will be a media circus. I've seen it before, and she'll end up dead."

"I have a couple of friends in the department, and they'll be discreet. I'll call them, and they will help us out, OK? We need cooperation from the hotel staff. The police will help us with that," Sam stated in a calming voice.

They made their way to the hotel and parked the BMW in the garage below. Sam had completed his calls by the time they arrived, and his two police buddies were on their way. It had been almost two hours since Will got the fake text, and he had no idea where Sarah could be. He hadn't calmed down yet. He was in full panic mode, blaming himself for not realizing right away that the text was a fake. It was his worst nightmare come true, and he didn't know how to find her. He just knew he had to find her fast.

Chapter Twenty-Six

Will and Sam rushed out of the car, still contemplating where to look for clues before the police arrived. They knew it could have been just some random fan, but they needed to explore all possibilities. Sam wondered who could have known that Will and Sarah would be at the hotel. He grilled Will on the people who may have had the opportunity or motive to harm Sarah. It was a more logical place to start than the vastness of crazy fandom.

"It could be anyone, but we should begin by looking at people you know. Let's start where she was last seen. Is there any reason to suspect the reporter?" Sam asked as they headed up the elevator from the garage.

"I don't think so. I've known her for more than three years, and she's never shown a psychotic side. She flirts, but I can't imagine what would motivate her to hurt Sarah. Maybe there's more she can tell us about why Sarah left," Jon answered as they entered the lobby. "I'm going to head up to Paris's to see if she can tell me anything more before your boys get here. I can't just sit around and wait."

"No, Jon, there may be some psycho loose in the building. I wouldn't be doing my job if I let you wander around the hotel by yourself. They'll be here soon," Sam said adamantly. "What about your old girlfriend,

Mia? She always seemed a bit unstable to me." He smirked slightly. "Could she be involved?"

"I don't know. She called over the holidays, but I missed her call, and she didn't leave a message. I don't even know if she knows I'm engaged. I never had a chance to tell her."

"Would it upset her to find out you're getting married?"

"I think it might freak her out a bit. I meant to tell her myself, but with Sarah's accident, I just forgot all about her. We've always kind of been there for each other, as friends. She might feel a little abandoned. She's got some issues with that, but how would she even know we were at the hotel?"

"Twitter?" Sam offered. "How about your publicist, Remi? Why was she so late?"

"I'm not sure. I never really found out."

"How does she feel about you getting engaged? Has she mentioned any concerns about how it's going to affect your image or marketability?" Sam asked as he stood up and unbuttoned his sports coat.

"Yeah, we've talked about it quite a bit, actually."

"You're her biggest client, and she wouldn't want anything or anyone screwing with her biggest moneymaker, would she?" Sam questioned.

"No. She thinks I'm too young to get married and is afraid that it will ruin my image. She doesn't think that my fans will accept me marrying anyone not in the business."

"How did she seem when you saw her?" asked Sam.

"She did appear a bit shaken, but I didn't ask her about it because I was so focused on catching up to Sarah. I could call her," Will said as he reached for his phone.

Sam held out his hand with his fingers spread. "No, that would just tip her off if she's involved. Is there anyone else who knew you were at the hotel?"

"Isaac knew about the interview. He isn't taking the engagement too well, either," admitted Will.

"Do you think he could be involved?"

"He does seem upset. Just yesterday, he asked me why we couldn't just shack up. He was practically screaming at me. I thought he was just being dramatic, as usual. He said I was making a huge mistake and I would regret getting married. I told him I was going to do what I wanted. I don't know. I've always trusted these people." He looked at Sam in anguish, not knowing what to do. He'd always worried about the crazy fans and paparazzi—not the few people he trusted.

"Jon, everyone is a suspect. We can't rule anyone out until we find Sarah, but we will find her. There are cameras everywhere in this hotel and in the parking garage. We just have to get access to the security tapes. That's why we need the police, and they will be here any minute."

They didn't have to wait long before Sam's buddies arrived, though it seemed like hours to Will. The two officers were dressed in street clothes, not uniforms. The four men sat down in a secluded corner of the lobby to talk discreetly. Will and Sam described the entire incident, and Will took out the one printed picture he had of Sarah in his wallet. He had forgotten it was there at first. It was the one he had downloaded off the Internet—the one of Sarah and the other guy at the fair. He quickly folded the stranger out of sight before handing it to the officers. The rest of his pictures were digital and on his phone, so he was relieved to have something to give them.

After watching Will fold the paper, one officer asked, "Who's this guy?" He flipped the paper over. "Could he be of interest?"

"No. He's nobody—doesn't even live here," answered Will.

The officers explained that they would talk to the staff and check the security camera footage. Having more than two hours of video from multiple cameras to review, they needed to get started right away. The tapes would provide the quickest, most accurate information. One officer would start with the hallway outside Paris's suite on the fifth floor, using the times Jon had given him as a reference and paying special attention to the thirty minutes of time when Jon was down at his car. The other officer would focus on the parking garage footage, looking for anything suspicious.

Will and Sam headed upstairs to see if Paris could give them any more information. She hadn't been ruled out as a suspect, and she ran a gossip site, so they were leery about how much information to share with her. Rather than let her know that Sarah was missing, they decided to see if she could give them any insight as to why Sarah had left in the first place. Paris seemed a little dazed when she first opened the suite door, but then joked that Jonathan had come back to complete the missed interview.

"Paris, what did you and Sarah talk about while I was gone? She refuses to talk about it, and I just want to understand why she is so upset," Will asked her as he sat down on the couch.

"Just small talk," she replied. "Do you want something to drink?"

Not waiting for a response, she slowly brushed her bottle-blonde hair to one side as she walked over to the small table, assembled three glasses in a line, and opened the ice bucket. She tweezed several cubes into each glass and filled them halfway with designer vodka.

"She's young. Give her some time. She probably just needs to think things through. God, Jon, you're a lot to take on." She offered one of the glasses to Will as she brought a second one to her lips and took a sip. "Take it. You look like you could use a drink."

He held up his hand, shaking his head. "Seriously, I just want to know why she was so upset. What exactly did you say?" Will, tired of playing games, didn't want to waste any more time. He wanted to know why Sarah would have left the suite at all. "What was said? That's all I want to know."

"It was nothing. We just talked a little about your man-whoring past. She seemed a bit intimidated by it."

Will stared at her in disbelief. "What?"

"I just wanted her to be prepared. She seemed like a nice girl, and I thought she should know what she would be facing if she married you. Everyone knows you won't be faithful. No one in Hollywood is," she said matter-of-factly, taking another sip of her drink.

"What the hell are you talking about? You don't know me." Will narrowed his eyes at her. Sarah didn't need anyone adding to her doubts. No wonder she'd left.

"What do you mean? I've known you for years, Jon. She deserves a heads-up, don't you think?"

Will turned to Sam, communicating that it was time to leave. Just then, Sam received a text. He glanced at it and casually passed the phone to Will. He read the message. His eyes met Sam's, and Will stood up. Sam headed for the suite entrance as Will made his way past Paris.

"Sarah?" Will roared as he crashed through the bedroom door and scanned the room. He flung open the closet door, not knowing what to expect. He stormed to the bathroom and pulled back the shower curtain. Sarah wasn't there. "Where is she?"

"What do you mean? Sarah isn't here. I told you, she left."

Will put his arm around Paris's shoulders and pulled the phone out of his jacket pocket. Grasping her shoulder tightly, he held the phone in front of Paris's face so she could read the text: *Be careful. Sarah never left the suite while Jon was at his car.* After he was sure she had read it, Will tossed the phone to Sam, who was standing in front of the only exit from the suite. Will slid his arm across Paris's neck, forcing her into a headlock. He was raging. He couldn't believe he'd left Sarah with her. How could he have been so stupid, so trusting?

"You're hurting me, Jon!" Paris gasped.

Will knew what he needed to do. He was an actor, after all, and could be very persuasive. "I'm going to snap your neck if you don't tell me what you did with her. You know I will," he said coolly, without emotion, though he was anything but emotionless. "Sam, you remember when I played that Special Forces agent? Great training. They taught me how to kill a man fifteen different ways. Killing her would be nothing. Tell me where she is, Paris," he demanded in a low, bone-chilling monotone.

"I don't know!" She wheezed as he tightened his grip.

"You know, no one would blame me. People expect celebrities to crack. It happens all the time. We have way too much pressure in our lives—always on show, constantly being picked apart by the press. This is your last chance," Will declared, his frigid voice breaking with a murderous tone.

"She wasn't good enough for you. She didn't deserve you," Paris blurted out in a raspy voice. "You're better off this way."

Will loosened his grasp as he noted her words. *Wasn't.* His heart plummeted. All hope of finding Sarah unharmed drained from his body. He stared right through Paris with a blank expression as she turned to face him. Will felt the blood drain from his face, and his throat started to constrict. His breathing became shallow; he stood locked in place, just staring into space.

"No," he whispered.

Chapter Twenty-Seven

Will continued to stare, numbly vacant, unable to believe that this could be happening. After all he and Sarah had been through, it couldn't end like this. It didn't make sense. They were meant to be together, Jack had said. Why would Paris hurt her? Sarah was so innocent, so naive when it came to the evils of the world. She never had a chance. Will knew it was entirely his fault. It was Jack's death all over again. He should have protected her. He should have had some security. He never should have let his guard down. Will was rigid, imagining the horror of what he had let happen.

"It wouldn't have worked. She wasn't right for you. It's supposed to be me," Paris proclaimed.

Will barely heard her comments.

Sam looked over at her in disbelief. "What the hell?"

Then his phone vibrated, the sound breaking Jon's trance. His eyes met Sam's as Sam took the call.

"They found Sarah. She's alive," Sam announced.

Jon ran his hand through his hair, taking a deep breath, and exhaled in an uninhibited release. Then he crossed the room toward Sam.

"It will never last. She's not good enough for—"

"Shut the *hell* up!" Jon interrupted, glaring at Paris, willing her dead.

"They found her in the trunk of a car in a hockey equipment bag. Who plays hockey in LA?" Sam asked, not knowing Paris's husband was a pro hockey player. "Go and see Sarah. They're in the garage. The ambulance just got there. I'll stay here with the Wicked Witch until the police come up. They're on their way."

Will nodded at Sam with gratitude.

"You can be pretty scary when you want to be, Jon," Sam added, patting him on the shoulder and opening the door.

"Thanks!" he yelled as he sprinted for the stairs. He wasn't going to wait for the elevator. His legs were like jelly, and he seemed detached from his body, but somehow, he managed to jog down five floors and then one more to the garage. The fog was thick in his head. Sarah was alive, but in what state, he didn't know.

As Will entered the parking garage, he was slowed by a uniformed police officer. The officer was instructed to keep everyone out of the crime scene, but when he recognized Will, he let him through. Obviously, the officer had been informed of his relationship to the victim. Will didn't even have to say anything, and now that Sarah had been located, he didn't care that more police were involved.

Will sprinted toward the flashing lights of the ambulance, where he knew he would find Sarah. When her silhouette came into view, his heart melted with relief. He slowed to catch his breath, just for a second. She was sitting up on a narrow gurney about a foot off the ground. When their eyes locked, Sarah began to cry. The tears were dripping off her cheek by the time he reached her. He sat down next to her on the gurney and wrapped both his arms around her. He touched his hand to her cheek, feeling the moisture against his palm, and gazed into her eyes. He tucked her hair behind her ears and held her in silence for several seconds.

"I'm sorry I took so long."

She chuckled with relief as she continued to sob. "I'm just glad you're OK. I kept asking where you were, but no one would tell me." Her body shuttered as she sucked in a breath. "Don't ever leave me again," she choked out between sobs.

He knew that she needed to cry, to let go of her emotions. She'd feel better in the end. He squished his eyes together in frustration, wishing he could take away all that had happened to her. He wanted to cry too, but he wanted to be strong for her, and there were so many watching eyes.

So he pulled her even closer and whispered in her ear. "I won't."

Will held her for several more minutes before one of the officers who had viewed the security footage approached him. The officer pulled Will aside to discreetly fill him in on what had transpired.

"I'll be right here, Sarah," Will said as he stood up. "They need to check you out again anyway." Will and the officer stood about six feet away from Sarah as the paramedics reassessed her, but Will did not take his eyes off her.

"As soon as we got access to the security office, we started with the tapes," the officer told Will. "No one was seen leaving the fifth-floor suite between the time you left and the time you returned. That's when we sent Sam the text. We wanted you to know Sarah still could be in the room and you might be in danger. Then, as we continued to watch, we saw a woman knock on the suite door. She went into the suite briefly and returned to her car in the garage."

"That was my publicist," Will admitted. "She went up to let Paris know that I wouldn't be back to do the interview."

"Shortly after the first woman left, a second woman came out of the suite. The second woman retrieved a bag from a vehicle in the garage and dragged a luggage cart back to the room. After about thirty minutes, she came out of the suite again, pulling the cart with a large canvas bag on top. It was definitely big enough to hide a body. The tape showed her heaving the bag into the trunk of a Mercedes, full this time. Once we located the black Mercedes seen on the video, we broke the window and popped the trunk release inside the car to find the hockey equipment bag. It was a huge bag, and Sarah is so small that she fit inside it easily.

"She was unconscious, and her respirations were pretty shallow when we got her out of the bag. The paramedics were pretty confident that Sarah had been drugged with some sort of narcotic, so they started an IV on her and gave her a drug called Narcan. It counteracts the opiate's effects, and it brought her out of her stupor. I've seen it used before on overdoses—it's like a miracle. It was a good thing we found her so quickly, because who knows where she could have ended up? In her state, she could have stopped breathing altogether. You and Sam did a great job figuring out that she was still at the hotel."

"It was all Sam. I'm such an idiot," Will replied. He was overwhelmed with the thought of what had happened and didn't want to imagine it any worse.

"She's safe now. That's all that matters."

"Thanks for all your help—and your discretion," Will added.

The ambulance staff finished checking over Sarah and wanted to bring her to the hospital as a precaution. Will was allowed to ride in the back with her, which was against company policy. Sometimes being famous had its perks, and he was glad he didn't have to break his promise about leaving her.

At the hospital, the emergency room doctor evaluated Sarah and ran some blood tests to see what kind of drugs were in her. As they waited for the results, Sarah quietly shared what had happened while she was in the suite with Paris. She told Will how she started feeling dizzy shortly after he'd left. She said Paris started telling her how she should go back home because she would never be good enough for him and how he was just going to cheat on her. So Sarah decided to go find him. When she stood up to leave, everything went black.

"It hurts back here. I think I may have hit my head," she said as she put her hand to the back of her head and rubbed it gingerly.

Will looked at the back of her head, parting her hair gently to see her scalp, but he didn't see anything. "I don't see a cut or bump, but we should ask the doctor."

Sarah continued. "When I woke up, I was lying on a gurney with an IV in my arm. Total déjà vu. Just like the accident. It was so bright, like I'd been shocked awake. I didn't know what had happened. All I knew was I didn't know where you were." She leaned her head against Will's chest, and he gently caressed the back of her head.

"I'm here now," he said.

As Sarah and Will waited for the blood test results, Sam joined them in the emergency room. Sarah was in an actual room with large glass windows overlooking the nurses' station, the kind of room usually reserved for large trauma cases. It reminded Will of the intensive care unit where Sarah had spent most of her last hospital stay, but at least it was private and the blinds on the windows were closed. Sam had driven Will's car to the hospital and had loads of information to share.

He told Will and Sarah how Paris had confessed to the police that she was just trying to keep her website afloat. Her husband had been injured in the fall and was worried that his hockey career might have been coming to an end. He didn't want to sink any more money into her hobby, and their finances were starting to cause stress in their marriage. He had already been caught cheating once, so Paris knew she needed to make the website work on her own.

The gossip site had fallen on hard times, and advertising dollars were more difficult to get. She knew if Jon got married, his female fans wouldn't be as interested in him, and that would drop the interest in her site. Her website was her baby, and she couldn't stand it if it went under. She hadn't planned on hurting Sarah. She hadn't planned anything, actually. But when she heard Sarah was already on medication, she thought she could just make her disappear for a while—long enough for Jon to realize he wasn't ready to get married. She had some painkillers of her husband's in her purse, and she slipped them into Sarah's Coke. Paris kept saying that she would never do anything to hurt Jon.

"She admitted that the engagement threw her off, that she just wanted you to be bitter enough about Sarah leaving that she would have the chance to seduce you." Sam shook his head. "Hell, she seemed pretty obsessed with you, Jon. I wouldn't be surprised if she has some shrine with your picture plastered all over it."

Sam also informed Will that there was a large group of paparazzi and reporters already amassed outside the hospital, and more were sure to come. It would be difficult to leave without running into the cameras, so Will called Remi for some advice. He filled her in on all that had happened at the hotel and the paparazzi problem.

After hearing the story of Paris's confession, Remi commented, "That's ironic because the interview probably would have brought Paris so much notoriety that she never would have had to worry about advertising dollars again. It must have been the potential sex that motivated her." Remi said she would meet them as soon as possible at the hospital and they would figure out how to deal with the press when she got there.

Will called Kate to let her know what had happened so she wouldn't have to hear about it in the press first. She had a lot of questions, and Will did his best to answer them honestly without frightening her. When Remi arrived, he handed the phone off to Sarah so she could continue to reassure her mother.

Remi had spoken to the police department to determine what information the police were going to release, if any, and shared that she was not surprised that the police were planning a press conference at the hospital at five. She knew it would make the network news if it was scheduled at that time, and that was the police department's intent.

"The press release will break through network programming across the country. It will be good publicity for the police to solve a case so quickly with no one hurt, and with your name attached, the story will be everywhere. So it might be a good time to announce your engagement. What do you think?" Remi looked at Will with a very earnest expression. "Or you can just call Sarah your girlfriend, and you can announce it on the red carpet in February. Either way, she needs a label for this press release."

"Remi, my brain is fried. I can't process anything else today. Just tell us what to do," Will pleaded. He was mentally exhausted and had lost the ability to make decisions hours ago.

"Let's just leave the announcement for another day, shall we? It'll give us another big day in the press, but I think you should announce it before the end of February. You can go on *Kimmel* or *Ellen*, make the announcement, and then show off Sarah and her ring on the red carpet."

"Fine. I don't care at this point. Just make it happen." Will didn't really hear what he was agreeing to. He just wanted to go home with Sarah.

"I'll put together our own statement for the press and get working on the other stuff." She pulled her phone out of her bag and sent a quick text. Then Remi sat on the only chair in the room and began typing on her electronic tablet.

"A ton of people have seen my ring today, but I didn't admit anything," Sarah confessed.

Remi looked up from her typing. "That's all right. It'll just keep them guessing and be good for publicity in the long run. Every talk show in the country will want to have Jon on to share the story of today's adventure and to find out if you two are engaged. It will be great exposure."

"Super," Will said sarcastically. "Actually, I think I'll be happier once it's all out there. After today, I can handle anything." He wasn't going to put up with any crap from the media anymore.

The doctor came back into the room with the test results and assured Sarah that she would be fine. Narcotics were found in her blood, but she shouldn't have any lasting effects. He cautioned her on taking her prescription pain medicine because of her reaction today and suggested that she try to manage her pain with Advil or Tylenol. Will had the doctor check the back of Sarah's head, but since he didn't see any obvious problem, he didn't order any more tests. He told Sarah to ice it and to come back to the ER if she was feeling dizzy or started vomiting. He said she was free to go once the nurse came in with some papers for her to sign.

It was nearing five when they were finally ready to leave. They planned to escape the hospital during the press conference, when the press was distracted. Remi would be out front with the police department giving her official statement, while Sam, Will, and Sarah would sneak out to Will's car. Hopefully, they would make it out to the ramp without being swamped. The press conference would not be long, so they needed to time their escape perfectly. Remi would text Jon as soon as the cameras were rolling.

They almost made it to Will's car without anyone spotting them, but of course, there were a couple of paparazzi who had anticipated their plan. So Will held Sarah's left hand determinedly, covering her ring as they made their way to the BMW, and once behind the darkly tinted windows of the car, they finally relaxed. After they dropped off Sam, they headed to their house, feeling mentally drained and famished.

Back at the house, Will and Sarah walked into the kitchen to find Leslie unpacking the Chinese takeout she'd picked up. The sweet and fiery aroma filled their lungs as they greeted her.

"Thought you might be hungry," Leslie said with a smile. "It's from Yang's—General Tao's chicken and Mongolian vegetable."

"Oh, Leslie, we love you!" Sarah said as she wrapped her arms around her in true sincerity.

"I know. Enjoy your meal. I have to go," she declared. "You can tell me all about it tomorrow." She disappeared quickly, and Will knew she had left to give him and Sarah time to recover.

Once they were alone, Will grabbed two forks from the drawer. Tossing one to Sarah, he said, "Let's dig in." Having no intention of making more work for themselves, they started to eat right out of the cardboard cartons, switching cartons back and forth as they stood in the kitchen.

When Will ate a snap pea right off Sarah's fork as she brought it up to her mouth, she said, "Hey, I want that back," and leaned in to kiss him.

Desire overtook Will, and he was powerless to fight it any longer. They hadn't been together in that way since September. He had been afraid of hurting her after the accident, and she still had time left on the no-physical-activity sentence imposed by her surgery, so he'd pushed it out of his mind, waiting for her body to heal, but he couldn't wait anymore.

It might have been sheer hunger pent up over months or just a desperate longing to break through the numbness left by the day's events. He wasn't sure, but he could tell Sarah felt it too. Sarah draped her arms around his neck and wove her fingers through his hair as he manipulated her snugly fitted dress up to the top of her thighs. Then he picked her up, wrapping her legs around his waist, and carried her up the stairs to the king-sized bed.

Chapter Twenty-Eight

The next day, the seriousness of what had happened to her at the hotel hit Sarah hard. It was like a dream that had actually happened. She couldn't believe it. This kind of stuff didn't occur in real life—yet it did. How many times had Will warned her? But could she have done anything differently to prevent it? She couldn't fathom how she could have changed anything. Maybe if she only drank from sealed bottles, it would prevent someone from drugging her. Was this the life she had chosen? Sarah had chosen to be with Will, but she didn't want to live her life in fear of others' actions, either. She decided it was time to share her secret with him. He needed to know, and she couldn't put it off any longer.

"I want you to read this, because the only way to make our life together work is if we are completely honest with each other and I don't want to keep any secrets from you. But before I let you read it, I want you to promise me that you will not freak out and we will still get married, no matter what it says." She held out her journal, waiting for him to agree.

He looked at her wide-eyed. "What did you do?"

"I didn't do anything. I just want you to know—so promise me."

"Are you sure about this?" He hesitated for a moment while he gazed into her eyes, where he must have seen that she really was sincere. "OK, I promise."

"What are you promising?" She wanted to reiterate what he was committing to.

"I promise that I will not freak out and we will still get married," he said, cocking his head to look at her as if asking, *Is this really necessary?*

"OK," she said as she handed him the journal, hoping she was doing the right thing. "I wrote this before everything happened yesterday, so keep that in mind when you read it. Start here and read to here." She opened the book to the correct page. Sarah had the pages well marked with fluorescent-pink sticky notes hanging over their edges. Watching him intently as he settled back on the couch, she nervously arranged the pillows.

❧

> *Everyone keeps asking me what I remember about the accident, and I don't know what to say. I don't want to lie to them, but if I tell them the truth, it could wreck everything. I don't know what to do.*
>
> *I saw the fear on Will's face last summer when he was worried about the paparazzi stalking me, and in the airport, when I stopped him from leaving, he made me feel so safe in his arms, but I could feel him trembling. It's scary the way they paralyze him. They drain him of common sense—everything goes out the window, and he can't see the options before him.*
>
> *I suppose it would be different if they hadn't killed Jack. Will would definitely be different if Jack's accident had never*

happened. He would probably be caught up in the mecca of Hollywood, like the rest. Would I have ever met him? I doubt it. The selfish part of me says I wouldn't change a thing about the day of his accident, because I never would have met him if it hadn't happened. I'm so selfish. SELFISH! SELFISH! SELFISH! But I can't imagine my life without him now. I don't have the power to change anything anyway—moot point.

I know why I didn't tell Will what led up to my accident. It's the selfishness again. I don't want him to leave me. It would freak him out, and he would run, trying to save me from the evil paparazzi. I guess it freaks me out a bit too, thinking about that guy stalking me like that. He was there at the airport when Will abandoned his flight, the guy with the goatee and the receding hairline. I don't think I will ever forget his face now. I wonder if he was the one who took the picture of me in the beer garden at the fair. I guess I'll never know for sure who took that picture, but part of me hopes that it was him. Otherwise, there is someone else out there stalking.

I remember when I first saw him after the airport incident. It was a Tuesday morning, as I was leaving for my writing lab. I didn't remember him at first. I was walking down to the corner to catch the bus. It was about a week after Will had left for Greece. I thought he was just asking for directions when he stopped me, but he knew my name. It made me nervous, and I raced through the filing cabinet in my skull, searching to make the connection. I thought I must have known him from somewhere. Maybe a professor, I thought, but I couldn't figure it out. He made small talk at first. Then he started to ask questions like, How long have you known Jonathan? and Where did you two meet? That's when I smiled and clammed up. I had made the connection by that point.

After that day, he was there outside the rental house several times a week. I would see his shiny Korean car parked along the street. It was very distinctive, with its squared back end and unusual green color. Sometimes it was right in front of the house. Sometimes it was farther down the street, but always within view of the house. He didn't always approach me, but I could feel him watching me when I left the rental. Several times, I spotted him other places too—outside the public library, inside a restaurant at the Mall of America, and on my parents' street. He would make eye contact and smile at me, as if we were old friends. He must have seen the horror on my face, but he made no reaction to it.

When he did approach me, it was always questions about Will and me. Once I said, "You can see he's not here. Why are you following me?"

His answer was, "I can tell you're special to him. I just want to get your inside story."

My response was clearly rude. I was irritated and tired of being followed. I don't remember exactly what I said, but expletives were involved. I tried to convince him we had broken up. It didn't faze him.

"Heard that before. I'll see you tomorrow," he said, chuckling as he walked back to his car.

I was furious, but at least he didn't seem dangerous, and after that day, I stopped being mortified every time I saw him. I thought it was funny that he kept wasting his time following me, and I would chuckle sometimes when I spotted him lurking. After all, Will was overseas for another month, until Christmas, and

I wasn't going to tell the stalker guy anything. I knew I couldn't tell Will about him. He probably would have left filming and flown back to find the guy. That wouldn't have helped, so I kept it to myself, hoping the guy would give up.

Then a week before we were supposed to leave for Colorado, there he was, waiting outside the rental when I got back from class.

"Sarah, are you and Jon planning a secret wedding?" he asked.

I remember his exact phrasing because it was so different from the questions he usually asked, and I wrote it down in my journal right away. He caught me off guard, and he must have seen it on my face because he continued.

"You do know that Jon has been spotted shopping for an engagement ring? It was all over the Internet."

I watched him study my face, and I tried not to react, but I'm sure my face was transparent. I kept silent as he continued.

"I know you're the one. Why do you think I've been following you?" he said smugly.

Will stopped reading and looked over at Sarah. "You knew?" She met his eyes. "It was just a rumor. I never believe gossip." His dimple appeared for just a second before he started reading again.

I looked to the sky for strength and hurried into the house. In truth, I was avoiding the Internet gossip. I had watched it at first after Will left, but after two weeks of seeing The Demigod's director tweet about what great chemistry Will and Rachel had, I stopped checking the Internet. The gossip sites were even worse, with sightings of Will and every girl in

Europe. They just made me miss him all the more, and it was all lies anyway.

I dealt with the nastiness of Will's fans at school already, the stares and pointing from other students. Girls would come up to me after class, telling me that I wasn't good enough for him, how ugly I was, how they knew someone who was actually dating him and I was just a liar, so I didn't need to read the tabloids. I was tortured enough at school. It felt like I was back in middle school.

Then there were the girls who tried to be my best friend. They buddied up to me thinking I'd introduce them to him. They'd ask me questions, very personal questions sometimes, and expect me to just tell them everything. When they realized I wasn't going to share our secrets, they'd fade away. The guys were worse— staring at me, sizing me up. I could see it in their eyes. Dissecting me, like there must be a good reason why such a big star would hook up with me, and their snide comments under their breath made me want to vomit.

I got at least a couple of letters a week from Will's fans. I had my mail forwarded to the rental house so my mom wouldn't see all of it. I eventually didn't even look at the mail unless I recognized the return address. I let my roommates go through it once in a while, but I didn't want to see it. It was all hate mail anyway. I even got calls on my cell phone from tabloid reporters. I don't know how they got the number, but I found this great app to filter my incoming calls, and it took care of the problem for the most part. With all the other hate I had to deal with, I definitely wasn't going to seek more on the Internet.

The stalker sat outside the house for two more days without approaching me. On the third day, I had my last final, and I needed to run errands before I left for Colorado. I didn't have time for his games, and I was starting to worry that he was going to follow me onto the plane. I stopped at the house after my final to eat lunch, and as I ate, I thought about what this guy was hoping to get from me. I couldn't imagine that he really expected me to spill personal information about our relationship.

My most important errand was to pick up my skis from the Sports Shack, which was all the way across town by my parents' house, so it was my first. I had dropped off the skis a week before to get them cleaned up and have the bindings checked. I have never been skiing out west, and I didn't want any problems on the slopes. I wanted to get to the Sports Shack before rush hour started, because I knew traffic would be relentless if the rain started to freeze.

When I went out to my car, there he was, leaning up against the passenger side like he owned it.

"So are you meeting here or somewhere else?" he asked.

I remember rolling my eyes at him and thinking, "Really? What a douche. Like I'm going to tell him just because he asked."

Then he said something like, "I can pay you—for your story. Everybody can use money. Even if you broke up, I'll pay you for the story. What do you have to lose?"

I didn't say a word as I slid into my Honda. An EXpireD song was on the radio when I started the car, and I cranked it as loud as it would go, trying to push the guy out of my head. Thinking back, I shouldn't have turned it up, because if Will and I had broken up, the last thing that I would have wanted to listen to is the band formed by his two best friends. I took off down the street toward the freeway. I was halfway across town before I spotted his car in my rearview mirror. For a split second, I thought maybe it was just a look-alike car, but no. As it got closer, I saw the shape of his head, and I knew he was following me.

I was in the far left lane, and I could see the green box approaching on my right. I tried to speed up so he couldn't catch up to me, but he was cruising faster than I was willing to go. As his car overtook mine, he began honking a high-pitched horn, not like an American car's horn. I looked over to see what his problem was, and he was holding up a piece of paper against the window. On the paper, he had handwritten in black marker, "$5,000 for your story." When I read it, I thought, "Well, that's an insult." It was. What was he thinking??? Then I saw the brake lights. He was watching me and not the road. The car in front of him slammed on his brakes, and for some reason, his green car slammed into my car's side. My little defenseless red CR-V careened into the cement barrier, smashed on both sides like a metal sandwich. There was nothing I could do. My air bags exploded, and I felt the jolting impact of two or three more vehicles joining the pileup. I remember feeling really cold, and that's about all I can recall.

When I woke up in the hospital, I was really angry at the stalker. He had wrecked my vacation—my time with Will. What a greedy asshole, I thought. I wanted to hurt him for almost killing me. I'm not usually violent, but he made me SO MAD. Then I saw the pictures of the accident, and I read that the guy in the green crossover had died. I felt kind of bad, just a little. I didn't really want him to die, but I guess if someone had to die, it should be the one whose stupidity and greed had caused the accident.

I don't know what I should tell Will about the stalker. If I tell him anything, it is going to get blown up into a big argument, and he will try to lock me up in some castle tower to protect me like I'm a princess in a fairy tale. This is real life. I don't know. Maybe I'm wrong. I hope I'm wrong. I really want to spend my life with him, but he better stop obsessing over what could happen and start living!

Will flipped through the rest of the journal, not thinking, until Sarah snatched it out of his hand. He looked up at her without saying a word. He could feel an uncontrollable rage growing inside him. He wasn't mad at Sarah, and he didn't want her to think he was mad at her. So he leaned in, touching his forehead to hers, and held it there in silence with his eyes closed, thinking about almost losing her. Gathering comfort from her touch, he took several deep breaths, then pulled back.

"It's a good thing he died, or I would have killed him, and that would have really messed up our lives." Will wasn't feeling much remorse for the man's death, and he wasn't going to hide that fact from Sarah.

Sarah watched him carefully as his anger subsided. "Are you all right?"

He nodded and smiled at her, although it wasn't genuine. She stared into his eyes questioningly.

"I'm fine. We're still getting married. I was just thinking that I'm responsible for another person's death."

"Cut it out, Will! You can't control what other people do."

"He wouldn't have been chasing you if it weren't for me."

"The guy would have found someone else to stalk if it wasn't me, and maybe he would have killed that person instead of himself. It was probably good that he was stalking me," she added, staring at him wide-eyed. "It's not your fault. Jack's death was not your fault. You're not responsible for any of this. You weren't even there."

"You are my responsibility. I should have been there, Sarah. I should have been there to protect you. What if he was an obsessed fan? What if he had killed you? I'd never be able to live with myself." He reached for her hand and brought it up to his lips. He kissed it and then pressed her palm against his cheek before dropping it, intertwined with his, to her lap.

"You can't protect me from everything, Will. I could be hit by a bus tomorrow, and there is nothing you could do to stop it. We are not in control of everything, so we just have to live our lives the best we can."

He knew she was right. It was the exact same advice his dad had told him. He forged a smile again. She was so damn smart, but so naive. He looked into her green eyes, and as he thought about all she had dealt with on her own, he realized that she was tougher than he gave her credit for.

He pulled her into a hug and, after several seconds, admitted, "Actually, you handled yourself pretty well. I'm impressed."

Will knew something was going to have to change. He would definitely have to get more security. Though she handled herself well, he wasn't going to leave her alone anymore, especially after what happened yesterday. It would be a lot more work, but she was his number one priority now, so he would make sure she was safe above all else.

Chapter Twenty-Nine

The rest of the week, Sarah and Will stayed locked in the house, their days filled with swimming in the courtyard and lounging in front of the television. A few people stopped by to visit, but Will and Sarah hadn't left the property since they got home from the hospital.

Sarah was sitting forward, straddling a cushioned lounge chair under the pergola, typing on her laptop, when Will slid in behind her. He nuzzled her neck, inhaling deeply as his arms enveloped her. She leaned her head to the side and pulled her hair over until it fell just right, opening her neck for Will to kiss.

As he kissed her and his hands began to roam, he whispered, "I love you, Sarah."

"I love you too." She stretched her neck to glimpse his face. Seeing the worry on his brow, she asked, "What's wrong?"

He greedily kissed her lips awkwardly from behind, reaffirming what she suspected. He had been on the phone with Isaac this morning, and ever since, he'd seemed off, uptight. Even his kisses seemed needy.

When he didn't answer, she closed her laptop and turned around into a kneeling position so she could read his face better. As she sat back on her heels, she asked, "What did Isaac want?"

He paused for a long second. "There's been more hate mail. He just wanted to make sure that Sam was beefing up security. We're hiring a couple of new full-time security people."

"Good, because you can't keep me a prisoner here much longer," she said as a joke, but froze when Will didn't laugh. She was looking forward to going to the set tomorrow for the first day of filming in LA, but Will's expression made her question whether she would be going.

"Just a few more days of confinement for you, OK? We don't have the new guys hired yet, and you can't come on set the first few days. I just don't know what I would do if something happened to you, Sarah." He brushed her hair back off her shoulder and gazed sincerely into her emerald eyes. "I almost lost you—twice—and it was my fault. It would kill me—"

"It was just a fluke. I don't even remember what happened with Paris, and I'm fine. I'll only drink from sealed bottles. I promise." This was exactly why she'd worried about him reading her journal. It just added to his guilt, and now he was even more paranoid about her safety. "I can't even go on set with you until more security is hired? You're letting them win."

"No, you can come to the set, but not until Thursday. I need you to stay at the house until then, and it doesn't have anything to do with lack of security."

"Why Thursday?"

"Because"—his mouth twisted like he was searching for the right words—"it's just bad form to have your significant other on set when you're filming a love scene. And I don't want you there. It's bad enough that you'll see it in the theater."

It bothered Sarah just a little that Will had set the limit, but she did her best to push it out of her mind, knowing it was his job and she would just have to let it go.

Sarah stayed back at the house those first couple of days, but on Thursday, when the love scenes were complete, she went to the set—a big giant warehouse with trailers parked outside. At first, she spent most of her time observing. It was exciting to witness the film process, but after a few days and a call from her mother, Sarah realized that she needed to focus on her schoolwork. Time was ticking away. So she stayed in Will's trailer, with Sam nearby. The trailer was clean and new. It was like a miniapartment. It had just about everything she needed, but mostly, it was a place to hang out and type on her laptop.

Her faculty adviser approved Sarah's main project right away and then assigned two smaller ones online. She thought her adviser was being lenient, allowing her to get six credits for the three assignments. It wasn't until Sarah had completed the two smaller tasks that she realized what an enormous undertaking the last project was going to be. Now she was panicking that she would never get the assignment done in time. She only had four months. But if by some miracle she made it believable and turned it in on time, she could get the six credits she needed to graduate. Then everyone would be off her case, especially her parents. So she confined herself to the trailer for as long as she could stand. She needed to get her work done. It gave Will peace of mind that Sam was with her, and Sarah knew he deserved that. She promised him that she wouldn't go running around town without Sam, and she stuck to her word.

The best part about hanging out in the trailer was that, when he had a break, Will always came back to spend time with her, and Sarah knew she wouldn't see him if she was at the house. The hours on set were always long, and they ate together when they were able.

Today, Sarah sat typing on the silver laptop that she had gotten for her birthday. She spread out on the couch, leaning against its arm with a pillow behind her and her stocking feet stretched across the cushions.

It seemed like a lifetime ago that Will had given her the computer. She barely knew him back then, though at the time she thought she knew him so well. Now he was like her right arm, so much a part of her that it would be impossible to be without him. Her mind raced as she typed on her project. Somehow, she had to link all these random thoughts together into scenes and build the scenes into an entire movie. Sarah didn't really know how to write a screenplay, but she had loads of help. Will had given her the original idea to propose to her adviser. He remembered the stories Kate had told him about Sarah writing plays as a young girl. He knew she could write a great movie, even if Sarah didn't, and he would assist her if she needed help.

Sarah got the idea for the story's plot from something Sam had said about Will slipping into a role as a Special Forces agent when he was interrogating Paris. In truth, Will had never done a movie that involved the Special Forces, but he wanted Paris to think he had. The screenplay Sarah was writing was about an actor who was under so much pressure from the press that he became delusional and actually thought he was the characters he played in movies. It was a psychological thriller with just a little comedic element that, of course, poked fun at the paparazzi.

Lara gave her ideas on special effects that would work to make the movie more exciting. Even Zander was helpful by giving Sarah pointers on which parts worked visually and which ones wouldn't. Sarah hoped that by the time Will's filming was wrapped, she would have a pretty good handle on her project and would mostly just be editing dialogue.

Besides her project, she still had a ton to do before the wedding.

The wedding.

They still had to plan the entire wedding. They would be meeting with a wedding planner when Will was done filming, and that would help. Sarah and Will wanted to get married as soon as possible, but everyone kept reminding them that it took a long time to plan a wedding. Will had most of his summer free, but would be back to work promoting *Demigod Forbidden* in the fall and would be starting another film as soon as the promotion ended. They definitely wanted to be married by then.

But right now, Sarah was concentrating on finishing school and finding her way in Hollywood. She had always thought that when she found her significant other, they would be equal partners, both bringing their gifts to the relationship table. Sarah was having doubts that she would ever be Will's equal here in Hollywood. Without a career, or even a job, all her apparent value came from Will. The press was already insinuating that she was a gold digger. Even Will's agent had implied it. She knew she wasn't after Will's money, and Will knew it too, but she hated that people saw her that way. It made it even more important to her that she finish her degree, so she had to focus on that before she could really work on the wedding.

By the beginning of February, when the engagement was announced, they still hadn't made any concrete wedding plans. Will went on the talk show circuit to publically declare the engagement. He did two shows in California before he, Sarah, Leslie, Remi, Sam, and the two new security guards hopped a plane to New York City. He did two more shows there. Sarah didn't go to the sets with him. Remi requested that she stay away from the studio sets so that her ring wouldn't be exposed before the red carpet in February. She said it would build anticipation in the press and would make a bigger impact when it was finally shown. Sarah obliged willingly and stayed, with a security guard, back at the hotel in New York and worked on her project. They were only there for one night, and getting through the airports was bad enough.

The shows turned out just as Remi had planned. Will got a teaser clip from *Demigod Forbidden*'s director. The short movie clip helped promote the film, and it gave Will a break from the private questions. He announced to the world that he was engaged and shared the story of how his original announcement was messed up by his fiancée's kidnapping. He wasn't able to give all the details because of the pending charges against the reporter, but he made light of the incident the best he could. He shared just a little heartfelt personal information about the experience and how fearing the worst had really forced him to prioritize his life. He mentioned that this wasn't the first time Sarah's life had been put in danger because of the paparazzi. He talked about the car accident that had almost killed her and how it was reminiscent of his brother's death. He poked fun at the press, but at the same time tried to promote stricter legislation to control the paparazzi problem. The stories helped draw the attention away from the obvious questions of how he and Sarah met and the wedding plans. Will was thankful for that. He really didn't want to talk about meeting Sarah on the Internet. It was embarrassing. He knew it would come out someday, but he really wished it wouldn't.

Every time Will and Sarah were spotted out over the next couple of weeks, the paparazzi went wild. Every photographer wanted to be the one to snap the first picture of Sarah's engagement ring. Such a picture would be worth a ton of money, so Will and Sarah were followed ceaselessly. There were hordes of photographers outside their house every day, just waiting for the ring to leave. Will and Sarah made sure no shots got leaked before the red carpet viewing. Whenever she was out, Sarah turned her ring around so just the band was visible. It drove the press crazy, and Will and Sarah relished the photographer's irritation. It became a game of cat and mouse where the cat always ended up frustrated that it couldn't catch the mouse. The reveal day was coming soon, though, and Will and Sarah were looking forward to getting some peace away from the constant attention.

Chapter Thirty

The preparation for the red carpet event started long before the actual day. The stylist worked hard to connect Sarah with the right dress. She met with Sarah several times over a period of a month, and together, they found two dresses with coordinating shoes that would work well. Sarah let Will pick from the two, and the one he chose looked absolutely gorgeous on her. At least Will thought he was making the decision. If need be, Sarah knew she could always trump his choice. The stylist also helped set up Sarah with the appropriate bling—not too much, though. Just a pair of dangling diamond earrings, a simple white-gold bracelet, and a small gem-encrusted clutch purse. She didn't think Sarah needed much more than her gorgeous engagement ring.

Sarah spent the morning being pampered. A petite dark-haired woman came first to do Sarah's nails. She soaked Sarah's feet and hands and gave her a full pedicure and manicure. The woman applied nail tips to Sarah's fingers and polished her nails in a glossy, silvery pink. Sarah knew everyone would be looking at her hands tonight—her left hand, at least—so she was happy to have her beat-up, broken nails made beautiful.

When the woman had finished with Sarah's nails, she gave Will a manicure too—just a buffing. Sarah was feeling a bit overwhelmed by all the pampering, and Will was making fun of her by the time the second woman arrived to do her makeup and hair. Sarah had met with this woman and the stylist a week ago to determine the most appropriate hairstyle to match her dress. Until last week, Sarah had never had a facial or a manicure before, and she was not used to other people touching her body so intimately. It made her uneasy, just a little, but she knew how important this night was, so she was willing to put up with the indulgence.

"You need to get used to it." Will chuckled as he watched the auburn-haired woman finish applying foundation to Sarah's face with a makeup wedge.

Sarah closed her eyes as the woman lightly painted her eyelids with three different shades. "I have to admit the pampering is kind of fun, but I can't wait to be able to eat again."

"We can stop for an In-N-Out burger on our way home if you're still hungry after the parties, but there will be plenty of food all night."

"I'm going to hold you to that, you know, because I won't be able to eat until I know no one will be snapping pictures of me. I don't want anyone saying I have a baby bump."

"How did you get so paranoid?" he asked with a smirk.

"I don't know. I think the people I hang around must influence me— or maybe it's the article I saw last week that said I had a baby bump." She smirked back at him. "The makeup isn't too much, is it?"

"No. It's very natural—perfect," he answered.

After Sarah had given her approval, the woman started on her hair. She gathered it beautifully on the back of Sarah's head, leaving gentle wisps framing her face. Then the woman sprayed her hair thoroughly to hold it in place all night. Sarah never wore hairspray. She cringed at the feel of it. It felt so unnatural. *It's only for tonight*, she thought.

She beamed at Will as the woman packed up her supplies. Sarah was excited and insanely nervous. She hoped to make a good impression with the press and all those she met tonight. She wanted the world to like her, but she knew the odds were stacked against her. Will would still love her even if she fell on her face, but she wanted to impress everyone else and prove that she could handle all the pressure.

Sarah ascended the steps, making sure to not jostle her head. She didn't want to ruin her hair before she even left the house. Why had she told Leslie that she didn't need any help tonight? What had she been thinking? She took a deep breath as she hit the landing of the second floor and counted to ten in her mind. She didn't have to time to panic; the limo would be here soon and she needed to get dressed. All the accoutrements had been laid out, waiting for her. She just needed to assemble them, like a 3-D puzzle. She had run through the steps with the stylist. She knew what to do.

The groan that escaped Will's throat when she floated down the stairs in her gown confirmed the way she felt in the dress. His reaction gave her confidence. She felt elegant for the first time in her life. The dress perfectly married deep sapphire blue with silver. It was long and shimmery with simple styling that elongated Sarah's figure. The gown's straps were narrower at the shoulders, but widened to cover her bustline, coming together at the fitted waist. The neckline plunged low in the front and even lower in the back. She was wearing Christian Louboutin stilettos and, for the most part, was pretty steady in them. She had practiced walking up and down the stairs in them for almost a week, just to make sure she could actually pull it off. The shoes raised her closer to Will's height. He still towered over her, but at least she wouldn't look like a child next to him on the red carpet.

Will stood at the bottom of the stairs waiting for her, looking like a god in his black tux. With his perfectly tousled hair and that oh-so-perfectly fitted tux, no one would even see her. She could be wearing a garbage bag and no one would notice. The thought calmed Sarah's nerves as she descended the last few steps.

"Finish zipping me, would you?" She spun to give him access.

His hand grazed her bare skin before he slid the zipper up. "Alfresco?"

"I'll never tell." Her gown caught air as she twirled back around to face him. She wanted Will to contemplate that while he was giving interviews on the red carpet.

He raised one eyebrow, and his lips curled, intrigued. He placed his hands on her waist and looked into her emerald eyes. Then he trailed a finger from her shoulder, down the strap of her gown, to her waist. A shiver bolted through her.

"How do you keep it all in the right…place?"

"Tape," she said with a grin. "And I don't even want to tell you what else I had to do." She looked up at him from under her lashes, and he laughed.

◌◌◌

When Remi arrived, they all loaded into the black limousine. During the ride, Remi reminded Sarah of what to expect on the red carpet.

"It will sound like you're standing next to a jet engine with all the announcers talking at once. You won't be able to hear anything, so just follow me. I'll make sure we hit all the important interviews. People can be extremely rude, so don't take anything personally. They will probably treat you like you're invisible. The photographers may want pictures of just Jon. Or if they know who you are, they will definitely want pictures of you two together. We should give them both. They will want you to turn this way and that way. No matter which way you turn, it won't be the right way, because there are just too many to please. Just do your best and follow Jon's lead. They will be very annoying, but please don't call them paparazzi. They're very sensitive about that. Speaking of annoying, where's Isaac?"

"Don't worry, he'll meet us. He would never let me go to a big event like this alone. He's very protective."

"Won't there be tons of security?" asked Sarah.

Will laughed. "Oh, he's not literally protecting me. He's like a guard dog making sure that no other agents can get close enough to talk to me."

"Wow, there's still a lot I don't know," added Sarah.

"Remember, just be yourself and don't let them see that you're nervous. You'll do great." Remi smiled at her. "You both have your IDs, right? You can't get in without them."

"Yes." Will handed out glasses of champagne. "Let's enjoy ourselves, shall we? To Sarah's first red carpet, may the world love her as much as I do." He clinked glasses with each woman and smiled his gorgeous one-dimple smile, and they all drank.

The rest of the ride echoed earlier discussions about interview questions and the who's who in Hollywood. Too quickly, they neared their destination, and Sarah's heart began to race. As the road blockades came into sight, the butterflies from her stomach moved to her head, and all she heard from the end of the conversation was Remi saying, "We're on."

When the car stopped, a greeter in a black tux and white gloves opened the door. Will stepped out first. There was a blast of flashes and roars from the mob outside that penetrated the quiet car. The smell of hot dogs and french fries from an unseen street vendor wafted into the limo, mixed with the pungent odor of car exhaust. Will waved to the crowd and then turned to offer Sarah his hand. Sarah inched her way to the edge of the seat and looked wide-eyed at the scene before her. The bright lights reflected in the shallow rain puddles atop the red carpet that stretched out into the street. Several clear umbrellas protectively hung in the air in anticipation, and under their shielding stood the most beautiful human being Sarah had ever known. Sarah switched her sparkling clutch to her right hand and extended her left hand toward him. She looked into his stunning pale eyes and smiled, realizing that he was there to catch her if she fell. She took a deep breath and stepped out onto the damp runner.

Once they were under the clear canopy of the red carpet, they made their way into the gauntlet of photographers. Will casually sauntered onto the other side of the rope barrier to face the cameras, but Sarah hesitated by the entrance. When Will reached back for her hand and pulled her with him, the flashes and yelling began. He snaked his arm around her waist, touching her bare back, and subtly directed Sarah which way to turn. She couldn't hear him over the roar of the press, so his touch was their only communication. Every five steps required a turn to the left, then to the right. The rapid-fire shouting continued as they progressed down the carpet together. Sarah felt embarrassed having so many people fawn for her and Will's photo. It was still hard to comprehend the whole celebrity concept, and this scene took it to another level. The whole experience was overwhelming her senses. Finally, they approached the last set of photographers, and then Remi coaxed them out of the press line.

Next on the agenda were the fans. Sarah knew they weren't here to see her, so she stood her ground and shrunk back along the velveteen rope when Will tried to pull her with him. He glanced at her questioningly, and she mouthed, "You go."

So he walked toward the edge of the carpet, to the black metal barricade in front of the risers, and braved the crowd. They shoved memorabilia and magazines in front of him to autograph, and he posed with fans for pictures until Remi informed him that they had to keep moving. Walking back to meet Sarah, he looked at her with a predatory smirk Sarah had seen before.

༄

Once he had joined her side, she spoke into his ear. "Stop looking at me like that."

"I was just thinking about the rain," Will confessed, knowing she would know exactly what he was thinking.

Sarah blushed and pressed her lips together.

Rain always brought him back to the night they first made love. He pictured her petite figure lying on the bed beneath him, her rain-drenched hair, and her surprised expression when she let it slip that she loved him. He could still feel the softness of her skin against his as they lay in the dark later that evening, the storm raging outside. It didn't matter that they were being watched right now. His thoughts were his own—and Sarah's.

They continued to walk, oblivious to where they were going, just following the guidance of those surrounding them and not worrying about the cameras pointed at them. As they rounded a curve on the carpet, they both noted the small puddle at their feet and looked up to see raindrops dancing across the clear canopy above their heads.

"I love the rain," she admitted with a grin.

Then he leaned in, cupped her chin in his hands, and kissed her sweetly, tenderly, on the lips, right there on the red carpet, as if there was no one else in the room. The crowd went wild, and the air exploded with a spray of camera flashes. After several seconds, Remi touched Will's shoulder to remind him that they needed to keep moving, and the crowd booed. Remi apologetically shrugged, and they started moving forward down the red carpet again.

As they made their way up the podium steps for a high-profile interview, a well-known redhead correspondent named Julia Masters greeted them. She was tall, thin, and flawless in her long gold sequined gown.

"Jonathan Williams, how have you been?"

Will kissed the woman's cheek. "Fantastic, Julia."

"It's been too long since we last spoke," the redhead stated as she flirtatiously caressed his shoulder. "You're a busy man, I hear."

"Yes, crazy busy." He curled his arm around Sarah's waist. "I'd like you to meet my fiancée, Sarah."

"Pleasure to meet you," Julia greeted, then dove right into questioning. "First of all, let's get it out of the way. Who are you wearing tonight?" Will and Sarah revealed their fashion choices, and the reporter continued. "I hear you've been engaged since the holidays. Until two weeks ago, you were denying your engagement, and now you're kissing on the red carpet. How do you explain your one-eighty with the press?"

"You saw that?" Will asked coyly.

"Yes, I think the whole world saw that. So why the change, Jon?"

"Look at her," Will said with his one-dimple smile, and the main camera panned to a full view of Sarah. "I'm only human—or a demigod. Either way, her powers are way beyond my ability to fight." Will and the reporter chuckled as Will's eyes met Sarah's.

"I'm sure everyone has heard about the nightmare you went through in January—being drugged and kidnapped by a deranged gossip columnist. That must have been horrific. So, Sarah, does it scare you that something like this could happen again, being with Jonathan?"

"Honestly, looking back at the ordeal, it was pretty scary. But I don't have power over other's actions, so I can't let them control me," she said confidently.

Will could see the relief in her eyes when she had finished answering. He knew she was trying to keep her answers short, concise, and under ten seconds long—that's what she had learned in her media training class.

"Well, it seems like you have power over Jonathan." The reporter smiled and winked. "We have to see that ring before our time is up."

Will wrapped his left arm tighter around Sarah's waist, and she placed her left hand on his chest, letting his black tux jacket provide the perfect backdrop to show off the ring, just like they had practiced with Remi.

"Oh my, that is plenty big to share with the rest of us. You wouldn't mind sharing Jonathan with the rest of us, would you?" questioned the reporter with a chuckle.

Sarah smiled and looked at her fiancé.

"All kidding aside, the rest of us women are just sad to see him off the market. So do you have a wedding date set?"

"No, not yet." Sarah shook her head slightly as she spoke and smiled, looking very elegant in her long gown. She stayed tucked in Will's arm and seemed to stand a little taller. She was doing so well, and he was so proud of her.

"Besides *Demigod Forbidden*, what projects are you working on, Jon?" the reporter asked hurriedly, trying to fit as many questions as possible into her limited time frame.

"I found this fantastic script from an up-and-coming writer about an actor dealing with the press. It's my next obsession," Will said, meeting Sarah's eyes. "I just have to find funding for it."

"Well, if anyone could make it happen, it would be you. You're a god. I can't wait to see it. Thank you for sharing with us, Jon, Sarah."

"You're welcome. Thank you for having us," answered Will.

As they made their way down the steps from the stage, Will knew that Sarah could handle this, and he could deal with anything as long as she was at his side. He wasn't going to sit back and let the press run his life anymore. He was taking control, as much as he could, and he was determined to enjoy his life with Sarah. He didn't know what the future had in store for them, but he knew they would be together, and together, they could handle whatever life threw at them.

Look for the continuing story of Will and Sarah—the next novel by Susan Schussler,

Between the Lies

Chapter One

The text read, *Call me when U have time 2 talk-ASAP.* Sarah pressed send and set her phone on the table next to the couch. She curled up her legs next to her and opened her laptop. The text was to her best friend and someday sister-in-law, Jessica. The "someday" came from the fact that Sarah's brother, Jeff, and Jessica had been talking about getting married for almost a year now, and Jeff still hadn't given her a ring. He was waiting for just the right moment to make it official. This detail had put the slightest rift in Sarah and Jessica's relationship. Not that anything could ruin their friendship. They had been best friends since middle school, and their friendship could withstand much worse. Sarah knew Jessica's ring was a sore point, so she tried to avoid mentioning engagement rings or wedding plans when talking to her, though this was getting more and more difficult to do.

Sarah missed Jessica. She missed all her friends. It seemed like so long since she had seen them. Several months had passed since Sarah left her family and friends back in the Midwest for her new life in Los Angeles. When she made the choice to leave, she hadn't really known what to expect once she got to California. All she really knew was that she couldn't live apart from Will any longer. Being with him was the only thing that mattered. She still called him Will sometimes, though lately she had gotten used to calling him Jon. It was just easier. No one knew him by his nickname except his good friends, and they weren't around that often. She equated it to adopting an accent. The people she interacted with every day called him Jon, and she picked it up like a drawl or Valley speak. Besides, she was tired of explaining who Will was as he stood next to her laughing.

She logged on to the Internet while she waited for Jessica's response. She buzzed through the gossip site's pictures of her movie star fiancé coming out of a hotel, followed by Natalie Lipka. The caption read, "Boys will be boys."

She knew Jon had gone to dinner with the gorgeous Ukrainian actress as part of a business meeting for an upcoming film, but why did it have to be at that particular hotel? The Hotel Freemont was known for celebrity hookups, and the photo of them walking out separately and then getting into the same car just made them look guiltier. Sarah knew it was just dinner, but she also knew she would have to explain the picture to her family and friends—like so many before them, and this week the whole world would think Jon was cheating.

At least it wasn't Mia Thompson. A picture of Jon with his ex would take much longer than a week to blow over, and it would drive Sarah crazy. She could imagine Mia staring back with her "I've got a secret and you're so screwed" expression. Mia made her completely irrational. She didn't know how to explain it. Maybe it was the way Mia carried herself around Jon, as if she owned him, or maybe it was that the fans hadn't fully accepted Sarah and still wanted Jon and Mia together. Sarah could put up with any other woman flirting with Jon, but if Mia was in the same room, sirens blared in her head.

She took a deep breath and glanced at her phone—nothing yet. She still had time. She maneuvered her way to the one site where she wasn't supposed to go. She couldn't save the site on her desktop or in her favorites because he would see it, so she made the extra effort to key in the address by hand. Then she typed in the user ID and password she remembered from when the account had been set up. A smile spread across her face as she caught up on the site's activity. He had been to the Mall of America and rode the roller coaster last week. He took the light-rail train to Nicollet Mall in downtown Minneapolis and bought some tulips from the Danish vendor who always gabbed too much. Sarah could almost smell the flowers. And last night, he ate dinner at Sarah's parents' house. The picture of him sitting at the table with her mom and dad made Sarah laugh.

Just then, Sarah's favorite song began to blare from the table next to her—or it used to be her favorite, until she set it as a ringtone. She picked up the phone and slid her finger across the touch screen.

"What's up? You haven't been abducted, have you?" Jessica's voice rang with mockery.

"No, not this week," Sarah said with a chuckle. "I see William was at my parents' for dinner last night?"

"Well, you know how much he likes your mom's lasagna."

"Plastic dolls don't really eat, but I liked the picture with Mom and Dad. I miss you guys. I miss school. I even miss our old run-down rental house. Do you want to go out for drinks on Friday? You can bring William."

"Are you going to be in town?"

"No, I wish! I won't be home until graduation weekend. Jon has a bunch of commitments, and you know how he is about me traveling by myself."

"I don't blame him, Sarah. Look at all the garbage that has happened to you, and that was before you announced the engagement."

"Well, it's not like him being with me makes it any easier to travel. He's always recognized. It takes twice as long as it should to go anywhere. At least I can slip in and out under the radar usually—not yesterday, though. Some idiot followed me all day long when I was meeting with the wedding planner." Sarah caught herself. She'd almost started talking about the wedding, and she had told herself she wasn't going to do that.

"That's exactly why he's so worried about you. There are crazies everywhere. He feels responsible for you being in danger all the time."

"It was just paparazzi. I'm not in danger. It's not like I'm ever alone, anyway. We have a whole team of security now, not just Sam. I mean, I can't even use the bathroom by myself."

"Ew, too much information."

"No, I just mean there's always someone standing outside the door, as if I'm going to be knifed in the bathroom stall or something."

"He's just worried about you."

"Shut up! You're supposed to be on my side."

"I am on your side, but I think Jon's right. You need to be cautious—at least until after the wedding. I read somewhere that the pop star Fretti got into her car one day and some psycho fan was waiting in her backseat with duct tape. If her boyfriend hadn't been three cars down and heard her scream, who knows what would have happened?"

"I'm *not* a pop star, and you know that ninety percent of what you read about celebrities is fake, right?"

"Yeah, but I saw her talk about it in an interview too. I know you would like to deny it, but most gossip is spawned by seeds in the real world."

"You've been cyber stalking us with my mom, haven't you?" Sarah could tell by Jessica's tone that she was holding back.

"Your mom isn't that bad, and yes, I see her all the time. She's worried about you."

"Did she see the pictures of Jon with Natalie?"

"Yeah," Jessica said in a subdued voice.

"You think that's why I called, don't you? He's not cheating on me. It was just a couple of business dinners. That's all. There were a bunch of people with them. They're going to be doing a film together."

"So, what's up, then?"

"I don't know. I'm bored—or lonely?" Sarah declared, not really sure what she was feeling.

"I know you and Jon go out all the time. I see you on *Celebrity News* every other night. The press wants more public displays of affection, by the way, just in case no one has told you."

"We really don't go out much because Jon is always mobbed. We definitely don't go out as much as I did back home, and I'm not PDAing on camera just so the press can dissect our every lip and hand movement. I love Jon, but I just need to hang out with the girls once in a while."

"No girls in California?"

"No, I just don't have any friends—not that I trust, anyway. Everyone acts like my best friend, but it's just because of Jon. I can talk to Leslie, but I never know how much is filtering back to Jon. Not that I keep secrets from him," Sarah assured. "But it's girl stuff, and his cousin shares everything with him."

"So come for a visit. Bring a bodyguard."

"Actually, I was wondering if you, Alli, and Megan could come out to LA for the weekend. I'll send you the plane tickets, and you can stay at the house with us."

"So you and Jon stopped arguing about money, then?"

315

"Yeah, I caved."

"So did he give you a credit card or something?"

"Yep, but that's not all. Jon added my name to all his bank accounts, and I added him to mine—like that mattered. It almost killed his accountant. The accountant wanted to set up an expense account for me like Leslie's, but Jon said no. He says we're equal partners and we need to mesh our lives completely. He doesn't want me to have to ask him for money, so I have full access. He says that I just have to accept that I don't really have an income right now, and since we're getting married, I have to get used to sharing. Besides, I know I'll never make as much money as he does, and everything is so expensive out here. He keeps telling me to stop worrying about money and just enjoy life. He's been bugging me to have you guys out. So what do you say?"

"I'm up for it, but let me ask Megan and Alli," said Jessica. "Sarah is on the phone and wants to know if we can come out to the coast for the weekend—on Jon's dime."

"Are you kidding? Yeah! I'm there," answered Megan. Sarah could hear her clearly in the background.

"Let me talk to Sarah." Alli grabbed the phone from Jessica. "Sarah, what's wrong?"

"Nothing is wrong. I just miss you guys."

"So, you gave up on the money thing?"

"It was futile. Can you come on Friday after class? We could go to the beach or just hang out at the pool. It's in the seventies and sunny. And the shopping is unbelievable."

"That sounds great. I think it was twenty-six this morning when I caught the bus. I had to wear mittens and my winter jacket. I'm putting you on speaker, OK?"

"Megan, you have the last class at two thirty, right?"

"No, I dropped that class. I didn't need it. Besides, I hate having class on Fridays, and the TA was a douche," admitted Megan.

"All teaching assistants are douches," Jessica proclaimed, and Sarah could hear the smile on her face.

"Hey!" Alli protested.

"Alli is dating her TA from organic chemistry. He's Indian," revealed Jessica.

"I'm pretty sure TAs aren't supposed to date undergrads. How did that happen?" asked Sarah.

"We're not dating, and he's not from India—his parents are."

"You meet him for coffee almost every day, and he calls you all the time. Most TAs don't do that, especially when you're not in their class anymore," Megan remarked.

"Well, at least I'm not back together with a guy I've been avoiding for four years," Alli stated.

Sarah groaned. "Please don't tell me you're back together with Chase. Megan, what are you thinking?" She got up and started pacing through the house. She couldn't believe Jessica and Alli could have let this happen.

"We're not back together. We were just catching up," claimed Megan.

"Yeah. I thought you said you would only meet with him in public. Your room with the door closed is not public," Alli snapped.

"Megan, how many times did you say never again? You can't get back with Chase. You promised," said Sarah.

"I'm not. I was tempted, but I'm not."

"Really? You've already given him more chances then you should give any guy. He's going to hurt you again." Sarah said.

"It's not the same."

"Just be careful. He's your kryptonite," Sarah warned, exasperated. She pulled her long dark hair into a loose bundle at her neck before sitting down at the kitchen table. She looked out into the courtyard at the shimmering pool, trying to figure out why Megan would even go near Chase after all the crap he had put her through.

The courtyard was blissful with stone paths methodically designed to look natural as they weaved their trails from one gathering spot to another. Jon's parents purchased the house when Jon was eight. Jon's dad had received a large monetary payout from a big studio movie he directed at the time and put almost all of his earnings toward the purchase and remodel of the house. The entire estate was gorgeous, but Sarah's favorite place was the courtyard.

She thought about her life back home. It still snowed this time of year in Minnesota—not that often, but she could remember at least a couple of big snowstorms in April in her twenty-one years. Her life was so different now, but part of her wished it wasn't.

"It's a good thing you guys are getting away for the weekend. It sounds like all hell is breaking loose there," she said.

"I can't wait to tell you everything. We can be at the airport anytime after two on Friday, our time," said Jessica.

"Great, I'll get it all set up and get back to you this afternoon," said Sarah. She listened to her old housemates chatter about what they were going to wear on the trip and what they needed to pack. She liked to hear them interact. It made her feel like she was back at home.

As she listened, she looked up to see Jonathan crossing the courtyard from the main house. He had been working out with his personal trainer for the last ninety minutes in the main house's weight room. He wore athletic shorts with no shirt and had a white towel draped over his shoulders. His dark hair curled up in its damp state, and he pushed it out of his eyes as he passed the pool's diving board. His well-defined muscles glistened with sweat, and Sarah forgot she was on the phone for a second as she watched him. His ice-blue eyes brightened when they met hers through the glass french doors, and when he opened the door, a warm breeze blew in with just a hint of the fragrant orange blossoms from the trees up on the hill.

Sarah held her hand over the mouthpiece for a second and mouthed, "It's the girls."

Jonathan leaned into the phone and said, "Hi, ladies," before touching his lips gently to Sarah's neck just below her left ear—her favorite spot.

Sarah chuckled as Jon continued to kiss her. "Jon says hi."

The girls all responded in unison. "Hey, Jon."

"So I'll talk to you guys soon." They said their good-byes, and Sarah set her phone on the table as she turned to Jon. "You are very distracting."

He smiled his perfect smile, revealing the single dimple on his right cheek. "Want to hit the pool? The water is warm, and I didn't see anyone at the gate."

"There are no paparazzi outside?"

Jon shook his head. "No one's at the main house, either. I'm going to rinse off and grab my trunks."

Sarah needed to line up the flight for her friends before she went swimming, so she was going to call Jon's assistant first for some help. "OK, I'll meet you out there after I call Leslie."

"In your bikini?" he pleaded with wide eyes. "Please?"

Sarah hadn't worn her bikini since the car accident that almost took her life. She didn't feel comfortable showing the ugly scars on her abdomen. She scrunched her nose and scowled just a little. "Not yet."

This wasn't the first time Jonathan had specifically asked her to wear her bikini and she refused. He sighed and walked into the living room without another word.

Jon knew that she was still self-conscious about the scars. He wished she wasn't. He felt responsible for the accident that had disfigured her, and it hurt him to see her so insecure.

He made his way toward the bedroom to change and paused when he saw her silver laptop open on the couch. Colorful bubbles danced across the screen, but he could see the website behind them. He stared at it a moment, picking it up to get a closer look. His engagement photo was clearly visible on the wall in the dining room at Sarah's parents' house. With his hands fisting tighter on either side of the keyboard, it took all his restraint to not smash the computer against the wall.

He and Sarah had talked about this. With all the trouble they had been having with their personal life being leaked to the press, why would she log on to this site? It was known for how easy it was to hack. And why was their engagement photo in the background? That was just asking for trouble. He almost called for Sarah to explain, but instead, he squished his eyes together and took a deep breath. He knew she missed her friends, and he felt guilty for stealing her from them. He set the laptop back on the couch, then clicked on the red box with the X in the corner of the screen to close the site before heading out of the room.

About the Author

S usan Schussler loves the happy endings found in fiction because they inspire real life dreams. Growing up the youngest of eight children in a small house helped her develop a strong understanding of and respect for others' points of view. As a labor and delivery nurse, with her first degree in Dietetics, she has worn many career hats, but staying home to raise her children has been her most rewarding, so far, and has allowed her pursue her passion for writing. Schussler draws upon her hectic childhood and the diverse individuals she encountered throughout her life to help formulate the unique characters within her stories.

Schussler currently lives near St. Paul/Minneapolis with her husband and three sons. She enjoys spending afternoons on the lakes with family and friends, and though she hates to admit it, when she's not writing or chauffeuring her children, you may find her catching up on celebrity news.

For updates on coming releases visit her at www.susanschussler.com.

Acknowledgements

First, I need to thank my lifelong friend and content editor, Marianne Lenz whom once told me, "Just write it. It doesn't matter if it gets published. You can always leave it for your kids to read as part of your legacy." *My Legacy? Do I have a legacy?* Your words made it sound less scary and were just what I needed to get started. Thank you for being the wall where I could bounce ideas and for always being honest with me. Thank you for hashing out chapters, well past the time normal people (including our families) went to bed, and for always encouraging me to keep going. You have made me a stronger person and a better writer.

Thank you to Mary Harycki, whose courage and sheer capacity to give all of herself to others has always inspired me. You are truly a remarkable woman. Thank you for your kind words, even on the earliest versions of this book and for pushing me to publish it. I don't think I could have made this journey without you. You always make time to cheer me on and help me with whatever I need, even when you have a million other life distractions to sort through, and I am so grateful to have you in my life.

Thank you to Cathy Endres, Stasia Harycki and Katya Harycki—your enthusiasm for not only *Between the Raindrops*, but for my other books, has kept me writing. I still laugh thinking about the fervor expressed as chapters and laptops were passed back and forth on our trip to San Antonio. You three are a great resource of information and I am thankful for all of your insight and assistance.

Thank you to Jan Keane, Leta Keane, Kavita Monteiro and Sara Corbin for your feedback and support. Whether it was over long distance calls, over drinks at Gordy's or on long walks—each, in your own way, has helped evolve this book and has kept me motivated. I am sorry about my comma dyslexia—thanks for deciphering. You are indispensable and I appreciate your very valuable time and wisdom.

Thank you to my mother for cultivating creativity in your children from an early age and for giving me your sense of humor. I wish cancer hadn't taken you. I still have so many questions about life.

Thank you to my sons for not making too much fun of me when I spoke about my characters as if they were real people, and for always asking for clarification when you were confused. "Is that your friend, Sara or your character?" Thank you for sharing your perspective and for always making me laugh.

Finally and most importantly, I want to thank my husband, Tom, for your infinite patience and your encouragement that allowed me to devote so many hours to *Between the Raindrops*. Without you, I would not know true love and this book would have been impossible to write. I love you.